SHORT STORIES
CHARACTERS IN CONFLICT

EDITED BY
JOHN E. WARRINER

Formerly, Chairman of the English Department,
Garden City High School, Garden City, New
York. Chief author of *English Grammar and
Composition,* coauthor of *English Workshop*
series, and general editor of *Composition:
Models and Exercises* series.

HARCOURT BRACE JOVANOVICH

New York   Chicago   San Francisco
Atlanta   Dallas   *and*   London

Printed in the United States of America

ISBN 0-15-348340-7

Acknowledgments   For permission to reprint copyrighted works, grateful acknowledgment is given to the following sources:

Brandt & Brandt Literary Agents, Inc.: "The Most Dangerous Game" by Richard Connell. Copyright, 1924 by Richard Connell. Copyright renewed © 1952 by Louise Fox Connell. "By the Waters of Babylon" by Stephen Vincent Benét from *The Selected Works of Stephen Vincent Benét*. Copyright, 1942 by Stephen Vincent Benét. Copyright renewed © 1966 by Thomas C. Benét, Stephanie B. Mahin and Rachael Benét Lewis.

Curtis Brown Ltd. (England) and Doubleday & Company, Inc.: "The Birds" from the book *Kiss Me Again, Stranger* by Daphne du Maurier. Copyright 1952 by Daphne du Maurier.

Curtis Brown Ltd. (England) and Simon & Schuster, a Division of Gulf & Western Corporation: "A Sunrise on the Veld" from *African Stories* by Doris Lessing. Copyright © 1951, 1953, 1954, 1957, 1958, 1962, 1963, 1964, 1965 by Doris Lessing.

The Borden Deal Family Trust (Borden Deal, Trustee): "Antaeus" by Borden Deal from *Southwest Review*, Spring 1961. Copyright © 1961 by Southern Methodist University Press.

Delacorte Press: "Peter Two" excerpted from the book *Irwin Shaw Short Stories: Five Decades*. Copyright © 1937, 1938, 1939, 1940, 1941, 1942, 1943, 1944, 1945, 1946, 1947, 1949, 1950, 1952, 1953, 1954, 1955, 1956, 1957, 1958, 1961, 1962, 1963, 1964, 1967, 1968, 1969, 1971, 1973, 1977, 1978 by Irwin Shaw.

Delacorte Press/Seymour Lawrence: "Harrison Bergeron" excerpted from the book *Welcome to the Monkey House* by Kurt Vonnegut, Jr. Copyright © 1961 by Kurt Vonnegut, Jr. Originally published in *Fantasy and Science Fiction*.

Doubleday & Company, Inc.: "Enemy Territory" from *Dancers on the Shore* by William Melvin Kelley. Copyright © 1964 by William Melvin Kelley. "Raymond's Run" from *Tales and Short Stories for Black Folks* by Toni Cade Bambara. Copyright © 1971 by Doubleday & Company, Inc.

Farrar, Straus and Giroux, Inc.: "The Fatalist" from *Passions* by Isaac Bashevis Singer. Copyright © 1970, 1973, 1974, 1975 by Isaac Bashevis Singer. "Bad Characters" from *Bad Characters* by Jean Stafford. Copyright © 1954, 1964 by Jean Stafford.

Frederick Fell Publishers, Inc., 386 Park Avenue South, New York, N.Y. 10016: "The Bridge" by Nicolai Chukovski, from the book *Treasury of Russian Stories 1900–1966*, translated by Selig O. Wassner, copyright 1968.

Harcourt Brace Jovanovich, Inc.: "The Animals' Fair" from *Children and Others* by James Gould Cozzens. Copyright 1937 by the Curtis Publishing Co.; renewed 1965 by James Gould Cozzens. "A Slander" by Anton Chekhov, translated by Nathalie Wollard, copyright © 1970 by Harcourt Brace Jovanovich, Inc.

Houghton Mifflin Company: "Old Mother Hubbard" from *The Big It and Other Stories* by A. B. Guthrie, Jr. Copyright © 1960 by A. B. Guthrie, Jr.

James Hurst and The Atlantic Monthly Company, Boston, Mass.: "The Scarlet Ibis" by James Hurst from *The Atlantic Monthly*, July 1960. Copyright © 1960 by The Atlantic Monthly Company.

Harold Matson Company, Inc.: "All Summer in a Day" by Ray Bradbury. © 1954 by Ray Bradbury.

McGraw-Hill Ryerson Limited, Toronto: "Red Dress – 1946" (retitled "Red Dress") from *Dance of the Happy Shades* by Alice Munro. Copyright 1968 by Alice Munro.

Helen W. Thurber: "The Secret Life of Walter Mitty" from *My World–And Welcome To It* by James Thurber, published by Harcourt Brace Jovanovich. Copyright © 1942 by James Thurber. Copyright © 1968 by Helen Thurber. Originally printed in *The New Yorker*.

Contents

To the Student

You will enjoy the stories in this book. The first question asked about every story considered for the book was: Will students want to read it? Only if the answer to that question was "yes," could a story qualify for inclusion.

You will learn from these stories. The second question asked about each story was: Is it worth reading? In other words, does it do more than just entertain? Great stories are worth reading because they contain important ideas about life and about people. From watching characters in conflict, we learn how people behave and why they do the things they do. We learn about human desires and motives, about how actions are determined by emotions like love, hate, anger, jealousy, pride, kindness, and humility. We learn about the nature of good and evil. In stories, we can share a range of experiences, from happiness to unhappiness, from comedy to tragedy.

Another pleasure we get from reading is the pleasure of discussing the ideas in a story. As we analyze and talk about the meaning of a story, we learn to appreciate good literature. To discuss a story, we need to understand some of the elements of storytelling—the ways writers make characters and conflicts come alive. You will acquire a useful knowledge of many of these elements of storytelling during your study of this book.

Most important of all, however, is that you enjoy your reading.

J. W.

The Most Dangerous Game

RICHARD CONNELL

When you first looked at the title of this story, perhaps you thought of football or hockey. By taking another meaning of the word **game,** *you might have thought of jaguars or grizzlies as game for hunters. Before you have read very far, however, you'll know exactly what is meant by "the most dangerous game."*

Many people say that this short story is one of their favorites. Perhaps it will become one of yours. Whatever else you may think about it, you will probably agree that Connell has written an exciting adventure story—one that grips you by suspense until the very last sentence.

"Off there to the right–somewhere–is a large island," said Whitney. "It's rather a mystery—"

"What island is it?" Rainsford asked.

"The old charts call it 'Ship-Trap Island,' " Whitney replied. "A suggestive name, isn't it? Sailors have a curious dread of the place. I don't know why. Some superstition—"

"Can't see it," remarked Rainsford, trying to peer through the dank tropical night that was palpable[1] as it pressed its thick, warm blackness in upon the yacht.

"You've good eyes," said Whitney, with a laugh, "and I've seen you pick off a moose moving in the brown fall bush at four hundred yards, but even you can't see four miles or so through a moonless Caribbean night."

"Nor four yards," admitted Rainsford. "Ugh! It's like moist black velvet."

"It will be light in Rio," promised Whitney. "We should make it in a few days. I hope the jaguar guns have come from Purdey's. We should have some good hunting up the Amazon. Great sport, hunting."

"The best sport in the world," agreed Rainsford.

"For the hunter," amended Whitney. "Not for the jaguar."

"Don't talk rot, Whitney," said Rainsford. "You're a big-game hunter, not a philosopher. Who cares how a jaguar feels?"

"Perhaps the jaguar does," observed Whitney.

"Bah! They've no understanding."

1. *palpable* (păl'pə-bəl): seeming as if it could be touched.

2

"Even so, I rather think they understand one thing—fear. The fear of pain and the fear of death."

"Nonsense," laughed Rainsford. "This hot weather is making you soft, Whitney. Be a realist. The world is made up of two classes—the hunters and the huntees. Luckily, you and I are hunters. Do you think we've passed that island yet?"

"I can't tell in the dark. I hope so."

"Why?" asked Rainsford.

"The place has a reputation—a bad one."

"Cannibals?" suggested Rainsford.

"Hardly. Even cannibals wouldn't live in such a Godforsaken place. But it's gotten into sailor lore, somehow. Didn't you notice that the crew's nerves seemed a bit jumpy today?"

"They were a bit strange, now you mention it. Even Captain Nielsen—"

"Yes, even that tough-minded old Swede, who'd go up to the devil himself and ask him for a light. Those fishy blue eyes held a look I never saw there before. All I could get out of him was: 'This place has an evil name among seafaring men, sir.' Then he said to me, very gravely: 'Don't you feel anything?'—as if the air about us was actually poisonous. Now, you mustn't laugh when I tell you this—I did feel something like a sudden chill.

"There was no breeze. The sea was as flat as a plate-glass window. We were drawing near the island then. What I felt was a—a mental chill; a sort of sudden dread."

"Pure imagination," said Rainsford. "One superstitious sailor can taint the whole ship's company with his fear."

"Maybe. But sometimes I think sailors have an extra sense that tells them when they are in danger. Sometimes I think evil is a tangible thing—with wavelengths, just as sound and light have. An evil place can, so to speak, broadcast vibrations of evil. Anyhow, I'm glad we're getting out of this zone. Well, I think I'll turn in now, Rainsford."

"I'm not sleepy," said Rainsford. "I'm going to smoke another pipe up on the afterdeck."

"Good night, then, Rainsford. See you at breakfast."

"Right. Good night, Whitney."

There was no sound in the night as Rainsford sat there, but the muffled throb of the engine that drove the yacht swiftly through the darkness, and the swish and ripple of the wash of the propeller.

Rainsford, reclining in a steamer chair, indolently[2] puffed on his favorite brier.[3] The sensuous drowsiness of the night was on him. "It's so dark," he thought, "that I could sleep without closing my eyes; the night would be my eyelids—"

An abrupt sound startled him. Off to the right he heard it, and his ears, expert in such matters, could not be mistaken. Again he heard the sound, and again. Somewhere, off in the blackness, someone had fired a gun three times.

Rainsford sprang up and moved quickly to the rail, mystified. He strained his eyes in the direction from which the reports had come, but it was like trying to see through a blanket. He leaped upon the rail and balanced himself there, to get greater elevation; his pipe, striking a rope, was knocked from his mouth. He lunged for it; a short, hoarse cry came from his lips as he realized he had reached too far and had lost his balance. The cry was pinched off short as the blood-warm waters of the Caribbean Sea closed over his head.

He struggled up to the surface and tried to cry out, but the wash from the speeding yacht slapped him in the face and the salt water in his open mouth made him gag and strangle. Desperately he struck out with strong strokes after the receding lights of the yacht, but he stopped before he had swum fifty feet. A certain cool-headedness had come to him; it was not the first time he had been in a tight place. There was a chance that his cries could be heard by someone aboard the yacht, but that

2. *indolently:* lazily.
3. *brier:* pipe.

chance was slender, and grew more slender as the yacht raced on. He wrestled himself out of his clothes, and shouted with all his power. The lights of the yacht became faint and ever-vanishing fireflies; then they were blotted out entirely by the night.

Rainsford remembered the shots. They had come from the right, and doggedly he swam in that direction, swimming with slow, deliberate strokes, conserving his strength. For a seemingly endless time he fought the sea. He began to count his strokes; he could do possibly a hundred more and then—

Rainsford heard a sound. It came out of the darkness, a high screaming sound, the sound of an animal in an extremity of anguish and terror.

He did not recognize the animal that made the sound; he did not try to; with fresh vitality he swam toward the sound. He heard it again; then it was cut short by another noise, crisp, staccato.

"Pistol shot," muttered Rainsford, swimming on.

Ten minutes of determined effort brought another sound to his ears—the most welcome he had ever heard—the muttering and growling of the sea breaking on a rocky shore. He was almost on the rocks before he saw them; on a night less calm he would have been shattered against them. With his remaining strength he dragged himself from the swirling waters. Jagged crags appeared to jut into the opaqueness;[4] he forced himself upward, hand over hand. Gasping, his hands raw, he reached a flat place at the top. Dense jungle came down to the very edge of the cliffs. What perils that tangle of trees and underbrush might hold for him did not concern Rainsford just then. All he knew was that he was safe from his enemy, the sea, and that utter weariness was on him. He flung himself down at the jungle edge and tumbled headlong into the deepest sleep of his life.

When he opened his eyes, he knew from the position of the sun that it was late in the afternoon. Sleep had given him new

---

4. *opaqueness* (ō-pāk′nĭs): darkness.

vigor; a sharp hunger was picking at him. He looked about him, almost cheerfully.

"Where there are pistol shots, there are men. Where there are men, there is food," he thought. But what kind of men, he wondered, in so forbidding a place? An unbroken front of snarled and ragged jungle fringed the shore.

He saw no sign of a trail through the closely knit web of weeds and trees; it was easier to go along the shore, and Rainsford floundered along by the water. Not far from where he had landed, he stopped.

Some wounded thing, by the evidence a large animal, had thrashed about in the underbrush; the jungle weeds were crushed down and the moss was lacerated; one patch of weeds was stained crimson. A small, glittering object not far away caught Rainsford's eye and he picked it up. It was an empty cartridge.

"A twenty-two," he remarked. "That's odd. It must have been a fairly large animal too. The hunter had his nerve with him to tackle it with a light gun. It's clear that the brute put up a fight. I suppose the first three shots I heard was when the hunter flushed his quarry and wounded it. The last shot was when he trailed it here and finished it."

He examined the ground closely and found what he had hoped to find—the print of hunting boots. They pointed along the cliff in the direction he had been going. Eagerly he hurried along, now slipping on a rotten log or a loose stone, but making headway; night was beginning to settle down on the island.

Bleak darkness was blacking out the sea and jungle when Rainsford sighted the lights. He came upon them as he turned a crook in the coastline, and his first thought was that he had come upon a village, for there were many lights. But as he forged along he saw, to his great astonishment, that all the lights were in one enormous building—a lofty structure with pointed towers plunging upward into the gloom. His eyes made out the shadowy outlines of a palatial chateau; it was set on a high bluff, and on three sides of it cliffs dived down to where the sea licked greedy lips in the shadows.

"Mirage," thought Rainsford. But it was no mirage, he found, when he opened the tall spiked iron gate. The stone steps were real enough; the massive door with a leering gargoyle[5] for a knocker was real enough; yet about it all hung an air of unreality.

He lifted the knocker, and it creaked up stiffly, as if it had never before been used. He let it fall, and it startled him with its booming loudness. He thought he heard steps within; the door remained closed. Again Rainsford lifted the heavy knocker, and let it fall. The door opened then, opened as suddenly as if it were on a spring, and Rainsford stood blinking in the river of glaring gold light that poured out. The first thing Rainsford's eyes discerned was the largest man Rainsford had ever seen—a gigantic creature, solidly made and black-bearded to the waist. In his hand the man held a long-barreled revolver, and he was pointing it straight at Rainsford's heart.

Out of the snarl of beard two small eyes regarded Rainsford.

"Don't be alarmed," said Rainsford, with a smile which he hoped was disarming. "I'm no robber. I fell off a yacht. My name is Sanger Rainsford of New York City."

The menacing look in the eyes did not change. The revolver pointed as rigidly as if the giant were a statue. He gave no sign that he understood Rainsford's words, or that he had even heard them. He was dressed in uniform, a black uniform trimmed with gray astrakhan.[6]

"I'm Sanger Rainsford of New York," Rainsford began again. "I fell off a yacht. I am hungry."

The man's only answer was to raise with his thumb the

5. *gargoyle* (gär'goil'): weirdly carved animal or creature of some sort.
6. *astrakhan*: lamb fur.

hammer of his revolver. Then Rainsford saw the man's free hand go to his forehead in a military salute, and he saw him click his heels together and stand at attention. Another man was coming down the broad marble steps, an erect, slender man in evening clothes. He advanced to Rainsford and held out his hand.

In a cultivated voice marked by a slight accent that gave it added precision and deliberateness, he said: "It is a very great pleasure and honor to welcome Mr. Sanger Rainsford, the celebrated hunter, to my home."

Automatically Rainsford shook the man's hand.

"I've read your book about hunting snow leopards in Tibet, you see," explained the man. "I am General Zaroff."

Rainsford's first impression was that the man was singularly handsome; his second was that there was an original, almost bizarre quality about the general's face. He was a tall man past middle age, for his hair was a vivid white; but his thick eyebrows and pointed military mustache were as black as the night from which Rainsford had come. His eyes, too, were black and very bright. He had high cheekbones, a sharp-cut nose, a spare, dark face—the face of a man used to giving orders, the face of an aristocrat. Turning to the giant in uniform, the general made a sign. The giant put away his pistol, saluted, withdrew.

"Ivan is an incredibly strong fellow," remarked the general, "but he has the misfortune to be deaf and dumb. A simple fellow, but, I'm afraid, like all his race, a bit of a savage."

"Is he Russian?"

"He is a Cossack," said the general, and his smile showed red lips and pointed teeth. "So am I."

"Come," he said, "we shouldn't be chatting here. We can talk later. Now you want clothes, food, rest. You shall have them. This is a most restful spot."

Ivan had reappeared, and the general spoke to him with lips that moved but gave forth no sound.

"Follow Ivan, if you please, Mr. Rainsford," said the general. "I was about to have my dinner when you came. I'll wait for you. You'll find that my clothes will fit you, I think."

It was to a huge, beam-ceilinged bedroom with a canopied bed big enough for six men that Rainsford followed the silent giant. Ivan laid out an evening suit, and Rainsford, as he put it on, noticed that it came from a London tailor who ordinarily cut and sewed for none below the rank of duke.

The dining room to which Ivan conducted him was, in many ways, remarkable. There was a medieval magnificence about it; it suggested a baronial hall of feudal times with its oaken panels, its high ceiling, its vast refectory table where twoscore men could sit down to eat. About the hall were the mounted heads of many animals—lions, tigers, elephants, moose, bears; larger or more perfect specimens Rainsford had never seen. At the great table the general was sitting, alone.

"You'll have a cocktail, Mr. Rainsford," he suggested. The cocktail was surpassingly good; and, Rainsford noted, the table appointments were of the finest—the linen, the crystal, the silver, the china.

They were eating *borsch*, the rich, red soup with sour cream so dear to Russian palates. Half apologetically General Zaroff said: "We do our best to preserve the amenities of civilization here. Please forgive any lapses. We are well off the beaten track, you know. Do you think the champagne has suffered from its long ocean trip?"

"Not in the least," declared Rainsford. He was finding the general a most thoughtful and affable host, a true cosmopolite.[7] But there was one small trait of the general's that made Rainsford uncomfortable. Whenever he looked up from his plate he found the general studying him, appraising him narrowly.

"Perhaps," said General Zaroff, "you were surprised that I

7. *cosmopolite* (kŏz-mŏp′ə-līt′): person of wide experience.

recognized your name. You see, I read all books on hunting published in English, French, and Russian. I have but one passion in my life, Mr. Rainsford, and it is the hunt."

"You have some wonderful heads here," said Rainsford as he ate a particularly well cooked filet mignon. "That Cape buffalo is the largest I ever saw."

"Oh, that fellow. Yes, he was a monster."

"Did he charge you?"

"Hurled me against a tree," said the general. "Fractured my skull. But I got the brute."

"I've always thought," said Rainsford, "that the Cape buffalo is the most dangerous of all big game."

For a moment the general did not reply; he was smiling his curious red-lipped smile. Then he said slowly: "No. You are wrong, sir. The Cape buffalo is not the most dangerous big game." He sipped his wine. "Here in my preserve on this island," he said in the same slow tone, "I hunt more dangerous game."

Rainsford expressed his surprise. "Is there big game on this island?"

The general nodded. "The biggest."

"Really?"

"Oh, it isn't here naturally, of course. I have to stock the island."

"What have you imported, General?" Rainsford asked. "Tigers?"

The general smiled. "No," he said. "Hunting tigers ceased to interest me some years ago. I exhausted their possibilities, you see. No thrill left in tigers, no real danger. I live for danger, Mr. Rainsford."

The general took from his pocket a gold cigarette case and offered his guest a long black cigarette with a silver tip; it was perfumed, and gave off a smell like incense.

"We will have some capital hunting, you and I," said the general. "I shall be most glad to have your society."

"But what game—" began Rainsford.

"I'll tell you," said the general. "You will be amused, I know. I think I may say, in all modesty, that I have done a rare thing. I have invented a new sensation. May I pour you another glass of port, Mr. Rainsford?"

"Thank you, General."

The general filled both glasses, and said: "God makes some men poets. Some He makes kings, some beggars. Me He made a hunter. My hand was made for the trigger, my father said. He was a very rich man with a quarter of a million acres in the Crimea,[8] and he was an ardent sportsman. When I was only five years old he gave me a little gun, specially made in Moscow for me, to shoot sparrows with. When I shot some of his prize turkeys with it, he did not punish me; he complimented me on my marksmanship. I killed my first bear in the Caucasus when I was ten. My whole life has been one prolonged hunt. I went into the army—it was expected of noblemen's sons—and for a time commanded a division of Cossack cavalry, but my real interest was always the hunt. I have hunted every kind of game in every land. It would be impossible for me to tell you how many animals I have killed."

The general puffed at his cigarette.

"After the debacle in Russia[9] I left the country, for it was imprudent for an officer of the Czar to stay there. Many noble Russians lost everything. I, luckily, had invested heavily in American securities, so I shall never have to open a tearoom in Monte Carlo or drive a taxi in Paris. Naturally, I continued to hunt—grizzlies in your Rockies, crocodiles in the Ganges, rhinoceroses in East Africa. It was in Africa that the Cape buffalo hit me and laid me up for six months. As soon as I recovered I started for the Amazon to hunt jaguars, for I had heard they were unusually cunning. They weren't." The Cossack sighed. "They were no match at all for a hunter with his wits about him, and a high-powered rifle. I was bitterly disappointed. I

8. *Crimea:* an area in Russia.
9. *debacle* (dǐ-bä′kəl) *in Russia:* a reference to the Russian Revolution of 1917, when the Czar was overthrown.

was lying in my tent with a splitting headache one night when a terrible thought pushed its way into my mind. Hunting was beginning to bore me! And hunting, remember, had been my life. I have heard that in America businessmen often go to pieces when they give up the business that has been their life."

"Yes, that's so," said Rainsford.

The general smiled. "I had no wish to go to pieces," he said. "I must do something. Now, mine is an analytical mind, Mr. Rainsford. Doubtless that is why I enjoy the problems of the chase."

"No doubt, General Zaroff."

"So," continued the general, "I asked myself why the hunt no longer fascinated me. You are much younger than I am, Mr. Rainsford, and have not hunted as much, but you perhaps can guess the answer."

"What was it?"

"Simply this: hunting had ceased to be what you call 'a sporting proposition.' It had become too easy. I always got my quarry. Always. There is no greater bore than perfection."

The general lit a fresh cigarette.

"No animal had a chance with me any more. That is no boast; it is a mathematical certainty. The animal had nothing but his legs and his instinct. Instinct is no match for reason. When I thought of this, it was a tragic moment for me, I can tell you."

Rainsford leaned across the table, absorbed in what his host was saying.

"It came to me as an inspiration what I must do," the general went on.

"And that was?"

The general smiled the quiet smile of one who has faced an obstacle and surmounted it with success. "I had to invent a new animal to hunt," he said.

"A new animal? You're joking."

"Not at all," said the general. "I never joke about hunting. I needed a new animal. I found one. So I bought this island, built this house, and here I do my hunting. The island is perfect for my purposes—there are jungles with a maze of trails in them, hills, swamps—"

"But the animal, General Zaroff?"

"Oh," said the general, "it supplies me with the most exciting hunting in the world. No other hunting compares with it for an instant. Every day I hunt, and I never grow bored now, for I have a quarry with which I can match my wits."

Rainsford's bewilderment showed in his face.

"I wanted the ideal animal to hunt," explained the general. "So I said: 'What are the attributes of an ideal quarry?' And the answer was, of course: 'It must have courage, cunning, and, above all, it must be able to reason.' "

"But no animal can reason," objected Rainsford.

"My dear fellow," said the general, "there is one that can."

"But you can't mean—" gasped Rainsford.

"And why not?"

"I can't believe you are serious, General Zaroff. This is a grisly joke."

"Why should I not be serious? I am speaking of hunting."

"Hunting? General Zaroff, what you speak of is murder."

The general laughed with entire good nature. He regarded Rainsford quizzically. "I refuse to believe that so modern and civilized a young man as you seem to be harbors romantic ideas about the value of human life. Surely your experiences in the war—"

"Did not make me condone[10] coldblooded murder," finished Rainsford stiffly.

Laughter shook the general. "How extraordinarily droll[11]

10. *condone:* pardon or overlook.
11. *droll:* amusing.

you are!" he said. "One does not expect nowadays to find a young man of the educated class, even in America, with such a naive, and, if I may say so, mid-Victorian point of view. It's like finding a snuffbox in a limousine. Ah, well, doubtless you had Puritan ancestors. So many Americans appear to have had. I'll wager you'll forget your notions when you go hunting with me. You've a genuine new thrill in store for you, Mr. Rainsford."

"Thank you, I'm a hunter, not a murderer."

"Dear me," said the general, quite unruffled, "again that unpleasant word. But I think I can show you that your scruples[12] are quite ill-founded."

"Yes?"

"Life is for the strong, to be lived by the strong, and, if need be, taken by the strong. The weak of the world were put here to give the strong pleasure. I am strong. Why should I not use my gift? If I wish to hunt, why should I not? I hunt the scum of the earth—sailors from tramp ships—lascars, blacks, Chinese, whites, mongrels—a thoroughbred horse or hound is worth more than a score of them."

"But they are men," said Rainsford hotly.

"Precisely," said the general. "That is why I use them. It gives me pleasure. They can reason, after a fashion. So they are dangerous."

"But where do you get them?"

The general's left eyelid fluttered down in a wink. "This island is called Ship-Trap," he answered. "Sometimes an angry god of the high seas sends them to me. Sometimes, when Providence is not so kind, I help Providence a bit. Come to the window with me."

Rainsford went to the window and looked out toward the sea.

"Watch! Out there!" exclaimed the general, pointing into

12. *scruples:* feelings that something is morally wrong.

the night. Rainsford's eyes saw only blackness, and then, as the general pressed a button, far out to sea Rainsford saw the flash of lights.

The general chuckled. "They indicate a channel," he said, "where there's none: giant rocks with razor edges crouch like a sea monster with wide-open jaws. They can crush a ship as easily as I crush this nut." He dropped a walnut on the hardwood floor and brought his heel grinding down on it. "Oh, yes," he said, casually, as if in answer to a question, "I have electricity. We try to be civilized here."

"Civilized? And you shoot down men?"

A trace of anger was in the general's black eyes, but it was there for but a second, and he said, in his most pleasant manner: "Dear me, what a righteous young man you are! I assure you I do not do the thing you suggest. That would be barbarous. I treat these visitors with every consideration. They get plenty of good food and exercise. They get into splendid physical condition. You shall see for yourself tomorrow."

"What do you mean?"

"We'll visit my training school," smiled the general. "It's in the cellar. I have about a dozen pupils down there now. They're from the Spanish bark *San Lucar* that had the bad luck to go on the rocks out there. A very inferior lot, I regret to say. Poor specimens and more accustomed to the deck than to the jungle."

He raised his hand, and Ivan, who served as waiter, brought thick Turkish coffee. Rainsford, with an effort, held his tongue in check.

"It's a game, you see," pursued the general blandly.[13] "I suggest to one of them that we go hunting. I give him a supply of food and an excellent hunting knife. I give him three hours' start. I am to follow, armed only with a pistol of the smallest caliber and range. If my quarry eludes me for three whole days,

13. *blandly:* mildly or agreeably.

he wins the game. If I find him"—the general smiled —"he loses."

"Suppose he refuses to be hunted?"

"Oh," said the general, "I give him his option, of course. He need not play that game if he doesn't wish to. If he does not wish to hunt, I turn him over to Ivan. Ivan once had the honor of serving as official knouter[14] to the Great White Czar, and he has his own ideas of sport. Invariably, Mr. Rainsford, invariably they choose the hunt."

"And if they win?"

The smile on the general's face widened. "To date I have not lost," he said.

Then he added, hastily: "I don't wish you to think me a braggart, Mr. Rainsford. Many of them afford only the most elementary sort of problem. Occasionally I strike a tartar.[15] One almost did win. I eventually had to use the dogs."

"The dogs?"

"This way, please. I'll show you."

The general steered Rainsford to a window. The lights from the windows sent a flickering illumination that made grotesque patterns on the courtyard below, and Rainsford could see moving about there a dozen or so huge black shapes; as they turned toward him, their eyes glittered greenly.

"A rather good lot, I think," observed the general. "They are let out at seven every night. If anyone should try to get into my house—or out of it—something extremely regrettable would occur to him." He hummed a snatch of song from the Folies Bergère.

"And now," said the general, "I want to show you my new collection of heads. Will you come with me to the library?"

"I hope," said Rainsford, "that you will excuse me tonight, General Zaroff. I'm really not feeling at all well."

"Ah, indeed?" the general inquired solicitously. "Well, I

14. *knouter:* flogger (a *knout* is a whip).
15. *tartar:* a violent person.

suppose that's only natural, after your long swim. You need a good, restful night's sleep. Tomorrow you'll feel like a new man, I'll wager. Then we'll hunt, eh? I've one rather promising prospect—"

Rainsford was hurrying from the room.

"Sorry you can't go with me tonight," called the general. "I expect rather fair sport—a big, strong fellow. He looks resourceful— Well, good night, Mr. Rainsford; I hope you have a good night's rest."

The bed was good, and the pajamas of the softest silk, and he was tired in every fiber of his being, but nevertheless, Rainsford could not quiet his brain with the opiate of sleep. He lay, eyes wide open. Once, he thought he heard stealthy steps in the corridor outside his room. He sought to throw open the door; it would not open. He went to the window and looked out. His room was high up in one of the towers. The lights of the chateau were out now, and it was dark and silent, but there was a fragment of sallow moon, and by its wan light he could see, dimly, the courtyard; there, weaving in and out in the pattern of shadow, were black, noiseless forms; the hounds heard him at the window and looked up, expectantly, with their green eyes. Rainsford went back to the bed and lay down. By many methods he tried to put himself to sleep. He had achieved a doze when, just as morning began to come, he heard, far off in the jungle, the faint report of a pistol.

General Zaroff did not appear until luncheon. He was dressed faultlessly in the tweeds of a country squire. He was solicitous about the state of Rainsford's health.

"As for me," sighed the general, "I do not feel so well. I am worried, Mr. Rainsford. Last night I detected traces of my old complaint."

To Rainsford's questioning glance the general said: "Ennui. Boredom."

Then, taking a second helping of crepes suzette, the general explained: "The hunting was not good last night. The fellow lost his head. He made a straight trail that offered no problems at all. That's the trouble with these sailors; they have dull brains to begin with, and they do not know how to get about in the woods. They do excessively stupid and obvious things. It's most annoying. Will you have another glass of Chablis, Mr. Rainsford?"

"General," said Rainsford firmly, "I wish to leave this island at once."

The general raised his thickets of eyebrows; he seemed hurt. "But, my dear fellow," the general protested, "you've only just come. You've had no hunting—"

"I wish to go today," said Rainsford. He saw the dead black eyes of the general on him, studying him. General Zaroff's face suddenly brightened.

He filled Rainsford's glass with venerable Chablis from a dusty bottle.

"Tonight," said the general, "we will hunt—you and I."

Rainsford shook his head. "No, General," he said. "I will not hunt."

The general shrugged his shoulders and delicately ate a hot-house grape. "As you wish, my friend," he said. "The choice rests entirely with you. But may I not venture to suggest that you will find my idea of sport more diverting than Ivan's?"

He nodded toward the corner to where the giant stood, scowling, his thick arms crossed on his hogshead of chest.

"You don't mean—" cried Rainsford.

"My dear fellow," said the general, "have I not told you I always mean what I say about hunting? This is really an inspiration. I drink to a foeman worthy of my steel—at last."

The general raised his glass, but Rainsford sat staring at him.

"You'll find this game worth playing," the general said enthusiastically. "Your brain against mine. Your woodcraft against mine. Your strength and stamina against mine. Out-door chess! And the stake is not without value, eh?"

"And if I win—" began Rainsford huskily.

"I'll cheerfully acknowledge myself defeated if I do not find you by midnight of the third day," said General Zaroff. "My sloop will place you on the mainland near a town."

The general read what Rainsford was thinking.

"Oh, you can trust me," said the Cossack. "I will give you my word as a gentleman and a sportsman. Of course you, in turn, must agree to say nothing of your visit here."

"I'll agree to nothing of the kind," said Rainsford.

"Oh," said the general, "in that case— But why discuss that now? Three days hence we can discuss it over a bottle of Veuve Cliquot, unless—"

The general sipped his wine.

Then a businesslike air animated him. "Ivan," he said to Rainsford, "will supply you with hunting clothes, food, a knife. I suggest you wear moccasins; they leave a poorer trail. I suggest too that you avoid the big swamp in the southeast corner of the island. We call it Death Swamp. There's quicksand there. One foolish fellow tried it. The deplorable part of it was that Lazarus followed him. You can imagine my feelings, Mr. Rainsford. I loved Lazarus; he was the finest hound in my pack. Well, I must beg you to excuse me now. I always take a siesta after lunch. You'll hardly have time for a nap, I fear. You'll want to start, no doubt. I shall not follow till dusk. Hunting at night is so much more exciting than by day, don't you think? Au revoir, Mr. Rainsford, au revoir."

General Zaroff, with a deep, courtly bow, strolled from the room.

From another door came Ivan. Under one arm he carried khaki hunting clothes, a haversack of food, a leather sheath containing a long-bladed hunting knife; his right hand rested on a cocked revolver thrust in the crimson sash about his waist. . . .

Rainsford had fought his way through the bush for two hours. "I must keep my nerve. I must keep my nerve," he said through tight teeth.

He had not been entirely clearheaded when the chateau gates snapped shut behind him. His whole idea at first was to put distance between himself and General Zaroff, and, to this end, he had plunged along, spurred on by the sharp rowels of something very like panic. Now he had got a grip on himself, had stopped, and was taking stock of himself and the situation.

He saw that straight flight was futile; inevitably it would bring him face to face with the sea. He was in a picture with a frame of water, and his operations, clearly, must take place within that frame.

"I'll give him a trail to follow," muttered Rainsford, and he struck off from the rude paths he had been following in the trackless wilderness. He executed a series of intricate loops; he doubled on his trail again and again, recalling all the lore of the fox hunt, and all the dodges of the fox. Night found him leg-weary, with hands and face lashed by the branches, on a thickly wooded ridge. He knew it would be insane to blunder on through the dark, even if he had the strength. His need for rest was imperative and he thought: "I have played the fox, now I must play the cat of the fable." A big tree with a thick trunk and outspread branches was nearby, and, taking care to leave not the slightest mark, he climbed up into the crotch, and stretching out on one of the broad limbs, after a fashion, rested. Rest brought him new confidence and almost a feeling of security. Even so zealous a hunter as General Zaroff could not trace him there, he told himself; only the devil himself could follow that complicated trail through the jungle after dark. But, perhaps, the general was a devil—

An apprehensive night crawled slowly by like a wounded snake, and sleep did not visit Rainsford, although the silence of a dead world was on the jungle. Toward morning, when a dingy gray was varnishing the sky, the cry of some startled bird focused Rainsford's attention in that direction. Something was coming through the bush, coming slowly, carefully, coming by the same winding way Rainsford had come. He flattened himself down on the limb, and through a screen of leaves almost as thick as tapestry, he watched. The thing that was approaching was a man.

It was General Zaroff. He made his way along with his eyes fixed in utmost concentration on the ground before him. He paused, almost beneath the tree, dropped to his knees, and studied the ground. Rainsford's impulse was to hurl himself down like a panther, but he saw that the general's right hand held something metallic—a small automatic pistol.

The hunter shook his head several times, as if he were puzzled. Then he straightened up and took from his case one of his black cigarettes; its pungent, incense-like smoke floated up to Rainsford's nostrils.

Rainsford held his breath. The general's eyes had left the ground and were traveling inch by inch up the tree. Rainsford froze there, every muscle tensed for a spring. But the sharp eyes of the hunter stopped before they reached the limb where Rainsford lay; a smile spread over his brown face. Very deliberately he blew a smoke ring into the air; then he turned his back on the tree and walked carelessly away, back along the trail he had come. The swish of the underbrush against his hunting boots grew fainter and fainter.

The pent-up air burst hotly from Rainsford's lungs. His first thought made him feel sick and numb. The general could follow a trail through the woods at night; he could follow an extremely difficult trail; he must have uncanny powers; only by the merest chance had the Cossack failed to see his quarry.

Rainsford's second thought was even more terrible. It sent a shudder of cold horror through his whole being. Why had the general smiled? Why had he turned back?

Rainsford did not want to believe what his reason told him was true, but the truth was as evident as the sun that had by now pushed through the morning mists. The general was playing with him! The general was saving him for another day's sport! The Cossack was the cat; he was the mouse. Then it was that Rainsford knew the full meaning of terror.

"I will not lose my nerve. I will not."

He slid down from the tree and struck off again into the woods. His face was set and he forced the machinery of his mind to function. Three hundred yards from his hiding place, he stopped where a huge, dead tree leaned precariously on a smaller, living one. Throwing off his sack of food, Rainsford took his knife from its sheath and began to work with all his energy.

The job was finished at last, and he threw himself down behind a fallen log a hundred feet away. He did not have to wait long. The cat was coming again to play with the mouse.

Following the trail with the sureness of a bloodhound came General Zaroff. Nothing escaped those searching black eyes, no crushed blade of grass, no bent twig, no mark, no matter how faint, in the moss. So intent was the Cossack on his stalking that he was upon the thing Rainsford had made before he saw it. His foot touched the protruding bough that was the trigger. Even as he touched it, the general sensed his danger and leaped back with the agility of an ape. But he was not quite quick enough: the dead tree, delicately adjusted to rest on the cut living one, crashed down and struck the general a glancing blow on the shoulder as it fell; but for his alertness, he must have been smashed beneath it. He staggered, but he did not fall; nor did he drop his revolver. He stood there, rubbing his injured shoulder, and Rainsford, with fear again gripping his heart, heard the general's mocking laugh ring through the jungle.

"Rainsford," called the general, "if you are within sound of my voice, as I suppose you are, let me congratulate you. Not many men know how to make a Malay man-catcher. Luckily for me, I too have hunted in Malacca. You are proving interesting, Mr. Rainsford. I am going now to have my wound dressed; it's only a slight one. But I shall be back. I shall be back."

When the general, nursing his bruised shoulder, had gone, Rainsford took up his flight again. It was flight now, a desperate, hopeless flight, that carried him on for some hours. Dusk came, then darkness, and still he pressed on. The ground grew softer under his moccasins; the vegetation grew ranker, denser; insects bit him savagely. Then, as he stepped forward, his foot sank into the ooze. He tried to wrench it back, but the muck sucked viciously at his foot as if it were a giant leech. With a violent effort, he tore his foot loose. He knew where he was now. Death Swamp and its quicksand.

His hands were tight closed as if his nerve were something tangible that someone in the darkness was trying to tear from his grip. The softness of the earth had given him an idea. He stepped back from the quicksand a dozen feet or so and, like some huge prehistoric beaver, he began to dig.

Rainsford had dug himself in in France when a second's delay meant death. That had been a placid pastime compared to his digging now. The pit grew deeper; when it was above his shoulders, he climbed out, and from some hard saplings cut stakes and sharpened them to a fine point. These stakes he planted in the bottom of the pit with the points sticking up. With flying fingers he wove a rough carpet of weeds and branches and with it he covered the mouth of the pit. Then, wet with sweat and aching with tiredness, he crouched behind the stump of a lightning-charred tree.

He knew his pursuer was coming; he heard the padding sound of feet on the soft earth, and the night breeze brought him the perfume of the general's cigarette. It seemed to Rainsford that the general was coming with unusual swiftness; he was not feeling his way along, foot by foot. Rainsford, crouching there, could not see the general, nor could he see the pit. He lived a year in a minute. Then he felt an impulse to cry aloud with joy, for he heard the sharp crackle of the breaking branches as the cover of the pit gave way; he heard the sharp scream of pain as the pointed stakes found their mark. He leaped up from his place of concealment. Then he cowered back. Three feet from the pit a man was standing, with an electric torch in his hand.

"You've done well, Rainsford," the voice of the general called. "Your Burmese tiger pit has claimed one of my best dogs. Again you score. I think, Mr. Rainsford, I'll see what you can do against my whole pack. I'm going home for a rest now. Thank you for a most amusing evening."

At daybreak Rainsford, lying near the swamp, was awakened by a sound that made him know that he had new things to learn about fear. It was a distant sound, faint and wavering, but he knew it. It was the baying of a pack of hounds.

Rainsford knew he could do one of two things. He could stay where he was and wait. That was suicide. He could flee. That was postponing the inevitable. For a moment he stood there, thinking. An idea that held a wild chance came to him, and, tightening his belt, he headed away from the swamp.

The baying of the hounds drew nearer, then still nearer, nearer, ever nearer. On a ridge Rainsford climbed a tree. Down a watercourse, not a quarter of a mile away, he could see the bush moving. Straining his eyes, he saw the lean figure of General Zaroff; just ahead of him Rainsford made out another figure whose wide shoulders surged through the tall jungle weeds; it was the giant Ivan, and he seemed pulled forward by some unseen force; Rainsford knew that Ivan must be holding the pack in leash.

They would be on him any minute now. His mind worked frantically. He thought of a native trick he had learned in Uganda. He slid down the tree. He caught hold of a springy young sapling and to it he fastened his hunting knife, with the blade pointing down the trail; with a bit of wild grapevine he tied back the sapling. Then he ran for his life. The hounds raised their voices as they hit the fresh scent. Rainsford knew now how an animal at bay feels.

He had to stop to get his breath. The baying of the hounds

stopped abruptly, and Rainsford's heart stopped too. They must have reached the knife.

He shinnied excitedly up a tree and looked back. His pursuers had stopped. But the hope that was in Rainsford's brain when he climbed died, for he saw in the shallow valley that General Zaroff was still on his feet. But Ivan was not. The knife, driven by the recoil of the springing tree, had not wholly failed.

Rainsford had hardly tumbled to the ground when the pack took up the cry again.

"Nerve, nerve, nerve!" he panted, as he dashed along. A blue gap showed between the trees dead ahead. Ever nearer drew the hounds. Rainsford forced himself on toward that gap. He reached it. It was the shore of the sea. Across a cove he could see the gloomy gray stone of the chateau. Twenty feet below him the sea rumbled and hissed. Rainsford hesitated. He heard the hounds. Then he leaped far out into the sea. . .

When the general and his pack reached the place by the sea, the Cossack stopped. For some minutes he stood regarding the blue-green expanse of water. He shrugged his shoulders. Then he sat down, took a drink of brandy from a silver flask, lit a perfumed cigarette, and hummed a bit from *Madame Butterfly*.

General Zaroff had an exceedingly good dinner in his great paneled dining hall that evening. With it he had a bottle of Pol Roger and half a bottle of Chambertin. Two slight annoyances kept him from perfect enjoyment. One was the thought that it would be difficult to replace Ivan; the other was that his quarry had escaped him; of course the American hadn't played the game—so thought the general as he tasted his after-dinner liqueur. In his library he read, to soothe himself, from the works of Marcus Aurelius. At ten he went up to his bedroom. He was deliciously tired, he said to himself, as he locked himself in. There was a little moonlight, so, before turning on his light, he went to the window and looked down at the court-yard. He could see the great hounds, and he called: "Better luck another time," to them. Then he switched on the light.

A man, who had been hiding in the curtains of the bed, was standing there.

"Rainsford!" screamed the general. "How did you get here?"

"Swam," said Rainsford. "I found it quicker than walking through the jungle."

The general sucked in his breath and smiled. "I congratulate you," he said. "You have won the game."

Rainsford did not smile. "I am still a beast at bay," he said, in a low, hoarse voice. "Get ready, General Zaroff."

The general made one of his deepest bows. "I see," he said. "Splendid! One of us is to furnish a repast for the hounds. The other will sleep in this very excellent bed. On guard, Rains-ford. . . ."

He had never slept in a better bed, Rainsford decided.

The Facts of the Story

Write short answers to the following questions. Answers may be one word or a phrase. You can probably answer all the questions without rereading the story, but look back if you wish.

1. The game that General Zaroff hunts is _____.

2. Why is this the "most dangerous" game?

3. What is Zaroff's island called?

4. What makes the island perfect for Zaroff's hunting?

5. Zaroff gives Rainsford two choices: he can be hunted, or _____.

6. To win the game, how many days must Rainsford survive the hunt?

7. To be set free on the mainland if he survives, Rainsford must agree not to _____.

8. Besides being the hunter, what other advantage does Zaroff give himself?

9. As a result of Rainsford's skill in setting traps on the trail, Zaroff loses a _____ and _____.

10. How does Rainsford finally avoid being caught?

The Ideas in the Story

Prepare to discuss the following questions in class.

1. At the beginning of the story, the author lets us know Rainsford's ideas about hunting and Whitney's reactions to these ideas. How do Whitney's and Rainsford's ideas differ? Why would the author want us to know about these ideas at the start of the story?

2. What are your reactions to the following ideas stated by two characters in the story?

Rainsford: "The world is made up of two classes—the hunters and the huntees." (Page 3)

Zaroff: "Life is for the strong, to be lived by the strong, and, if need be, taken by the strong. The weak of the world were put here to give the strong pleasure. I am strong. Why should I not use my gift?" (Page 14)

3. At first, Rainsford's ideas about hunting are similar to Zaroff's. Do you think Rainsford's ideas are changed by his experience with Zaroff? Why or why not?

The Art of the Storyteller

Plot

Plot is a series of connected events which are brought to some kind of conclusion—sometimes a happy one, sometimes an unhappy one. Most plots contain a *problem* to be solved; a *conflict* (or struggle) involving one or more *characters; suspense;* and a *climax.*

A Problem to Be Solved

The first requirement for a plot is a problem that the main character faces and wants to solve. If the character can solve the problem quickly and easily, we say the story does not have much of a plot. But if the main character must overcome a number of difficult obstacles to solve the problem, the plot becomes more interesting.

Conflict, or Struggle

To solve the problem, the character becomes involved in a *conflict,* or struggle, of some kind. A person can be in conflict with another person, or with some natural force (such as a shark or an earthquake), or with society as a whole, or even with different ideas or desires within himself or herself. From the time he falls from the yacht, Rainsford's problem is to survive. The first obstacle he faces is the sea. He wins his struggle against the sea only to be faced with other obstacles in the life-or-death struggle with General Zaroff. Where does Rainsford also struggle against his own mounting terror?

Characters: Protagonist and Antagonist

In most stories, the conflict is between two characters. The character who faces the problem and must overcome obstacles in order to solve it is called the *protagonist.* The character or the force that opposes the protagonist is called the *antagonist.* The antagonist stands in the way of the protagonist's getting what he or she wants. This does not mean that the protagonist is always a "good guy" and the antagonist always a "bad guy," though that's usually the case. A bank robber trying to solve the problem that all bank robbers try to solve could be the protagonist, and a detective trying to prevent the robbery could be the antagonist. *Protagonist* and *antagonist* are simply handy terms to use in identifying the principal characters or forces involved in a story's conflict. How does this writer make Zaroff seem like a totally evil antagonist?

Suspense

Many good stories, especially action stories, hold us in suspense. *Suspense* is our feeling that we have to keep on reading to find out what happens next. It is a feeling composed of a number of emotions–curiosity, fear, worry. When the suspense is great, we say we "can't put the book down" or, if the story is on television, we "can't turn off the set." "The Most Dangerous Game" creates suspense in the opening lines. The first thing that Whitney says about the island is that it's "rather a mystery." What other details about the island are supposed to arouse our curiosity and keep us reading?

The author builds suspense again in the dinner scene, when Zaroff begins to talk about his new "game." At what point in the scene did you realize what "game" Zaroff hunts on his island?

Suspense again mounts during "the chase." You are familiar with "the chase" from the "cops-and-robbers" kind of story so common on television: cars racing through city streets; squealing tires; near collisions; the sudden stop; the slamming of car doors; the attempted escape, perhaps over rooftops; the blazing guns. In "The Most Dangerous Game," the manhunt is a form of "the chase," a sure-fire method of creating suspense. Were there any moments during the chase when you thought Rainsford had lost the game?

Climax

Usually an author makes us sympathize with one character in the story. We want this character to succeed, but we are afraid he or she may fail. The point at which we learn whether this character succeeds or fails is the *climax* of the story. In a well-plotted story, the climax is the point of greatest interest and emotional intensity. It is the moment toward which all the action in the story has led us. In "The Most Dangerous Game," we do not reach the climax until we come to the very last line: "He had never slept in a better bed, Rainsford decided." In fact, Connell has been so skillful in plotting his story that we are not sure of the outcome until the last two words, *"Rainsford* decided." What were your feelings when you came to these last two words?

Composition

Narrating an Imagined Action

In telling a story, writers cannot give a detailed account of everything that happens. They must decide which events to describe in detail and which events to omit. Two important events are omitted from "The Most Dangerous Game." One is Rainsford's second swim, after which he hides in Zaroff's bedroom. The other is the final fight between the two men, which determines who is "to furnish a repast for the hounds."

Assuming the role of author, write a brief account of one of these events. Either describe Rainsford's swim and tell how he got into Zaroff's bedroom, or describe the final fight. Before you write, take time to imagine *in detail* exactly what happened. Keep your readers in suspense. Your story should be fast-moving and exciting, not wordy or long-winded.

Write as though you are the author telling the story, not as though you are answering a question. How *not* to begin: "I think Rainsford would have . . ."; "One thing that might have happened is . . ." Begin by describing the action: "For the second time in three days, Rainsford felt the warm waters of the Caribbean close over him."

Write about 200 words.

Richard Connell

As a boy in Poughkeepsie, New York, Richard Connell (1893 -1949) learned something about writing when he tried his hand as a sportswriter for the newspaper his father edited. He continued his writing at Harvard, where he was the editor of the *Lampoon.* After his discharge from the Army following World War I, he worked for a newspaper and later for an advertising firm. In addition to hundreds of short stories, Connell wrote novels and screenplays. He is best known today as the author of "The Most Dangerous Game."

To Build a Fire

JACK LONDON

This famous story takes place in the Yukon Territory, a vast area in northwest Canada on the eastern border of Alaska. In the 1890's part of the Yukon Territory, called the Klondike, was the scene of a gold rush. Travel in this harsh country was possible only over the rivers, using a boat in summer and trails on the frozen surface of the rivers in winter. This far north, the sun does not rise above the horizon in the dead of winter, and the temperature drops as low as seventy-five degrees below zero (sixty degrees below zero Celsius). As you will see, survival on the trail in such cold requires not only great physical endurance, but also intelligence and good judgment.

As you read, think about the following questions: Why is the man making this journey? Which of the man's problems are partly of his own making? Why did London put the dog in the story?

Day had broken cold and gray, exceedingly cold and gray, when the man turned aside from the main Yukon trail and climbed the high earth bank, where a dim and little-traveled trail led eastward through the fat spruce timberland. It was a steep bank, and he paused for breath at the top, excusing the act to himself by looking at his watch. It was nine o'clock. There was no sun or hint of sun, though there was not a cloud in the sky. It was a clear day, and yet there seemed an intangible pall over the face of things, a subtle gloom that made the day dark, and that was due to the absence of sun. This fact did not worry the man. He was used to the lack of sun. It had been days since he had seen the sun, and he knew that a few more days must pass before that cheerful orb, due south, would just peep above the skyline and dip immediately from view.

The man flung a look back along the way he had come. The Yukon lay a mile wide and hidden under three feet of ice. On top of this ice were as many feet of snow. It was all pure white, rolling in gentle undulations where the ice jams of the freeze-up had formed. North and south, as far as his eye could see, it was unbroken white, save for a dark hairline that curved and twisted from around the spruce-covered island to the south, and that curved and twisted away into the north, where it disappeared behind another spruce-covered island. This dark hairline was the trail—the main trail—that led south five hundred miles to the Chilkoot Pass, Dyea, and salt water; and that led north seventy miles to Dawson, and still on to the north a thousand miles to Nulato, and finally to St. Michael on the Bering Sea, a thousand miles and half a thousand more.

But all this—the mysterious, far-reaching hairline trail, the absence of sun from the sky, the tremendous cold, and the strangeness and weirdness of it all—made no impression on the

man. It was not because he was long used to it. He was a
newcomer in the land, a cheechako, and this was his first
winter. The trouble with him was that he was without imagination. He was quick and alert in the things of life, but only in
the things, and not in the significances. Fifty degrees below
zero meant eighty-odd degrees of frost. Such fact impressed
him as being cold and uncomfortable, and that was all. It did
not lead him to meditate upon his frailty as a creature of temperature, and upon man's frailty in general, able only to live
within certain narrow limits of heat and cold, and from there
on it did not lead him to the conjectural field of immortality
and man's place in the universe. Fifty degrees below zero stood
for a bite of frost that hurt and that must be guarded against by
the use of mittens, earflaps, warm moccasins, and thick socks.
Fifty degrees below zero was to him just precisely fifty degrees
below zero. That there should be anything more to it than that
was a thought that never entered his head.

As he turned to go on, he spat speculatively. There was a
sharp, explosive crackle that startled him. He spat again. And
again, in the air, before it could fall to the snow, the spittle
crackled. He knew that at fifty below, spittle crackled on the
snow, but this spittle had crackled in the air. Undoubtedly it
was colder than fifty below—how much colder he did not
know. But the temperature did not matter. He was bound for
the old claim on the left fork of Henderson Creek, where the
boys were already. They had come over across the divide from
the Indian Creek country, while he had come the roundabout
way to take a look at the possibilities of getting out logs in the
spring from the islands in the Yukon. He would be into camp
by six o'clock; a bit after dark, it was true, but the boys would be
there, a fire would be going, and a hot supper would be ready.
As for lunch, he pressed his hand against the protruding bundle under his jacket. It was also under his shirt, wrapped up in
a handkerchief and lying against the naked skin. It was the only
way to keep the biscuits from freezing. He smiled agreeably to

himself as he thought of those biscuits, each cut open and sopped in bacon grease, and each enclosing a generous slice of fried bacon.

He plunged in among the big spruce trees. The trail was faint. A foot of snow had fallen since the last sled had passed over, and he was glad he was without a sled, traveling light. In fact, he carried nothing but the lunch wrapped in the hand-kerchief. He was surprised, however, at the cold. It certainly was cold, he concluded, as he rubbed his numb nose and cheekbones with his mittened hand. He was a warm-whiskered man, but the hair on his face did not protect the high cheek-bones and the eager nose that thrust itself aggressively into the frosty air.

At the man's heels trotted a dog, a big native husky, the proper wolf dog, gray-coated and without any visible or tem-peramental difference from its brother, the wild wolf. The ani-mal was depressed by the tremendous cold. It knew that it was no time for traveling. Its instinct told it a truer tale than was told to the man by the man's judgment. In reality, it was not merely colder than fifty below zero; it was colder than sixty below, than seventy below. It was seventy-five below zero. Since the freezing point is thirty-two above zero, it meant that one hundred and seven degrees of frost obtained. The dog did not know anything about thermometers. Possibly in its brain there was no sharp consciousness of a condition of very cold such as was in the man's brain. But the brute had its instinct. It experienced a vague but menacing apprehension that subdued it and made it slink along at the man's heels, and that made it question eagerly every unwonted[1] movement of the man, as if expecting him to go into camp or to seek shelter somewhere and build a fire. The dog had learned fire, and it wanted fire, or else to burrow under the snow and cuddle its warmth away from the air.

---

1. *unwonted*: unusual.

The frozen moisture of its breathing had settled on its fur in a fine powder of frost, and especially were its jowls, muzzle, and eyelashes whitened by its crystaled breath. The man's red beard and mustache were likewise frosted, but more solidly, the deposit taking the form of ice and increasing with every warm, moist breath he exhaled. Also, the man was chewing tobacco, and the muzzle of ice held his lips so rigidly that he was unable to clear his chin when he expelled the juice. The result was that a crystal beard of the color and solidity of amber was increasing its length on his chin. If he fell down it would shatter itself, like glass, into brittle fragments. But he did not mind the appendage. It was the penalty all tobacco-chewers paid in that country, and he had been out before in two cold snaps. They had not been so cold as this, he knew, but by the spirit thermometer[2] at Sixty Mile he knew they had been registered at fifty below and at fifty-five.

He held on through the level stretch of woods for several miles, crossed a wide flat, and dropped down a bank to the frozen bed of a small stream. This was Henderson Creek, and he knew he was ten miles from the forks. He looked at his watch. It was ten o'clock. He was making four miles an hour, and he calculated that he would arrive at the forks at half past twelve. He decided to celebrate that event by eating his lunch there.

The dog dropped in again at his heels, with a tail drooping discouragement, as the man swung along the creek bed. The furrow of the old sled trail was plainly visible, but a dozen inches of snow covered the marks of the last runners. In a month no man had come up or down that silent creek. The man held steadily on. He was not much given to thinking, and just then particularly, he had nothing to think about save that he would eat lunch at the forks and that at six o'clock he would be in camp with the boys. There was nobody to talk to; and, had

2. *spirit thermometer:* alcohol thermometer.

there been, speech would have been impossible because of the ice muzzle on his mouth. So he continued monotonously to chew tobacco and to increase the length of his amber beard.

Once in a while the thought reiterated itself that it was very cold and that he had never experienced such cold. As he walked along he rubbed his cheekbones and nose with the back of his mittened hand. He did this automatically, now and again changing hands. But rub as he would, the instant he stopped his cheekbones went numb, and the following instant the end of his nose went numb. He was sure to frost his cheeks; he knew that, and experienced a pang of regret that he had not devised a nose strap of the sort Bud wore in the cold snaps. Such a strap passed across the cheeks, as well, and saved them. But it didn't matter much, after all. What were frosted cheeks? A bit painful, that was all; they were never serious.

Empty as the man's mind was of thought, he was keenly observant, and he noticed the changes in the creek, the curves and bends and timber jams, and always he sharply noted where he placed his feet. Once, coming around a bend, he shied abruptly, like a startled horse, curved away from the place where he had been walking, and retreated several paces back along the trail. The creek, he knew, was frozen clear to the bottom—no creek could contain water in that arctic winter—but he knew also that there were springs that bubbled out from the hillsides and ran along under the snow and on top of the ice of the creek. He knew that the coldest snaps never froze these springs, and he knew likewise their danger. They were traps. They hid pools of water under the snow that might be three inches deep, or three feet. Sometimes a skin of ice half an inch thick covered them, and in turn was covered by the snow. Sometimes there were alternate layers of water and ice skin, so that when one broke through he kept on breaking through for a while, sometimes wetting himself to the waist.

That was why he had shied in such panic. He had felt the give under his feet and heard the crackle of a snow-hidden ice skin. And to get his feet wet in such a temperature meant trouble and danger. At the very least it meant delay, for he would be forced to stop and build a fire, and under its protection to bare his feet while he dried his socks and moccasins. He stood and studied the creek bed and its banks, and decided that the flow of water came from the right. He reflected awhile, rubbing his nose and cheeks, then skirted to the left, stepping gingerly and testing the footing for each step. Once clear of the danger, he took a fresh chew of tobacco and swung along at his four-mile gait.

In the course of the next two hours he came upon several similar traps. Usually the snow above the hidden pools had a sunken, candied appearance that advertised the danger. Once again, however, he had a close call; and once, suspecting danger, he compelled the dog to go on in front. The dog did not want to go. It hung back until the man shoved it forward, and then it went quickly across the white, unbroken surface. Suddenly it broke through, floundered to one side, and got away to firmer footing. It had wet its forefeet and legs, and almost immediately the water that clung to it turned to ice. It made quick efforts to lick the ice off its legs, then dropped down in the snow and began to bite out the ice that had formed between the toes. This was a matter of instinct. To permit the ice to remain would mean sore feet. It did not know this. It merely obeyed the mysterious prompting that arose from the deep crypts[3] of its being. But the man knew, having achieved a judgment on the subject, and he removed the mitten from his right hand and helped tear out the ice particles. He did not expose his fingers more than a minute, and was astonished at the swift numbness that smote them. It certainly was cold. He pulled on the mitten hastily, and beat the hand savagely across his chest.

At twelve o'clock the day was at its brightest. Yet the sun was

---

3. *crypts* (krĭpts): literally, underground chambers.

too far south on its winter journey to clear the horizon. The bulge of the earth intervened between it and Henderson Creek, where the man walked under a clear sky at noon and cast no shadow. At half past twelve, to the minute, he arrived at the forks of the creek. He was pleased at the speed he had made. If he kept it up, he would certainly be with the boys by six. He unbuttoned his jacket and shirt and drew forth his lunch. The action consumed no more than a quarter of a minute, yet in that brief moment the numbness laid hold of the exposed fingers. He did not put the mitten on, but instead struck the fingers a dozen sharp smashes against his leg. Then he sat down on a snow-covered log to eat. The sting that followed upon the striking of his fingers against his leg ceased so quickly that he was startled. He had had no chance to take a bite of biscuit. He struck the fingers repeatedly and returned them to the mitten, baring the other hand for the purpose of eating. He tried to take a mouthful, but the ice muzzle prevented. He had forgotten to build a fire and thaw out. He chuckled at his foolishness, and as he chuckled he noted the numbness creeping into the exposed fingers. Also, he noted that the stinging which had first come to his toes when he sat down was already passing away. He wondered whether the toes were warm or numb. He moved them inside the moccasins and decided that they were numb.

He pulled the mitten on hurriedly and stood up. He was a bit frightened. He stamped up and down until the stinging returned into the feet. It certainly was cold, was his thought. That man from Sulfur Creek had spoken the truth when telling how cold it sometimes got in the country. And he had laughed at him at the time! That showed one must not be too sure of things. There was no mistake about it, it *was* cold. He strode up and down, stamping his feet and threshing his arms, until reassured by the returning warmth. Then he got out matches and proceeded to make a fire. From the undergrowth, where high water of the previous spring had lodged a supply of seasoned twigs, he got his firewood. Working carefully from a small beginning, he soon had a roaring fire, over which he thawed the ice from his face and in the protection of which he ate his biscuits. For the moment the cold of space was outwitted. The dog took satisfaction in the fire, stretching out close enough for warmth and far enough away to escape being singed.

When the man had finished, he filled his pipe and took his comfortable time over a smoke. Then he pulled on his mittens, settled the earflaps of his cap firmly about his ears, and took the creek trail up the left fork. The dog was disappointed and yearned back toward the fire. This man did not know cold. Possibly all the generations of his ancestry had been ignorant of cold, of real cold, of cold one hundred and seven degrees below freezing point. But the dog knew; all its ancestry knew, and it had inherited the knowledge. And it knew that it was not good to walk abroad in such fearful cold. It was the time to lie snug in a hole in the snow and wait for a curtain of cloud to be drawn across the face of outer space whence this cold came. On the other hand, there was no keen intimacy between the dog and the man. The one was the toil slave of the other, and the only caresses it had ever received were the caresses of the whiplash and of harsh and menacing throat sounds that threatened the whiplash. So the dog made no effort to communicate its apprehension to the man. It was not concerned in the welfare of the man; it was for its own sake that it yearned back toward the fire. But the man whistled, and spoke to it with the sound of whiplashes, and the dog swung in at the man's heels and followed after.

The man took a chew of tobacco and proceeded to start a new amber beard. Also, his moist breath quickly powdered with white his mustache, eyebrows, and lashes. There did not seem to be so many springs on the left fork of the Henderson, and for half an hour the man saw no signs of any. And then it happened. At a place where there were no signs, where the soft, unbroken snow seemed to advertise solidity beneath, the man broke through. It was not deep. He wet himself halfway to the knees before he floundered out to the firm crust.

He was angry, and cursed his luck aloud. He had hoped to get into camp with the boys at six o'clock, and this would delay him an hour, for he would have to build a fire and dry out his footgear. This was imperative at that low temperature—he knew that much; and he turned aside to the bank, which he climbed. On top, tangled in the underbrush about the trunks of several small spruce trees, was a high-water deposit of dry firewood—sticks and twigs, principally, but also larger portions of seasoned branches and fine, dry, last year's grasses. He threw down several large pieces on top of the snow. This served for a foundation and prevented the young flame from drowning itself in the snow it otherwise would melt. The flame he got by touching a match to a small shred of birch bark that he took from his pocket. This burned even more readily than paper. Placing it on the foundation, he fed the young flame with wisps of dry grass and with the tiniest dry twigs.

He worked slowly and carefully, keenly aware of his danger. Gradually, as the flame grew stronger, he increased the size of the twigs with which he fed it. He squatted in the snow, pulling the twigs out from their entanglement in the brush and feeding directly to the flame. He knew there must be no failure. When it is seventy-five below zero, a man must not fail in his first attempt to build a fire—that is, if his feet are wet. If his feet are dry, and he fails, he can run along the trail for a half a mile and restore his circulation. But the circulation of wet and freezing feet cannot be restored by running when it is seventy-five below. No matter how fast he runs, the wet feet will freeze the harder.

All this the man knew. The old-timer on Sulfur Creek had told him about it the previous fall, and now he was appreciating the advice. Already all sensation had gone out of his feet. To build the fire, he had been forced to remove his mittens, and the fingers had quickly gone numb. His pace of four miles an hour had kept his heart pumping blood to the surface of his body and to all the extremities. But the instant he stopped, the action of the pump eased down. The cold of space smote the unprotected tip of the planet, and he, being on that unprotected tip, received the full force of the blow. The blood of his body recoiled before it. The blood was alive, like the dog, and like the dog it wanted to hide away and cover itself up from the fearful cold. So long as he walked four miles an hour, he pumped that blood, willy-nilly, to the surface; but now it ebbed away and sank down into the recesses of his body. The extremities were the first to feel its absence. His wet feet froze the faster, and his exposed fingers numbed the faster, though they had not yet begun to freeze. Nose and cheeks were already freezing, while the skin of all his body chilled as it lost its blood.

But he was safe. Toes and nose and cheeks would be only touched by the frost, for the fire was beginning to burn with strength. He was feeding it with twigs the size of his finger. In another minute he would be able to feed it with branches the size of his wrist, and then he could remove his wet footgear, and, while it dried, he could keep his naked feet warm by the fire, rubbing them at first, of course, with snow. The fire was a success. He was safe. He remembered the advice of the old-timer on Sulfur Creek, and smiled. The old-timer had been very serious in laying down the law that no man must travel alone in the Klondike after fifty below. Well, here he was; he had had the accident; he was alone; and he had saved himself. Those old-timers were rather womanish, some of them, he thought. All a man had to do was to keep his head and he was all right. Any man who was a man could travel alone. But it was surprising, the rapidity with which his cheeks and nose were freezing. And he had not thought his fingers could go lifeless in so short a time. Lifeless they were, for he could scarcely make them move together to grip a twig, and they seemed remote from his body and from him. When he touched a twig, he had to look and see whether or not he had hold of it. The wires were pretty well down between him and his finger ends.

All of which counted for little. There was the fire, snapping and crackling and promising life with every dancing flame. He started to untie his moccasins. They were coated with ice; the thick German socks were like sheaths of iron halfway to the knees; and the moccasin strings were like rods of steel all twisted and knotted as by some conflagration. For a moment he tugged with his numb fingers, then, realizing the folly of it, he drew his sheath knife.

But before he could cut the strings it happened. It was his own fault, or, rather, his mistake. He should not have built the fire under the spruce tree. He should have built it in the open. But it had been easier to pull the twigs from the bush and drop them directly on the fire. Now the tree under which he had done this carried a weight of snow on its boughs. No wind had blown for weeks, and each bough was fully freighted. Each time he had pulled a twig he had communicated a slight agitation to the tree—an imperceptible agitation, so far as he was concerned, but an agitation sufficient to bring about the disaster. High up in the tree one bough capsized its load of snow. This fell on the boughs beneath, capsizing them. This process continued, spreading out and involving the whole tree. It grew like an avalanche, and it descended without warning upon the man and the fire, and the fire was blotted out! Where it had burned was a mantle of fresh and disordered snow.

The man was shocked. It was as though he had just heard his own sentence of death. For a moment he sat and stared at the spot where the fire had been. Then he grew very calm. Perhaps the old-timer on Sulfur Creek was right. If he had only had a trail mate, he would have been in no danger now. The trail mate could have built the fire. Well, it was up to him to build the fire over again, and this second time there must be no failure. Even if he succeeded, he would most likely lose some toes. His feet must be badly frozen by now, and there would be some time before the second fire was ready.

Such were his thoughts, but he did not sit and think them. He was busy all the time they were passing through his mind. He made a new foundation for a fire, this time in the open, where no treacherous tree could blot it out. Next he gathered dry grasses and tiny twigs from the high-water flotsam. He could not bring his fingers together to pull them out, but he was able to gather them by the handful. In this way he got many rotten twigs and bits of green moss that were undesirable, but it was the best he could do. He worked methodically, even collecting an armful of the larger branches to be used later when the fire gathered strength. And all the while the dog sat and watched him, a certain yearning wistfulness in its eyes, for it looked upon him as the fire provider, and the fire was slow in coming.

When all was ready, the man reached in his pocket for a second piece of birch bark. He knew the bark was there, and, though he could not feel it with his fingers, he could hear its crisp rustling as he fumbled for it. Try as he would, he could not clutch hold of it. And all the time, in his consciousness, was the knowledge that each instant his feet were freezing. This thought tended to put him in a panic, but he fought against it and kept calm. He pulled on his mittens with his teeth, and threshed his arms back and forth, beating his hands with all his might against his sides. He did this sitting down, and he stood up to do it; and all the while the dog sat in the snow, its wolf brush of a tail curled around warmly over its forefeet, its sharp wolf ears pricked forward intently as it watched the man. And the man, as he beat and threshed with his arms and hands, felt a great surge of envy as he regarded the creature that was warm and secure in its natural covering.

After a time he was aware of the first faraway signals of sensation in his beaten fingers. The faint tingling grew stronger till it evolved into a stinging ache that was excruciating, but which the man hailed with satisfaction. He stripped the mitten from his right hand and fetched forth the birch bark. The exposed fingers were quickly going numb again. Next he brought out his bunch of sulfur matches. But the tremendous cold had already driven the life out of his fingers. In his effort to separate one match from the others, the whole bunch fell in the snow. He tried to pick it out of the snow, but failed. The dead fingers could neither touch nor clutch. He was very careful. He drove the thought of his freezing feet, and nose, and cheeks, out of his mind, devoting his whole soul to the matches. He watched, using the sense of vision in place of that of touch, and when he saw his fingers on each side of the bunch, he closed them—that is, he willed to close them, for the wires were down, and the fingers did not obey. He pulled the mitten on the right hand, and beat it fiercely against his knee. Then, with both mittened hands, he scooped the bunch of matches, along with much snow, into his lap. Yet he was no better off.

After some manipulation he managed to get the bunch between the heels of his mittened hands. In this fashion he carried it to his mouth. The ice crackled and snapped when by a violent effort he opened his mouth. He drew the lower jaw in, curled the upper lip out of the way, and scraped the bunch with his upper teeth in order to separate a match. He succeeded in getting one, which he dropped on his lap. He was no better off. He could not pick it up. Then he devised a way. He picked it up in his teeth and scratched it on his leg. Twenty times he scratched before he succeeded in lighting it. As it flamed he held it with his teeth to the birch bark. But the burning brimstone went up his nostrils and into his lungs, causing him to cough spasmodically. The match fell into the snow and went out.

The old-timer on Sulfur Creek was right, he thought in the moment of controlled despair that ensued: after fifty below, a man should travel with a partner. He beat his hands, but failed in exciting any sensation. Suddenly he bared both hands, removing the mittens with his teeth. He caught the whole bunch between the heels of his hands. His arm muscles, not being frozen, enabled him to press the hand heels tightly against the matches. Then he scratched the bunch along his leg. It flared into flame, seventy sulfur matches at once! There was no wind to blow them out. He kept his head to one side to escape the strangling fumes, and held the blazing bunch to the birch bark. As he so held it, he became aware of sensation in his hand. His flesh was burning. He could smell it. Deep down below the surface he could feel it. The sensation developed into pain that grew acute. And still he endured it, holding the flame of the matches clumsily to the bark that would not light readily because his own burning hands were in the way, absorbing most of the flame.

At last, when he could endure no more, he jerked his hands apart. The blazing matches fell sizzling into the snow, but the birch bark was alight. He began laying dry grass and the tiniest twigs on the flame. He could not pick and choose, for he had to lift the fuel between the heels of his hands. Small pieces of rotten wood and green moss clung to the twigs, and he bit them off as well as he could with his teeth. He cherished the flame carefully and awkwardly. It meant life, and it must not perish. The withdrawal of blood from the surface of his body now made him begin to shiver, and he grew more awkward. A large piece of green moss fell squarely on the little fire. He tried to poke it out with his fingers, but his shivering frame made him poke too far, and he disrupted the nucleus of the little fire, the burning grasses and tiny twigs separating and scattering. He tried to poke them together again, but in spite of the tenseness of the effort, his shivering got away with him, and the twigs were hopelessly scattered. Each twig gushed a puff of smoke and went out. The fire provider had failed. As he looked apathetically about him, his eyes chanced on the dog, sitting across the ruins of the fire from him, in the snow, making restless, hunching movements, slightly lifting one forefoot and then the other, shifting its weight back and forth on them with wistful eagerness.

The sight of the dog put a wild idea into his head. He remembered the tale of the man, caught in a blizzard, who killed a steer and crawled inside the carcass, and so was saved. He would kill the dog and bury his hands in the warm body until the numbness went out of them. Then he could build another fire. He spoke to the dog, calling it to him; but in his voice was a strange note of fear that frightened the animal, who had never known the man to speak in such a way before. Something was the matter, and its suspicious nature sensed danger—it knew not what danger, but somewhere, somehow, in its brain arose an apprehension of the man. It flattened its ears down at the sound of the man's voice, and its restless, hunching movements and the liftings and shiftings of its fore-feet became more pronounced; but it would not come to the man. He got on his hands and knees and crawled toward the dog. This unusual posture again excited suspicion, and the animal sidled mincingly away.

The man sat up in the snow for a moment and struggled for calmness. Then he pulled on his mittens, by means of his teeth, and got up on his feet. He glanced down at first in order to assure himself that he was really standing up, for the absence of sensation in his feet left him unrelated to the earth. His erect position in itself started to drive the webs of suspicion from the dog's mind; and when he spoke peremptorily, with the sound of whiplashes in his voice, the dog rendered its customary alle-giance and came to him. As it came within reaching distance, the man lost his control. His arms flashed out to the dog, and he experienced genuine surprise when he discovered that his hands could not clutch, that there was neither bend nor feeling in the fingers. He had forgotten for the moment that they were frozen and that they were freezing more and more. All this happened quickly, and before the animal could get away, he encircled its body with his arms. He sat down in the snow, and in this fashion held the dog, while it snarled and whined and struggled.

But it was all he could do, hold its body encircled in his arms and sit there. He realized that he could not kill the dog. There was no way to do it. With his helpless hands he could neither draw nor hold his sheath knife nor throttle the animal. He released it, and it plunged wildly away, its tail between its legs and still snarling. It halted forty feet away and surveyed him curiously, with ears sharply pricked forward. The man looked down at his hands in order to locate them, and found them hanging on the ends of his arms. It struck him as curious that one should have to use his eyes in order to find out where his hands were. He began threshing his arms back and forth, beating the mittened hands against his sides. He did this for five minutes, violently, and his heart pumped enough blood up to the surface to put a stop to his shivering. But no sensation was aroused in his hands. He had an impression that they hung like weights on the ends of his arms, but when he tried to run the impression down, he could not find it.

A certain fear of death, dull and oppressive, came to him. This fear quickly became poignant as he realized that it was no longer a mere matter of freezing his fingers and toes, or of losing his hands and feet, but that it was a matter of life and death, with the chances against him. This threw him into a panic, and he turned and ran up the creek bed along the old, dim trail. The dog joined in behind and kept up with him. He ran blindly, without intention, in fear such as he had never known in his life. Slowly, as he plowed and floundered through the snow, he began to see things again—the banks of the creek, the old timber jams, the leafless aspens, and the sky. The running made him feel better. He did not shiver. Maybe, if he ran on, his feet would thaw out; and, anyway, if he ran far enough, he would reach the camp and the boys. Without doubt he would lose some fingers and toes and some of his face; but the boys would take care of him, and save the rest of him when he got there. And, at the same time, there was another thought in his mind that said he would never get to the camp and the boys; that it was too many miles away, that the freezing had too great a start on him, and that he would soon be stiff and dead. This thought he kept in the background and refused to consider. Sometimes it pushed itself forward and demanded to be heard, but he thrust it back and strove to think of other things.

It struck him as curious that he could run at all on feet so frozen that he could not feel them when they struck the earth and took the weight of his body. He seemed to himself to skim along above the surface, and to have no connection with the earth. Somewhere he had once seen a winged Mercury,[4] and he wondered if Mercury felt as he felt when skimming over the earth.

His theory of running until he reached camp and the boys had one flaw in it: he lacked the endurance. Several times he stumbled, and finally he tottered, crumpled up, and fell. When he tried to rise, he failed. He must sit and rest, he decided, and next time he would merely walk and keep on going. As he sat and regained his breath, he noted that he was feeling quite warm and comfortable. He was not shivering, and it even seemed that a warm glow had come to his chest and trunk. And yet, when he touched his nose or cheeks, there was no sensation. Running would not thaw them out. Nor would it thaw out his hands and feet. Then the thought came to him that the frozen portions of his body must be extending. He tried to keep this thought down, to forget it, to think of something else; he was aware of the panicky feeling that it caused, and he was afraid of the panic. But the thought asserted itself, and persisted, until it produced a vision of his body totally frozen.

4. *Mercury:* the messenger of the gods in Roman mythology. He wore winged sandals and a winged hat.

This was too much, and he made another wild run along the trail. Once he slowed down to a walk, but the thought of the freezing extending itself made him run again.

And all the time the dog ran with him, at his heels. When he fell down a second time, it curled its tail over its forefeet and sat in front of him, facing him, curiously eager and intent. The warmth and security of the animal angered him, and he cursed it till it flattened down its ears appeasingly. This time the shivering came more quickly upon the man. He was losing in his battle with the frost. It was creeping into his body from all sides. The thought of it drove him on, but he ran no more than a hundred feet when he staggered and pitched headlong. It was his last panic. When he had recovered his breath and control, he sat up and entertained in his mind the conception of meeting death with dignity. However, the conception did not come to him in such terms. His idea of it was that he had been making a fool of himself, running around like a chicken with its head cut off—such was the simile that occurred to him. Well, he was bound to freeze anyway, and he might as well take it decently. With this new-found peace of mind came the first glimmerings of drowsiness. A good idea, he thought, to sleep off to death. It was like taking an anesthetic. Freezing was not so bad as people thought. There were lots worse ways to die.

He pictured the boys finding his body next day. Suddenly he found himself with them, coming along the trail and looking for himself. And, still with them, he came around a turn in the trail and found himself lying in the snow. He did not belong with himself any more, for even then he was out of himself, standing with the boys and looking at himself in the snow. It certainly was cold, was his thought. When he got back to the States, he could tell the folks what real cold was. He drifted on from this to a vision of the old-timer on Sulfur Creek. He could see him quite clearly, warm and comfortable, and smoking a pipe.

"You were right, old hoss; you were right," the man mumbled to the old-timer of Sulfur Creek.

Then the man drowsed off into what seemed to him the most comfortable and satisfying sleep he had ever known. The dog sat facing him and waiting. The brief day drew to a close in a long, slow twilight. There were no signs of a fire to be made, and, besides, never in the dog's experience had it known a man to sit like that in the snow and make no fire. As the twilight drew on, its eager yearning for the fire mastered it, and with a great lifting and shifting of forefeet, it whined softly, then flattened its ears down in anticipation of being chidden[5] by the man. But the man remained silent. Later, the dog whined loudly. And still later it crept close to the man and caught the scent of death. This made the animal bristle and back away. A little longer it delayed, howling under the stars that leaped and dancing and shone brightly in the cold sky. Then it turned and trotted up the trail in the direction of the camp it knew, where were the other food providers and fire providers.

5. *chidden:* scolded.

The Facts of the Story

Write short answers to the following questions. Answers may be one word or a phrase. You can probably answer all the questions without rereading the story, but look back if you wish. To answer some questions, you may quote from the story.

1. Why is the man making this journey?

2. At first, why doesn't the cold make an impression on the man?

3. Why can't the man eat until he builds a fire?

4. What advice had the old-timer on Sulfur Creek given the man?

5. In what way does the dog help the man?

6. Why does the man's danger increase when he stops exercising?

7. What serious accident does the man suffer?

8. What serious mistake does the man make?

9. Why does the dog survive?

10. Why is the story called "To Build a Fire"?

The Ideas in the Story

For class discussion, prepare answers to the following questions.

1. In "The Most Dangerous Game," General Zaroff explains why he has become bored with hunting animals. He says: " 'No animal had a chance with me any more. . . . The animal had nothing but his legs and his instinct. *Instinct* is no match for reason.' " Early in "To Build a Fire," London says about the dog: "The animal was depressed

by the tremendous cold. It knew that it was no time for traveling. Its *instinct* told it a truer tale than was told to the man by the man's judgment." London's story seems to suggest that the *lack* of animal instinct is a human frailty. London probably included the dog in the story so that he could make this observation about instinct and reason. Referring to specific passages in the story, tell how instinct becomes a more important quality than reason, or judgment. What do you think of this idea?

2. London says that the man lacked imagination. He did not meditate upon "his frailty as a creature of temperature, and upon man's frailty in general . . ." By referring to events in the story, explain how London shows that people are physically frail, or weak. On the other hand, where does he show that the dog is equipped to survive where humans cannot?

3. In this story, the man's weaknesses are chiefly physical. They are revealed by his struggle against the physical force of nature. But human beings often suffer because of other frailties. Name some of these other nonphysical weaknesses, and explain how they also can cause problems.

The Art of the Storyteller

Plot

The plot of "To Build a Fire" is simple, yet it illustrates many of the elements of plot explained in the discussion of "The Most Dangerous Game" (page 28). Obviously the protagonist is the man. His problem is to reach the camp on Henderson Creek. What is the antagonist—the force that opposes the protagonist? (You know that it is not a person, since there is only one person in the story.) What problems does the protagonist have to overcome to get what he wants? Why does he fail?

You probably will agree that the story is full of suspense and that the suspense builds steadily to the climax—the moment of greatest emotional intensity, when we know how the conflict will turn out. In "The Most Dangerous Game," the climax comes with the last sentence, where we learn that Rainsford wins his struggle against Zaroff. Until then we cannot be sure of the outcome—we are still gripped by suspense. The climax in "To Build a Fire" occurs earlier in the story. At what point do you strongly suspect that the man will not survive? At what moment do you know for certain he does not survive?

The story moves on from the climax to the conclusion. What does the storyteller tell you after you know for certain that the man is dead? What were your feelings as you read the conclusion of the story?

Foreshadowing

Suspense is often increased when the writer hints at what will happen later in the story. This is called *foreshadowing.* For example, the final sentences in the third paragraph hint that *we* are going to find out something about survival in extreme cold, something this man does not understand: "Fifty degrees below zero was to him just precisely fifty degrees below zero. That there should be anything more to it than that was a thought that never entered his head." Indeed, as you know, later events in the story show how dangerous such extreme cold really is.

How does each of the following statements foreshadow events that occur later in the story?

> 1. . . . there seemed an intangible pall over the face of things, a subtle gloom . . . (Page 33)
>
> 2. And to get his feet wet in such a temperature meant trouble and danger. (Page 38)
>
> 3. But the dog knew . . . that it was not good to walk abroad in such fearful cold. (Page 40)

Look over the opening pages of "The Most Dangerous Game." Find an example of foreshadowing there.

Composition

Developing a Paragraph

A well-constructed paragraph often begins with a *topic sentence* –that is, a statement of the subject to be discussed. The writer develops the paragraph by giving information to support the idea in the topic sentence. Using facts from "To Build a Fire," write a paragraph developing one of the following topic sentences.

1. In "To Build a Fire," Jack London uses details that make us feel the effects of the severe cold. (Search through the story for examples of how London does this. Use these examples in developing your paragraph.)

2. If the man in "To Build a Fire" had had more imagination, he would not have frozen to death.

3. A wolf dog is better-equipped than a human being to survive at seventy-five degrees below zero.

Write approximately 100 words.

Jack London

Born in poverty in San Francisco, Jack London (1876-1916) grew up having more experience with the rough life of the waterfront than with the inside of a classroom. His great love of reading made up for his lack of schooling. He was probably better known at the public library than at the high school. Adventurer, vagabond, sailor, prospector for gold in the Klondike, London acquired fame and fortune as a writer of fiction. Although his participation in the Klondike gold rush yielded him no gold, it did give him something more valuable –material for the stories that made him, at one time, America's best-paid and most popular writer. Two of his novels, *The Call of the Wild* and *White Fang,* are among the greatest dog stories ever written.

The Birds

DAPHNE du MAURIER

Before you read this nightmarish story, consider the situation it is built on. Suppose all the birds in the world decide without warning to attack human beings, with the intention, apparently, of destroying the human race. Now let your imagination go. What do you imagine the birds' attack would be like? How would you protect yourself? Which birds would you fear most? How could governments protect their people? Do you think the birds could succeed?

In developing this unlikely situation, du Maurier shows what a remarkable imagination she has. Perhaps in your own imagining, you thought of some things she did not.

The story is set on a farm in England.

On December the third the wind changed overnight and it was winter. Until then the autumn had been mellow, soft. The leaves had lingered on the trees, golden-red, and the hedgerows were still green. The earth was rich where the plow had turned it.

Nat Hocken, because of a wartime disability, had a pension and did not work full time at the farm. He worked three days a week, and they gave him the lighter jobs: hedging, thatching, repairs to the farm buildings.

Although he was married, with children, his was a solitary disposition; he liked best to work alone. It pleased him when he was given a bank to build up, or a gate to mend at the far end of the peninsula, where the sea surrounded the farmland on either side. Then, at midday, he would pause and eat the pasty that his wife had baked for him, and, sitting on the cliff's edge, would watch the birds. Autumn was best for this, better than spring. In spring the birds flew inland, purposeful, intent; they knew where they were bound; the rhythm and ritual of their life brooked no delay. In autumn those that had not migrated overseas but remained to pass the winter were caught up in the same driving urge, but because migration was denied them, followed a pattern of their own. Great flocks of them came to the peninsula, restless, uneasy, spending themselves in motion; now wheeling, circling in the sky, now settling to feed on the rich, new-turned soil; but even when they fed, it was as though they did so without hunger, without desire. Restlessness drove them to the skies again.

Black and white, jackdaw and gull, mingled in strange partnership, seeking some sort of liberation, never satisfied, never still. Flocks of starlings, rustling like silk, flew to fresh pasture, driven by the same necessity of movement, and the smaller birds, the finches and the larks, scattered from tree to hedge as if compelled.

Nat watched them, and he watched the sea birds too. Down in the bay they waited for the tide. They had more patience. Oyster catchers, redshank, sanderling, and curlew watched by the water's edge; as the slow sea sucked at the shore and then withdrew, leaving the strip of seaweed bare and the shingle churned, the sea birds raced and ran upon the beaches. Then that same impulse to flight seized upon them too. Crying, whistling, calling, they skimmed the placid sea and left the shore. Make haste, make speed, hurry and begone; yet where, and to what purpose? The restless urge of autumn, unsatisfying, sad, had put a spell upon them and they must flock, and wheel, and cry; they must spill themselves of motion before winter came.

"Perhaps," thought Nat, munching his pasty by the cliff's edge, "a message comes to the birds in autumn, like a warning. Winter is coming. Many of them perish. And like people who, apprehensive of death before their time, drive themselves to work or folly, the birds do likewise."

The birds had been more restless than ever this fall of the year, the agitation more marked because the days were still. As the tractor traced its path up and down the western hills, the figure of the farmer silhouetted on the driving seat, the whole machine and the man upon it, would be lost momentarily in the great cloud of wheeling, crying birds. There were many more than usual; Nat was sure of this. Always, in autumn, they followed the plow, but not in great flocks like these, nor with such clamor.

Nat remarked upon it when hedging was finished for the day. "Yes," said the farmer, "there are more birds about than usual; I've noticed it too. And daring, some of them, taking no notice of the tractor. One or two gulls came so close to my head this afternoon I thought they'd knock my cap off! As it was, I could scarcely see what I was doing, when they were overhead and I had the sun in my eyes. I have a notion the weather will change. It will be a hard winter. That's why the birds are restless."

Nat, tramping home across the fields and down the lane to his cottage, saw the birds still flocking over the western hills, in the last glow of the sun. No wind, and the gray sea calm and full. Campion in bloom yet in the hedges, and the air mild. The farmer was right, though, and it was that night the weather turned. Nat's bedroom faced east. He woke just after two and heard the wind in the chimney. Not the storm and bluster of a sou'westerly gale, bringing the rain, but east wind, cold and dry. It sounded hollow in the chimney, and a loose slate rattled on the roof. Nat listened, and he could hear the sea roaring in the bay. Even the air in the small bedroom had turned chill: a draft came under the skirting of the door, blowing upon the bed. Nat drew the blanket round him, leant closer to the back of his sleeping wife, and stayed wakeful, watchful, aware of misgiving without cause.

Then he heard the tapping on the window. There was no creeper on the cottage walls to break loose and scratch upon the pane. He listened, and the tapping continued until, irritated by the sound, Nat got out of bed and went to the window. He opened it, and as he did so something brushed his hand, jabbing at his knuckles, grazing the skin. Then he saw the flutter of the wings and it was gone, over the roof, behind the cottage.

It was a bird; what kind of bird he could not tell. The wind must have driven it to shelter on the sill.

He shut the window and went back to bed, but, feeling his knuckles wet, put his mouth to the scratch. The bird had drawn blood. Frightened, he supposed, and bewildered, the bird, seeking shelter, had stabbed at him in the darkness. Once more he settled himself to sleep.

Presently the tapping came again, this time more forceful,

more insistent, and now his wife woke at the sound and, turning in the bed, said to him, "See to the window, Nat, it's rattling."

"I've already seen to it," he told her; "there's some bird there trying to get in. Can't you hear the wind? It's blowing from the east, driving the birds to shelter."

"Send them away," she said, "I can't sleep with that noise."

He went to the window for the second time, and now when he opened it, there was not one bird upon the sill but half a dozen; they flew straight into his face, attacking him.

He shouted, striking out at them with his arms, scattering them; like the first one, they flew over the roof and disappeared. Quickly he let the window fall and latched it.

"Did you hear that?" he said. "They went for me. Tried to peck my eyes." He stood by the window, peering into the darkness, and could see nothing. His wife, heavy with sleep, murmured from the bed.

"I'm not making it up," he said, angry at her suggestion. "I tell you the birds were on the sill, trying to get into the room."

Suddenly a frightened cry came from the room across the passage where the children slept.

"It's Jill," said his wife, roused at the sound, sitting up in bed. "Go to her, see what's the matter."

Nat lit the candle, but when he opened the bedroom door to cross the passage the draft blew out the flame.

There came a second cry of terror, this time from both children, and stumbling into their room, he felt the beating of wings about him in the darkness. The window was wide open. Through it came the birds, hitting first the ceiling and the walls, then swerving in midflight, turning to the children in their beds.

"It's all right, I'm here," shouted Nat, and the children flung themselves, screaming, upon him, while in the darkness the birds rose and dived and came for him again.

"What is it, Nat, what's happened?" his wife called from the further bedroom, and swiftly he pushed the children through the door to the passage and shut it upon them, so that he was alone now in their bedroom with the birds.

He seized a blanket from the nearest bed and, using it as a weapon, flung it to right and left about him in the air. He felt the thud of bodies, heard the fluttering of wings, but they were not yet defeated, for again and again they returned to the assault, jabbing his hands, his head, the little stabbing beaks sharp as pointed forks. The blanket became a weapon of defense; he wound it about his head, and then in greater darkness beat at the birds with his bare hands. He dared not stumble to the door and open it, lest in doing so the birds should follow him.

How long he fought with them in the darkness he could not tell, but at last the beating of the wings about him lessened and then withdrew, and through the density of the blanket he was aware of light. He waited, listened; there was no sound except the fretful crying of one of the children from the bedroom beyond. The fluttering, the whirring of the wings had ceased.

He took the blanket from his head and stared about him. The cold gray morning light exposed the room. Dawn and the open window had called the living birds; the dead lay on the floor. Nat gazed at the little corpses, shocked and horrified. They were all small birds, none of any size; there must have been fifty of them lying there upon the floor. There were robins, finches, sparrows, blue tits, larks, and bramblings, birds that by nature's law kept to their own flock and their own territory, and now, joining one with another in their urge for battle, had destroyed themselves against the bedroom walls, or in the strife had been destroyed by him. Some had lost feathers in the fight; others had blood, his blood, upon their beaks.

Sickened, Nat went to the window and stared out across his patch of garden to the fields.

It was bitter cold, and the ground had all the hard, black

look of frost. Not white frost, to shine in the morning sun, but the black frost that the east wind brings. The sea, fiercer now with the turning tide, white-capped and steep, broke harshly in the bay. Of the birds there was so sign. Not a sparrow chattered in the hedge beyond the garden gate, no early missel thrush or blackbird pecked on the grass for worms. There was no sound at all but the east wind and the sea.

Nat shut the window and the door of the small bedroom, and went back across the passage to his own. His wife sat up in bed, one child asleep beside her, the smaller in her arms, his face bandaged. The curtains were tightly drawn across the window, the candles lit. Her face looked garish in the yellow light. She shook her head for silence.

"He's sleeping now,"she whispered, "but only just. Something must have cut him, there was blood at the corner of his eyes. Jill said it was the birds. She said she woke up, and the birds were in the room."

His wife looked up at Nat, searching his face for confirmation. She looked terrified, bewildered, and he did not want her to know that he was also shaken, dazed almost, by the events of the past few hours.

"There are birds in there," he said, "dead birds, nearly fifty of them. Robins, wrens, all the little birds from hereabouts. It's as though a madness seized them, with the east wind." He sat down on the bed beside his wife, and held her hand. "It's the weather," he said, "it must be that, it's the hard weather. They aren't the birds, maybe, from here around. They've been driven down from upcountry."

"But, Nat," whispered his wife, "it's only this night that the weather turned. There's been no snow to drive them. And they can't be hungry yet. There's food for them out there in the fields."

"It's the weather," repeated Nat. "I tell you, it's the weather."

His face, too, was drawn and tired, like hers. They stared at one another for a while without speaking.

"I'll go downstairs and make a cup of tea," he said.

The sight of the kitchen reassured him. The cups and saucers, neatly stacked upon the dresser, the table and chairs, his wife's roll of knitting on her basket chair, the children's toys in a corner cupboard.

He knelt down, raked out the old embers, and relit the fire. The glowing sticks brought normality, the steaming kettle and the brown teapot comfort and security. He drank his tea, carried a cup up to his wife. Then he washed in the scullery, and, putting on his boots, opened the back door.

The sky was hard and leaden, and the brown hills that had gleamed in the sun the day before looked dark and bare. The east wind, like a razor, stripped the trees, and the leaves, crackling and dry, shivered and scattered with the wind's blast. Nat stubbed the earth with his boot. It was frozen hard. He had never known a change so swift and sudden. Black winter had descended in a single night.

The children were awake now. Jill was chattering upstairs and young Johnny crying once again. Nat heard his wife's voice, soothing, comforting. Pesently they came down. He had breakfast ready for them, and the routine of the day began.

"Did you drive away the birds?" asked Jill, restored to calm because of the kitchen fire, because of day, because of breakfast.

"Yes, they've all gone now," said Nat. "It was the east wind brought them in. They were frightened and lost, they wanted shelter."

"They tried to peck us," said Jill. "They went for Johnny's eyes."

"Fright made them do that," said Nat. "They didn't know where they were in the dark bedroom."

"I hope they won't come again," said Jill. "Perhaps if we put bread for them outside the window they will eat that and fly away."

She finished her breakfast and then went for her coat and hood, her schoolbooks and her satchel. Nat said nothing, but his wife looked at him across the table. A silent message passed between them.

"I'll walk with her to the bus," he said. "I don't go to the farm today."

And while the child was washing in the scullery he said to his wife, "Keep all the windows closed, and the doors too. Just to be on the safe side. I'll go to the farm. Find out if they heard anything in the night." Then he walked with his small daughter up the lane. She seemed to have forgotten her experience of the night before. She danced ahead of him, chasing the leaves, her face whipped with the cold and rosy under the pixie hood.

"Is it going to snow, Dad?" she said. "It's cold enough."

He glanced up at the bleak sky, felt the wind tear at his shoulders.

"No," he said, "it's not going to snow. This is a black winter, not a white one."

All the while he searched the hedgerows for the birds, glanced over the top of them to the fields beyond, looked to the small wood above the farm where the rooks and jackdaws gathered. He saw none.

The other children waited by the bus stop, muffled, hooded like Jill, the faces white and pinched with cold.

Jill ran to them, waving. "My dad says it won't snow," she called, "it's going to be a black winter."

She said nothing of the birds. She began to push and struggle with another little girl. The bus came ambling up the hill. Nat saw her onto it, then turned and walked back towards the farm. It was not his day for work, but he wanted to satisfy himself that all was well. Jim, the cowman, was clattering in the yard.

"Boss around?" asked Nat.

"Gone to market," said Jim. "It's Tuesday, isn't it?"

He clumped off round the corner of a shed. He had no time for Nat. Nat was said to be superior. Read books, and the like.

Nat had forgotten it was Tuesday. This showed how the events of the preceding night had shaken him. He went to the back door of the farmhouse and heard Mrs. Trigg singing in the kitchen, the wireless[1] making a background to her song.

"Are you there, missus?" called out Nat.

She came to the door, beaming, broad, a good-tempered woman.

"Hullo, Mr. Hocken," she said. "Can you tell me where this cold is coming from? Is it Russia? I've never seen such a change. And it's going on, the wireless says. Something to do with the Arctic Circle."

"We didn't turn on the wireless this morning," said Nat. "Fact is, we had trouble in the night."

"Kiddies poorly?"

"No . . ." He hardly knew how to explain it. Now, in daylight, the battle of the birds would sound absurd.

He tried to tell Mrs. Trigg what had happened, but he could see from her eyes that she thought his story was the result of a nightmare.

"Sure they were real birds," she said, smiling, "with proper feathers and all? Not the funny-shaped kind that the men see after closing hours on a Saturday night?"

"Mrs. Trigg," he said, "there are fifty dead birds, robins, wrens, and such, lying low on the floor of the children's bedroom. They went for me; they tried to go for young Johnny's eyes."

Mrs. Trigg stared at him doubtfully.

"Well there, now," she answered, "I suppose the weather brought them. Once in the bedroom, they wouldn't know where they were to. Foreign birds maybe, from that Arctic Circle."

"No," said Nat, "they were the birds you see about here every day."

---

1. *wireless:* radio.

"Funny thing," said Mrs. Trigg, "no explaining it, really. You ought to write up and ask the *Guardian.* They'd have some answer for it. Well, I must be getting on."

She nodded, smiled, and went back into the kitchen.

Nat, dissatisfied, turned to the farm gate. Had it not been for those corpses on the bedroom floor, which he must now collect and bury somewhere, he would have considered the tale exaggeration too.

Jim was standing by the gate.

"Had any trouble with the birds?" asked Nat.

"Birds? What birds?"

"We got them up our place last night. Scores of them, came in the children's bedroom. Quite savage they were."

"Oh?" It took time for anything to penetrate Jim's head. "Never heard of birds acting savage," he said at length. "They get tame, like, sometimes. I've seen them come to the windows for crumbs."

"These birds last night weren't tame."

"No? Cold, maybe. Hungry. You put out some crumbs."

Jim was no more interested than Mrs. Trigg had been. It was, Nat thought, like air raids in the war. No one down this end of the country knew what the Plymouth folk had seen and suffered. You had to endure something yourself before it touched you. He walked back along the lane and crossed the stile to his cottage. He found his wife in the kitchen with young Johnny.

"See anyone?" she asked.

"Mrs. Trigg and Jim," he answered. "I don't think they believed me. Anyway, nothing wrong up there."

"You might take the birds away," she said. "I daren't go into the room to make the beds until you do. I'm scared."

"Nothing to scare you now," said Nat. "They're dead, aren't they?"

He went up with a sack and dropped the stiff bodies into it, one by one. Yes, there were fifty of them, all told. Just the ordinary, common birds of the hedgerow, nothing as large even as a thrush. It must have been fright that made them act the way they did. Blue tits, wrens—it was incredible to think of the power of their small beaks jabbing at his face and hands the night before. He took the sack out into the garden and was faced now with a fresh problem. The ground was too hard to dig. It was frozen solid, yet no snow had fallen, nothing had happened in the past hours but the coming of the east wind. It was unnatural, queer. The weather prophets must be right. The change was something connected with the Arctic Circle.

The wind seemed to cut him to the bone as he stood there uncertainly, holding the sack. He could see the white-capped seas breaking down under in the bay. He decided to take the birds to the shore and bury them.

When he reached the beach below the headland he could scarcely stand, the force of the east wind was so strong. It hurt to draw breath, and his bare hands were blue. Never had he known such cold, not in all the bad winters he could remember. It was low tide. He crunched his way over the shingle[2] to the softer sand and then, his back to the wind, ground a pit in the sand with his heel. He meant to drop the birds into it, but as he opened up the sack the force of the wind carried them, lifted them, as though in flight again, and they were blown away from him along the beach, tossed like feathers, spread and scattered, the bodies of the fifty frozen birds. There was something ugly in the sight. He did not like it. The dead birds were swept away from him by the wind.

"The tide will take them when it turns," he said to himself.

He looked out to sea and watched the crested breakers, combing green. They rose stiffly, curled, and broke again, and because it was ebb tide the roar was distant, more remote, lacking the sound and thunder of the flood.

Then he saw them. The gulls. Out there, riding the seas.

2. *shingle:* pebbly beach.

What he had thought at first to be the white caps of the
waves were gulls. Hundreds, thousands, tens of thousands . . .
They rose and fell in the trough of the seas, heads to the wind,
like a mighty fleet at anchor, waiting on the tide. To eastward,
and to the west, the gulls were there. They stretched as far as
his eye could reach, in close formation, line upon line. Had
the sea been still, they would have covered the bay like a white
cloud, head to head, body packed to body. Only the east wind,
whipping the sea to breakers, hid them from the shore.

Nat turned and, leaving the beach, climbed the steep path
home. Someone should know of this. Someone should be
told. Something was happening, because of the east wind and
the weather, that he did not understand. He wondered if he
should go to the call box by the bus stop and ring up the police.
Yet what could they do? What could anyone do? Tens of thousands of gulls riding the sea there in the bay because of storm,
because of hunger. The police would think him mad, or
drunk, or take the statement from him with great calm.
"Thank you. Yes, the matter has already been reported. The
hard weather is driving the birds inland in great numbers." Nat
looked about him. Still no sign of any other bird. Perhaps the
cold had sent them all from upcountry? As he drew near to the
cottage his wife came to meet him at the door. She called to
him, excited. "Nat," she said, "it's on the wireless. They've
just read out a special news bulletin. I've written it down."

"What's on the wireless?" he said.

"About the birds," she said. "It's not only here, it's everywhere. In London, all over the country. Something has happened to the birds."

Together they went into the kitchen. He read the piece of
paper lying on the table.

"Statement from the Home Office at 11 A.M. today. Reports
from all over the country are coming in hourly about the vast
quantity of birds flocking above towns, villages, and outlying
districts, causing obstruction and damage and even attacking

individuals. It is thought that the Arctic air stream, at present covering the British Isles, is causing birds to migrate south in immense numbers, and that intense hunger may drive these birds to attack human beings. Householders are warned to see to their windows, doors, and chimneys, and to take reasonable precautions for the safety of their children. A further statement will be issued later."

A kind of excitement seized Nat; he looked at his wife in triumph.

"There you are," he said. "Let's hope they'll hear that at the farm. Mrs. Trigg will know it wasn't any story. It's true. All over the country. I've been telling myself all morning there's something wrong. And just now, down on the beach, I looked out to sea and there are gulls, thousands of them, tens of thousands—you couldn't put a pin between their heads—and they're all out there, riding on the sea, waiting."

"What are they waiting for, Nat?" she asked.

He stared at her, then looked down again at the piece of paper.

"I don't know," he said slowly. "It says here the birds are hungry."

He went over to the drawer where he kept his hammer and tools.

"What are you going to do, Nat?"

"See to the windows and the chimneys too, like they tell you."

"You think they would break in, with the windows shut? Those sparrows and robins and such? Why, how could they?"

He did not answer. He was not thinking of the robins and the sparrows. He was thinking of the gulls. . . .

He went upstairs and worked there the rest of the morning, boarding the windows of the bedrooms, filling up the chimney bases. Good job it was his free day and he was not working at the farm. It reminded him of the old days, at the beginning of the war. He was not married then, and he had made all the blackout boards for his mother's house in Plymouth. Made the shelter too. Not that it had been of any use when the moment came. He wondered if they would take these precautions up at the farm. He doubted it. Too easygoing, Harry Trigg and his missus. Maybe they'd laugh at the whole thing. Go off to a dance or a whist drive.[3]

"Dinner's ready." She called him, from the kitchen.

"All right. Coming down."

He was pleased with his handiwork. The frames fitted nicely over the little panes and at the bases of the chimneys.

When dinner was over and his wife was washing up, Nat switched on the one o'clock news. The same announcement was repeated, the one which she had taken down during the morning, but the news bulletin enlarged upon it. "The flocks of birds have caused dislocation in all areas," read the announcer, "and in London the sky was so dense at ten o'clock this morning that it seemed as if the city was covered by a vast black cloud.

"The birds settled on rooftops, on window ledges, and on chimneys. The species included blackbird, thrush, the common house sparrow, and, as might be expected in the metropolis, a vast quantity of pigeons and starlings, and that frequenter of the London river, the black-headed gull. The sight has been so unusual that traffic came to a standstill in many thoroughfares, work was abandoned in shops and offices, and the streets and pavements were crowded with people standing about to watch the birds."

Various incidents were recounted, the suspected reason of cold and hunger stated again, and warnings to householders repeated. The announcer's voice was smooth and suave. Nat had the impression that this man, in particular, treated the whole business as he would an elaborate joke. There would be others like him, hundreds of them, who did not know what it

---

3. *whist drive:* a marathon card game.

was to struggle in darkness with a flock of birds. There would be parties tonight in London, like the ones they gave on election nights. People standing about, shouting and laughing, getting drunk. "Come and watch the birds!"

Nat switched off the wireless. He got up and started work on the kitchen windows. His wife watched him, young Johnny at her heels.

"What, boards for down here too?" she said. "Why, I'll have to light up before three o'clock. I see no call for boards down here."

"Better be sure than sorry," answered Nat. "I'm not going to take any chances."

"What they ought to do," she said, "is to call the Army out and shoot the birds. That would soon scare them off."

"Let them try," said Nat. "How'd they set about it?"

"They have the Army to the docks," she answered, "when the dockers strike. The soldiers go down and unload the ships."

"Yes," said Nat, "and the population of London is eight million or more. Think of all the buildings, all the flats and houses. Do you think they've enough soldiers to go round shooting birds from every roof?"

"I don't know. But something should be done. They ought to do something."

Nat thought to himself that "they" were no doubt considering the problem at that very moment, but whatever "they" decided to do in London and the big cities would not help the people here, three hundred miles away. Each householder must look after his own.

"How are we off for food?" he said.

"Now, Nat, whatever next?"

"Never mind. What have you got in the larder?"

"It's shopping day tomorrow, you know that. I don't keep uncooked food hanging about, it goes off. Butcher doesn't call till the day after. But I can bring back something when I go in tomorrow."

Nat did not want to scare her. He thought it possible that she might not go to town tomorrow. He looked in the larder for himself, and in the cupboard where she kept her tins. They would do for a couple of days. Bread was low.

"What about the baker?"

"He comes tomorrow too."

He saw she had flour. If the baker did not call she had enough to bake one loaf.

"We'd be better off in old days," he said, "when the women baked twice a week, and had pilchards[4] salted, and there was food for a family to last a siege, if need be."

"I've tried the children with tinned fish, they don't like it," she said.

Nat went on hammering the boards across the kitchen windows. Candles. They were low in candles too. That must be another thing she meant to buy tomorrow. Well, it could not be helped. They must go early to bed tonight. That was, if . . .

He got up and went out of the back door and stood in the garden, looking down towards the sea. There had been no sun all day, and now, at barely three o'clock, a kind of darkness had already come, the sky sullen, heavy, colorless like salt. He could hear the vicious sea drumming on the rocks. He walked down the path, halfway to the beach. And then he stopped. He could see the tide had turned. The rock that had shown in midmorning was now covered, but it was not the sea that held his eyes. The gulls had risen. They were circling, hundreds of them, thousands of them, lifting their wings against the wind. It was the gulls that made the darkening of the sky. And they were silent. They made not a sound. They just went on soaring and circling, rising, falling, trying their strength against the wind.

---

4. *pilchards:* a kind of fish.

Nat turned. He ran up the path, back to the cottage.

"I'm going for Jill," he said. "I'll wait for her at the bus stop."

"What's the matter?" asked his wife. "You've gone quite white."

"Keep Johnny inside," he said. "Keep the door shut. Light up now, and draw the curtains."

"It's only just gone three," she said.

"Never mind. Do what I tell you."

He looked inside the toolshed outside the back door. Nothing there of much use. A spade was too heavy, and a fork no good. He took the hoe. It was the only possible tool, and light enough to carry.

He started walking up the lane to the bus stop, and now and again glanced back over his shoulder.

The gulls had risen higher now; their circles were broader, wider; they were spreading out in huge formation across the sky.

He hurried on; although he knew the bus would not come to the top of the hill before four o'clock, he had to hurry. He passed no one on the way. He was glad of this. No time to stop and chatter.

At the top of the hill he waited. He was much too soon. There was half an hour still to go. The east wind came whipping across the fields from the higher ground. He stamped his feet and blew upon his hands. In the distance he could see the clay hills, white and clean, against the heavy pallor of the sky. Something black rose from behind them, like a smudge at first, then widening, becoming deeper, and the smudge became a cloud, and the cloud divided again into five other clouds, spreading north, east, south, and west, and they were not clouds at all; they were birds. He watched them travel across the sky, and as one section passed overhead, within two or three hundred feet of him, he knew, from their speed, they were bound inland, upcountry; they had no business with the people here on the peninsula. They were rooks, crows, jackdaws, magpies, jays, all birds that usually preyed upon the smaller species; but this afternoon they were bound on some other mission.

"They've been given the towns," thought Nat; "they know what they have to do. We don't matter so much here. The gulls will serve for us. The others go to the towns."

He went to the call box, stepped inside, and lifted the receiver. The exchange would do. They would pass the message on.

"I'm speaking from Highway," he said, "by the bus stop. I want to report large formations of birds traveling upcountry. The gulls are also forming in the bay."

"All right," answered the voice, laconic, weary.

"You'll be sure and pass this message on to the proper quarter?"

"Yes . . . yes . . ." Impatient now, fed-up. The buzzing note resumed.

"She's another," thought Nat, "she doesn't care. Maybe she's had to answer calls all day. She hopes to go to the pictures tonight. She'll squeeze some fellow's hand, and point up at the sky, and say 'Look at all them birds!' She doesn't care."

The bus came lumbering up the hill. Jill climbed out, and three or four other children. The bus went on towards the town.

"What's the hoe for, Dad?"

They crowded around him, laughing, pointing.

"I just brought it along," he said. "Come on now, let's get home. It's cold, no hanging about. Here, you. I'll watch you across the fields, see how fast you can run."

He was speaking to Jill's companions, who came from different families, living in the council houses.[5] A shortcut would take them to the cottages.

5. *council houses:* public housing.

"We want to play a bit in the lane," said one of them.

"No, you don't. You go off home or I'll tell your mammy."

They whispered to one another, round-eyed, then scuttled off across the fields. Jill stared at her father, her mouth sullen.

"We always play in the lane," she said.

"Not tonight, you don't," he said. "Come on now, no dawdling."

He could see the gulls now, circling the fields, coming in towards the land. Still silent. Still no sound.

"Look, Dad, look over there, look at all the gulls."

"Yes. Hurry, now."

"Where are they flying to? Where are they going?"

"Upcountry, I dare say. Where it's warmer."

He seized her hand and dragged her after him along the lane.

"Don't go so fast. I can't keep up."

The gulls were copying the rooks and crows. They were spreading out in formation across the sky. They headed, in bands of thousands, to the four compass points.

"Dad, what is it? What are the gulls doing?"

They were not intent upon their flight, as the crows, as the jackdaws had been. They still circled overhead. Nor did they fly so high. It was as though they waited upon some signal. As though some decision had yet to be given. The order was not clear.

"Do you want me to carry you, Jill? Here, come pick-a-back."

This way he might put on speed; but he was wrong. Jill was heavy. She kept slipping. And she was crying too. His sense of urgency, of fear, had communicated itself to the child.

"I wish the gulls would go away. I don't like them. They're coming closer to the lane."

He put her down again. He started running, swinging Jill

after him. As they went past the farm turning, he saw the
farmer backing his car out of the garage. Nat called to him.

"Can you give us a lift?" he said.

"What's that?"

Mr. Trigg turned in the driving seat and stared at them.
Then a smile came to his cheerful, rubicund face.

"It looks as though we're in for some fun," he said. "Have
you seen the gulls? Jim and I are going to take a crack at them.
Everyone's gone bird-crazy, talking of nothing else. I hear you
were troubled in the night. Want a gun?"

Nat shook his head.

The small car was packed. There was just room for Jill, if she
crouched on top of petrol tins on the back seat.

"I don't want a gun," said Nat, "but I'd be obliged if you'd
run Jill home. She's scared of the birds."

He spoke briefly. He did not want to talk in front of Jill.

"OK," said the farmer, "I'll take her home. Why don't you
stop behind and join the shooting match? We'll make the
feathers fly."

Jill climbed in, and, turning the car, the driver sped up the
lane. Nat followed after. Trigg must be crazy. What use was a
gun against a sky of birds?

Now Nat was not responsible for Jill, he had time to look
about him. The birds were circling still above the fields. Most-
ly herring gull, but the black-backed gull amongst them. Usually they kept apart. Now they were united. Some bond had
brought them together. It was the black-backed gull that
attacked the smaller birds, and even newborn lambs, so he'd
heard. He'd never seen it done. He remembered this now,
though, looking above him in the sky. They were coming in
toward the farm. They were circling lower in the sky, and the
black-backed gulls were to the front, the black-backed gulls
were leading. The farm, then, was their target. They were
making for the farm.

Nat increased his pace towards his own cottage. He saw the farmer's car turn and come back along the lane. It drew up beside him with a jerk.

"The kid has run inside," said the farmer. "Your wife was watching for her. Well, what do you make of it? They're saying in town the Russians have done it. The Russians have poisoned the birds."

"How could they do that?" asked Nat.

"Don't ask me. You know how stories get around. Will you join my shooting match?"

"No, I'll get along home. The wife will be worried else."

"My missus says if you could eat gull there'd be some sense in it," said Trigg, "we'd have roast gull, baked gull, and pickle 'em into the bargain. You wait until I let off a few barrels into the brutes. That'll scare 'em."

"Have you boarded your windows?" asked Nat.

"No. Lot of nonsense. They like to scare you on the wireless. I've had more to do today than to go round boarding up my windows."

"I'd board them now, if I were you."

"Garn. You're windy. Like to come to our place to sleep?"

"No, thanks all the same."

"All right. See you in the morning. Give you a gull breakfast."

The farmer grinned and turned his car to the farm entrance.

Nat hurried on. Past the little wood, past the old barn, and then across the stile to the remaining field.

As he jumped the stile he heard the whir of wings. A black-backed gull dived down at him from the sky, missed, swerved in flight, and rose to dive again. In a moment it was joined by others, six, seven, a dozen, black-backed and herring mixed. Nat dropped his hoe. The hoe was useless. Covering his head with his arms, he ran toward the cottage. They kept coming at him from the air, silent save for the beating wings. The terrible, fluttering wings. He could feel the blood on his hands, his wrists, his neck. Each stab of a swooping beak tore his flesh. If only he could keep them from his eyes. Nothing else mattered. He must keep them from his eyes. They had not learnt yet how to cling to a shoulder, how to rip clothing, how to dive in mass upon the head, upon the body. But with each dive, with each attack, they became bolder. And they had no thought for themselves. When they dived low and missed, they crashed bruised and broken, on the ground. As Nat ran he stumbled, kicking their spent bodies in front of him.

He found the door; he hammered upon it with his bleeding hands. Because of the boarded windows no light shone. Everything was dark.

"Let me in," he shouted, "it's Nat. Let me in."

He shouted loud to make himself heard above the whir of the gulls' wings.

Then he saw the gannet, poised for the dive, above him in the sky. The gulls circled, retired, soared, one after another, against the wind. Only the gannet remained. One single gannet above him in the sky. The wings folded suddenly to its body. It dropped like a stone. Nat screamed, and the door opened. He stumbled across the threshold, and his wife threw her weight against the door.

They heard the thud of the gannet as it fell.

His wife dressed his wounds. They were not deep. The backs of his hands had suffered most, and his wrists. Had he not worn a cap they would have reached his head. As to the gannet . . . the gannet could have split his skull.

The children were crying, of course. They had seen the blood on their father's hands.

"It's all right now," he told them. "I'm not hurt. Just a few scratches. You play with Johnny, Jill. Mammy will wash these cuts."

He half shut the door to the scullery so that they could not see. His wife was ashen. She began running water from the sink.

"I saw them overhead," she whispered. "They began collecting just as Jill ran in with Mr. Trigg. I shut the door fast, and it jammed. That's why I couldn't open it at once when you came."

"Thank God they waited for me," he said. "Jill would have fallen at once. One bird alone would have done it.'

Furtively, so as not to alarm the children, they whispered together as she bandaged his hands and the back of his neck.

"They're flying inland," he said, "thousands of them. Rooks, crows, all the bigger birds. I saw them from the bus stop. They're making for the towns."

"But what can they do, Nat?"

"They'll attack. Go for everyone out in the streets. Then they'll try the windows, the chimneys."

"Why don't the authorities do something? Why don't they get the Army, get machine guns, anything?"

"There's been no time. Nobody's prepared. We'll hear what they have to say on the six o'clock news."

Nat went back into the kitchen, followed by his wife. Johnny was playing quietly on the floor. Only Jill looked anxious.

"I can hear the birds," she said. "Listen, Dad."

Nat listened. Muffled sounds came from the windows, from the door. Wings brushing the surface, sliding, scraping, seeking a way of entry. The sound of many bodies, pressed together, shuffling on the sills. Now and again came a thud, a crash, as some bird dived and fell. "Some of them will kill themselves that way," he thought, "but not enough. Never enough."

"All right," he said aloud. "I've got boards over the windows, Jill. The birds can't get in."

He went and examined all the windows. His work had been thorough. Every gap was closed. He would make extra certain, however. He found wedges, pieces of old tin, strips of wood and metal, and fastened them at the sides to reinforce the boards. His hammering helped to deafen the sound of the birds, the shuffling, the tapping, and more ominous—he did not want his wife or the children to hear it—the splinter of cracked glass.

"Turn on the wireless," he said, "let's have the wireless."

This would drown the sound also. He went upstairs to the bedrooms and reinforced the windows there. Now he could hear the birds on the roof, the scraping of claws, a sliding, jostling sound.

He decided they must sleep in the kitchen, keep up the fire, bring down the mattresses, and lay them out on the floor. He was afraid of the bedroom chimneys. The boards he had placed at the chimney bases might give way. In the kitchen they would be safe because of the fire. He would have to make a joke of it. Pretend to the children they were playing at camp. If the worst happened, and the birds forced an entry down the bedroom chimneys, it would be hours, days perhaps, before they could break down the doors. The birds would be imprisoned in the bedrooms. They could do no harm there. Crowded together, they would stifle and die.

He began to bring the mattresses downstairs. At sight of them his wife's eyes widened in apprehension. She thought the birds had already broken in upstairs.

"All right," he said cheerfully, "we'll all sleep together in the kitchen tonight. More cozy here by the fire. Then we shan't be worried by those silly old birds tapping at the windows."

He made the children help him rearrange the furniture, and he took the precaution of moving the dresser, with his wife's help, across the window. It fitted well. It was an added safeguard. The mattresses could now be lain, one beside the other, against the wall where the dresser had stood.

"We're safe enough now," he thought. "We're snug and tight, like an air-raid shelter. We can hold out. It's just the food that worries me. Food, and coal for the fire. We've enough for two or three days, not more. By that time . . ."

No use thinking ahead as far as that. And they'd be giving directions on the wireless. People would be told what to do. And now, in the midst of many problems, he realized that it was dance music only, coming over the air. Not Children's Hour, as it should have been. He glanced at the dial. Yes, they were on the Home Service all right. Dance records. He switched to the Light program. He knew the reason. The usual programs had been abandoned. This only happened at exceptional times. Elections and such. He tried to remember if it had happened in the war, during the heavy raids on London. But of course. The BBC[6] was not stationed in London during the war. The programs were broadcast from other, temporary quarters. "We're better off here," he thought; "we're better off here in the kitchen, with the windows and the doors boarded, than they are up in the towns. Thank God we're not in the towns."

At six o'clock the records ceased. The time signal was given. No matter if it scared the children, he must hear the news. There was a pause after the pips. Then the announcer spoke. His voice was solemn, grave. Quite different from midday.

"This is London," he said. "A national emergency was proclaimed at four o'clock this afternoon. Measures are being taken to safeguard the lives and property of the population, but it must be understood that these are not easy to effect immediately, owing to the unforeseen and unparalleled nature of the present crisis. Every householder must take precautions to his own building, and where several people live together, as in flats and apartments, they must unite to do the utmost they can to prevent entry. It is absolutely imperative that every individual stay indoors tonight and that no one at all remain on the

6. *BBC*: British Broadcasting Corporation.

streets, or roads, or anywhere withoutdoors. The birds, in vast numbers, are attacking anyone on sight, and have already begun an assault upon buildings; but these, with due care, should be impenetrable. The population is asked to remain calm and not to panic. Owing to the exceptional nature of the emergency, there will be no further transmission from any broadcasting station until 7 A.M. tomorrow."

They played the national anthem. Nothing more happened. Nat switched off the set. He looked at his wife. She stared back at him.

"What's it mean?" said Jill. "What did the news say?"

"There won't be any more programs tonight," said Nat. "There's been a breakdown at the BBC."

"Is it the birds?" asked Jill. "Have the birds done it?"

"No," said Nat, "it's just that everyone's very busy, and then of course they have to get rid of the birds, messing everything up, in the towns. Well, we can manage without the wireless for one evening."

"I wish we had a gramophone,"[7] said Jill, "that would be better than nothing."

She had her face turned to the dresser backed against the windows. Try as they did to ignore it, they were all aware of the shuffling, the stabbing, the persistent beating and sweeping of wings.

"We'll have supper early," suggested Nat, "something for a treat. Ask Mammy. Toasted cheese, eh? Something we all like?"

He winked and nodded at his wife. He wanted the look of dread, of apprehension, to go from Jill's face.

He helped with the supper, whistling, singing, making as much clatter as he could, and it seemed to him that the shuffling and the tapping were not so intense as they had been at first. Presently he went up to the bedrooms and listened, and he no longer heard the jostling for place upon the roof.

7. *gramophone:* phonograph.

"They've got reasoning powers," he thought; "they know it's hard to break in here. They'll try elsewhere. They won't waste their time with us."

Supper passed without incident, and then, when they were clearing away, they heard a new sound, droning, familiar, a sound they all knew and understood.

His wife looked up at him, her face alight. "It's planes," she said; "they're sending out planes after the birds. That's what I said they ought to do all along. That will get them. Isn't that gunfire? Can't you hear guns?"

It might be gunfire out at sea. Nat could not tell. Big naval guns might have an effect upon the gulls out at sea, but the gulls were inland now. The guns couldn't shell the shore because of the population.

"It's good, isn't it," said his wife, "to hear the planes?" And Jill, catching her enthusiasm, jumped up and down with Johnny. "The planes will get the birds. The planes will shoot them."

Just then they heard a crash about two miles distant, followed by a second, then a third. The droning became more distant, passed away out to sea.

"What was that?" asked his wife. "Were they dropping bombs on the birds?"

"I don't know," answered Nat. "I don't think so."

He did not want to tell her that the sound they had heard was the crashing of aircraft. It was, he had no doubt, a venture on the part of the authorities to send out reconnaissance forces, but they might have known the venture was suicidal. What could aircraft do against birds that flung themselves to death against propeller and fuselage, but hurtle to the ground themselves? This was being tried now, he supposed, over the whole country. And at a cost. Someone high up had lost his head.

"Where have the planes gone, Dad?" asked Jill.

"Back to base," he said. "Come on, now, time to tuck down for bed."

It kept his wife occupied, undressing the children before the fire, seeing to the bedding, one thing and another, while he went round the cottage again, making sure that nothing had worked loose. There was no further drone of aircraft, and the naval guns had ceased. "Waste of life and effort," Nat said to himself. "We can't destroy enough of them that way. Cost too heavy. There's always gas. Maybe they'll try spraying with gas, mustard gas. We'll be warned first, of course, if they do. There's one thing, the best brains of the country will be onto it tonight."

Somehow the thought reassured him. He had a picture of scientists, naturalists, technicians, and all those chaps they called the back-room boys, summoned to a council; they'd be working on the problem now. This was not a job for the government, for the chiefs of staff—they would merely carry out the orders of the scientists.

"They'll have to be ruthless," he thought. "Where the trouble's worst they'll have to risk more lives, if they use gas. All the livestock, too, and the soil—all contaminated. As long as everyone doesn't panic. That's the trouble. People panicking, losing their heads. The BBC was right to warn us of that."

Upstairs in the bedrooms all was quiet. No further scraping and stabbing at the windows. A lull in battle. Forces regrouping. Wasn't that what they called it in the old wartime bulletins? The wind hadn't dropped, though. He could still hear it roaring in the chimneys. And the sea breaking down on the shore. Then he remembered the tide. The tide would be on the turn. Maybe the lull in battle was because of the tide. There was some law the birds obeyed, and it was all to do with the east wind and the tide.

He glanced at his watch. Nearly eight o'clock. It must have gone high water an hour ago. That explained the lull: the birds attacked with the flood tide. It might not work that way inland, upcountry, but it seemed as if it was so this way on the coast. He reckoned the time limit in his head. They had six hours to go without attack. When the tide turned again, around one twenty in the morning, the birds would come back. . . .

There were two things he could do. The first to rest, with his wife and the children, and all of them snatch what sleep they could, until the small hours. The second to go out, see how they were faring at the farm, see if the telephone was still working there, so that they might get news from the exchange.

He called softly to his wife, who had just settled the children. She came halfway up the stairs and he whispered to her.

"You're not to go," she said at once, "you're not to go and leave me alone with the children. I can't stand it."

Her voice rose hysterically. He hushed her, calmed her.

"All right," he said, "all right. I'll wait till morning. And we'll get the wireless bulletin then too, at seven. But in the morning, when the tide ebbs again, I'll try for the farm, and they may let us have bread and potatoes, and milk too."

His mind was busy again, planning against emergency. They would not have milked, of course, this evening. The cows would be standing by the gate, waiting in the yard, with the household inside, battened behind boards, as they were here at the cottage. That is, if they had time to take precautions. He thought of the farmer, Trigg, smiling at him from the car. There would have been no shooting party, not tonight.

The children were asleep. His wife, still clothed, was sitting on her mattress. She watched him, her eyes nervous.

"What are you going to do?" she whispered.

He shook his head for silence. Softly, stealthily, he opened the back door and looked outside.

It was pitch dark. The wind was blowing harder than ever, coming in steady gusts, icy, from the sea. He kicked at the step outside the door. It was heaped with birds. There were dead birds everywhere. Under the windows, against the walls. These were the suicides, the divers, the ones with broken necks. Wherever he looked he saw dead birds. No trace of the living.

The living had flown seaward with the turn of the tide. The gulls would be riding the seas now, as they had done in the forenoon.

In the far distance, on the hill where the tractor had been two days before, something was burning. One of the aircraft that had crashed; the fire, fanned by the wind, had set light to a stack.

He looked at the bodies of the birds, and he had a notion that if he heaped them, one upon the other, on the windowsills they would make added protection for the next attack. Not much, perhaps, but something. The bodies would have to be clawed at, pecked, and dragged aside before the living birds could gain purchase on the sills and attack the panes. He set to work in the darkness. It was queer; he hated touching them. The bodies were still warm and bloody. The blood matted their feathers. He felt his stomach turn, but he went on with his work. He noticed grimly that every windowpane was shattered. Only the boards had kept the birds from breaking in. He stuffed the cracked panes with the bleeding bodies of the birds.

When he had finished he went back into the cottage. He barricaded the kitchen door, made it doubly secure. He took off his bandages, sticky with the birds' blood, not with his own cuts, and put on fresh plaster.

His wife had made him cocoa and he drank it thirstily. He was very tired.

"All right," he said, smiling, "don't worry. We'll get through."

He lay down on his mattress and closed his eyes. He slept at once. He dreamt uneasily, because through his dreams there ran a thread of something forgotten. Some piece of work, neglected, that he should have done. Some precaution that he had known well but had not taken, and he could not put a name to it in his dreams. It was connected in some way with the burning aircraft and the stack upon the hill. He went on sleeping, though; he did not awake. It was his wife shaking his shoulder that awoke him finally.

"They've begun," she sobbed, "they've started this last hour. I can't listen to it any longer alone. There's something smelling bad too, something burning."

Then he remembered. He had forgotten to make up the fire. It was smoldering, nearly out. He got up swiftly and lit the lamp. The hammering had started at the windows and the doors, but it was not that he minded now. It was the smell of singed feathers. The smell filled the kitchen. He knew at once what it was. The birds were coming down the chimney, squeezing their way down to the kitchen range.

He got sticks and paper and put them on the embers, then reached for the can of paraffin.

"Stand back," he shouted to his wife. "We've got to risk this."

He threw the paraffin onto the fire. The flame roared up the pipe, and down upon the fire fell the scorched, blackened bodies of the birds.

The children woke, crying. "What is it?" said Jill. "What's happened?"

Nat had no time to answer. He was raking the bodies from the chimney, clawing them out onto the floor. The flames still roared, and the danger of the chimney catching fire was one he had to take. The flames would send away the living birds from the chimney top. The lower joint was the difficulty, though. This was choked with the smoldering, helpless bodies of the birds caught by fire. He scarcely heeded the attack on the windows and the door: let them beat their wings, break their beaks, lose their lives, in the attempt to force an entry into his home. They would not break in. He thanked God he had one of the old cottages, with small windows, stout walls. Not like the new council houses. Heaven help them up the lane in the new council houses.

"Stop crying," he called to the children. "There's nothing to be afraid of, stop crying."

He went on raking at the burning, smoldering bodies as they fell into the fire.

"This'll fetch them," he said to himself, "the draft and the flames together. We're all right, as long as the chimney doesn't catch. I ought to be shot for this. It's all my fault. Last thing, I should have made up the fire. I knew there was something."

Amid the scratching and tearing at the window boards came the sudden homely striking of the kitchen clock. Three A.M. A little more than four hours yet to go. He could not be sure of the exact time of high water. He reckoned it would not turn much before half past seven, twenty to eight.

"Light up the Primus,"[8] he said to his wife. "Make us some tea, and the kids some cocoa. No use sitting around doing nothing."

That was the line. Keep her busy, and the children too. Move about, eat, drink; always best to be on the go.

He waited by the range. The flames were dying. But no more blackened bodies fell from the chimney. He thrust his poker up as far as it could go and found nothing. It was clear. The chimney was clear. He wiped the sweat from his forehead.

"Come on now, Jill," he said, "bring me some more sticks. We'll have a good fire going directly." She wouldn't come near him, though. She was staring at the heaped singed bodies of the birds.

"Never mind them," he said, "we'll put those in the passage when I've got the fire steady."

The danger of the chimney was over. It could not happen again, not if the fire was kept burning day and night.

"I'll have to get more fuel from the farm tomorrow," he thought. "This will never last. I'll manage, though. I can do all that with the ebb tide. It can be worked, fetching what we need, when the tide's turned. We've just got to adapt ourselves, that's all."

They drank tea and cocoa and ate slices of bread and Bovril.[9]

8. *Primus:* small portable stove.
9. *Bovril:* a kind of instant beef broth.

Only half a loaf left, Nat noticed. Never mind, though, they'd get by.

"Stop it," said young Johnny, pointing to the windows with his spoon, "stop it, you old birds."

"That's right," said Nat, smiling, "we don't want the old beggars, do we? Had enough of 'em."

They began to cheer when they heard the thud of the suicide birds.

"There's another, Dad," cried Jill, "he's done for."

"He's had it," said Nat. "There he goes, the blighter."

This was the way to face up to it. This was the spirit. If they could keep this up, hang on like this until seven, when the first news bulletin came through, they would not have done too badly.

"Give us a cigarette," he said to his wife. "A bit of a smoke will clear away the smell of the scorched feathers."

'There's only two left in the packet," she said. "I was going to buy you some from the co-op."

"I'll have one," he said, "t'other will keep for a rainy day."

No sense trying to make the children rest. There was no rest to be got while the tapping and the scratching went on at the windows. He sat with one arm round his wife and the other round Jill, with Johnny on his mother's lap and the blankets heaped about them on the mattress.

"You can't help admiring the beggars," he said; "they've got persistence. You'd think they'd tire of the game, but not a bit of it."

Admiration was hard to sustain. The tapping went on and on and a new rasping note struck Nat's ear, as though a sharper beak than any hitherto had come to take over from its fellows. He tried to remember the names of birds; he tried to think which species would go for this particular job. It was not the tap of the woodpecker. That would be light and frequent. This was more serious, because if it continued long the wood would splinter, as the glass had done. Then he remembered the hawks. Could the hawks have taken over from the gulls? Were there buzzards now upon the sills, using talons as well as beaks? Hawks, buzzards, kestrels, falcons—he had forgotten the birds of prey. He had forgotten the gripping power of the birds of prey. Three hours to go, and while they waited, the sound of the splintering wood, the talons tearing at the wood.

Nat looked about him, seeing what furniture he could destroy to fortify the door. The windows were safe because of the dresser. He was not certain of the door. He went upstairs, but when he reached the landing he paused and listened. There was a soft patter on the floor of the children's bedroom. The birds had broken through. . . . He put his ear to the door. No mistake. He could hear the rustle of wings and the light patter as they searched the floor. The other bedroom was still clear. He went into it and began bringing out the furniture, to pile at the head of the stairs should the door of the children's bedroom go. It was a preparation. It might never be needed. He could not stack the furniture against the door, because it opened inward. The only possible thing was to have it at the top of the stairs.

"Come down, Nat, what are you doing?" called his wife.

"I won't be long," he shouted. "Just making everything ship-shape up here."

He did not want her to come; he did not want her to hear the pattering of the feet in the children's bedroom, the brushing of those wings against the door.

At five thirty he suggested breakfast, bacon and fried bread, if only to stop the growing look of panic in his wife's eyes and to calm the fretful children. She did not know about the birds upstairs. The bedroom, luckily, was not over the kitchen. Had it been so, she could not have failed to hear the sound of them up there, tapping the boards. And the silly, senseless thud of the suicide birds, the death and glory boys, who flew into the bedroom, smashing their heads against the walls. He knew them of old, the herring gulls. They had no brains. The black-backs were different; they knew what they were doing. So did the buzzards, the hawks . . .

He found himself watching the clock, gazing at the hands that went so slowly round the dial. If his theory was not correct, if the attack did not cease with the turn of the tide, he knew they were beaten. They could not continue through the long day without air, without rest, without more fuel, without . . . His mind raced. He knew there were so many things they needed to withstand siege. They were not fully prepared. They were not ready. It might be that it would be safer in the towns, after all. If he could get a message through on the farm telephone to his cousin, only a short journey by train upcountry, they might be able to hire a car. That would be quicker—hire a car between tides . . .

His wife's voice, calling his name, drove away the sudden, desperate desire for sleep.

"What is it? What now?" he said sharply.

"The wireless," said his wife. "I've been watching the clock. It's nearly seven."

"Don't twist the knob," he said, impatient for the first time. "It's on the Home where it is. They'll speak from the Home."

They waited. The kitchen clock struck seven. There was no sound. No chimes, no music. They waited until a quarter past, switching to the Light. The result was the same. No news bulletin came through.

"We've heard wrong," he said. "They won't be broadcasting until eight o'clock."

They left it switched on, and Nat thought of the battery, wondered how much power was left in it. It was generally recharged when his wife went shopping in the town. If the battery failed they would not hear the instructions.

"It's getting light," whispered his wife. "I can't see it, but I can feel it. And the birds aren't hammering so loud."

She was right. The rasping, tearing sound grew fainter every moment. So did the shuffling, the jostling for place upon the step, upon the sills. The tide was on the turn. By eight there was no sound at all. Only the wind. The children, lulled at last by the stillness, fell asleep. At half past eight Nat switched the wireless off.

"What are you doing? We'll miss the news," said his wife.

"There isn't going to be any news," said Nat. "We've got to depend upon ourselves."

He went to the door and slowly pulled away the barricades. He drew the bolts and, kicking the bodies from the step outside the door, breathed the cold air. He had six working hours before him, and he knew he must reserve his strength for the right things, not waste it in any way. Food, and light, and fuel; these were the necessary things. If he could get them in sufficiency, they could endure another night.

He stepped into the garden, and as he did so he saw the living birds. The gulls had gone to ride the sea, as they had done before; they sought sea food, and the buoyancy of the tide, before they returned to the attack. Not so the land birds. They waited and watched. Nat saw them, on the hedgerows, on the soil, crowded in the trees, outside in the field, line upon line of birds, all still, doing nothing.

He went to the end of his small garden. The birds did not move. They went on watching him.

"I've got to get food," said Nat to himself. "I've got to go to the farm to find food."

He went back to the cottage. He saw to the windows and the doors. He went upstairs and opened the children's bedroom. It was empty, except for the dead birds on the floor. The living were out there, in the garden, in the fields. He went downstairs.

"I'm going to the farm," he said.

His wife clung to him. She had seen the living birds from the open door.

"Take us with you," she begged. "We can't stay here alone. I'd rather die than stay here alone."

He considered the matter. He nodded.

"Come on, then," he said. "Bring baskets, and Johnny's pram. We can load up the pram."

They dressed against the biting wind, wore gloves and scarves. His wife put Johnny in the pram. Nat took Jill's hand.

"The birds," she whimpered, "they're all out there in the fields."

"They won't hurt us," he said, "not in the light."

They started walking across the field towards the stile, and the birds did not move. They waited, their heads turned to the wind.

When they reached the turning to the farm, Nat stopped and told his wife to wait in the shelter of the hedge with the two children.

"But I want to see Mrs. Trigg," she protested. "There are lots of things we can borrow if they went to market yesterday; not only bread, and . . ."

"Wait here," Nat interrupted. "I'll be back in a moment."

The cows were lowing, moving restlessly in the yard, and he could see a gap in the fence where the sheep had knocked their way through, to roam unchecked in the front garden before the farmhouse. No smoke came from the chimneys. He was filled with misgiving. He did not want his wife or the children to go down to the farm.

"Don't gib[10] now," said Nat, harshly, "do what I say."

She withdrew with the pram into the hedge, screening herself and the children from the wind.

He went down alone to the farm. He pushed his way through the herd of bellowing cows, which turned this way and

10. *gib:* look threateningly.

that, distressed, their udders full. He saw the car standing by the gate, not put away in the garage. The windows of the farmhouse were smashed. There were many dead gulls lying in the yard and around the house. The living birds perched on the group of trees behind the farm and on the roof of the house. They were quite still. They watched him.

Jim's body lay in the yard . . . what was left of it. When the birds had finished, the cows had trampled him. His gun was beside him. The door of the house was shut and bolted, but as the windows were smashed, it was easy to lift them and climb through. Trigg's body was close to the telephone. He must have been trying to get through to the exchange when the birds came for him. The receiver was hanging loose, the instrument torn from the wall. No sign of Mrs. Trigg. She would be upstairs. Was it any use going up? Sickened, Nat knew what he would find.

"Thank God," he said to himself, "there were no children."

He forced himself to climb the stairs, but halfway he turned and descended again. He could see her legs protruding from the open bedroom door. Beside her were the bodies of the black-backed gulls, and an umbrella, broken.

"It's no use," thought Nat, "doing anything. I've only got five hours, less than that. The Triggs would understand. I must load up with what I can find."

He tramped back to his wife and children.

"I'm going to fill up the car with stuff," he said. "I'll put coal in it, and paraffin for the Primus. We'll take it home and return for a fresh load."

"What about the Triggs?" asked his wife.

"They must have gone to friends," he said.

"Shall I come and help you, then?"

"No; there's a mess down there. Cows and sheep all over the place. Wait, I'll get the car. You can sit in it."

Clumsily he backed the car out of the yard and into the lane.

His wife and the children could not see Jim's body from there.

"Stay here," he said, "never mind the pram. The pram can be fetched later. I'm going to load the car."

Her eyes watched his all the time. He believed she understood; otherwise she would have suggested helping him to find the bread and groceries.

They made three journeys altogether, backwards and forwards between their cottage and the farm, before he was satisfied they had everything they needed. It was surprising, once he started thinking, how many things were necessary. Almost the most important of all was planking for the windows. He had to go round searching for timber. He wanted to renew the boards on all the windows at the cottage. Candles, paraffin, nails, tinned stuff; the list was endless. Besides all that, he milked three of the cows. The rest, poor brutes, would have to go on bellowing.

On the final journey he drove the car to the bus stop, got out, and went to the telephone box. He waited a few minutes, jangling the receiver. No good, though. The line was dead. He climbed onto a bank and looked over the countryside, but there was no sign of life at all, nothing in the fields but the waiting, watching birds. Some of them slept—he could see the beaks tucked into the feathers.

"You'd think they'd be feeding," he said to himself, "not just standing in that way."

Then he remembered. They were gorged with food. They had eaten their fill during the night. That was why they did not move this morning. . . .

No smoke came from the chimneys of the council houses. He thought of the children who had run across the fields the night before.

"I should have known," he thought; "I ought to have taken them home with me."

He lifted his face to the sky. It was colorless and gray. The bare trees on the landscape looked bent and blackened by the east wind. The cold did not affect the living birds waiting out there in the fields.

"This is the time they ought to get them," said Nat; "they're a sitting target now. They must be doing this all over the country. Why don't our aircraft take off now and spray them with mustard gas? What are all our chaps doing? They must know, they must see for themselves."

He went back to the car and got into the driver's seat.

"Go quickly past that second gate," whispered his wife. "The postman's lying there. I don't want Jill to see."

He accelerated. The little Morris bumped and rattled along the lane. The children shrieked with laughter.

"Up-a-down, up-a-down," shouted young Johnny.

It was a quarter to one by the time they reached the cottage. Only an hour to go.

"Better have cold dinner," said Nat. "Hot up something for yourself and the children, some of that soup. I've no time to eat now. I've got to unload all this stuff."

He got everything inside the cottage. It could be sorted later. Give them all something to do during the long hours ahead. First he must see to the windows and the doors.

He went round the cottage methodically, testing every window, every door. He climbed onto the roof also, and fixed boards across every chimney, except the kitchen. The cold was so intense he could hardly bear it, but the job had to be done. Now and again he would look up, searching the sky for aircraft. None came. As he worked he cursed the inefficiency of the authorities.

"It's always the same," he muttered, "they always let us down. Muddle, muddle, from the start. No plan, no real organization. And we don't matter down here. That's what it is. The people upcountry have priority. They're using gas up there, no doubt, and all the aircraft. We've got to wait and take what comes."

He paused, his work on the bedroom chimney finished, and

looked out to sea. Something was moving out there. Something gray and white amongst the breakers.

"Good old Navy," he said, "they never let us down. They're coming down-channel, they're turning in the bay."

He waited, straining his eyes, watering in the wind, towards the sea. He was wrong, though. It was not ships. The Navy was not there. The gulls were rising from the sea. The massed flocks in the fields, with ruffled feathers, rose in formation from the ground and, wing to wing, soared upwards to the sky.

The tide had turned again.

Nat climbed down the ladder and went inside the kitchen. The family were at dinner. It was a little after two. He bolted the door, put up the barricade, and lit the lamp.

"It's nighttime," said young Johnny.

His wife had switched on the wireless once again, but no sound came from it.

"I've been all round the dial," she said, "foreign stations, and that lot. I can't get anything."

"Maybe they have the same trouble," he said, "maybe it's the same right through Europe."

She poured out a plateful of the Triggs' soup, cut him a large slice of the Triggs' bread, and spread their dripping upon it.

They ate in silence. A piece of the dripping ran down young Johnny's chin and fell onto the table.

"Manners, Johnny," said Jill, "you should learn to wipe your mouth."

The tapping began at the windows, at the door. The rustling, the jostling, the pushing for position on the sills. The first thud of the suicide gulls upon the step.

"Won't America do something?" said his wife. "They've always been our allies, haven't they? Surely America will do something?"

Nat did not answer. The boards were strong against the windows, and on the chimneys too. The cottage was filled with stores, with fuel, with all they needed for the next few days.

When he had finished dinner he would put the stuff away, stack it neatly, get everything shipshape, handy like. His wife could help him, and the children too. They'd tire themselves out, between now and a quarter to nine, when the tide would ebb; then he'd tuck them down on their mattresses, see that they slept good and sound until three in the morning.

He had a new scheme for the windows, which was to fix barbed wire in front of the boards. He had brought a great roll of it from the farm. The nuisance was, he'd have to work at this in the dark, when the lull came between nine and three. Pity he had not thought of it before. Still, as long as the wife slept, and the kids, that was the main thing.

The smaller birds were at the window now. He recognized the light tap-tapping of their beaks and the soft brush of their wings. The hawks ignored the windows. They concentrated their attack upon the door. Nat listened to the tearing sound of splintering wood, and wondered how many million years of memory were stored in those little brains, behind the stabbing beaks, the piercing eyes, now giving them this instinct to destroy mankind with all the deft precision of machines.

"I'll smoke that last cigarette," he said to his wife. "Stupid of me, it was the one thing I forgot to bring back from the farm."

He reached for it, switched on the silent wireless. He threw the empty packet on the fire, and watched it burn.

The Facts of the Story

Write short answers to the following questions. Answers may be one word or a phrase. You can probably answer all the questions without rereading the story, but look back if you wish.

1. At what time of year do the events in this story happen?

2. At first, how does Nat account for the vast numbers of birds?

3. What kinds of birds are the first to attack?

4. Why does Nat especially fear attacks by the gulls and, later, by the hawks?

5. What regular occurrence in nature seems to determine when the birds attack and when they rest?

6. What happens to the Triggs, who do not take Nat's warning seriously?

7. What important thing does Nat forget to do before going to sleep the second night?

8. What attempt does the government make to drive away the birds?

9. What happens to the planes that attempt to kill the birds?

10. What does the final failure of the wireless suggest?

The Ideas in the Story

For class discussion, prepare answers to the following questions.

1. In "To Build a Fire" (page 32), Jack London refers to human frailty. The man in his story is too frail to cope with

the severe cold. In its ability to survive the cold, the dog is stronger than the man. In her story, Daphne du Maurier also seems to be saying something about human frailty. Her story reminds us of how fragile we really are, of how thin the barrier is that protects us from other creatures. What powers of the birds make it possible for them to win? Can you think of ways that the people might defeat the birds?

2. Is there any hint in the story as to what is *causing* the birds to behave in this way?

3. In this story, the result of the birds' attack could be the destruction of the human race. Throughout history, people have wondered if–and how–the human race could be destroyed. Many possibilities have been suggested: a drastic change in temperature–return of the ice age; destruction by fire from the sun; destruction by water; attack by insects, by rodents, by reptiles, by disease, by machines that have the ability to think, by nuclear warfare. The possibilities are fascinating–in a gruesome way. What other stories, television shows, or movies deal with this question of a threat to the entire human race? Who wins the conflict in these other accounts?

The Art of the Storyteller

Plot

Like the plot of "To Build a Fire," the plot of "The Birds" is simple. The conflict is between Nat, the protagonist, and the birds, the antagonist; the plot is composed of Nat's struggle to survive the birds' attacks. Much of Nat's struggle must be devoted to making the house safe. He also must try to get help. He also must get food and light and fuel to withstand a siege. Du Maurier plants two questions in the mind of the reader: Will the struggle be a losing one? Is there any way that Nat can win?

Climax

The outcome of this horror story is not stated, but it is force-fully suggested. Explain how each of the following passages suggests the same outcome. Which of these passages suggests most clearly to you that the birds will succeed in destroying the human race? That passage marks the climax.

1. No smoke came from the chimneys of the council houses. (Page 95)

2. He lifted his face to the sky. It was colorless and gray. The bare trees on the landscape looked bent and blackened by the east wind. The cold did not affect the living birds waiting out there in the fields.

"This is the time they ought to get them," said Nat; "they're a sitting target now. They must be doing this all over the country. Why don't our aircraft take off now and spray them with mustard gas? What are all our chaps doing? They must know, they must see for themselves." (Pages 95-96)

3. His wife had switched on the wireless once again, but no sound came from it.

"I've been all round the dial," she said, "foreign stations, and that lot. I can't get anything." (Page 97)

4. The hawks ignored the windows. They concentrated their attack upon the door. (Page 98)

Foreshadowing

Very early in this story (page 68), the author includes a piece of foreshadowing that not only states the problem of the protag-onist, but also suggests the outcome of the conflict. Nat has just seen tens of thousands of gulls riding the waves. His reaction foreshadows what is to come: "Someone should know of this. . . . Something was happening, because of the east wind and the weather, that he did not understand. He wondered if he should go to the call box by the bus stop and ring up the police. Yet what could they do? What could anyone do?" The answer to this final question is suggested by everything that happens in the story. What is that answer?

Fantasy

While you were reading "The Birds," you probably had a feeling that these events could never happen. Birds would never behave this way. The whole story is so contrary to experience that it simply is not to be believed. This kind of story is called *fantasy*. All of us have read and enjoyed fantasies—such as fables, fairy tales, and children's stories in which animals talk and behave like people. Another popular kind of fantasy is science fiction, which usually is set in another world or in a future time, and which features gadgets that no one has ever seen.

Although a fantasy is not factually true, a skillfull writer makes us almost *believe* the story while we are reading it. Daphne du Maurier has imagined what would happen if all the birds in the world set out to destroy the human race. By concentrating on the experience of one family in rural England, she shows, in marvelously imagined detail, what might happen, and does it so convincingly that, for the moment, we believe it is happening.

While the situation du Maurier describes is fictional, she is careful to make the characters believable. Our knowledge of human nature tells us that, should such a fantastic and horrible event occur, people probably would react exactly as her characters do. What reactions of the Triggs, for example, seem true to life? What explanations for the birds' unnatural behavior are offered by Nat, and by the government over the wireless? Are these explanations the kind you would expect? How does the story show that people are inclined to turn to the government for help? How would you explain Nat's refusal to give up, even when he knows the odds against him are overwhelming? Would you expect human beings to act this way?

Composition

Writing a "What If" Story

One reason that "The Birds" is so effective is that du Maurier has imagined the events in great detail. We might call a fantasy like this a "what if" story. *What if* all the birds in the world suddenly decided to destroy us? *What if* one of the other disasters listed on page 100 should occur? What would the results be? Select a disaster and, following the pattern of "The Birds," write your own fantasy, imagining the events in detail. You should not write such a long story, of course; but in three or four pages, you should be able to describe what you think it would be like to experience such a disaster.

Putting "The Birds" in a Different Setting

In "The Birds," the author tells what happens on a farm. Imagine what the birds' attack would be like in a city. For instance, how would the defensive measures taken by apartment dwellers differ from those taken by country people? When you have imagined fully what the situation in the city would be like, write your own brief version of the birds' attack as experienced by a city dweller.

Write approximately 300 words.

Daphne du Maurier

Daphne du Maurier (1907-   ) was born into the London world of artists and writers. She is the daughter of a famous English actor, Sir Gerald du Maurier, and granddaughter of George du Maurier, an artist and a novelist. Although she has written several books of short stories, she is best known for her novels, in particular, for the Gothic romance *Rebecca,* which was made into an Academy Award-winning movie under the direction of Alfred Hitchcock. "The Birds," typical of du Maurier's fiction in its fast-moving action, its use of suspense, and its inescapable tragedy, was also made into a famous horror movie under Hitchcock's direction. In Hollywood's version, the story is set in California.

The Cask of Amontillado

EDGAR ALLAN POE

Of all the motives that spur people to action, revenge, while understandable, is certainly not the most admirable. It is a motive that sometimes leads to cruelty, even to murder. "The Cask of Amontillado" is a story of revenge.

In this story the setting—the place and time of the action—is important. Beneath the streets of some European cities are ancient cemeteries, long winding tunnels lined with recesses and shelves used for centuries to bury the dead. These are the catacombs. A noble family would sometimes have its own underground cemetery, referred to as the family vaults. As you will find out when you read this story, the catacombs are dark and damp, not a safe place to go if you are suffering from a cold, but not a bad place to store wine—or commit a murder.

The story takes place in Italy during the "supreme madness of the carnival season," which comes just before Lent. At carnival time, people take to the streets in pursuit of pleasure. They dress in grotesque and colorful costumes and wear masks to disguise their identity. Some people drink too much. Amontillado, in the title of this story, is a kind of wine.

The thousand injuries of Fortunato I had borne as I best could; but when he ventured upon insult, I vowed revenge. You, who so well know the nature of my soul, will not suppose, however, that I gave utterance to a threat. At *length* I would be avenged; this was a point definitively settled – but the very definitiveness with which it was resolved, precluded the idea of risk. I must not only punish, but punish with impunity. A wrong is unredressed when retribution overtakes its redresser. It is equally unredressed when the avenger fails to make himself felt as such to him who has done the wrong.

It must be understood that neither by word nor deed had I given Fortunato cause to doubt my good will. I continued, as was my wont, to smile in his face, and he did not perceive that my smile *now* was at the thought of his immolation.

He had a weak point – this Fortunato – although in other regards he was a man to be respected and even feared. He prided himself on his connoisseurship in wine. Few Italians have the true virtuoso spirit. For the most part their enthusiasm is adopted to suit the time and opportunity – to practice imposture upon the British and Austrian millionaires. In painting and gemmary Fortunato, like his countrymen, was a quack – but in the matter of old wines he was sincere. In this respect I did not differ from him materially: I was skillful in the Italian vintages myself, and bought largely whenever I could.

It was about dusk, one evening during the supreme madness of the carnival season, that I encountered my friend. He accosted me with excessive warmth, for he had been drinking much. The man wore motley.[1] He had on a tight-fitting parti-striped dress, and his head was surmounted by the conical cap and bells. I was so pleased to see him that I thought I should never have done wringing his hand.

I said to him: "My dear Fortunato, you are luckily met. How remarkably well you are looking today! But I have received a pipe[2] of what passes for Amontillado, and I have my doubts."

"How?" said he. "Amontillado? A pipe? Impossible! And in the middle of the carnival!"

"I have my doubts," I replied; "and I was silly enough to pay the full Amontillado price without consulting you in the matter. You were not to be found, and I was fearful of losing a bargain."

"Amontillado!"

"I have my doubts."

"Amontillado!"

"And I must satisfy them."

"Amontillado!"

"As you are engaged, I am on my way to Luchesi. If anyone has a critical turn, it is he. He will tell me—"

"Luchesi cannot tell Amontillado from sherry."

"And yet some fools will have it that his taste is a match for your own."

"Come, let us go."

"Whither?"

"To your vaults."

"My friend, no; I will not impose upon your good nature. I perceive you have an engagement. Luchesi—"

"I have no engagement—come."

"My friend, no. It is not the engagement, but the severe cold

1. *motley:* jester costume, of many colors.
2. *pipe:* cask.

with which I perceive you are afflicted. The vaults are insufferably damp. They are encrusted with niter."[3]

"Let us go, nevertheless. The cold is merely nothing. Amontillado! You have been imposed upon. And as for Luchesi, he cannot distinguish sherry from Amontillado."

Thus speaking, Fortunato possessed himself of my arm. Putting on a mask of black silk, and drawing a *roquelaure*[4] closely about my person, I suffered him to hurry me to my palazzo.[5]

There were no attendants at home; they had absconded to make merry in honor of the time. I had told them that I should not return until the morning, and had given them explicit orders not to stir from the house. These orders were sufficient, I well knew, to insure their immediate disappearance, one and all, as soon as my back was turned.

I took from their sconces two flambeaux,[6] and giving one to Fortunato, bowed him through several suites of rooms to the archway that led into the vaults. I passed down a long and winding staircase, requesting him to be cautious as he followed. We came at length to the foot of the descent, and stood together on the damp ground of the catacombs of the Montresors.

The gait of my friend was unsteady, and the bells upon his cap jingled as he strode.

"The pipe?" said he.

"It is farther on," said I; "but observe the white webwork which gleams from these cavern walls."

He turned toward me, and looked into my eyes with two filmy orbs that distilled the rheum of intoxication.

"Niter?" he asked, at length.

"Niter," I replied. "How long have you had that cough?"

---

3. *niter:* mineral deposit.
4. *roquelaure:* (rŏk'ə-lôr): cloak.
5. *palazzo:* palace (or very elegant house).
6. *flambeaux:* torches.

"Ugh! ugh! ugh!—ugh! ugh! ugh!—ugh! ugh! ugh!—ugh! ugh! ugh!—ugh! ugh! ugh!"

My poor friend found it impossible to reply for many minutes.

"It is nothing," he said, at last.

"Come," I said with decision, "we will go back; your health is precious. You are rich, respected, admired, beloved; you are happy, as once I was. You are a man to be missed. For me it is no matter. We will go back; you will be ill, and I cannot be responsible. Besides, there is Luchesi—"

"Enough," he said; "the cough is a mere nothing; it will not kill me. I shall not die of a cough."

"True—true," I replied; "and, indeed, I had no intention of alarming you unnecessarily; but you should use all proper caution. A draft of this Medoc will defend us from the damps."

Here I knocked off the neck of a bottle which I drew from a long row of its fellows that lay upon the mold.

"Drink," I said, presenting him the wine.

He raised it to his lips with a leer. He paused and nodded to me familiarly, while his bells jingled.

"I drink," he said, "to the buried that repose around us."

"And I to your long life."

He again took my arm, and we proceeded.

"These vaults," he said, "are extensive."

"The Montresors," I replied, "were a great and numerous family."

"I forget your arms."

"A huge human foot d'or,[7] in a field azure; the foot crushes a serpent rampant whose fangs are imbedded in the heel."

"And the motto?"

"*Nemo me impune lacessit.*"[8]

"Good!" he said.

The wine sparkled in his eyes and the bells jingled. My own

7. *d'or:* of gold.
8. Latin for "No one injures me without punishment."

fancy grew warm with the Medoc. We had passed through walls of piled bones, with casks and puncheons[9] intermingling, into the inmost recesses of the catacombs. I paused again, and this time I made bold to seize Fortunato by an arm above the elbow.

"The niter!" I said; "see, it increases. It hangs like moss upon the vaults. We are below the river's bed. The drops of moisture trickle among the bones. Come, we will go back ere it is too late. Your cough—"

"It is nothing," he said; "let us go on. But first, another draft of the Medoc."

I broke and reached him a flagon of De Grâve. He emptied it at a breath. His eyes flashed with a fierce light. He laughed and threw the bottle upward with a gesticulation I did not understand.

I looked at him in surprise. He repeated the movement—a grotesque one.

"You do not comprehend?" he said.

"Not I," I replied.

"Then you are not of the brotherhood."

"How?"

"You are not of the masons."[10]

"Yes, yes," I said; "yes, yes."

"You? Impossible! A mason?"

"A mason," I replied.

"A sign," he said.

"It is this," I answered, producing a trowel from beneath the folds of my *roquelaure.*

"You jest," he exclaimed, recoiling a few paces. "But let us proceed to the Amontillado."

"Be it so," I said, replacing the tool beneath the cloak, and again offering him my arm. He leaned upon it heavily. We continued our route in search of the Amontillado. We passed

9. *puncheons:* large casks.
10. *masons:* a secret organization, originally started by masons, or stoneworkers.

through a range of low arches, descended, passed on, and descending again, arrived at a deep crypt, in which the foulness of the air caused our flambeaux rather to glow than flame.

At the most remote end of the crypt there appeared another less spacious. Its walls had been lined with human remains, piled to the vault overhead, in the fashion of the great catacombs of Paris. Three sides of this interior crypt were still ornamented in this manner. From the fourth the bones had been thrown down, and lay promiscuously upon the earth, forming at one point a mound of some size. Within the wall thus exposed by the displacing of the bones, we perceived a still interior recess, in depth about four feet, in width three, in height six or seven. It seemed to have been constructed for no especial use within itself, but formed merely the interval between two of the colossal supports of the roof of the catacombs, and was backed by one of their circumscribing walls of solid granite.

It was in vain that Fortunato, uplifting his dull torch, endeavored to pry into the depth of the recess. Its termination the feeble light did not enable us to see.

"Proceed," I said; "herein is the Amontillado. As for Luchesi—"

"He is an ignoramus," interrupted my friend, as he stepped unsteadily forward, while I followed immediately at his heels. In an instant he had reached the extremity of the niche, and finding his progress arrested by the rock, stood stupidly bewildered. A moment more and I had fettered[11] him to the granite. In its surface were two iron staples, distant from each other about two feet, horizontally. From one of these depended a short chain, from the other a padlock. Throwing the links about his waist, it was but the work of a few seconds to secure it. He was too much astounded to resist. Withdrawing the key I stepped back from the recess.

11. *fettered:* chained.

"Pass your hand," I said, "over the wall; you cannot help feeling the niter. Indeed it is *very* damp. Once more let me *implore* you to return. No? Then I must positively leave you. But I must first render you all the little attentions in my power."

"The Amontillado!" ejaculated my friend, not yet recovered from his astonishment.

"True," I replied; "the Amontillado."

As I said these words I busied myself among the pile of bones of which I have before spoken. Throwing them aside, I soon uncovered a quantity of building stone and mortar. With these materials and with the aid of my trowel, I began vigorously to wall up the entrance of the niche.

I had scarcely laid the first tier of the masonry when I discovered that the intoxication of Fortunato had in a great measure worn off. The earliest indication I had of this was a low moaning cry from the depth of the recess. It was *not* the cry of a drunken man. There was then a long and obstinate silence. I laid the second tier, and the third, and the fourth; and then I heard the furious vibrations of the chain. The noise lasted for several minutes, during which, that I might hearken to it with the more satisfaction, I ceased my labors and sat down upon the bones. When at last the clanking subsided, I resumed the trowel, and finished without interruption the fifth, the sixth, and the seventh tier. The wall was now nearly upon a level with my breast. I again paused, and holding the flambeaux over the masonwork, threw a few feeble rays upon the figure within.

A succession of loud and shrill screams, bursting suddenly from the throat of the chained form, seemed to thrust me violently back. For a brief moment I hesitated—I trembled. Unsheathing my rapier,[12] I began to grope with it about the recess; but the thought of an instant reassured me. I placed my hand upon the solid fabric of the catacombs, and felt satisfied. I

---

12. *rapier:* long sword.

reapproached the wall. I replied to the yells of him who clamored. I re-echoed—I aided—I surpassed them in volume and in strength. I did this, and the clamorer grew still.

It was now midnight, and my task was drawing to a close. I had completed the eighth, the ninth, and the tenth tier. I had finished a portion of the last and the eleventh; there remained but a single stone to be fitted and plastered in. I struggled with its weight; I placed it partially in its destined position. But now there came from out the niche a low laugh that erected the hairs upon my head. It was succeeded by a sad voice, which I had difficulty in recognizing as that of the noble Fortunato. The voice said: "Ha! ha! ha!—he! he!—a very good joke indeed—an excellent jest. We will have many a rich laugh about it at the palazzo—he! he! he!—over our wine—he! he! he!"

"The Amontillado!" I said.

"He! he! he!—he! he! he!—yes, the Amontillado. But is it not getting late? Will not they be awaiting us at the palazzo, the Lady Fortunato and the rest? Let us be gone."

"Yes," I said, "let us be gone."

"For the love of God, Montresor!"

"Yes," I said, "for the love of God!"

But to these words I hearkened in vain for a reply. I grew impatient. I called aloud: "Fortunato!"

No answer. I called again: "Fortunato!"

No answer still. I thrust a torch through the remaining aperture and let it fall within. There came forth in return only a jingling of the bells. My heart grew sick—on account of the dampness of the catacombs. I hastened to make an end of my labor. I forced the last stone into its position; I plastered it up. Against the new masonry I re-erected the old rampart of bones. For half of a century no mortal has disturbed them. *In pace requiescat!*[13]

---

13. Latin for "May he rest in peace!"

The Facts of the Story

For class discussion, prepare answers to the following questions.

1. Why does Montresor want to kill Fortunato? Is there any hint that Montresor might be insane?

2. At the beginning of the story, Montresor says there are two requirements for an effective act of revenge. What are these requirements? Explain how Montresor makes sure that his act of revenge meets them.

3. What specific details describing the setting (the catacombs) help to create a sense of horror and disgust?

4. Montresor himself narrates the story of his grisly deed. How do we know what his victim is feeling? When does Fortunato first suspect that something is very wrong with this trip to the catacombs?

5. What is the climax of this story?

The Art of the Storyteller

Plot

Plot, you will recall, is the series of related events that make up a story. In general, the main ingredient of a plot is a *problem* that must be solved by the protagonist. The protagonist's attempts to overcome obstacles involve him or her in a *conflict,* or a struggle. As we read a story, our feeling of *suspense* intensifies steadily as the action moves toward a *climax,* the point at which we know whether the protagonist succeeds or fails.

In "The Cask of Amontillado," Montresor, who is the protagonist, must get revenge on Fortunato by murdering him without being caught or even suspected. The conflict lies in Montresor's struggle to solve four problems:

1. He must make sure that he and Fortunato are not seen together.

2. He must devise a way to get Fortunato into the vaults without arousing his suspicions.

3. He must be sure he can control Fortunato once he gets him into the vault.

4. He must be certain the body is never found.

How does Montresor solve each of his problems?

A Single Effect

Poe believed that a good short story should produce a *single effect*. Most readers agree that the effect produced in "The Cask of Amontillado" is a feeling of horror. Everything Poe includes in the story makes us feel the horror. Montresor states his grisly goal in the first sentence. Then he proceeds, without letup, to tell us how he achieved his goal. Our horror grows as we see Fortunato, drunk and sick, led to his death without offering any opposition because he does not understand what is happening until it is too late. Our horror reaches its peak in the next-to-last sentence. What final shocking fact do we learn there?

Irony

When you mean the opposite of what you say, you are using *irony*; you are being *ironic*. For example, if you meet a friend while sloshing miserably through a heavy rain, and you say, "Hi, nice sunny day, isn't it?" your remark is ironic. You mean the opposite of what you are saying. This kind of irony is common. It appears in Poe's story when Montresor, as he encounters Fortunato, remarks, "My dear Fortunato, you are luckily met." Luckily for whom?

When events turn out contrary to the way we would normally expect, we say the situation is ironic. It is ironic, for example, that Fortunato, who is obviously out for a good time at the carnival, should have such a very bad time.

Sometimes when we are reading a story, we know something that a person in the story does not know. Such a situation frequently produces irony. Explaining that he is not worried about his cough, Fortunato says, "I shall not die of a cough." Montresor replies, "True, true." This conversation is ironic since we know that Montresor plans to kill Fortunato.

Fortunato exclaims "Good!" when he learns that the motto on the Montresors' coat of arms is "No one injures me without punishment." What is ironic about Fortunato's remark?

What is ironic about Montresor saying to his victim: ". . . your health is precious"? What is ironic about the victim's name–Fortunato?

Composition

Creating a Single Effect

Write a descriptive paragraph that will give your reader a single strong impression. For example, suppose you are describing your room. Do you want to give an impression of messiness, peacefulness, tidiness, or coziness? If describing a room does not appeal to you, try one of these scenes:

Scene	Single Effect
a peaceful outdoor setting	happiness
a severe storm	discomfort or misery
a crowd	confusion
an attack	fear
an accident	horror
a stage performance	nervousness
a close game	excitement

Your success will depend on how many details you can use to build up the single effect. Omit details, no matter how interesting, that do not contribute to the emotional impact. If there is action in the scene, think of your paragraph as a brief narrative which must be told in *chronological order*–that is, in the order in which the events occur. If the scene is static, or without action, like the description of a bedroom, follow a spatial order, making clear where each item in the scene is located. You will need such locating expressions as *on the floor, on the bed, on the right wall, under the desk, beside the mirror.* For an outdoor scene, you might need to use locating expressions like *in the valley, near the mall, across the street, in the gutter, in the gravel.*

Write approximately 150 words.

Edgar Allan Poe

Edgar Allan Poe (1809-1849) was born in Boston, the son of traveling actors. His father deserted the family and his mother died in Richmond, Virginia, when Edgar was three years old. The child was brought up by John Allan, a wealthy Richmond merchant. Poe was given a superior education, but he broke with his guardian because the older man disapproved of his literary ambitions. During his adult life, Poe lived in the big cities of the East Coast—Richmond, Baltimore, Philadelphia, New York, and Boston—where he struggled to support himself as a magazine writer and editor. Although Poe suffered from poverty and poor health, he achieved in his short life a position of the highest rank among American writers. He succeeded in realizing his early ambition to become a poet, but he is best known for his short stories, which reflect his intense, nightmarish imagination. "The Cask of Amontillado" is one of his horror stories, which have been popular with generations of readers. Other famous tales of horror are "The Tell-Tale Heart," "The Black Cat," and "The Pit and the Pendulum." Poe is often said to have originated the modern detective story. His detective, Dupin, is seen at work in "The Purloined Letter" and "The Murders in the Rue Morgue."

Antaeus

BORDEN DEAL

This story is about T. J., a boy from the rural South, who, with his family, moves to a Northern city. You can imagine the difficulties such a boy would experience in adjusting to life in a poor and crowded section of a big industrial city. When he meets the neighborhood gang, T. J. asks in disbelief: "Don't you-all have no woods around here? . . . You mean you ain't got no fields to raise nothing in?"

The title of the story refers to a character in Greek mythology. Antaeus was a powerful giant who forced any stranger who entered his land to wrestle with him. The giant's one-sided condition was that if he won, he would kill the stranger. There couldn't have been any strangers in the land of Antaeus, because Antaeus always won.

But Antaeus had a weakness, as giants often do. He was the son of Terra, goddess of the earth, and the secret of his strength was that he drew it from the earth. Every time Antaeus fell to the ground, he rose stronger than ever. Finally, Hercules, with his usual brilliance, settled the matter by lifting Antaeus into the air so that he could not get strength from the ground. Then Hercules strangled him. In this story, you will find a line that explains why the author chose the title "Antaeus."

This was during the wartime, when lots of people were coming North for jobs in factories and war industries, when people moved around a lot more than they do now and sometimes kids were thrown into new groups and new lives that were completely different from anything they had ever known before. I remember this one kid; T. J. his name was, from somewhere down South, whose family moved into our building during that time. They'd come North with everything they owned piled into the back seat of an old-model sedan that you wouldn't expect could make the trip, with T. J. and his three younger sisters riding shakily atop the load of junk.

Our building was just like all the others there, with families crowded into a few rooms, and I guess there were twenty-five or thirty kids about my age in that one building. Of course, there were a few of us who formed a gang and ran together all the time after school, and I was the one who brought T. J. in and started the whole thing.

The building right next door to us was a factory where they made walking dolls. It was a low building with a flat, tarred roof that had a parapet[1] all around it about head-high and we'd found out a long time before that no one, not even the watchman, paid any attention to the roof because it was higher than any of the other buildings around. So my gang used the roof as a headquarters. We could get up there by crossing over to the fire escape from our own roof on a plank and then going on up. It was a secret place for us, where nobody else could go without our permission.

I remember the day I first took T. J. up there to meet the gang. He was a stocky, robust kid with a shock of white hair,

1. *parapet:* wall.

118

nothing sissy about him except his voice—he talked different from any of us and you noticed it right away. But I liked him anyway, so I told him to come on up.

We climbed up over the parapet and dropped down on the roof. The rest of the gang were already there.

"Hi," I said. I jerked my thumb at T. J. "He just moved into the building yesterday."

He just stood there, not scared or anything, just looking, like the first time you see somebody you're not sure you're going to like.

"Hi," Blackie said. "Where you from?"

"Marion County," T. J. said.

We laughed. "Marion County?" I said. "Where's that?"

He looked at me like I was a stranger, too. "It's in Alabama," he said, like I ought to know where it was.

"What's your name?" Charley said.

"T. J.," he said, looking back at him. He had pale blue eyes that looked washed-out but he looked directly at Charley, waiting for his reaction. He'll be all right, I thought. No sissy in him . . . except that voice. Who ever talked like that?

"T. J.," Blackie said. "That's just initials. What's your real name? Nobody in the world has just initials."

"I do," he said. "And they're T. J. That's all the name I got."

His voice was resolute with the knowledge of his rightness and for a moment no one had anything to say. T. J. looked around at the rooftop and down at the black tar under his feet. "Down yonder where I come from," he said, "we played out in the woods. Don't you-all have no woods around here?"

"Naw," Blackie said. "There's the park a few blocks over, but it's full of kids and cops and old women. You can't do a thing."

T. J. kept looking at the tar under his feet. "You mean you ain't got no fields to raise nothing in? No watermelons or nothing?"

"Naw," I said scornfully. "What do you want to grow something for? The folks can buy everything they need at the store."

He looked at me again with that strange, unknowing look. "In Marion County," he said, "I had my own acre of cotton and my own acre of corn. It was mine to plant ever' year."

He sounded like it was something to be proud of, and in some obscure way it made the rest of us angry. "Heck!" Blackie said. "Who'd want to have their own acre of cotton and corn? That's just work. What can you do with an acre of cotton and corn?"

T. J. looked at him. "Well, you get part of the bale offen your acre," he said seriously. "And I fed my acre of corn to my calf."

We didn't really know what he was talking about, so we were more puzzled than angry; otherwise, I guess, we'd have chased him off the roof and wouldn't let him be part of our gang. But he was strange and different and we were all attracted by his stolid sense of rightness and belonging, maybe by the strange softness of his voice contrasting our own tones of speech into harshness.

He moved his foot against the black tar. "We could make our own field right here," he said softly, thoughtfully. "Come spring we could raise us what we want to . . . watermelons and garden truck and no telling what all."

"You'd have to be a good farmer to make these tar roofs grow any watermelons," I said. We all laughed.

But T. J. looked serious. "We could haul us some dirt up here," he said. "And spread it out even and water it and before you know it we'd have us a crop in here." He looked at us intently. "Wouldn't that be fun?"

"They wouldn't let us," Blackie said quickly.

"I thought you said this was you-all's roof," T. J. said to me. "That you-all could do anything you wanted up here."

"They've never bothered us," I said. I felt the idea beginning to catch fire in me. It was a big idea and it took a while for it to sink in, but the more I thought about it the better I liked it. "Say," I said to the gang, "he might have something there. Just make us a regular roof garden, with flowers and grass and trees and everything. And all ours, too," I said. "We wouldn't let anybody up here except the ones we wanted to."

"It'd take a while to grow trees," T. J. said quickly, but we weren't paying any attention to him. They were all talking about it suddenly, all excited with the idea after I'd put it in a way they could catch hold of it. Only rich people had roof gardens, we knew, and the idea of our own private domain excited them.

"We could bring it up in sacks and boxes," Blackie said. "We'd have to do it while the folks weren't paying any attention to us. We'd have to come up to the roof of our building and then cross over with it."

"Where could we get the dirt?" somebody said worriedly.

"Out of those vacant lots over close to school," Blackie said. "Nobody'd notice if we scraped it up."

I slapped T. J. on the shoulder. "Man, you had a wonderful idea," I said, and everybody grinned at him, remembering he had started it. "Our own private roof garden."

He grinned back. "It'll be ourn," he said. "All ourn." Then he looked thoughtful again. "Maybe I can lay my hands on some cotton seed, too. You think we could raise us some cotton?"

We'd started big projects before at one time or another, like any gang of kids, but they'd always petered out for lack of organization and direction. But this one didn't . . . somehow or other T. J. kept it going all through the winter months. He kept talking about the watermelons and the cotton we'd raise, come spring, and when even that wouldn't work he'd switch around to my idea of flowers and grass and trees, though he was always honest enough to add that it'd take a while to get any trees started. He always had it on his mind and he'd mention it in school, getting them lined up to carry dirt that afternoon, saying, in a casual way, that he reckoned a few more weeks ought to see the job through.

Our little area of private earth grew slowly. T. J. was smart enough to start in one corner of the building, heaping up the carried earth two or three feet thick, so that we had an immediate result to look at, to contemplate with awe. Some of the evenings T. J. alone was carrying earth up to the building, the rest of the gang distracted by other enterprises or interests, but T. J. kept plugging along on his own and eventually we'd all come back to him again, and then our own little acre would grow more rapidly.

He was careful about the kind of dirt he'd let us carry up there and more than once he dumped a sandy load over the parapet into the areaway below because it wasn't good enough. He found out the kinds of earth in all the vacant lots for blocks around. He'd pick it up and feel it and smell it, frozen though it was sometimes, and then he'd say it was good growing soil or it wasn't worth anything and we'd have to go on somewhere else.

Thinking about it now, I don't see how he kept us at it. It was hard work, lugging paper sacks and boxes of dirt all the way up the stairs of our own building, keeping out of the way of the grown-ups so they wouldn't catch on to what we were doing. They probably wouldn't have cared, for they didn't pay much attention to us, but we wanted to keep it secret anyway. Then we had to go through the trapdoor to our roof, teeter over a plank to the fire escape, then climb two or three stories to the parapet and drop down onto the roof. All that for a small pile of earth that sometimes didn't seem worth the effort. But T. J. kept the vision bright within us, his words shrewd and calculated toward the fulfillment of his dream; and he worked harder than any of us. He seemed driven toward a goal that we couldn't see, a particular point in time that would be definitely marked by signs and wonders that only he could see.

The laborious earth just lay there during the cold months, inert and lifeless, the clods lumpy and cold under our feet when we walked over it. But one day it rained, and afterward there was a softness in the air and the earth was alive and giving again with moisture and warmth. That evening T. J. smelled the air, his nostrils dilating with the odor of the earth under his feet.

"It's spring," he said, and there was a gladness rising in his voice that filled us all with the same feeling. "It's mighty late for it, but it's spring. I'd just about decided it wasn't never gonna get here at all."

We were all sniffing at the air, too, trying to smell it the way that T. J. did, and I can still remember the sweet odor of the earth under our feet. It was the first time in my life that spring and spring earth had meant anything to me. I looked at T. J. then, knowing in a faint way the hunger within him through the toilsome winter months, knowing the dream that lay behind his plan. He was a new Antaeus, preparing his own bed of strength.

"Planting time," he said. "We'll have to find us some seed."

"What do we do?" Blackie said. "How do we do it?"

"First we'll have to break up the clods," T. J. said. "That won't be hard to do. Then we plant the seed, and after a while they come up. Then you got you a crop." He frowned. "But you ain't got it raised yet. You got to tend it and hoe it and take care of it and all the time it's growing and growing while you're awake and while you're asleep. Then you lay it by when it's growed and let it ripen and then you got you a crop."

"There's those wholesale seed houses over on Sixth," I said. "We could probably swipe some grass seed over there."

T. J. looked at the earth. "You-all seem mighty set on raising some grass," he said. "I ain't never put no effort into that. I spent all my life trying not to raise grass."

"But it's pretty," Blackie said. "We could play on it and take sunbaths on it. Like having our own lawn. Lots of people got lawns."

"Well," T. J. said. He looked at the rest of us, hesitant for the first time. He kept on looking at us for a moment. "I did have it in mind to raise some corn and vegetables. But we'll plant grass."

He was smart. He knew where to give in. And I don't suppose it made any difference to him, really. He just wanted to grow something, even if it was grass.

"Of course," he said, "I do think we ought to plant a row of watermelons. They'd be mighty nice to eat while we was a-laying on that grass."

We all laughed. "All right," I said. "We'll plant us a row of watermelons."

Things went very quickly then. Perhaps half the roof was covered with the earth, the half that wasn't broken by ventilators, and we swiped pocketfuls of grass seed from the open bins in the wholesale seed house, mingling among the buyers on Saturdays and during the school lunch hour. T. J. showed us how to prepare the earth, breaking up the clods and smoothing it and sowing the grass seed. It looked rich and black now with moisture, receiving of the seed, and it seemed that the grass sprang up overnight, pale green in the early spring.

We couldn't keep from looking at it, unable to believe that we had created this delicate growth. We looked at T. J. with understanding now, knowing the fulfillment of the plan he had carried alone within his mind. We had worked without full understanding of the task, but he had known all the time.

We found that we couldn't walk or play on the delicate blades, as we had expected to, but we didn't mind. It was enough just to look at it, to realize that it was the work of our own hands, and each evening the whole gang was there, trying to measure the growth that had been achieved that day.

One time a foot was placed on the plot of ground . . . one time only, Blackie stepping onto it with sudden bravado. Then he looked at the crushed blades and there was shame in his face. He did not do it again. This was his grass, too, and not to be desecrated. No one said anything, for it was not necessary.

T. J. had reserved a small section for watermelons and he was still trying to find some seed for it. The wholesale house didn't have any watermelon seed and we didn't know where we could lay our hands on them. T. J. shaped the earth into mounds, ready to receive them, three mounds lying in a straight line along the edge of the grass plot.

We had just about decided that we'd have to buy the seed if we were to get them. It was a violation of our principles, but we were anxious to get the watermelons started. Somewhere or other, T. J. got his hands on a seed catalog and brought it one evening to our roof garden.

"We can order them now," he said, showing us the catalog. "Look!"

We all crowded around, looking at the fat, green watermelons pictured in full color on the pages. Some of them were split open, showing the red, tempting meat, making our mouths water.

"Now we got to scrape up some seed money," T. J. said, looking at us. "I got a quarter. How much you-all got?"

We made up a couple of dollars between us and T. J. nodded his head. "That'll be more than enough. Now we got to decide what kind to get. I think them Kleckley Sweets. What do you-all think?"

He was going into esoteric matters, beyond our reach. We hadn't even known there were different kinds of melons. So we just nodded our heads and agreed that yes, we thought the Kleckley Sweets, too.

"I'll order them tonight," T. J. said. "We ought to have them in a few days."

Then an adult voice said behind us: "What are you boys doing up here?"

It startled us, for no one had ever come up here before, in all the time we had been using the roof of the factory. We jerked around and saw three men standing near the trapdoor at the other end of the roof. They weren't policemen, or night watchmen, but three men in plump business suits, looking at us. They walked toward us.

"What are you boys doing up here?" the one in the middle said again.

We stood still, guilt heavy among us, levied by the tone of voice, and looked at the three strangers.

The men stared at the grass flourishing behind us. "What's this?" the man said. "How did this get up here?"

"Sure is growing good, ain't it?" T. J. said conversationally. "We planted it."

The men kept looking at the grass as if they didn't believe it. It was a thick carpet over the earth now, a patch of deep greenness startling in the sterile industrial surroundings.

"Yes, sir," T. J. said proudly. "We toted that earth up here and planted that grass." He fluttered the seed catalog. "And we're just fixing to plant us some watermelon."

The man looked at him then, his eyes strange and faraway. "What do you mean, putting this on the roof of my building?" he said. "Do you want to go to jail?"

T. J. looked shaken. The rest of us were silent, frightened by the authority of his voice. We had grown up aware of adult authority, of policemen and night watchmen and teachers, and this man sounded like all the others. But it was a new thing to T. J.

"Well, you wan't using the roof," T. J. said. He paused a moment and added shrewdly, "So we just thought to pretty it up a little bit."

"And sag it so I'd have to rebuild it," the man said sharply. He turned away, saying to a man beside him, "See that all that junk is shoveled off by tomorrow."

"Yes, sir," the man said.

T. J. started forward. "You can't do that," he said. "We toted it up here and it's our earth. We planted it and raised it and toted it up here."

The man stared at him coldly. "But it's my building," he said. "It's to be shoveled off tomorrow."

"It's our earth," T. J. said desperately. "You ain't got no right!"

The men walked on without listening and descended clumsily through the trapdoor. T. J. stood looking after them, his body tense with anger, until they had disappeared. They wouldn't even argue with him, wouldn't let him defend his earth-rights.

He turned to us. "We won't let 'em do it," he said fiercely. "We'll stay up here all day tomorrow and the day after that and we won't let 'em do it."

We just looked at him. We knew that there was no stopping it. He saw it in our faces and his face wavered for a moment before he gripped it into determination.

"They ain't got no right," he said. "It's our earth. It's our land. Can't nobody touch a man's own land."

We kept on looking at him, listening to the words but knowing that it was no use. The adult world had descended on us even in our richest dream, and we knew there was no calculating the adult world, no fighting it, no winning against it.

We started moving slowly toward the parapet and the fire escape, avoiding a last look at the green beauty of the earth that T. J. had planted for us . . . had planted deeply in our minds as well as in our experience. We filed slowly over the edge and down the steps to the plank, T. J. coming last, and all of us could feel the weight of his grief behind us.

"Wait a minute," he said suddenly, his voice harsh with the effort of calling. We stopped and turned, held by the tone of his voice, and looked up at him standing above us on the fire escape.

"We can't stop them?" he said, looking down at us, his face

strange in the dusky light. "There ain't no way to stop 'em?"

"No," Blackie said with finality. "They own the building."

We stood still for a moment, looking up at T. J., caught into inaction by the decision working in his face. He stared back at us and his face was pale and mean in the poor light, with a bald nakedness in his skin like cripples have sometimes.

"They ain't gonna touch my earth," he said fiercely. "They ain't gonna lay a hand on it! Come on."

He turned around and started up the fire escape again, almost running against the effort of climbing. We followed more slowly, not knowing what he intended. By the time we reached him, he had seized a board and thrust it into the soil, scooping it up and flinging it over the parapet into the areaway below. He straightened and looked us squarely in the face.

"They can't touch it," he said. "I won't let 'em lay a dirty hand on it!"

We saw it then. He stooped to his labor again and we followed it, the gusts of his anger moving in frenzied labor among us as we scattered along the edge of earth, scooping it and throwing it over the parapet, destroying with anger the growth we had nurtured with such tender care. The soil carried so laboriously upward to the light and the sun cascaded swiftly into the dark areaway, the green blades of grass crumpled and twisted in the falling.

It took less time than you would think . . . the task of destruction is infinitely easier than that of creation. We stopped at the end, leaving only a scattering of loose soil, and when it was finally over, a stillness stood among the group and over the factory building. We looked down at the bare sterility of black tar, felt the harsh texture of it under the soles of our shoes, and the anger had gone out of us, leaving only a sore aching in our minds like overstretched muscles.

T. J. stooped for a moment, his breathing slowing from anger and effort, caught into the same contemplation of destruction as all of us. He stooped slowly, finally, and picked up a lonely blade of grass left trampled under our feet, and put it between his teeth, tasting it, sucking the greenness out of it into his mouth. Then he started walking toward the fire escape, moving before any of us were ready to move, and disappeared over the edge while we stared after him.

We followed him but he was already halfway down to the ground, going on past the board where we crossed over, climbing down into the areaway. We saw the last section swing down with his weight and then he stood on the concrete below us, looking at the small pile of anonymous earth scattered by our throwing. Then he walked across the place where we could see him and disappeared toward the street without glancing back, without looking up to see us watching him.

They did not find him for two weeks. Then the Nashville police caught him just outside the Nashville freight yards. He was walking along the railroad track; still heading south, still heading home.

As for us, who had no remembered home to call us . . . none of us ever again climbed the escapeway to the roof.

The Facts of the Story

Write answers to the following questions. Answers should be complete sentences. You can probably answer all the questions without rereading the story, but look back if you wish.

1. The plot of this story is based on the attempts of the boys to solve a problem. What is the problem?

2. What obstacles must they overcome to solve the problem?

3. Why do they fail?

4. What is the climax of this story?

5. There are two settings in this story– the roof garden and the city. How do the two settings contrast?

The Ideas in the Story

Prepare to discuss orally, in class, the following questions.

1. On page 123, the author says that T. J. was "a new Antaeus, preparing his own bed of strength." What does this mean? Why does T. J. leave the city when the roof garden is destroyed?

2. In the final sentence of the story, the narrator says that he and the other boys "had no remembered home to call us." What do you think he means by this? Do you think people need "green worlds" such as the one created on the rooftop? What does the narrator mean when he says that T. J. had planted "the green beauty of the earth . . . deeply in our minds"?

3. In "The Birds" (page 56), you saw that people like the Triggs often cannot understand what they have not experienced themselves. Explain how and where this same human characteristic appears in "Antaeus."

4. A major problem faced by all young people is how to adjust to the demands of the adult world. What in their experience made the other boys react differently from T. J. to the orders of the factory owner?

The Art of the Storyteller

Characters and Characterization

Characters in a story may be people like ourselves, or they may be very different, not only from us, but from anyone we have ever known or heard about. One of a writer's jobs is to make the personalities of the characters clear and believable to the reader. The process by which a writer does this is called *characterization.*

Characterization is more important in some stories than in others. Plot is the main element in both "The Most Dangerous Game" and "To Build a Fire." But characterization is also important in "The Most Dangerous Game." The peculiarities of General Zaroff must be made clear to the reader because he is a very different person, and the whole story hinges on his "different" taste in games. The principal character in "To Build a Fire," on the contrary, doesn't even have a name. He could be any ordinary man. His personality is not important, except that London wants us to know that the man lacks imagination, a deficiency that does make a difference in the story.

In some stories, the characters are more interesting and memorable than the plot. "Antaeus" is this kind of story. While you are not likely to forget what happened in the story, the chances are that you will remember more vividly T. J. himself. It is his ideas and his personality that determine the action. Where does T. J. demonstrate these qualities of a natural leader?

Imagination

Ability to persuade

Ability to organize and plan

Willingness to compromise, to give in, on occasion

Willingness to set an example for others

Composition

Writing a Character Sketch

A writer may portray an interesting person by writing a short story about him or her, as Borden Deal did when he wrote about T. J. Or a writer may portray the person in an article of the kind found in newspapers or popular magazines about important people in the news or people prominent in theater, television, movies, or sports. Such an article is called a *character sketch.*

Write a character sketch of someone you know or once knew. In planning your sketch, follow these steps:

1. Jot down the principal character traits of the person. Then select the traits you want to emphasize.

2. Think of at least one interesting anecdote telling about something that the person did. (An *anecdote* is a very brief story.) Remember that it is through their *actions* that we learn what people are like.

3. Physical characteristics are normally not very important. Describe the person, of course, but don't spend a lot of time doing it. Your sketch should concentrate on your subject's personality and actions, not on his or her appearance.

You may choose to write about someone you admire or about someone you heartily dislike, but make sure your sketch clearly shows why you feel the way you do. Open the character sketch with a topic sentence introducing your subject.

Write approximately 150 words.

Borden Deal

Borden Deal (1922-   ) was born into a farm family in Pontotoc, Mississippi. He knows well what life was like in Southern farming communities during the hard years of the 1930's Depression and during World War II. Many of his stories and novels are about similar communities. Deal witnessed the migration of families from farms in the South to cities in the North, where jobs were available in war industries. Note that his story "Antaeus" begins, "This was during the wartime . . ."

The Bridge

NICOLAI CHUKOVSKI
Translated by Selig O. Wassner

Anyone who has ever had a problem with shyness or awkwardness or poor marks in school will sympathize with Kostya, who has been deeply affected by all three of these problems. Because of his poor marks in high school, this seventeen-year-old Russian cannot qualify for college, so he must travel alone to distant Siberia to work for his uncle.

Kostya dreads leaving his sheltered life at home. His aunt and grandmother, who live with him, are sure that he will be a failure, and so is Kostya. But on the day before his departure, something happens that changes Kostya. Watch how Chukovski builds up suspense as he describes this event in "The Bridge."

"I just can't see him going," Gramma said, turning over the potato cake in the pan with a knife. "He's scared of everything."

"He'll go," Aunt Nadya replied from the depth of the kitchen. "He has to go. He'll be better off there."

Gramma sighed loudly. She wasn't at all convinced Kostya would be better off there.

Kostya had heard every word. He stood not far from the open window amid the currant shrubs, quickly picking the berries and shoving them into his mouth. Since it had been decided he would have to go away, Kostya was spending hours at a time in these shrubs, their luxurious, end-of-July growth serving as an excellent hiding place. He liked to be alone, and not have to talk to anyone. Through the branches creeping over the windowsill into the shade-filled kitchen, he could see Gramma's hands moving over the kerosene burner, and hear the sizzling of the frying pancakes.

"He's scared of everything . . . everything," Gramma repeated. "He's afraid to buy a stamp in the post office. How'll he go?"

Kostya's mouth was getting sour from the berries. He worked his way out of the shrubbery, found his bicycle on the dark porch, and he opened the kitchen door. Aunt Nadya was peeling potatoes—since it was Sunday she hadn't gone to work in the factory but was helping Gramma. The peels coiled like spirals over Aunt Nadya's thick, manlike fingers. Gramma, a squat, little woman, had just turned over another sizzling pancake. She looked up at the boy. Kostya knew that the mountain of potato cakes piled up in a plate at the burner was being baked for him—one more sign that his going-away was final.

"I'm going for a little ride," he said glumly, hoisting the small bicycle over his shoulder.

Gramma sighed, stepping heavily from foot to foot. "Go on, have your last ride," Aunt Nadya told him without lifting her face from the potatoes. "You won't be doing it there."

Kostya walked the bicycle through the open wicket[1] and threw his long leg over the frame. The bike, a juvenile size bought a long time ago, had become too small for him. This year he had shot up to almost twice his previous height, though otherwise he remained the same: narrow shoulders, a thin neck with a protruding Adam's apple, and slightly protuberant, translucent ears. Mechanically Kostya rode out into the alley, hedged by dusty elder thickets. His sharp knees almost touched his chin but he didn't mind—he was much too used to it. Mechanically he swerved to his left to cut into the open fields; he didn't want to meet anybody and didn't want anybody to disturb his thoughts.

Last spring after he was graduated from high school, barely getting promoted, Kostya had decided that going to the institute was out of the question. There had been a time his marks were no worse than anybody else's, but after his mother had died, a year and a half ago, he hadn't attended school for several months, and he had fallen too far behind to catch up. Everybody in class had known that Kostya never learned his lessons. He had become shy and unsure of himself, and the shyness had compounded his confusion whenever he'd been called to the blackboard.

And then his awkwardness. In company he'd either keep quiet or blurt out anything that came to his mind, then feel ashamed of himself. He had begun to avoid people, go swimming by himself, had even given up the soccer team. Once he had been shortchanged in the bakery shop and instead of reminding the saleswoman that she had made a mistake, he had told his grandmother that he had lost the money. Gramma

1. *wicket:* gate.

was the only one with whom he felt at ease, unafraid. But now he'd have to leave her. . . .

This was the third year Gramma hadn't worked in the factory but had lived on her pension. Aunt Nadya had four little children; her husband had gone into construction work somewhere on the Volga;[2] and there were rumors he had himself another woman—for the last year he hadn't sent home a kopeck.[3] The whole settlement where Kostya had been born and lived all his starless seventeen years was made up of people working in the factory. It was a women's factory where a true man wouldn't be caught working. Lads would leave the settlement as soon as they were graduated, and Kostya, too, would have to leave and stop living at Gramma's and Aunt Nadya's expense. But where? Uncle Vassily Petrovitch, Gramma's brother, had asked him to come, promising Gramma to take good care of him and find him a job. Everybody had thought that this was good and right, that a bright future was ahead of him . . . everybody but Kostya. Deep inside he was afraid nothing would come out of it, yet he didn't dare tell anybody.

He didn't dare confess to anybody how frightening was the thought of leaving Gramma. Uncle Vassily Petrovitch loomed in Kostya's mind like a cold, strict old man of whom even Gramma was afraid. Quite often she had warned him "not to do anything to spite your uncle." Uncle Vasya[4] had left for Siberia many years ago, before Kostya was even born, when his mother was still a little girl. He had been a tugboat captain on that great Siberian river that flows into the Arctic Ocean, but now he was more than that—he was a chief over a whole fleet of boats. Kostya often saw this river on a large map hanging in the classroom; with all its winding tributaries it reminded him of some strange plant with many weird roots stretching and

2. *Volga:* a major river of Russia.
3. *kopeck:* a Russian coin. This is like saying he hadn't sent home a cent.
4. *Vasya:* a nickname for Vassily.

stretching. . . . Uncle Vasya often asked that Kostya come. "I'll enter him in the River Technicum[5] together with my son Kolya," he wrote. "They will drill them there so that in three years both of them will become fine navigators." When Gramma had read that letter she flinched, and cast Kostya a frightened look at the word *drill*. And yet tonight they would go to the railroad station and wait for the Moscow train arriving at five in the morning. He would leave all by himself for Moscow, the unfamiliar big city he had never seen before, and in Moscow he'd have to find his way to another railroad station, board another train leaving for Siberia, and he'd be all by himself with nothing to remind him of Gramma's comfort apart from the potato pancakes in the basket. . . .

It was a warm but sunless, overcast day. Kostya rode out of the settlement and turned onto the highway running amid wavy fields. To the right, about three kilometers away, stretched the river—wide at times, hiding at times behind soft hills. The cloud-covered sky seemed to be hanging low over the usually busy highway, now deserted because it was Sunday. A warm, hay-scented breeze caressed the boy's face, as though careful not to disturb his thinking.

Deep in his thoughts, Kostya pushed the pedals, unaware of a little bird that kept perching on a telegraph post ahead of him, swinging its long tail, and seeming to wait until he caught up with it, then flying up again, perching on another post, farther away, and waiting again. The boy did not notice it, nor the old, thick-leaved linden trees—the remnants of an old road on which this highway was constructed—shooting up here and there like petrified explosions. Kostya pedaled onward where the gray ribbon of the macadam ran into the sunless twilight, rising softly or sloping gently.

Each time Kostya reached a crest of the wavy road, he had an excellent view to the next crest. Each time he was on the top

---

5. *River Technicum:* a technical school, specializing in naval training.

of a hill he could see a green depression through which the road made a straight cut, first running down, then up toward the crest, where it butted against the sky and disappeared.

Hurdling one of these crests, Kostya sighted in the distance a minute, colored dot moving in the same direction. It occurred to him he might have noticed it before but had paid it no attention. There might have been a two-kilometer span between them—he only had a glimpse of it, looming blue and yellow, before it reached the next crest and vanished.

Kostya began to pedal faster. He dashed downhill, bouncing over a little bridge that spanned the two banks of a gully, then climbed the uphill stretch, using the impetus gained from the down-drive. He hurdled the crest and saw again the yellow-blue dot—bigger now, just beginning to move up the next rise. The distance between them had been shortened considerably; he could see it was somebody on a bicycle. How odd, he thought, so gaily dressed, yellow on top, blue below. Quite intrigued, Kostya leaned forward, pumping harder and harder, trying for greater speed.

As soon as he came over the next crest he realized that the cyclist ahead of him was a girl wearing a blue skirt and yellow blouse, her fair hair falling down her back. She had been ped-aling unhurriedly until she heard him coming from behind. As she turned her face to him, the glimpse Kostya caught was brief: a round, babyish face. There were still about two hun-dred meters separating them, and when she turned away again, her plump little calves in the white socks began to push hard-er—the girl didn't want to be outdistanced.

She spurted ahead. Kostya leaned forward on the bars, pumping with all his might. Yet he was unable to cut the distance by much—she seemed to be quite good. On the next rise he appeared to gain a little, but when they came down the slope and the bikes rolled on their own, he stayed back some-what. Her bike's better than mine, he thought. Yet the excite-ment of the chase added will to his strength—on the next rise he gained considerably, and covered the next downhill stretch, long as it was, without giving in a meter. Now he could see her well: no more than thirteen or fourteen. At times the girl turned her head slightly, seeming to try to catch a glimpse of him from the corner of her eye. Then he saw her chubby cheek, and a moment later he'd see her trying desperately to keep him from catching up with her. But he was drawing inexorably closer.

The girl's hair fluttered in the wind, exposing the back of her neck. They sped out of the fields, plunging into a forest of aspen, spruce, and birch trees that seemed to rise into a solid wall. As the distance between the bicycles stubbornly decreased, Kostya was overcome by a sense of triumph. The girl's glances were more frequent; every time she tried to have a look at him her bike made a little zigzag, and he gained a few meters. He was sure now to catch up with her, probably on the next rise.

A recently laid asphalt road turned off the highway into the forest, right at the start of the rise. Kostya knew where it led: toward the river, where a new bridge was being built to connect the state farms on both sides. But what he did not suspect was that the pursued bicycle would turn off to that road.

The girl made the turn abruptly. It was so sudden that he almost flashed by. She might have thought he would follow the highway and stop pursuing her. But Kostya had become so intensely elated that all he could think of now was catching up with her. He, too, swerved from the highway and spurted after her.

The road was downhill all the way. Both bicycles were tearing down at their maximum speeds, the girl steadily about ten meters ahead of Kostya. But he didn't care any more—the road only led to the bridge now under construction and she'd have no choice but to stop there.

The road approached the bridge at an angle; through the tree trunks at the right the mirror of the river flashed far below under its steep bank. Cement barrels, sifters, and wooden scaffolding loomed before their eyes together with piles upon piles of scrap concrete – the unfinished structure was right in front of them.

The bridgework had no top layer yet but it spanned both banks. It looked like a net scaled by a formless hodgepodge of wood in which the future metallic slickness could only be vaguely surmised. Now, because it was Sunday, instead of the unceasing hum of work, a deep silence stood over the river.

Everything happened so fast that Kostya had no time to consider the danger. Suddenly he saw that the asphalt was coming to an end, and a four-plank trestle, laid over a sand embankment, led to the bridge. The girl pedaled ahead at top speed. Kostya was so shocked that before he had time to recover his wits he found himself, too, bouncing along those planks. He gripped the bar firmly to avoid veering off onto the sand. But the sand wasn't what bothered him. What frightened him was the realization that the trestle ran from the embankment onto the truss, across the unfenced iron girders which served as a narrow path for the bridgeworkers – high above the water. Was she insane? She was coming to the end of the embankment without slowing down!

"Brake! Brake!" he managed to shout out. But then he choked on his own words.

The girl half turned at the sound of his voice. Again she glanced at him from the corner of one eye. Her bicycle, making a slight zigzag, almost pulled her off the planks. But she managed to straighten out the wheel and spurt straight ahead, onto the truss, over the narrow path suspended high above the water.

Something is terribly wrong here, flashed through Kostya's mind. He should have braked short of the bridge but for some uncanny reason he hadn't done so. His bike carried him onto the truss, onto those same planks, high above the water. . . .

There was no more time to stop, turn, or look back. The

only way was straight ahead—with no letup of speed. His hand must not jerk. He knew he couldn't stand the suspense; he'd weaken from fear. But he must go on . . . because of her . . . because her bike was straight ahead. . . .

Kostya couldn't tear his eyes away from the girl. She rode evenly, unswervingly, yet he sensed a desperate tension in that straightness. How can she stand it! Oh, if she only doesn't get it into her head to look back! How far is it to the end of the bridge? If she can only keep her hand from jerking! If only she'll not try to look back! She's over more than half—one more minute, and it'll be all over. Just that she doesn't look back!

The girl did look back.

She turned her head just slightly, just to make sure from the corner of her eye that he was behind. As she turned, her front wheel gave a slight jerk. A second, a long eternity, she struggled with it, trying to make it straight. But she couldn't. Her bike veered into the air, into emptiness. . . .

He didn't see her fall. She simply disappeared from the bridge—she and her bike. Abruptly he did something he had thought was impossible—he put on the brakes and jumped off onto the planks. He looked down. The water was way, way down, glistening with a dull, firm shine like a metal—streaming away, somewhere beyond the bridge. He saw her bike, caught by its frame at the end of a beam, sticking out from behind the rough scaffolding, still swinging slightly. But the girl was nowhere in sight.

Stunned, Kostya put down his bike and dived.

He pierced the surface of the water with his hands and felt it close above him as he was dragged down by the current. Although stung by the fall, he had the presence of mind to open his eyes and look for her. All he could see were hazy outlines of some huge blocks and posts. After touching the bottom, he felt himself pulled up. He turned over under the water and surfaced.

The current pulled him to the bridge span. He came close to

a concrete abutment not cleared yet of some wooden casing and piles of lumber. Above, fragments of the cloudy sky seemed to be peeking through the many-storied net of girders, crossbeams, and timbering. The current was strong, too strong for any resistance. Kostya drifted with it, turning, whirling, not even trying to fight it until . . . he saw her, just around the bend.

The top of her head appeared behind a pile of timber sticking out of the water at the bridge span. Up to her mouth in water, the girl clutched the pile with both hands, right in front of a foaming whirl. Kostya couldn't see her whole face but her cheek and one eye, and from the look of that eye—large, frightened—he knew that she was holding with her last strength. One more moment and the current would carry her away.

"Hold on!" he shouted, choking on a mouthful of water. Now there was only one thing to be afraid of, that the current would carry him by her. He'd never be able to get back to her against it. Kostya tried desperately to gain control of his movements. His wet breeches and canvas slippers hampered his effort. Nonetheless, he managed to throw out his left arm and grab that same pile. As the current whirled him around and around he hung on, his shoulder touching hers.

The girl's pale, wet face was close to his, her wide-open eyes bright with tension. He hoped she would believe that he would be able to save her. But how? He didn't have the slightest idea himself what to do next.

High up, the concrete abutment towered like a tremendous giant. Its surface was too smooth to offer a hold. Kostya looked back—behind them the river grew wide.

"You know how to swim?" he asked.

She shook her head.

Kostya knew that the girl couldn't hold on much longer. He looked back again; the left bank was not too far away. By himself he'd probably make it. To the right, in the direction of the current, the river made a bend. To the left, oblong stones jutted out of the water. There, he should try to get over there. . . .

He looked at the girl again. He'd have to act fast, as long as she still had some strength left. "Let go," he ordered.

"No, no."

"You must listen to me," he said gravely. He pulled her hand away from the pile and tried to put it on his shoulder. Immediately her other hand slipped off the pile and now the girl clung to him with both hands. Under the burden Kostya let go, and both of them began to sink. The whirl pulled them under. In desperation he forcibly pried open her hands and pushed her away. Thrashing wildly, the girl rose to the surface by herself. He, too, came up, snorted, and looked around. The girl kept thrashing right beside him. Her round face rose for a moment out of the water; her mouth gasped for air before she began to sink again. The bridge with all its mass of iron and wood seemed to be rapidly backing away.

Kostya wound her short, chubby arm around his neck. Her other arm, which was about to clutch him, he pushed aside. "Don't you dare," he said sternly. "You must obey me."

She obeyed and stopped clinging to him. As they began to float more steadily, Kostya struggled stubbornly, stroking with one arm and cutting across the current toward the stones. The girl's soft arm rested confidently though heavily against his neck, pressing his face into the water. But Kostya knew how to handle himself. As long as her face remained above water, he'd be able to lift his head for a breath of air, then let it be submerged.

The girl stopped struggling. She calmed down and obviously had more confidence in him than he had in himself. "I'll do whatever you say," she whispered into his ear. But he felt he was weakening, and he was afraid the current would not let them reach the stones. He tried to drift to the shore but the whirls carried him to the right, around the stones, toward the rapids. Two times he tried to reach bottom with his feet; on the third try he touched it.

Although the water reached above his ears, he managed to keep afloat. The shallow from which the stones protruded had apparently extended quite far. Seeing him stand, the girl tried to stand up, too. After she swallowed some water and choked, Kostya picked her up and, stepping carefully, he carried her to the shore.

Fifteen minutes later they were sitting on the sloping bank amid elm trees, watching the water through the branches. Their clothes were hung on the trees to dry—he had only his trunks on, she had on panties and a white undershirt. Her seminakedness embarrassed him; he tried not to sit too close to her, nor glance at her too often. She, however, seemed not to mind. Her innocent, bright eyes were full of confidence as they admired him through strands of wet hair that kept falling onto her face.

Their bicycles lay side by side on the grass. Kostya had removed them from the bridge by himself. The zeal of achievement had made him feel light and fearless. It hadn't been too difficult to get his bicycle, although when he had stepped onto those planks once again he had asked himself how he was able to ride on that narrow, unfenced path. An hour ago he'd probably not have had the courage to walk on it; but now he ambled without fear, without having to look at his feet. To recover the girl's bike wasn't that easy; he had to clamber down the timbering and hoist the thing with his feet while hanging on the girder with his hands. He had enjoyed his work, however, knowing that she stood there on the shore, watching him, admiring him. He hadn't been afraid to fall into the water because that would have only been a repeat jump. But he had been concerned he might drop the bicycle. He hadn't. He rolled them both up onto the shore, toward the elm tree where their clothes were hung to dry.

"You can do everything." The girl looked at Kostya with admiring eyes.

"I can," he confirmed. "Had I dropped your bike I'd have given you mine." He felt like being extremely generous; as a matter of fact, he was sorry he couldn't give her his bike.

"I'd not have taken it for anything," she said. "You are leaving?"

"Yes, tonight."

"For long?"

"Forever."

"And when will you come back?" she asked.

"Probably never."

The impression his words made on her affected him too.

"Never," the girl repeated slowly. "How far are you going?"

"Very far," he replied. "I'm taking the Moscow train tonight."

She asked if he was going to the district capital. She had apparently thought the district capital was very far.

"Uh-uh," Kostya said. "The day after tomorrow I'll be in Moscow."

"In Moscow?" she asked respectfully.

"But only for a day," he explained. "Got to do some sightseeing."

"You're going even farther?" she asked incredulously.

He nodded. "To Siberia."

She became quiet. He sensed how impressive that name sounded to her.

"Who's going with you?" she asked again.

"I'm going by myself."

While he answered her questions, Kostya began to see his trip in a new light. He had suddenly made a discovery—he found out something about himself he had never known: he could accomplish tasks. The future, which up to now had appeared fearful, suddenly became a grandiose adventure within reach.

"I'll guide big ships," Kostya said, getting up from excitement. "Diesel motor ships."

"Where to?"

"To the Arctic Ocean. Beyond the Arctic Circle and back. Through the taiga, tundra,[6] all kinds of animals," Kostya recalled what he knew about Siberia. He was waiting for her to ask if he really knew how to guide diesel motor ships, but she didn't. Perhaps she had some doubts if he really could do everything. He, too, had some doubts.

"I'll learn," he said, thinking of Uncle Vasya. "What one man can do another man can, too."

There was silence for a while. Narrow-shouldered, long-legged, upright, Kostya stared into the water glistening through the trees. Absorbed in his new ideas, he seemed to have forgotten about the girl who sat with her arms around her round knees, glancing at him timidly from time to time.

"Is somebody coming to see you off?" she asked softly.

"They are." He nodded.

"Who?"

Kostya knew that Gramma and Aunt Nadya would come with him to the station, but somehow he didn't feel like telling it to the girl. He made no reply.

"I'll come too, may I?" she asked in a pattering whisper, brushing off her wet hair from her forehead. "We live next to the station, I'll just jump out of the window and run up. May I?" The girl talked fast, as if she were afraid he might stop her. "I won't be in anybody's way, they won't even see me. I'll just watch. May I, may I?"

Kostya didn't answer. He looked at her with a joyous wonderment in his heart—it was a hitherto unknown tenderness which he realized was also a new discovery.

---

6. *taiga:* coniferous forest; *tundra:* treeless plain.

The Facts of the Story

Write answers to the following questions. Answers should be complete sentences. Look at the story if you wish.

1. There are two conflicts in this story—an external conflict and an internal conflict. What internal conflict, or struggle within himself, does Kostya face?

2. What external conflict presents itself on the bridge?

3. How does Kostya resolve the external conflict?

4. How is his internal conflict resolved?

5. From the final pages, select the sentence that you think best describes the change that comes over Kostya as a result of his experience on the bridge.

The Art of the Storyteller

Theme

You have learned that, in addition to plot and characters, a short story contains ideas. The main idea or insight about life is the *theme* of the story. Sometimes the theme is stated directly by the author. More often, however, the author tells the story and leaves it to the reader to grasp the theme.

In "The Bridge," the theme is simple and obvious. It is not stated in so many words, but a careful reader will understand it at once. This story of Kostya's experience at the bridge reveals that one experience may change the personality, indeed the entire life, of a person.

By his characterization of Kostya at the beginning of the story and by his account of Kostya's heroism later, Chukovski dramatizes his theme. Timid, withdrawn, immature, Kostya has, for more than a year, moped around home, tied to his grandmother's apron strings. He does not accomplish anything because he never does anything. The thought of leaving home frightens him. Then he is faced with an emergency that calls for action and quick thinking. He finds that he is, after all, capable of heroic deeds. His self-confidence is restored. Stated another way, the theme reveals that growing up is a matter not only of age, but also of experience.

If you are inclined to be skeptical, you may wonder whether the change in Kostya will be lasting. Do you think the change will survive the journey to Siberia and improve Kostya's chances of success there, or that Kostya eventually will revert to his old ways? Explain your answer.

The Flashback

The *flashback* is a device frequently used by short-story writers. It gives the reader a quick look back at events that happened earlier, even before the beginning of the story. "The Bridge" contains a good example of a flashback.

As the story begins, Kostya is hiding outside the kitchen window listening to his aunt and his grandmother talking about him. Through their conversation, we learn that Kostya is "scared of everything" and that he is going away. The story gets under way when Kostya decides to take a ride on his bicycle. However, there is still much that we need to know about him. This information is given in a four-paragraph flashback, which interrupts the account of the bicycle ride. Glance over the first four pages of the story. With which paragraph does the flashback begin? Where does it end?

At what places in the flashback do you find information about the following?

1. The reason Kostya has fallen behind in his schoolwork.

2. The reason he has to go away to find work.

3. The character of Uncle Vasya.

4. The plans for Kostya's departure.

Chukovski could have begun the story with a straight account of these matters and then introduced the bicycle ride. Why do you think he chose instead to begin where he did?

Composition

Supporting a Topic Sentence with Examples

Like Kostya, you have undoubtedly undergone changes in personality and character as the result of certain unforgettable experiences. Write a paragraph about one such experience. Begin with the topic sentence "A single experience brought about an important change in me." Tell what happened and explain how it changed you.

If you wish, develop the paragraph by giving more than one example: "I can remember three experiences that changed me." If you prefer, use someone else as your subject: "Jane Doe's personality was changed by one unforgettable experience."

Change, of course, need not be for the better. People often change for the worse.

Write approximately 100 words.

Nicolai Chukovski

Nicolai Chukovski (1904-1965) was a Russian. He wrote historical fiction, short stories, and books on exploration. "The Bridge" is one of the few writings of his that have been translated into English.

Enemy Territory

WILLIAM MELVIN KELLEY

Writers seem to enjoy writing stories based on their childhood experiences. In this story, William Melvin Kelley writes about an experience he had when he was six years old and living in New York City. Many children like to play soldier, especially when their country is at war, as the United States was with Japan when Kelley was six. To a six-year-old child in a city, however, a real enemy may be the "gang" on the next block, which is "enemy territory," not to be invaded. To Tommy's Cuban grandfather, a bar in the nearby Irish section of the city was "enemy territory," as you will soon discover.

You will follow this story more easily if you understand that it is really two stories, one "inside" the other. There is the story of Tommy, with which "Enemy Territory" begins and ends, and there is the story of his grandfather, which is told "inside" Tommy's story by his grandmother.

I peered over a rotting tree stump and saw him moving, without a helmet, in the bushes. I got his forehead in my sights, squeezed the trigger, and imagined I saw the bullet puncture his head and blood trickle out. "I got you, Jerome. I got you!"

"Awh, you did not."

"I got you; you're dead."

I must have sounded very definite because he compromised. "You only wounded me."

"Tommy? Tommy! Come here." Her voice came from high above me.

I scrambled to my knees. "What, Ma?" She was on the porch of our house, next to the vacant lot where we were playing.

"Come here a minute, dear. I want you to do something for me." She was wearing a yellow dress. The porch was red brick.

I hopped up and ran to the foot of our steps. She came to the top. "Mister Bixby left his hat."

As I had waited in ambush for Jerome, I had seen Mister Bixby climb and, an hour later, chug down the steps. He was one of my father's poker-playing friends. It was only after she mentioned it that I remembered Mister Bixby had been wearing, when he arrived, a white, wide-brimmed panama hat with a black band.

Entering my parents' room on the second floor, I saw it on their bed. My mother picked it up. "Walk it around to his house. Now walk, I say. Don't run because you'll probably drop it and ruin it." It was so white a speck of dirt would have shone like a black star in a white sky. "So walk! Let me see your hands."

I extended them palms up and she immediately sent me to the bathroom to wash. Then she gave me the hat. I did not really grip it; rather, with my finger in the crown, I balanced it, as if about to twirl it.

When I stepped onto the porch again, I saw them playing on their corner – Valentine's Gang. Well, in this day of street gangs organized like armies, I cannot rightly call Joey Valentine, who was eight, and his acquaintances, who ranged in age from five to seven, a gang. It was simply that they lived on the next block, and since my friends and I were just at the age when we were allowed to cross the street, but were not yet used to this new freedom, we still stood on opposite sides of the asphalt strip that divided us and called each other names. It was not until I got onto the porch that I realized, with a sense of dread that only a six-year-old can conjure up, that Mister Bixby lived one block beyond Valentine's Territory.

Still, with faith that the adult nature of my mission would give me unmolested passage, I approached the corner, which was guarded by a red fire-alarm box, looked both ways for the cars that seldom came, and, swallowing, began to cross over.

They were playing with toy soldiers and tin tanks in the border of dry yellow dirt that separated the flagstones from the gutter. I was in the middle of the street when they first realized I was invading; they were shocked. At the time, I can remember thinking they must have been awed that I should have the unequaled courage to cross into their territory. But looking back, I realize it probably had little to do with me. It was the hat, a white panama hat. A more natural target for abuse has never existed.

I was two steps from the curb when Joey Valentine moved into my path. "Hey, what you got?"

Since he was obviously asking the question to show off, I bit my lips and did not answer. I saw myself as one of my radio heroes resisting Japanese interrogation. I was aloof. However, the white panama hat was not at all aloof. Before I knew it, Joey Valentine reached out a mud-caked hand and knocked the hat off my finger to a resounding chorus of cheers and laughter.

I scooped up the hat before any of them, retreated at a run across the street, and stopped beside the red alarm box. Wanting to save some small amount of my dignity, I screamed at them: "I'll get you guys! I'll get you. I'm not really an American. I'm an African and Africans are friends of the Japs and I'll get them to *bomb your house!*"

But even as I ranted at them, I could see I was doing so in vain. Across the way, Valentine's Gang lounged with the calm of movie Marines listening to Japanese propaganda on the radio. I turned toward my house, inspecting the hat for smudges. There were none; it was as blinding white as ever. Already I felt tears inching down my cheeks.

Not until I was halfway up the porch steps did I see my grandmother sitting in her red iron chair. But before I could say anything, before I could appeal for understanding and comfort, she lifted herself out of the chair and disappeared into the house. She had seen it all—I knew that—and she was too ashamed of me to face me.

Suddenly, she was coming back, holding a broom handle. She had never before lifted a hand to me, but in my state, I felt sure that many things would change. I closed my eyes and waited.

Instead of the crunch of hard wood on bone, I heard her chair creak. I opened my eyes and found the end of the broom handle under my nose.

"You know if you don't go back and deliver that hat, you'll feel pretty bad tonight."

I nodded.

"Well, take this. We don't like you fighting. But sometimes you have to. So now you march down there and tell those boys if they don't let you alone, you'll have to hit them with this. Here." She pushed the broom handle at me.

I took it, but was not very happy about it. I studied her; she looked the same, her white hair bunned at her neck, her blue eyes large behind glasses, her skin the color of unvarnished wood. But something inside must have changed for her actually to tell me to hit someone. I had been in fights, fits and starts of temper that burned out in a second. But to walk deliberately down to the corner, threaten someone, and hit him if he did not move aside, this was completely different, and, as my parents and grandmother had raised me, downright evil. She must have realized what I was thinking.

"You know who Teddy Roosevelt was?"

I nodded.

"Well, he once said: *Speak softly and carry a big stick; you will go far.*"

I understood her, but to do something like this was still alien to my nature. I held back.

"Come on." She stood abruptly and took my hand. We went into the house, down the hall, and into her bedroom. "I have to see to the mulatto rice. You sit on my bed and look at the picture on the wall." She went on to the kitchen. I was still holding the broom handle and now put it down across the bed, and climbed up beside it, surrounded by her room, an old woman's room with its fifty years of perfume, powder, and sweet soap. I felt a long way from the corner and Valentine's Gang.

There were three pictures on the wall and I was not certain which she wanted me to study. The smallest was of my granduncle Wilfred, who lived on Long Island and came to Thanksgiving dinner. The largest was of Jesus, the fingers of His right hand crossed and held up, His left hand baring His chest, in the middle of which was His heart, red and dripping blood. In the cool darkness of the room, He looked at me with gentle eyes, a slight smile on His lips. The third was my grandmother's husband, who had died so long before that I had never known him and had no feeling for him as my grandfather. He was light, like my grandmother, but more like some of the short, sallow Italian men who lived on the block. His black hair was parted in the middle. He wore a big mustache which hid his mouth. His jaw was square and dimpled. With black eyes, he seemed to look at something just above my head.

"Well, all right now." My grandmother came in, sweating from standing over the stove, and sat in a small armchair beside the bed. "Did you look at the picture?"

"I didn't know which one." I looked at Jesus again.

"No, not Him this time. This one." She indicated her husband. "I meant him."

Now Pablo Cortés, your grandfather—she started—was just like you, as gentle as a milkweed flower settling into honey, and as friendly as ninety-seven puppy dogs. He was from Cuba, which is an island in the Atlantic Ocean.

He was so kind that he'd meet every boat coming in from Cuba and talk to all of the people getting off, and if he found that one of them didn't have a place to stay, and no money for food, he'd bring him home. He'd lead his new friend into the kitchen and say: "Jennie, this is a countryman. He got no place to sleep, and he's hungry." And I'd sigh and say: "All right. Dinner'll be ready in ten minutes." They'd go into the living room and sing and roll cigars.

That's what he did for a living, roll cigars, working at home. The leaves were spread out all over the floor like a rug and I never did like cigars because I know somebody's been walking all over the leaves, sometimes in bare feet like your mother did when she was a little girl.

Pablo was so friendly he gave a party every day while I was at work. I'd come home and open the door and the cigar smoke would tumble out, and through the haze I would see twenty drunken Cubans, most with guitars, others rolling cigars, and all of them howling songs.

So now fifty years ago, I'd come from down South to stay with my brother Wilfred, and I was so dumb that the first time

I saw snow I thought somebody upstairs'd broken open a pillow out the window. So my brother Wilfred had to explain a lot of things to me. And the first thing was about the neighborhoods. The Italians lived in one neighborhood, and the Polish in another, and the Negroes and Cubans someplace else. After Pablo and I got married, we lived with the Negroes. And if you walked two blocks one way, you'd come to the Irish neighborhood, and if you were smart, you'd turn around and come back because if the Irish caught you, they'd do something terrible to you.

I don't know if Pablo knew this or not, or if he just thought he was so friendly that everybody would just naturally be friendly right back. But one day he went for a walk. He got over into the Irish neighborhood and got a little thirsty—which he did pretty often—so he went into an Irish bar and asked for a drink. I guess they thought he was new in this country because the bartender gave him his drink. So Pablo, smiling all the time, and waiting for them to smile back, stood there in that Irish bar and drank slow. When he was finished, the bartender took the glass, and instead of washing it, he smashed it down on the floor and stepped on it and crushed the pieces under his heel. What he meant was that it was pretty bad to be a Cuban and no Irishman would want to touch a glass a Cuban had drunk from.

I don't know if Pablo knew that either. He asked for another drink. And he got it. And after he finished this one, the bartender smashed it in the sink and glared at him.

Pablo was still thirsty and ordered again.

The bartender came and stood in front of him. He was a big man, with a face as red as watermelon. "Say, buddy, can't you take a hint?"

Pablo smiled. "What hint?"

The bartender was getting pretty mad. "Why you think I'm breaking them glasses?"

"I thought you like to break glasses. You must got a high bill on glasses."

The bartender got an ax handle from under the bar. "Get out of here, Cuban!"

So now Pablo knew the bartender didn't want him in the bar. "Now, let me get this straight. If I ask you for drink, and you give me drink, you would break that glass too?"

"That's right. But you better not order again."

Pablo sighed. He was sad. "Well, then we will pretend I got drunk in this bar." And the next thing anybody knew Pablo was behind the bar, breaking all the glasses he could reach.

"And we will pretend that I look at myself in your mirror." He picked up a bottle and cracked the big mirror they had.

By now there was a regular riot going on with all the men in the bar trying to catch and hold him, and Pablo running around, breaking chairs and tables. Finally, just before they caught and tied him up, he tipped over their piano. "We will pretend I played a Cuban song on this piano!"

They called the police and held him until the wagon came. And the next time I saw him was in court the next morning, where the judge kept looking at Pablo like he really didn't believe that a man who seemed so kind and gentle could do such things. But it was plain Pablo had wrecked the Irishman's bar. The judge sentenced him to thirty days in the city jail, and fifty dollars damages, which Pablo couldn't pay. So the judge gave him thirty extra days.

I didn't see Pablo for the next two months. When he came home, he was changed. He wasn't smiling at all, and you remember that he used to smile all the time. As soon as he came in the house he told me he was going out again. I knew where and I got mad. "Do you want to spend another two months in jail? Is that what you want?"

He didn't understand me. "Why you ask me that?"

"Why! You're going over there to that white man's bar and get into a fight and go on back to jail. Did you like it that much? Did jail change you so much?"

"Jennie, don't you see? I try not to change." He picked up five boxes of cigars he'd made before he went to jail and put them into a brown paper bag, and tucked the bag under his arm.

I watched him go out the door and then started to cry. I loved him, you see, and didn't want him back in jail. And I cried because I didn't understand him now and was afraid of that.

When the Irishmen saw him coming into their bar, they were stunned. Their mouths dropped open and they all got very quiet. Pablo didn't pay them any mind, just walked up to the bar and put his foot on the brass rail.

The bartender picked up his ax handle. "What you want here, Cuban? Ain't you had enough?"

"No." Pablo didn't smile. He took the brown paper bag and put it gently on the counter. Cigars, he said, are delicate and shouldn't be tossed around.

The bartender looked at the bag. "What you got there?"

"Maybe you find out." He touched the box with his fingers. "I like a drink."

The bartender stared at him for a second and then at the paper bag for a long time. He started to sweat. "All right." He set the drink down in front of Pablo.

For a minute, Pablo just looked at it. Then he lifted it to his lips and drank it down and pushed it across the bar to the bartender.

The bartender picked it up and studied it. Finally, he looked at Pablo again. "What the . . . ! I had to close up for a week after you was here the first time." He took the glass to the sink, washed it with soap and water, and put it with the other clean glasses. Then he looked at Pablo again. "Satisfied?"

"Not yet." Pablo grabbed the paper bag and started to open it.

"Watch out, fellows!" the bartender yelled in his ear. When Pablo looked up, all the men in the bar were lying on their stomachs covering their heads. The bartender was behind the bar on his knees, his hands over his ears.

Pablo took a cigar box out of the bag, opened it, pulled

himself up and across the bar, and reached the box down to the bartender. "Hey, you want fine, handmade Havana cigar?" He was smiling.

☐ ☐ ☐

"Are you going back down to that corner?" My grandmother took my hand.

I looked into her face and then at the picture of her husband. He was still studying something just above my head. "I guess so." I did not really want to do it.

"You may not even have to use that." She pointed at the broom handle. "But you should know you can."

I knew this was true, and climbed off the bed and picked up the white hat and the broom handle. "Okay."

"I'll be waiting on the porch for you." She smiled, got up, and, sighing, went out to the kitchen.

For a while, I listened to pots knocking and being filled with water. Then I stood in her room and practiced what I would say to Valentine's Gang: "If you guys don't let me go by, I'll have to hit you with this." There was a quake in my voice the first time I said it out loud, but, if I had to, I thought I would actually be able to say it and then use the stick. I went down the hall, onto the porch, and looked down toward the corner.

It was empty. The mothers of the members of Valentine's Gang had summoned them home to supper.

The Facts of the Story

Write answers to the following questions. Answers may be one word or a phrase. You can probably answer all the questions without rereading the story, but look back if you wish.

1. Tommy's mother sends him to return Mr. Bixby's _____.

2. He does not complete the errand because his trip is interrupted by _____.

3. The author thinks that the gang is surprised, not so much by Tommy's entering its territory, as by the _____.

4. What does Tommy's grandmother give him to use as a weapon?

5. Why does the grandmother tell Tommy the story of his grandfather Pablo?

6. According to his grandmother, in what way is Tommy like his grandfather?

7. What is in the bag that Pablo takes with him to the bar after his jail term?

8. What do the other men in the bar think is in the bag?

9. What friendly gesture does Pablo make to the bartender when he goes to the bar the second time?

10. Why are no boys defending the enemy territory when Tommy goes off on his errand the second time?

The Ideas in the Story

Tommy's grandmother suggests that he follow Theodore Roosevelt's slogan for overcoming opposition: "Speak softly and carry a big stick." People often argue about this idea. The following questions might help you analyze this slogan and express your own reactions to it.

1. How is the story of Pablo related to the idea of the "big stick"?

2. Do you think Pablo should simply have left the bar when the bartender told him to? Why, or why not?

3. Is it important that someone like Tommy actually use the broom handle, or is it enough that he be ready to use it? Explain.

4. Does this story suggest that the way to settle an argument is by violence? Or is the point of the grandmother's story something else?

Composition

Telling a Story That Illustrates a Lesson

In "Enemy Territory," William Melvin Kelley tells how, at the age of six, he learned a lesson from his grandmother. The lesson is expressed in Theodore Roosevelt's slogan "Speak softly and carry a big stick." You know other sayings that express truths learned from experience. Some of these are listed below. Select one and write a brief story about an experience of your own, telling how it taught you the truth of the saying. If you wish, use a saying not included in the list.

A stitch in time saves nine.

People who live in glass houses shouldn't throw stones.

Too many cooks spoil the soup.

An idle mind is the devil's workshop.

A soft answer turns away wrath.

Write approximately 100 words.

William Melvin Kelley

Having grown up in New York City, William Melvin Kelley (1937-   ) knows well the people and the place he writes about in "Enemy Territory." Kelley went to Harvard University and published his first novel when he was twenty-four. *Dancers on the Shore,* the collection of short stories that includes "Enemy Territory," is dedicated to his grandmother, Jesse Garcia. She was the one who encouraged his interest in becoming a writer, and was, Kelley says, "the only family I had."

Peter Two

IRWIN SHAW

"Peter Two" is about a thirteen-year-old boy who watches a lot of television. The story is humorous in tone—except for one tense moment when matters become extremely serious. Whether or not you find Peter to be a typical thirteen-year-old, or even a believable one, you will probably be interested in watching his actions and following his thoughts.

Peter is watching television at the beginning and at the end of this story. But you will see how a disturbing encounter with the "incomprehensible" adult world changes the way he feels about TV's fearless heroes.

It was Saturday night and people were killing each other by the hour on the small screen. Policemen were shot in the line of duty, gangsters were thrown off roofs, and an elderly lady was slowly poisoned for her pearls, and her murderer brought to justice by a cigarette company after a long series of discussions in the office of a private detective. Brave, unarmed actors leaped at villains holding forty-fives, and ingénues were saved from death by the knife by the quick thinking of various handsome and intrepid young men.

Peter sat in the big chair in front of the screen, his feet up over the arm, eating grapes. His mother wasn't home, so he ate the seeds and all as he stared critically at the violence before him. When his mother was around, the fear of appendicitis hung in the air and she watched carefully to see that each seed was neatly extracted and placed in an ashtray. Too, if she were home, there would be irritated little lectures on the quality of television entertainment for the young, and quick-tempered fiddling with the dials to find something that was vaguely defined as educational. Alone, daringly awake at eleven o'clock, Peter ground the seeds between his teeth, enjoying the impolite noise and the solitude and freedom of the empty house. During the television commercials Peter closed his eyes and imagined himself hurling bottles at large unshaven men with pistols and walking slowly up dark stairways toward the door behind which everyone knew the Boss was waiting, the bulge of his shoulder holster unmistakable under the cloth of his pencil-striped flannel jacket.

Peter was thirteen years old. In his class there were three other boys with the same given name, and the history teacher, who thought he was a funny man, called them Peter One,

165

Peter Two (now eating grapes, seeds and all), Peter Three, and Peter the Great. Peter the Great was, of course, the smallest boy in the class. He weighed only sixty-two pounds, and he wore glasses, and in games he was always the last one to be chosen. The class always laughed when the history teacher called out "Peter the Great," and Peter Two laughed with them, but he didn't think it was so awfully funny.

He had done something pretty good for Peter the Great two weeks ago, and now they were what you might call friends. All the Peters were what you might call friends, on account of that comedian of a history teacher. They weren't *real* friends, but they had something together, something the other boys didn't have. They didn't like it, but they had it, and it made them responsible for each other. So two weeks ago, when Charley Blaisdell, who weighed a hundred and twenty, took Peter the Great's cap at recess and started horsing around with it, and Peter the Great looked as if he was going to cry, he, Peter Two, grabbed the cap and gave it back and faced Blaisdell. Of course, there was a fight, and Peter thought it was going to be his third defeat of the term, but a wonderful thing happened. In the middle of the fight, just when Peter was hoping one of the teachers would show up (they sure showed up plenty of times when you didn't need them), Blaisdell let a hard one go. Peter ducked and Blaisdell hit him on the top of the head and broke his arm. You could tell right off he broke his arm, because he fell to the ground yelling, and his arm just hung like a piece of string. Walters, the gym teacher, finally showed up and carried Blaisdell off, yelling all the time, and Peter the Great came up and said admiringly, "Boy, one thing you have to admit, you sure have a hard head."

Blaisdell was out of class two days, and he still had his arm in the sling, and every time he was excused from writing on the blackboard because he had a broken arm, Peter got a nice warm feeling all over. Peter the Great hung around him all the time, doing things for him and buying him sodas, because

Peter the Great's parents were divorced and gave him all the money he wanted, to make up to him. And that was OK.

But the best thing was the feeling he'd had since the fight. It was like what the people on the television must feel after they'd gone into a room full of enemies and come out with the girl or with the papers or with the suspect, leaving corpses and desolation behind them. Blaisdell weighed a hundred and twenty pounds but that hadn't stopped Peter any more than the fact that the spies all had two guns apiece ever stopped the FBI men on the screen. They saw what they had to do and they went in and did it, that was all. Peter couldn't phrase it for himself, but for the first time in his life he had a conscious feeling of confidence and pride in himself.

"Let them come," he muttered obscurely, munching grape seeds and watching the television set through narrowed eyes, "just let them come."

He was going to be a dangerous man, he felt, when he grew up, but one to whom the weak and the unjustly hunted could safely turn. He was sure he was going to be six feet tall, because his father was six feet tall, and all his uncles, and that would help. But he would have to develop his arms. They were just too thin. After all, you couldn't depend on people breaking their bones on your head every time. He had been doing push-ups each morning and night for the past month. He could only do five and a half at a time so far, but he was going to keep at it until he had arms like steel bars. Arms like that really could mean the difference between life and death later on, when you had to dive under the gun and disarm somebody. You had to have quick reflexes, too, of course, and be able to feint to one side with your eyes before the crucial moment. And, most important of all, no matter what the odds, you had to be fearless. One moment of hesitation and it was a case for the morgue. But now, after the battle of Peter the Great's cap, he didn't worry about that part of it, the fearless part. From now on, it would just be a question of technique.

Comedians began to appear all over the dial, laughing with a lot of teeth, and Peter went into the kitchen and got another bunch of grapes and two tangerines from the refrigerator. He didn't put on the light in the kitchen and it was funny how mysterious a kitchen could be near midnight when nobody else was home, and there was only the beam of the light from the open refrigerator, casting shadows from the milk bottles onto the linoleum. Until recently he hadn't liked the dark too much and he always turned on lights wherever he went, but you had to practice being fearless, just like anything else.

He ate the two tangerines standing in the dark in the kitchen, just for practice. He ate the seeds, too, to show his mother. Then he went back into the living room, carrying the grapes.

The comedians were still on and still laughing. He fiddled with the dial, but they were wearing funny hats and laughing and telling jokes about the income tax on all the channels. If his mother hadn't made him promise to go to sleep by ten o'clock, he'd have turned off the set and gone to bed. He decided not to waste his time and got down on the floor and began to do push-ups, trying to be sure to keep his knees straight. He was up to four and slowing down when he heard the scream. He stopped in the middle of a push-up and waited, just to make sure. The scream came again. It was a woman and it was real loud. He looked up at the television set. There was a man there talking about floor wax, a man with a mustache and a lot of teeth, and it was a cinch *he* wasn't doing any screaming.

The next time the scream came, there was moaning and talking at the end of it, and the sound of fists beating on the front door. Peter got up and turned off the television, just to be sure the sounds he was hearing weren't somehow being broadcast.

The beating on the door began again and a woman's voice cried "Please, please, *please* . . ." and there was no doubt about it any more.

Peter looked around him at the empty room. Three lamps
were lit and the room was nice and bright and the light was
reflected off the grapes and off the glass of the picture of the
boats on Cape Cod that his Aunt Martha painted the year she
was up there. The television set stood in the corner, like a big
blind eye now that the light was out. The cushions of the soft
chair he had been sitting in to watch the programs were pushed
in and he knew his mother would come and plump them out
before she went to sleep, and the whole room looked like a
place in which it was impossible to hear a woman screaming at
midnight and beating on the door with her fists and yelling,
"Please, please, *please* . . ."

The woman at the door yelled "Murder, murder, he's killing
me!" and for the first time Peter was sorry his parents had gone
out that night.

"Open the door!" the woman yelled. "Please, *please* open
the door!" You could tell she wasn't saying please just to be
polite by now.

Peter looked nervously around him. The room, with all its
lights, seemed strange, and there were shadows behind everything. Then the woman yelled again, just noise this time.
Either a person is fearless, Peter thought coldly, or he isn't
fearless. He started walking slowly toward the front door. There
was a long mirror in the foyer and he got a good look at himself. His arms looked very thin.

The woman began hammering once more on the front door
and Peter looked at it closely. It was a big steel door, but it was
shaking minutely, as though somebody with a machine was
working on it. For the first time he heard another voice. It was
a man's voice, only it didn't sound quite like a man's voice. It
sounded like an animal in a cave, growling and deciding to do
something unreasonable. In all the scenes of threat and violence on the television set, Peter had never heard anything at
all like it. He moved slowly toward the door, feeling the way he
had felt when he had the flu, remembering how thin his arms

looked in the mirror, regretting that he had decided to be fear-less.

"Oh, God!" the woman yelled, "Oh, God, don't do it!"

Then there was some more hammering and the low, animal sound of the beast in the cave that you never heard over the air, and he threw the door open.

Mrs. Chalmers was there in the vestibule, on her knees, facing him, and behind her Mr. Chalmers was standing, lean-ing against the wall, with the door to his own apartment open behind him. Mr. Chalmers was making that funny sound and he had a gun in his hand and he was pointing it at Mrs. Chal-mers.

The vestibule was small and it had what Peter's mother called Early American wallpaper and a brass light fixture. There were only the two doors opening on the vestibule, and the Chalmers had a mat in front of theirs with "Welcome" written on it. The Chalmers were in their mid-thirties, and Peter's mother always said about them, "One thing about our neighbors, they *are* quiet." She also said that Mrs. Chalmers put a lot of money on her back.

Mrs. Chalmers was kind of fat and her hair was pretty blond and her complexion was soft and pink and she always looked as though she had been in the beauty parlor all afternoon. She always said "My, you're getting to be a big boy" to Peter when she met him in the elevator, in a soft voice, as though she was just about to laugh. She must have said that fifty times by now. She had a good, strong smell of perfume on her all the time, too.

Mr. Chalmers wore pince-nez glasses most of the time and he was getting bald and he worked late at his office a good many evenings of the week. When he met Peter in the elevator he would say, "It's getting colder," or "It's getting warmer," and that was all, so Peter had no opinion about him, except that he looked like the principal of a school.

But now Mrs. Chalmers was on her knees in the vestibule and her dress was torn and she was crying and there were black streaks on her cheeks and she didn't look as though she'd just come from the beauty parlor. And Mr. Chalmers wasn't wearing a jacket and he didn't have his glasses on and what hair he had was mussed all over his head and he was leaning against the Early American wallpaper making this animal noise, and he had a big, heavy pistol in his hand and he was pointing it right at Mrs. Chalmers.

"Let me in!" Mrs. Chalmers yelled, still on her knees. "You've got to let me in. He's going to kill me. *Please!*"

"Mrs. Chalmers . . ." Peter began. His voice sounded as though he were trying to talk underwater, and it was very hard to say the *s* at the end of her name. He put out his hands uncertainly in front of him, as though he expected somebody to throw him something.

"Get inside, you," Mr. Chalmers said.

Peter looked at Mr. Chalmers. He was only five feet away and without his glasses he was squinting. Peter feinted with his eyes, or at least later in his life he thought he had feinted with his eyes. Mr. Chalmers didn't do anything. He just stood there, with the pistol pointed, somehow, it seemed to Peter, at both Mrs. Chalmers and himself at the same time. Five feet was a long distance, a long, long distance.

"Good night," Peter said, and he closed the door.

There was a single sob on the other side of the door and that was all.

Peter went in and put the uneaten grapes back in the refrigerator, flicking on the light as he went into the kitchen and leaving it on when he went out. Then he went back to the living room and got the stems from the first bunch of grapes and threw them into the fireplace, because otherwise his mother would notice and look for the seeds and not see them and give him four tablespoons of milk of magnesia the next day.

Then, leaving the lights on in the living room, although he knew what his mother would say about that when she got home, he went into his room and quickly got into bed. He waited for the sound of shots. There were two or three noises that might have been shots, but in the city it was hard to tell.

He was still awake when his parents came home. He heard his mother's voice, and he knew from the sound she was complaining about the lights in the living room and kitchen, but he pretended to be sleeping when she came into his room to look at him. He didn't want to start in with his mother about the Chalmers, because then she'd ask when it had happened and she'd want to know what he was doing up at twelve o'clock.

He kept listening for shots for a long time, and he got hot and damp under the covers and then freezing cold. He heard several sharp, ambiguous noises in the quiet night, but nothing that you could be sure about, and after a while he fell asleep.

In the morning, Peter got out of bed early, dressed quickly, and went silently out of the apartment without waking his parents. The vestibule looked just the way it always did, with the brass lamp and the flowered wallpaper and the Chalmers' doormat with "Welcome" on it. There were no bodies and no blood. Sometimes when Mrs. Chalmers had been standing there waiting for the elevator, you could smell her perfume for a long time after. But now there was no smell of perfume, just the dusty, apartment-house usual smell. Peter stared at the Chalmers' door nervously while waiting for the elevator to come up, but it didn't open and no sound came from within.

Sam, the man who ran the elevator and who didn't like him, anyway, only grunted when Peter got into the elevator, and Peter decided not to ask him any questions. He went out into the chilly, bright Sunday-morning street, half expecting to see the morgue wagon in front of the door, or at least two or three prowl cars. But there was only a sleepy woman in slacks airing a boxer and a man with his collar turned up hurrying up from the corner with the newspapers under his arm.

Peter went across the street and looked up to the sixth floor, at the windows of the Chalmers' apartment. The Venetian blinds were pulled shut in every room and all the windows were closed.

A policeman walked down the other side of the street, heavy, blue, and purposeful, and for a moment Peter felt close to arrest. But the policeman continued on toward the avenue and turned the corner and disappeared and Peter said to himself, They never know anything.

He walked up and down the street, first on one side, then on the other, waiting, although it was hard to know what he was waiting for. He saw a hand come out through the blinds in his parents' room and slam the window shut, and he knew he ought to get upstairs quickly with a good excuse for being out, but he couldn't face them this morning, and he would invent an excuse later. Maybe he would even say he had gone to the museum, although he doubted that his mother would swallow that. Some excuse. Later.

Then, after he had been patrolling the street for almost two hours, and just as he was coming up to the entrance of his building, the door opened and Mr. and Mrs. Chalmers came out. He had on his pince-nez and a dark gray hat, and Mrs. Chalmers had on her fur coat and a red hat with feathers on it. Mr. Chalmers was holding the door open politely for his wife, and she looked, as she came out the door, as though she had just come from the beauty parlor.

It was too late to turn back or avoid them, and Peter just stood still, five feet from the entrance.

"Good morning," Mr. Chalmers said as he took his wife's arm and they started walking past Peter.

"Good morning, Peter," said Mrs. Chalmers in her soft voice, smiling at him. "Isn't it a nice day today?"

"Good morning," Peter said, and he was surprised that it came out and sounded like good morning.

The Chalmers walked down the street toward Madison Avenue, two married people, arm in arm, going to church or to a big hotel for Sunday breakfast. Peter watched them, ashamed.

He was ashamed of Mrs. Chalmers for looking the way she did the night before, down on her knees, and yelling like that and being so afraid. He was ashamed of Mr. Chalmers for making the noise that was not like the noise of a human being, and for threatening to shoot Mrs. Chalmers and not doing it. And he was ashamed of himself because he had been fearless when he opened the door, but had not been fearless ten seconds later, with Mr. Chalmers five feet away with the gun. He was ashamed of himself for not taking Mrs. Chalmers into the apartment, ashamed because he was not lying now with a bullet in his heart. But most of all he was ashamed because they had all said good morning to each other and the Chalmers were walking quietly together, arm in arm, in the windy sunlight, toward Madison Avenue.

It was nearly eleven o'clock when Peter got back to the apartment, but his parents had gone back to sleep. There was a pretty good program on at eleven, about counterspies in Asia, and he turned it on automatically, while eating an orange. It was pretty exciting, but then there was a part in which an Oriental held a ticking bomb in his hand in a roomful of Americans, and Peter could tell what was coming. The hero, who was fearless and who came from California, was beginning to feint with his eyes, and Peter reached over and turned the set off. It closed down with a shivering, collapsing pattern. Blinking a little, Peter watched the blind screen for a moment.

Ah, he thought in sudden, permanent disbelief, after the night in which he had faced the incomprehensible, shameless, weaponed grown-up world and had failed to disarm it, ah, they can have that, that's for kids.

The Facts of the Story

For class discussion, prepare answers to the following questions.

1. How do television programs affect Peter?

2. How did the battle for Peter the Great's cap affect Peter Two's opinion of himself?

3. According to Peter, what is the most important quality a person should possess in order to be someone to whom "the weak and the unjustly hunted could safely turn"? Does Peter think he has this quality?

4. What important physical characteristic needed by a defender of the weak does Peter think he lacks? What is he doing to correct this shortcoming?

5. How does the frightening experience with Mr. and Mrs. Chalmers change Peter's view of himself? How does it change his opinion of television programs?

6. Why doesn't Peter tell his parents what happened when they were out?

The Ideas in the Story

For class discussion, prepare answers to the following questions.

1. In this story, Irwin Shaw says something about how we grow out of our childhood. Peter at thirteen is in some ways still a child. Which of Peter's actions during the evening suggest that he is still a child?

2. The story shows that the real adult world is different from what, as children, we might imagine it to be. When we are young, all of us, perhaps under the influence of our

television experiences, enjoy imagining what we will be like and what feats we will perform when we enter the adult world. Usually we picture ourselves as heroes of one kind or another. After all, if we are going to daydream, we might as well have satisfying dreams.

One dramatic experience with the real adult world, however, can awaken us. The story of Peter is clearly about such an experience. At the end, Peter is ashamed of adults and of himself. "But most of all he was ashamed because they had all said good morning to each other and the Chalmers were walking quietly together, arm in arm, in the windy sunlight, toward Madison Avenue." Why do you think Peter considers the Chalmers' actions that morning shameful? What disturbing fact about adults has Peter learned from the Chalmers' behavior?

3. Irwin Shaw makes fun of television programs, especially of the crime shows that Peter watches. What characteristics of these shows does Shaw consider ridiculous? Why does Peter turn off the set when the comedians come on? Why do you think he would dislike the comedians?

4. Reread the last two paragraphs of the story. What does the final paragraph reveal about the way Peter has changed in the course of this story?

The Art of the Storyteller

The Character Story

Like "Antaeus" (page 117), "Peter Two" is a *character story* – that is, a story in which character is more important than the action. Shaw concentrates on Peter. There is a plot, but the events are important only because of what they tell us about Peter.

Shaw uses two methods of characterization. He tells us what Peter *does,* and he tells us what Peter *thinks.* The following passage is a good example of how he uses these two methods of characterization. Actions are in regular type; thoughts are printed in italics.

> Comedians began to appear all over the dial, laughing with a lot of teeth, and Peter went into the kitchen and got another bunch of grapes and two tangerines from the refrigerator. He didn't put on the light in the kitchen and *it was funny how mysterious a kitchen could be near midnight when nobody else was home, and there was only the beam of the light from the open refrigerator, casting shadows from the milk bottles onto the linoleum. Until recently he hadn't liked the dark too much* and he always turned on lights wherever he went, but *you had to practice being fearless, just like anything else.*
>
> He ate the two tangerines standing in the dark in the kitchen, *just for practice.* He ate the seeds, too, *to show his mother.* Then he went back into the living room, carrying the grapes.

Find two other passages in the story where the author tells us what Peter is *thinking.*

Do you find Peter believable? Do you think that the change in Peter's attitude toward adults and television programs would happen to a real thirteen-year-old in this same situation? Explain.

Irony

As you learned when you read "The Cask of Amontillado" (page 104), one kind of irony occurs when a story turns out in a way opposite to what the reader or a character in the story expects. For example, it is ironic that Fortunato's visit to the catacombs turns out to be such a disaster. (He expected a taste of rare wine, but he is entombed behind a wall instead.)

Shaw uses this kind of irony in "Peter Two." Notice how Peter responds to the violence he sees on television: "During the television commercials Peter closed his eyes and imagined himself hurling bottles at large unshaven men with pistols and walking slowly up dark stairways toward the door behind which everyone knew the Boss was waiting, the bulge of his shoulder holster unmistakable under the cloth of his pencil-striped flannel jacket." Peter expects that he would respond to actual violence in the same fearless way. Yet, ironically, what does he do when confronted by Mr. Chalmers' pistol?

Notice also what Peter feels he will be like when he is a man: "one to whom the weak and the unjustly hunted could safely turn." In view of this belief, what is ironic about Peter's reactions to Mrs. Chalmers' plea for help?

Composition

Supporting an Opinion with Facts

Knowing thirteen-year-olds as well as you do, you should have a definite opinion as to whether Peter is a believable character. Write a paragraph beginning with one of the following topic sentences:

> Peter is a believable thirteen-year-old.

> Peter's thoughts and actions are not those of a believable thirteen-year-old.

Glance through the story to find facts to support your topic sentence. Then use these facts about Peter, his actions and thoughts, to support your view of him.

Write approximately 150 words.

Irwin Shaw

Irwin Shaw (1913-   ) grew up in New York City and is a graduate of Brooklyn College. His Army experiences in World War II were fully used in his early fiction. He is a prolific writer, having produced short stories, novels, and plays. In light of his description of television programs in "Peter Two," it is interesting to note that one of Shaw's novels, *Rich Man, Poor Man,* was made into a television serial in 1977. A book published in 1978 contains sixty-three of the eighty-four stories Shaw had written up to that time. In the introduction to that book, he wrote, "I have written stories in Brooklyn, Greenwich Village, on Fifth Avenue, in *The New Yorker* office on Forty-third Street, in Connecticut, Cairo, Algiers, London, Paris, Rome, the Basque country, on ships, in the Alps, in the Mojave Desert, and bits and pieces on transcontinental trains. All these things, in one way or another, are reflected in my stories, which I now see as a record of the events of almost sixty years, all coming together in the imagination of one American."

Raymond's Run

TONI CADE BAMBARA

"Raymond's Run" doesn't have very much to do with either Raymond or his run. The story is about Raymond's ten-year-old sister, Hazel Elizabeth Deborah Parker, nicknamed Squeaky, who minds Raymond because he is "not quite right." She tells you about herself, her brother, her friends, and her ability to run: "I'm the fastest thing on two feet. There is no track meet that I don't win the first-place medal. . . . The big kids call me Mercury cause I'm the swiftest thing in the neighborhood." But Squeaky has more important qualities than her ability to win the fifty-yard dash. Whether or not you like her, you will probably admire her, and think that Raymond is lucky to have such a sister.

I don't have much work to do around the house like some girls. My mother does that. And I don't have to earn my pocket money; George runs errands for the big boys and sells Christmas cards. And anything else that's got to get done, my father does. All I have to do in life is mind my brother Raymond, which is enough.

Sometimes I slip and say my little brother Raymond. But as any fool can see he's much bigger and he's older too. But a lot of people call him my little brother cause he needs looking after cause he's not quite right. And a lot of smart mouths got lots to say about that too, especially when George was minding him. But now, if anybody has anything to say to Raymond, anything to say about his big head, they have to come by me. And I don't play the dozens[1] or believe in standing around with somebody in my face doing a lot of talking. I much rather just knock you down and take my chances even if I am a little girl with skinny arms and a squeaky voice, which is how I got the name Squeaky. And if things get too rough, I run. And as anybody can tell you, I'm the fastest thing on two feet.

There is no track meet that I don't win the first-place medal. I used to win the twenty-yard dash when I was a little kid in kindergarten. Nowadays, it's the fifty-yard dash. And tomorrow I'm subject to run the quarter-meter relay all by myself and come in first, second, and third. The big kids call me Mercury cause I'm the swiftest thing in the neighborhood. Everybody knows that—except two people who know better, my father and me. He can beat me to Amsterdam Avenue with me having a two fire-hydrant head start and him running with his hands in

---

1. *the dozens:* a game in which the players trade insults. The first one to show anger loses the game.

his pockets and whistling. But that's private information. Cause can you imagine some thirty-five-year-old man stuffing himself into PAL shorts to race little kids? So as far as everyone's concerned, I'm the fastest and that goes for Gretchen, too, who has put out the tale that she is going to win the first-place medal this year. Ridiculous. In the second place, she's got short legs. In the third place, she's got freckles. In the first place, no one can beat me and that's all there is to it.

I'm standing on the corner admiring the weather and about to take a stroll down Broadway so I can practice my breathing exercises, and I've got Raymond walking on the inside close to the buildings, cause he's subject to fits of fantasy and starts thinking he's a circus performer and that the curb is a tightrope strung high in the air. And sometimes after a rain he likes to step down off his tightrope right into the gutter and slosh around getting his shoes and cuffs wet. Then I get hit when I get home. Or sometimes if you don't watch him he'll dash across traffic to the island in the middle of Broadway and give the pigeons a fit. Then I have to go behind him apologizing to all the old people sitting around trying to get some sun and getting all upset with the pigeons fluttering around them, scattering their newspapers and upsetting the wax-paper lunches in their laps. So I keep Raymond on the inside of me, and he plays like he's driving a stagecoach which is OK by me so long as he doesn't run me over or interrupt my breathing exercises, which I have to do on account of I'm serious about my running, and I don't care who knows it.

Now some people like to act like things come easy to them, won't let on that they practice. Not me. I'll high-prance down 34th Street like a rodeo pony to keep my knees strong even if it does get my mother uptight so that she walks ahead like she's not with me, don't know me, is all by herself on a shopping trip, and I am somebody else's crazy child. Now you take Cynthia Procter for instance. She's just the opposite. If there's a test tomorrow, she'll say something like, "Oh, I guess I'll play handball this afternoon and watch television tonight," just to let you know she ain't thinking about the test. Or like last week when she won the spelling bee for the millionth time, "A good thing you got *receive*, Squeaky, cause I would have got it wrong. I completely forgot about the spelling bee." And she'll clutch the lace on her blouse like it was a narrow escape. Oh, brother. But of course when I pass her house on my early morning trots around the block, she is practicing the scales on the piano over and over and over and over. Then in music class she always lets herself get bumped around so she falls accidentally on purpose onto the piano stool and is so surprised to find herself sitting there that she decides just for fun to try out the ole keys. And what do you know—Chopin's waltzes just spring out of her fingertips and she's the most surprised thing in the world. A regular prodigy. I could kill people like that. I stay up all night studying the words for the spelling bee. And you can see me any time of day practicing running. I never walk if I can trot, and shame on Raymond if he can't keep up. But of course he does, cause if he hangs back someone's liable to walk up to him and get smart, or take his allowance from him, or ask him where he got that great big pumpkin head. People are so stupid sometimes.

So I'm strolling down Broadway breathing out and breathing in on counts of seven, which is my lucky number, and here comes Gretchen and her sidekicks: Mary Louise, who used to be a friend of mine when she first moved to Harlem from Baltimore and got beat up by everybody till I took up for her on account of her mother and my mother used to sing in the same choir when they were young girls, but people ain't grateful, so now she hangs out with the new girl Gretchen and talks about me like a dog; and Rosie, who is as fat as I am skinny and has a big mouth where Raymond is concerned and is too stupid to know that there is not a big deal of difference between herself and Raymond and that she can't afford to throw stones. So they are steady coming up Broadway and I see right away that it's going to be one of those Dodge City scenes cause the street ain't that big and they're close to the buildings just as we are. First I think I'll step into the candy store and look over the new comics and let them pass. But that's chicken and I've got a reputation to consider. So then I think I'll just walk straight on through them or even over them if necessary. But as they get to me, they slow down. I'm ready to fight, cause like I said I don't feature a whole lot of chitchat, I much prefer to just knock you down right from the jump and save everybody a lotta precious time.

"You signing up for the May Day races?" smiles Mary Louise, only it's not a smile at all. A dumb question like that doesn't deserve an answer. Besides, there's just me and Gretchen standing there really, so no use wasting my breath talking to shadows.

"I don't think you're going to win this time," says Rosie, trying to signify with her hands on her hips all salty, completely forgetting that I have whupped her behind many times for less salt than that.

"I always win cause I'm the best," I say straight at Gretchen who is, as far as I'm concerned, the only one talking in this ventriloquist-dummy routine. Gretchen smiles, but it's not a smile, and I'm thinking that girls never really smile at each other because they don't know how and don't want to know how and there's probably no one to teach us how, cause grown-up girls don't know either. Then they all look at Raymond who has just brought his mule team to a standstill. And they're about to see what trouble they can get into through him.

"What grade you in now, Raymond?"

"You got anything to say to my brother, you say it to me, Mary Louise Williams of Raggedy Town, Baltimore."

"What are you, his mother?" sasses Rosie.

"That's right, Fatso. And the next word out of anybody and I'll be *their* mother too." So they just stand there and Gretchen shifts from one leg to the other and so do they. Then Gretchen puts her hands on her hips and is about to say something with her freckle-face self but doesn't. Then she walks around me looking me up and down but keeps walking up Broadway, and her sidekicks follow her. So me and Raymond smile at each other and he says, "Gidyap" to his team and I continue with my breathing exercises, strolling down Broadway toward the ice man on 145th with not a care in the world cause I am Miss Quicksilver herself.

I take my time getting to the park on May Day because the track meet is the last thing on the program. The biggest thing on the program is the May Pole dancing, which I can do without, thank you, even if my mother thinks it's a shame I don't take part and act like a girl for a change. You'd think my mother'd be grateful not to have to make me a white organdy dress with a big satin sash and buy me new white baby-doll shoes that can't be taken out of the box till the big day. You'd think she'd be glad her daughter ain't out there prancing around a May Pole getting the new clothes all dirty and sweaty and trying to act like a fairy or a flower or whatever you're supposed to be when you should be trying to be yourself, whatever that is, which is, as far as I am concerned, a poor black girl who really can't afford to buy shoes and a new dress you only wear once a lifetime cause it won't fit next year.

I was once a strawberry in a Hansel and Gretel pageant when I was in nursery school and didn't have no better sense than to dance on tiptoe with my arms in a circle over my head doing umbrella steps and being a perfect fool just so my mother and father could come dressed up and clap. You'd think they'd know better than to encourage that kind of nonsense. I am not a strawberry. I do not dance on my toes. I run. That is what I am all about. So I always come late to the May Day program, just in time to get my number pinned on and lay in the grass till they announce the fifty-yard dash.

I put Raymond in the little swings, which is a tight squeeze this year and will be impossible next year. Then I look around for Mr. Pearson, who pins the numbers on. I'm really looking for Gretchen if you want to know the truth, but she's not around. The park is jam-packed. Parents in hats and corsages and breast-pocket handkerchiefs peeking up. Kids in white dresses and light-blue suits. The parkees unfolding chairs and chasing the rowdy kids from Lenox as if they had no right to be there. The big guys with their caps on backwards, leaning against the fence swirling the basketballs on the tips of their fingers, waiting for all these crazy people to clear out the park so they can play. Most of the kids in my class are carrying bass drums and glockenspiels and flutes. You'd think they'd put in a few bongos or something for real like that.

Then here comes Mr. Pearson with his clipboard and his cards and pencils and whistles and safety pins and fifty million other things he's always dropping all over the place with his clumsy self. He sticks out in a crowd because he's on stilts. We used to call him Jack and the Beanstalk to get him mad. But I'm the only one that can outrun him and get away, and I'm too grown for that silliness now.

"Well, Squeaky," he says, checking my name off the list and handing me number seven and two pins. And I'm thinking he's got no right to call me Squeaky, if I can't call him Beanstalk.

"Hazel Elizabeth Deborah Parker," I correct him and tell him to write it down on his board.

"Well, Hazel Elizabeth Deborah Parker, going to give someone else a break this year?" I squint at him real hard to see if he is seriously thinking I should lose the race on purpose just to give someone else a break. "Only six girls running this time," he continues, shaking his head sadly like it's my fault all of New York didn't turn out in sneakers. "That new girl should give you a run for your money." He looks around the park for Gretchen like a periscope in a submarine movie. "Wouldn't it be a nice gesture if you were . . . to ahhh . . ."

I give him such a look he couldn't finish putting that idea

into words. Grown-ups got a lot of nerve sometimes. I pin number seven to myself and stomp away, I'm so burnt. And I go straight for the track and stretch out on the grass while the band winds up with "Oh, the Monkey Wrapped His Tail Around the Flag Pole," which my teacher calls by some other name. The man on the loudspeaker is calling everyone over to the track and I'm on my back looking at the sky, trying to pretend I'm in the country, but I can't, because even grass in the city feels hard as sidewalk, and there's just no pretending you are anywhere but in a "concrete jungle" as my grandfather says.

The twenty-yard dash takes all of two minutes cause most of the little kids don't know no better than to run off the track or run the wrong way or run smack into the fence and fall down and cry. One little kid, though, has got the good sense to run straight for the white ribbon up ahead so he wins. Then the second-graders line up for the thirty-yard dash and I don't even bother to turn my head to watch cause Raphael Perez always wins. He wins before he even begins by psyching the runners, telling them they're going to trip on their shoelaces and fall on their faces or lose their shorts or something, which he doesn't really have to do since he is very fast, almost as fast as I am. After that is the forty-yard dash which I use to run when I was in first grade. Raymond is hollering from the swings cause he knows I'm about to do my thing cause the man on the loudspeaker has just announced the fifty-yard dash, although he might just as well be giving a recipe for angel food cake cause you can hardly make out what he's sayin for the static. I get up and slip off my sweat pants and then I see Gretchen standing at the starting line, kicking her legs out like a pro. Then as I get into place I see that ole Raymond is on line on the other side of the fence, bending down with his fingers on the ground just like he knew what he was doing. I was going to yell at him but then I didn't. It burns up your energy to holler.

Every time, just before I take off in a race, I always feel like

I'm in a dream, the kind of dream you have when you're sick with fever and feel all hot and weightless. I dream I'm flying over a sandy beach in the early morning sun, kissing the leaves of the trees as I fly by. And there's always the smell of apples, just like in the country when I was little and used to think I was a choo-choo train, running through the fields of corn and chugging up the hill to the orchard. And all the time I'm dreaming this, I get lighter and lighter until I'm flying over the beach again, getting blown through the sky like a feather that weighs nothing at all. But once I spread my fingers in the dirt and crouch over the Get on Your Mark, the dream goes and I am solid again and am telling myself, Squeaky you must win, you must win, you are the fastest thing in the world, you can even beat your father up Amsterdam if you really try. And then I feel my weight coming back just behind my knees then down to my feet then into the earth and the pistol shot explodes in my blood and I am off and weightless again, flying past the other runners, my arms pumping up and down and the whole world is quiet except for the crunch as I zoom over the gravel in the track. I glance to my left and there is no one. To the right, a blurred Gretchen, who's got her chin jutting out as if it would win the race all by itself. And on the other side of the fence is Raymond with his arms down to his side and the palms tucked up behind him, running in his very own style, and it's the first time I ever saw that and I almost stop to watch my brother Raymond on his first run. But the white ribbon is bouncing toward me and I tear past it, racing into the distance till my feet with a mind of their own start digging up footfuls of dirt and brake me short. Then all the kids standing on the side pile on me, banging me on the back and slapping my head with their May Day programs, for I have won again and everybody on 151st Street can walk tall for another year.

"In first place . . ." the man on the loudspeaker is clear as a bell now. But then he pauses and the loudspeaker starts to whine. Then static. And I lean down to catch my breath and here comes Gretchen walking back, for she's overshot the finish line too, huffing and puffing with her hands on her hips, taking it slow, breathing in steady time like a real pro, and I sort of like her a little for the first time. "In first place . . ." and then three or four voices get all mixed up on the loudspeaker and I dig my sneaker into the grass and stare at Gretchen who's staring back, we both wondering just who did win. I can hear old Beanstalk arguing with the man on the loudspeaker and then a few others running their mouths about what the stopwatches say. Then I hear Raymond yanking at the fence to call me and I wave to shush him, but he keeps rattling the fence like a gorilla in a cage like in them gorilla movies, but then like a dancer or something he starts climbing up nice and easy but very fast. And it occurs to me, watching how smoothly he climbs hand over hand and remembering how he looked running with his arms down to his side and with the wind pulling his mouth back and his teeth showing and all, it occurred to me that Raymond would make a very fine runner. Doesn't he always keep up with me on my trots? And he surely knows how to breathe in counts of seven cause he's always doing it at the dinner table, which drives my brother George up the wall. And I'm smiling to beat the band cause if I've lost this race, or if me and Gretchen tied, or even if I've won, I can always retire as a runner and begin a whole new career as a coach with Raymond as my champion. After all, with a little more study I can beat Cynthia and her phony self at the spelling bee. And if I bugged my mother, I could get piano lessons and become a star. And I have a big rep as the baddest thing around. And I've got a roomful of ribbons and medals and awards. But what has Raymond got to call his own?

So I stand there with my new plans, laughing out loud by this time as Raymond jumps down from the fence and runs over with his teeth showing and his arms down to the side, which no one before him has quite mastered as a running style. And by the time he comes over I'm jumping up and down so glad to see him—my brother Raymond, a great runner in the family tradition. But of course everyone thinks I'm jumping up and down because the men on the loudspeaker have finally gotten themselves together and compared notes and are announcing "In first place—Miss Hazel Elizabeth Deborah Parker." (Dig that.) "In second place—Miss Gretchen P. Lewis." And I look over at Gretchen wondering what the "P" stands for. And I smile. Cause she's good, no doubt about it. Maybe she'd like to help me coach Raymond; she obviously is serious about running, as any fool can see. And she nods to congratulate me and then she smiles. And I smile. We stand there with this big smile of respect between us. It's about as real a smile as girls can do for each other, considering we don't practice real smiling every day, you know, cause maybe we too busy being flowers or fairies or strawberries instead of something honest and worthy of respect . . . you know . . . like being people.

The Facts of the Story

Write the numbers 1 to 10 in a column on a piece of paper. Write the letter of the answer that best completes each of the following statements after the proper number.

1. Squeaky lets us in on the secret that the only person who can beat her in a race is (a) Gretchen (b) Raymond (c) her father.

2. She keeps herself in condition for racing by (a) practicing breathing exercises (b) running secretly every morning (c) doing push-ups in secret.

3. Raymond, she tells us, is "not quite right." His most noticeable physical feature is his (a) arms (b) height (c) head.

4. Toward her brother Raymond, Squeaky seems to feel (a) protective (b) jealous (c) embarrassed.

5. On the sidewalk, Squeaky keeps Raymond close to the buildings and away from the curb because (a) she doesn't want anyone to see him (b) he likes to look in store windows (c) she wants to keep him out of the street.

6. Squeaky doesn't like people who (a) play the piano well (b) won't let on that they ever practice (c) do well in school.

7. Squeaky's attitude toward the other girls seems to be (a) timid (b) friendly (c) quarrelsome.

8. Mr. Pearson suggests to Squeaky that she (a) let another girl win the race (b) enter the May Pole dancing (c) make a runner out of Raymond.

9. As a result of Raymond's run, Squeaky (a) decides to train Raymond to become a runner (b) tells her mother she won't care for Raymond any more (c) discovers Raymond is not a very good runner at all.

10. After the race, Squeaky and Gretchen (a) hate each other (b) become mortal enemies (c) respect each other.

The Art of the Storyteller

Believable Characters

In presenting characters, a writer must be careful to make them believable, to make them seem true to life. For example, the language a character uses must be the kind that a person with the same background, living in the same environment, and of the same age would use in actual life. Since Squeaky tells this story, the author had to pay close attention to her language, in order to make her believable. Squeaky should speak the way a ten-year-old girl living in Harlem would really speak. If you think that Squeaky's grammar, vocabulary, and use of slang are believable, find examples to prove it. If you think her speech is not true to life, find examples to support that opinion.

Not only must the characters' language be true, but so must their actions. If their actions are not what we expect from a real person, we find it difficult to believe the story. Tell whether you find Squeaky's actions and opinions in this story believable. Do you find her feelings toward Gretchen at the end believable?

What is your opinion of Squeaky's evaluation of girls and smiling?

Point of View

A writer can choose one of several different *points of view* in telling a story. To understand the names usually given to these different points of view, think of the meaning of *person* as it is applied in grammar to the various pronouns. In grammar, a pronoun is in the first person when it refers to the person speaking–*I, me, we.* A pronoun is in the second person when it refers to the person spoken to–*you.* A pronoun is in the third person when it refers to someone or something other than the speaker or the person spoken to–*he, she, it, they.*

When a story is told by a character in the story, it is said to be told from the *first-person point of view.* Since Squeaky, who tells the story, is one of its characters, "Raymond's Run" is told from the first-person point of view. Because first-person point of view requires regular use of the pronoun *I,* it is sometimes called the "I" point of view.

When writers choose to tell a story from the first-person point of view, they are limited in what they can tell us. Their whole story must be told from the narrator's point of view. In "Raymond's Run," Squeaky can tell only what she herself thinks, feels, and sees. She cannot look into the minds of other characters and tell their thoughts and feelings, although she may guess at them. Neither can she describe what is happening someplace else, unless her part as a character in the story takes her to the place and allows her to see the action.

When a story is told not by a character in the story, but by the writer as an outsider, it is told from the *third-person point of view.* This is the most commonly used method of storytelling. Writers using the third-person point of view have complete freedom. They see all and know all. They know what all their characters are thinking and feeling at all times. They can record events that happen anywhere at any time.

Another term for the third-person point of view is the *omniscient* point of view. *Omniscient* means "knowing all." It comes from two Latin words, *omnis,* which means "all," and *sciens,* which means "knowing."

Is "Peter Two" (page 164) told from the first-person or the third-person point of view?

Composition

Developing a Topic Sentence

It is apparent that the other girls in the story did not like Squeaky very much. What were your reactions to this character? Did you identify with her, did you admire her, did you find her funny, or did you dislike her for some reason? Write a paragraph answering these questions. Make up your own topic sentence. Use facts that Squeaky reveals about herself to support your opinions.

Write approximately 100 words.

Toni Cade Bambara

As you would judge from reading "Raymond's Run," Toni Cade Bambara knows well the people who live in the sections of New York City where she grew up—Harlem and Bedford-Stuyvesant. Two of her books are *Tales and Stories for Black Folks* and *Gorilla, My Love,* a collection of stories which contains "Raymond's Run." In addition to being a writer, Bambara has been a social worker and a college professor.

Old Mother Hubbard

A. B. GUTHRIE, JR.

When Clem Randell replaces Curly as foreman of the R-5 Ranch, Clem knows he may have trouble with the ranch hands, who had liked Curly. Some of the hands are tough and stubborn and could make life difficult for a new boss. Clem knows he will have to prove he can be a strong foreman, even if it means a fight when Curly returns to the ranch. What Clem does not know is that on his first day at the ranch, the men will insult him with the name "Old Mother Hubbard."

If it hadn't been for the turkeys, maybe Clem Randell would have got off to a better start as foreman of the R-5. Still, it would have been tough for him. The boys didn't want anyone taking Curly's place, let alone this big pie-faced man who wore a sodbuster's[1] outfit and looked at you slow and unwinking as if he was trying to get his mind in gear.

I remember him from that first evening when the crew found out that Curly had got his time and wouldn't be back. I can see the broad face with the two deep lines running from the corners of the nose down below the mouth. I can see the calm, slow look he gave us, the lips that didn't smile but weren't unfriendly, either. I remember thinking of him as a man with a face that nothing ever happened to.

Some of us around the supper table grunted at him, meeting him that first time, and all of us got up pretty soon and went outside, leaving him and Rivers, the man cook, in the house. We went to the woodpile, where we were used to sitting on upended blocks and whittling and chewing the rag when the work was done.

"For Lord's sake!" Swede Jorgenson said. "A clodhopper! A regular sodbuster! For foreman!" He got up and put on an act, walking duck-footed, trying to look like one of those sugar-beet farmers that had just moved in on the bench.

"Bib overalls," said Slim Bethune, "and ditch-digger's shoes and a two-bit straw hat. On the R-5!"

We're a hay-and-cattle ranch, the R-5 is, but pretty well mechanized. But most of the boys keep to a sort of cowboy rigging even now, big hats and levis and maybe some brass on their belts. Nobody ever wears bib overalls.

John Goodin was older than most of us by fifteen or twenty years. He picked at his teeth with a hay stem while he talked. "It ain't the duds, boys. You're sore about Curly."

1. *sodbuster's:* farmer's. Clem didn't dress like a cowhand.

"What if we are?" asked Swede, looking down at John from his lanky six foot two.

"Curly's a good fellow, but mighty unreliable lately." Goodin's voice was low and slow. "You can't put up with a foreman going off on a bender at hayin' time. What kind of a way is that to run a ranch?"

Swede said, "Curly knows more in a minute than this honyacker will ever learn."

"Maybe so." Goodin was quiet for a minute. "How's Curly going to take this, full of tea like he is?"

"That would be something to see," said Slim. "Curly and this sodbuster meetin' up. There'd be bib overalls from here to breakfast."

Goodin was still working at the doubt in his mind. "After a while a man feels like he owns a job."

I think it was then I knew Curly would come back to the ranch, would come back soon, just as quick as he learned about Randell from one of the barflies in town. He was a forward man, even when he was sober.

Looking beyond Goodin, I saw Rivers come out of the house, carrying the black-snake whip he kept hung on the wall, and between me and him I saw the reason for it. A couple of turkey gobblers that roamed the barnyard had got into a fight again. Behind Rivers, Randell came, flopping in those big overalls.

Maybe you've never seen gobblers fight. They get their long warty necks all twisted around each other, like the strands of a rope, until you can't tell which head belongs to which, and they stand and sway while they peck at each other, taking shorter and shorter jabs as their necks coil around.

Rivers always seemed to get a heap of pleasure out of separating them. Soon's he'd see a fight he'd grab his black-snake whip and come running out and crack it around those ropy necks, until it finally came home to the gobblers that something was hurting them worse than they were hurting themselves. They'd flop about and beat the air with their wings and finally get unraveled and run away, sometimes with the blood dripping.

It was pretty funny, all right, except once in a while the lash of Rivers' whip would hit too high and flick out an eye. As far as that goes, though, sometimes they'd pick each other's eyes out.

Well, what I was saying, Rivers came out, with Randell not far behind him, and brought back the whip and snapped it around the turkeys' necks. He flipped it loose and drew it back and lashed again, and flipped it loose and drew back, and then Randell stepped in.

Another man would have hung back, I guess, being new like Randell was, thinking he better get his feet on the ground before he acted, but Randell moved in, almost like he was pushed, and put his hand on Rivers' arm. We couldn't hear what he said, but we saw Rivers jerk his head around and saw his mouth working, and we got up and lagged over to where they were.

"They peck their own eyes out," Rivers was saying.

"That isn't a reason to knock 'em out."

They stood there looking at each other. Rivers had his stubbly chin out, like a terrier.

Swede put in his oar. "Maybe you got a better way, Randell?"

"Why—" he said, "why—" and moved over and began untwisting the turkey necks with his hands. When he got them untwisted he kneed the birds apart and said, "Shoo now," waving with his hands. The gobblers trotted out from him, each in a little half-circle that brought them bumping back together again about ten feet from him. He got them apart and said "Shoo" again—and it was the same old story. I guess he separated them six times before he finally got one headed one way and one another.

It was sure funny, seeing that big man sweating over those birds, flopping after them and getting between them and saying

"Shoo" and having to do it over and over again. It was a fool business that just by accident had got to be important.

When Randell came back to us, Swede Jorgenson said in a voice as mild as milk, "You know, it ain't so easy, puttin' a stop to a turkey fight?"

Randell looked around, his eyes wide like an owl's. "It's no good makin' things suffer," he said.

Afterwards, I went to the barn to turn the teams out. It was just getting dark, I remember, because at first, looking out from the stalls, I couldn't see who was leaning over the half door. He swung it open for me and the horses trotted through and one by one lay down outside and began to roll.

"Stock's in good shape," Randell said.

"Always was," I answered, "under Curly."

"Yeah?"

And then, because I was just a pup and smart-alecky and loyal to Curly, I said, "You'll be seein' him."

"You think he'll show up, eh?"

"Sure."

In the dusk I could see those winkless eyes fixed on me.

"What if I whip him, kid?"

"You won't."

"But if I do? What would it do to me here?"

For the first time I felt uneasy under his gaze.

"It would set the men against me more than ever."

"What if you lose to him—which you will?"

"I'd have to leave. Don't you see?"

"Heads I win, tails you lose."

"Yeah." He was silent for a long time, standing big and dark and thoughtful as the light died out of the west. When he spoke again it was as if I wasn't there. "I don't know. I don't know. A man has to fight, though, if it comes to that."

His "I don't know" was knocking around in my head when I went to the bunk room, where Swede gave me hell when he learned I had been talking to Randell. "Leave him alone, kid.

Hear? We'll handle Old Mother Hubbard." It was the first time I had heard the new name.

Jorgenson and Bethune didn't waste any time setting their trap. I caught snatches of their plan that night, lying there in the dark on my bunk and hearing them mutter to each other.

"You think he'll fall for it, sure enough, Swede?"

"Sure. He can't stand to see a dumb brute beat. He said so himself. Anyhow, we can't hurt anything by trying. Oh, it'll be funny to see that clodhopper on Bullet."

I heard Slim chuckle and Swede say, "I knew a guy like him once, so all-fired gentle with animals, and he was a mean man with men." And then sleep washed over me and I didn't think about things any more until after breakfast next morning when the bunch of us started to get the horses and gear into the field. There was Slim and Swede inside the corral with Bullet, a half bronc that nobody had been able to stick except Slim, who had won second in the riding contest at the Great Falls Fair the year before.

What made us all stop to look was the way they were handling Bullet. They had snubbed him up short, and Swede was working him over with a club, and every once in a while Slim would kick him in the belly and jerk at the cinch, as if he was trying to knock the wind out of him so he could snug up the saddle, and both of them were cussing and making a racket.

Randell had gone to the truck, but he halted with one foot on the running board and watched. After a while, while I held my breath, the foot came off the running board and moved ahead of the other, and then the other moved ahead of it, toward the corral. We all started that way then.

Bullet was plunging from one side to the other and trying to rear, and with every plunge Swede socked him, yelling, "Stand still, you jughead!" And then Slim would kick him again. You could hardly see Bullet's eye for the white in it.

Randell said, "What's the idea?"

Jorgenson stopped with the club held over his head. "Ol' Cap's too stove up to use for wranglin' any more, so we're gentlin' this one."

"You have to beat him to death first?"

Swede let the club come down slow and leaned on it. "Mister," he said, "you never twisted this here bronc."

Slim seemed to have the cinch tight now. He turned around. "You got to knock the meanness out of him, or he'll buck you."

"I never heard of a bronc like that. You're puttin' meanness into him."

"Well!" said Slim. "Maybe you know better. Maybe you would like to top off this Bullet horse."

They had him then. He looked at us for a minute with that still face of his, and then he took a breath and said, "All right."

Along with the rest of the boys I climbed quick to the top rail of the corral. Slim and Swede mounted up with us to watch as Randell tested the cinch, untied Bullet and snugged the reins up in his left hand. He lifted his foot for the stirrup, looking more like a plow jockey than a rider. It was a narrow stirrup, and his shoe was wide, and Bullet kept dancing away from him just as he was about to get his toe in. He hopped as the horse danced, his left foot raised, his right hand twisting the stirrup for it.

From behind his hand Swede said, "This here is known as the clodhopper's waltz."

"Gobble, gobble," said Slim.

I thought we would fall off the rail laughing, but just then Randell got his toe in the stirrup and heaved himself up. At the same time, Bullet got his head down. There was a bow in his back like an angle iron. He was off the ground before Randell ever found his seat, up high and twisting, coming down with a jar that shook your bones just watching. Then he pitched again and the big flopping figure of Randell went over his right shoulder and thumped on the ground. We could hear the breath go out of him.

He lay there a minute while we perched on the rail, and then he picked himself up and went after the horse again. His face wasn't twisted, or frowning, or smiling, or even set. He didn't say anything. But somehow you could see purpose sticking out from him like a flag. He caught the horse and spoke once to him and turned the stirrup.

Broncs are funny. Sometimes they'll buck and sometimes they won't, and sometimes they'll just give a couple of crow hops and then gentle down like a dog. Maybe Bullet was being that way, just notionable, but I had the feeling that in the face of that purpose he knew he was licked. Anyhow, he stood quiet as an old cow horse and let the man mount. Randell rode him around the corral and later through the east field and came back and unsaddled him and turned him out. Slim Bethune said, "I'll be damned!" and that went for all twenty of us.

It must have been a long day for Randell. We had one trouble after another. A team ran away, breaking the pole on a sulky rake.[2] It just happened, of course, that the driver was safe on the ground, getting himself a drink, when the horses decided to break. Every engine in the field coughed and spit and died at one time or another. With most of them, it was gas-line trouble. Somehow or other, hay had got into the tanks. The stacker broke, under a big load of wet hay that one of the bull rakers had pushed in from a slough. And it was pitiful how little we knew about motors or repairs. We stood around while Randell fixed things up.

He spent the day keeping things in order, going from one piece of machinery to another, not getting impatient or mad, not showing he suspected us, but just doing job after job and doing all of them well. We kept thinking he would flare out at us, giving us something more to hang our dislike on. We kept hoping he would chuck it, finding things too tough. We yelled

2. *sulky rake:* rake drawn by a horse.

"Gobble, gobble!" when we were off from him, knowing our voices would carry.

Maybe we would have liked him better if we could have got under his skin. Maybe we would have liked him better if he hadn't been capable. And it's certain we would have liked him better if we hadn't been thinking about Curly. Curly would have been shouting or cussing, or singing, putting new life into you, asking you how you'd like a beer along about four o'clock when the sun got below your hat brim and peeled your lips. Curly was a character, all right.

I got to the barn first that night, being a teamster, and was unhooking my horses when here came Curly out of the house, walking briskly. "Hi, ol' hoss," he said.

Closer up, I could see that his eyes were red and sunk in his head. Maybe you've studied the face of a man who's been punishing the whiskey hard for five or six days, and seen something strange there and walled off from you, so that you didn't know how to figure him and felt kind of uneasy. That was the way it was with Curly.

The other men were coming in now in the pickup, on sulky rakes, and loaded in the flatbed stacker truck, and Curly was hollering "Hi!" to them. I heard Swede Jorgenson give a regular war whoop and saw him and Slim jump off the truck and shake Curly's hand, like he'd been away for a long time. They stood there talking.

Randell climbed out of the cab of the truck, moving slow and thoughtful as if his mind was far off. Swede made a little gesture toward him, and Curly stuck his head out and started for him. Randell didn't pay him any heed, maybe he didn't even see him, until Curly was right in front of him, saying something I didn't hear. He looked up then, just in time to get Curly's fist in the mouth. He faltered back, shaken but still not looking as if he understood, and Curly swung again.

This time Randell went down. "Steal my job, will you?" Curly asked, cussing.

Randell got up, and Curly hit him again, and Randell fell again. There was blood running from the corner of his mouth.

He turned over slow and got on his knees and lifted himself up again and stood there, and you would have thought he didn't intend to fight back, but as Curly charged in he struck one heavy, clumsy blow, and Curly went over as if he had been hit by a log. He went over on his back, not quite flat, supporting himself by his elbows while his eyes swam in his head. Randell stood a little piece from him, his hands down, as if he didn't know what to do next.

At first I didn't see. I just heard a gasp, as if everyone had sucked in air at once, and then I saw it, the revolver shining blue-black in Curly's hand, its nose pointed at Randell. It leaped in Curly's hand, and a puff of smoke went out of it, and the bark of it rang in my ears. The bullet knocked a wisp of dust from Randell's shirt, under the shoulder. It shook him, as maybe you've seen a tree shaken by a heavy blow. I thought he would go down.

Curly was sitting up. His mouth was tight and drawn over to the side. The revolver in his hand moved and his eyes narrowed over the sights, and I knew, without being able to stir, that he was going to shoot again.

All of us were paralyzed, I guess, standing there with our mouths open and our eyes wide while a man was being murdered. But Randell was not finished yet. For a big slow man he moved like a streak. He dropped below the line of the barrel and threw himself ahead. His fist swung as he smothered Curly, and Curly went out, lying there motionless, the revolver resting a foot from his loose hand after Randell got up. Jorgenson stepped over and took possession of the pistol.

Swede turned to me. "Take the pickup, kid. Quick! Get a doctor." His eyes went down to Curly, and it was as if he had something bitter in his mouth. "You'll have to bring the sheriff, too."

"No! You hear? No!" It was Randell speaking, speaking louder than ever I had heard him.

"Go on, kid."

"No. I won't appear against him. I won't testify." He got hold of his voice and spoke slow, as if to make sure we understood. "He's young and drunk." I didn't really know, until I put things together afterwards, why my mind flashed back to Rivers and the gobblers and Randell saying, "It's no good makin' things suffer," but afterwards I did know it all went part and parcel with the man.

Randell turned and started for the house, while we stood rooted to the ground. He had taken a dozen steps, maybe, when his legs began to give down. He straightened himself once and forged on, but they went weak again and he stumbled and fell forward in a big, sprawling heap.

We ran to him, Swede, Slim, John, and I. We picked Randell up and carried him into the house and laid him on his bunk. "Hot water! Lots of it!" Swede yelled, and we could hear Rivers banging buckets around and working the pump handle and shaking down the range.

We straightened Randell out and got his bloody shirt loose while he looked at us out of a pale sick face, not saying anything. The hole looked pretty high, but a good deal of blood had run out of it front and back.

"Rags! Clean ones!" Swede said to John Goodin.

The boys had all crowded into the bunk room and stood there silent. By and by one of them took off his hat, and one by one they all did, as if at a funeral or something. It struck me sudden and strange that deep in my gizzard I was hoping for Randell not to die.

Then the screen door banged, and it was Curly, coming in wild-eyed and red in the face. Our eyes went to him, and our silence broke against him; he pulled himself up, and his mouth began to run with words. "I thought he had a gun. He made as if to pull a pistol."

Nobody said a word. Jorgenson looked at Curly long and slow. There was hurt in that big Swede's face and something else, something old and sad and wise.

He didn't speak to Curly, but he turned and put his hand on Randell and said, "Take it easy, old-timer. You're gonna be OK." I felt a shout leaping into my throat, for all at once I just knew in my bones he had to be OK, but I didn't let the shout out, because just then Jorgenson's eyes came around and saw me and his voice rose big and stormy in the room. "Damn you, kid! I told you once. Get goin' for the doc!"

The Facts of the Story

Write short answers to the following questions. Answers may be one word or a phrase. You can probably answer all the questions without rereading the story, but look back if you wish.

1. Why was Curly fired?

2. Some of the men like Curly because _____.

3. Why did the turkey fight get Clem off to a bad start as foreman?

4. Clem knows that if he beats Curly in a fight, the men will _____.

5. On the other hand, if Curly beats him, Clem knows he will have to _____.

6. Copy a line from the story that expresses Clem's attitude toward animals.

7. How do the men make Clem's job more difficult?

8. What does Curly accuse Clem of, as an excuse for attacking him?

9. How does Curly try to explain his shooting Randell?

10. Who objects to Jorgenson's sending for the sheriff? Why does he object?

The Ideas in the Story

For class discussion, prepare answers to the following questions.

1. Curly is the antagonist in this story; he is also the "bad guy." He had gone on a bender at haying time, and, as John Goodin asks, "What kind of a way is that to run a ranch?" Even so, the hands like Curly until he commits two

violations of their honor code. He does not fight fair, and he lies. How is Curly's fighting unfair? What lie does he tell? How is all of this supposed to make you feel about Curly?

2. The ranch hands make fun of Clem's clothes because they are the clothes of a farmer, not a cowboy. They also ridicule him for his soft attitude toward animals. However, Clem shows personal qualities that the hands respect, even though they don't like to admit it. Name these qualities, and describe how Clem's actions reveal them. How does the storyteller make you feel about Clem?

3. The title of the story is the mocking name that the men give Clem. Why do you think they call him "Old Mother Hubbard"? Do you think it makes a good title?

4. The appeal of this kind of story might lie in the fact that we are relieved when decent, civilized people manage to defeat the bullies of the world. What movies, television shows, or other stories use this sort of conflict?

The Art of the Storyteller

Plot

"Old Mother Hubbard" is a well-planned, tightly written story. The problem to be solved by the protagonist, Clem Randell, is indicated in the first paragraph. He has to win the respect of the men who work under him in his new job. To do this, he must overcome a series of obstacles. What are these obstacles? Overcoming them is, for Clem, like passing a series of tests. How does Clem prove himself in each test?

Point of View

Like "Raymond's Run" (page 180), "Old Mother Hubbard" is told from the first-person point of view. In "Old Mother Hubbard," you can see how writers using the first-person point of view must limit themselves to telling only what the person telling the story can see and hear. Read the following excerpt and explain how the italicized lines show the limitations of the first-person point of view. Explain how a writer using the third-person (omniscient) point of view could have described the scene.

> Another man would have hung back, I guess, being new like Randell was, thinking he better get his feet on the ground before he acted, but Randell moved in, almost like he was pushed, and put his hand on Rivers' arm. *We couldn't hear what he said, but we saw Rivers jerk his head around and saw his mouth working,* and we got up and lagged over to where they were.

Composition

Writing Dialogue

A good part of many stories is told through *dialogue*–that is, through the conversations of the characters. In writing dialogue, a good storyteller must make the characters talk the way actual people would talk. In other words, the speech must be realistic. A skillful writer of dialogue also lets us see what the characters are doing as they talk, and often tells what they are feeling.

Sometimes a writer follows a speech with such dialogue tags as "he said" or "she replied." Sometimes it is not necessary to include any tags at all. The dialogue between the narrator and Randell on page 199, for example, has no tags. Look back at the dialogue between the ranch hands and Clem, beginning on page 200 with Swede's yelling, "Stand still, you jughead!" and ending on page 201 with Clem's "All right." Ask yourself as you read the passage whether the language is the kind of language ranch hands would use. Find two places where Guthrie describes what the characters are doing as they talk.

Imagine a situation in which two or three persons are talking. Think of a subject for them to discuss, preferably to disagree about. Write an account of their conversation in realistic dialogue. Add enough description to make clear where the speakers are and what they are doing as they talk and as they listen. Include some descriptions of facial expressions, tone of voice, etc. If you wish, use the first-person point of view and be a participant in the conversation yourself. Here are some suggestions for getting started:

Students discussing a teacher or teachers

Teachers discussing students

Two people deciding how to spend ten dollars

A parent and child discussing behavior, schoolwork, money, social life – or whatever parents and children have to discuss

A coach talking with a discouraged player

Two shoppers deciding what to buy

Friends disagreeing over last night's party

Write approximately 200 words.

A. B. Guthrie, Jr.

For much of his life A. B. Guthrie, Jr. (1901-   ), was a newspaper editor and a university professor in Lexington, Kentucky. His novels and short stories, however, portray a different part of the country, the Far West, and particularly the state of Montana, where he grew up and went to college and where he now lives. Guthrie's best-known works are two Western novels, *The Big Sky* and *The Way West*. He was awarded the Pulitzer Prize in 1950 for *The Way West*. Both of these novels were made into movies. Guthrie wrote the screenplay for another famous Western, *Shane.*

The Scarlet Ibis

JAMES HURST

Suppose you had a brother six years younger than you, who has been physically handicapped since birth. What do you think your attitude toward him would be? Would you accept his physical disability even though you wished your brother could be like you? Would your own pride affect the way you feel toward him?

This story is about Doodle, a handicapped child. It is told by his older brother, who at times feels love and tenderness for the younger boy, but who also, at other times, feels angry with him. The story shows how these two emotional attitudes affect not only the brothers' relationship, but also Doodle's life itself.

It was in the clove of seasons, summer was dead but autumn had not yet been born, that the ibis lit in the bleeding tree. The flower garden was stained with rotting brown magnolia petals and ironweeds grew rank amid the purple phlox. The five o'clocks by the chimney still marked time, but the oriole nest in the elm was untenanted and rocked back and forth like an empty cradle. The last graveyard flowers were blooming, and their smell drifted across the cotton field and through every room of our house, speaking softly the names of our dead.

It's strange that all this is still so clear to me, now that that summer has long since fled and time has had its way. A grindstone stands where the bleeding tree stood, just outside the kitchen door, and now if an oriole sings in the elm, its song seems to die up in the leaves, a silvery dust. The flower garden is prim, the house a gleaming white, and the pale fence across the yard stands straight and spruce. But sometimes (like right now), as I sit in the cool, green-draped parlor, the grindstone begins to turn, and time with all its changes is ground away—and I remember Doodle.

Doodle was just about the craziest brother a boy ever had. Of course, he wasn't a crazy crazy like old Miss Leedie, who was in love with President Wilson and wrote him a letter every day, but was a nice crazy, like someone you meet in your dreams. He was born when I was six and was, from the outset, a disappointment. He seemed all head, with a tiny body which was red and shriveled like an old man's. Everybody thought he was going to die—everybody except Aunt Nicey, who had delivered him. She said he would live because he was born in a caul and cauls were made from Jesus' nightgown. Daddy had Mr. Heath, the carpenter, build a little mahogany coffin for him. But he didn't die, and when he was three months old Mama and Daddy decided they might as well name him. They named him William Armstrong, which was like tying a big tail on a small kite. Such a name sounds good only on a tombstone.

I thought myself pretty smart at many things, like holding my breath, running, jumping, or climbing the vines in Old Woman Swamp, and I wanted more than anything else someone to race to Horsehead Landing, someone to box with, and someone to perch with in the top fork of the great pine behind the barn, where across the fields and swamps you could see the sea. I wanted a brother. But Mama, crying, told me that even if William Armstrong lived, he would never do these things with me. He might not, she sobbed, even be "all there." He might, as long as he lived, lie on the rubber sheet in the center of the bed in the front bedroom, where the white marquisette curtains billowed out in the afternoon sea breeze, rustling like palmetto fronds.

It was bad enough having an invalid brother, but having one who possibly was not all there was unbearable, so I began to make plans to kill him by smothering him with a pillow. However, one afternoon as I watched him, my head poked between the iron posts of the foot of the bed, he looked straight at me and grinned. I skipped through the rooms, down the echoing halls, shouting, "Mama, he smiled. He's all there! He's all there!" and he was.

When he was two, if you laid him on his stomach, he began to try to move himself, straining terribly. The doctor said that with his weak heart this strain would probably kill him, but it didn't. Trembling, he'd push himself up, turning first red, then a soft purple, and finally collapse back onto the bed like an old worn-out doll. I can still see Mama watching him, her hand pressed tight across her mouth, her eyes wide and unblinking. But he learned to crawl (it was his third winter), and we brought him out of the front bedroom, putting him on the rug before the fireplace. For the first time he became one of us.

As long as he lay all the time in bed, we called him William Armstrong, even though it was formal and sounded as if we were referring to one of our ancestors, but with his creeping around on the deerskin rug and beginning to talk, something had to be done about his name. It was I who renamed him. When he crawled, he crawled backward, as if he were in reverse and couldn't change gears. If you called him, he'd turn around as if he were going in the other direction, then he'd back right up to you to be picked up. Crawling backward made him look like a doodle-bug, so I began to call him Doodle, and in time even Mama and Daddy thought it was a better name than William Armstrong. Only Aunt Nicey disagreed. She said caul babies should be treated with special respect since they might turn out to be saints. Renaming my brother was perhaps the kindest thing I ever did for him, because nobody expects much from someone called Doodle.

Although Doodle learned to crawl, he showed no signs of walking, but he wasn't idle. He talked so much that we all quit listening to what he said. It was about this time that Daddy built him a go-cart and I had to pull him around. At first I just paraded him up and down the piazza, but then he started crying to be taken out into the yard and it ended up by my having to lug him wherever I went. If I so much as picked up my cap, he'd start crying to go with me and Mama would call from wherever she was, "Take Doodle with you."

He was a burden in many ways. The doctor had said that he mustn't get too excited, too hot, too cold, or too tired and that he must always be treated gently. A long list of don'ts went with him, all of which I ignored once we got out of the house. To discourage his coming with me, I'd run with him across the ends of the cotton rows and careen him around corners on two wheels. Sometimes I accidentally turned him over, but he never told Mama. His skin was very sensitive, and he had to wear a big straw hat whenever he went out. When the going got rough and he had to cling to the sides of the go-cart, the hat slipped all the way down over his ears. He was a sight. Finally, I could see I was licked. Doodle was my brother and he was going to cling to me forever, no matter what I did, so I dragged him across the burning cotton field to share with him the only beauty I knew, Old Woman Swamp. I pulled the go-cart through the sawtooth fern, down into the green dimness where the palmetto fronds whispered by the stream. I lifted him out and set him down in the soft rubber grass beside a tall pine. His eyes were round with wonder as he gazed about him, and his little hands began to stroke the rubber grass. Then he began to cry.

"For heaven's sake, what's the matter?" I asked, annoyed.

"It's so pretty," he said. "So pretty, pretty, pretty."

After that day Doodle and I often went down into Old Woman Swamp. I would gather wildflowers, wild violets, honeysuckle, yellow jasmine, snakeflowers, and water lilies, and with wire grass we'd weave them into necklaces and crowns. We'd bedeck ourselves with our handiwork and loll about thus beautified, beyond the touch of the everyday world. Then when the slanted rays of the sun burned orange in the tops of the pines, we'd drop our jewels into the stream and watch them float away toward the sea.

There is within me (and with sadness I have watched it in others) a knot of cruelty borne by the stream of love, much as our blood sometimes bears the seed of our destruction, and at times I was mean to Doodle. One day I took him up to the barn loft and showed him his casket, telling him how we all had believed he would die. It was covered with a film of Paris green[1] sprinkled to kill the rats, and screech owls had built a nest inside it.

Doodle studied the mahogany box for a long time, then said, "It's not mine."

"It is," I said. "And before I'll help you down from the loft, you're going to have to touch it."

"I won't touch it," he said sullenly.

---

1. *Paris green:* a poisonous bright-green powder.

"Then I'll leave you here by yourself," I threatened, and made as if I were going down.

Doodle was frightened of being left. "Don't go leave me, Brother," he cried, and he leaned toward the coffin. His hand, trembling, reached out, and when he touched the casket he screamed. A screech owl flapped out of the box into our faces, scaring us and covering us with Paris green. Doodle was paralyzed, so I put him on my shoulder and carried him down the ladder, and even when we were outside in the bright sunshine, he clung to me, crying, "Don't leave me. Don't leave me."

When Doodle was five years old, I was embarrassed at having a brother of that age who couldn't walk, so I set out to teach him. We were down in Old Woman Swamp and it was spring and the sick-sweet smell of bay flowers hung everywhere like a mournful song. "I'm going to teach you to walk, Doodle," I said.

He was sitting comfortably on the soft grass, leaning back against the pine. "Why?" he asked.

I hadn't expected such an answer. "So I won't have to haul you around all the time."

"I can't walk, Brother," he said.

"Who says so?" I demanded.

"Mama, the doctor—everybody."

"Oh, you can walk," I said, and I took him by the arms and stood him up. He collapsed onto the grass like a half-empty flour sack. It was as if he had no bones in his little legs.

"Don't hurt me, Brother," he warned.

"Shut up. I'm not going to hurt you. I'm going to teach you to walk." I heaved him up again, and again he collapsed.

This time he did not lift his face up out of the rubber grass. "I just can't do it. Let's make honeysuckle wreaths."

"Oh yes you can, Doodle," I said. "All you got to do is try. Now come on," and I hauled him up once more.

It seemed so hopeless from the beginning that it's a miracle I didn't give up. But all of us must have something or someone to be proud of, and Doodle had become mine. I did not know then that pride is a wonderful, terrible thing, a seed that bears two vines, life and death. Every day that summer we went to the pine beside the stream of Old Woman Swamp, and I put him on his feet at least a hundred times each afternoon. Occasionally I too became discouraged because it didn't seem as if he was trying, and I would say, "Doodle, don't you *want* to learn to walk?"

He'd nod his head, and I'd say, "Well, if you don't keep trying, you'll never learn." Then I'd paint for him a picture of us as old men, white-haired, him with a long white beard and me still pulling him around in the go-cart. This never failed to make him try again.

Finally one day, after many weeks of practicing, he stood alone for a few seconds. When he fell, I grabbed him in my arms and hugged him, our laughter pealing through the swamp like a ringing bell. Now we knew it could be done. Hope no longer hid in the dark palmetto thicket but perched like a cardinal in the lacy toothbrush tree, brilliantly visible. "Yes, yes," I cried, and he cried it too, and the grass beneath us was soft and the smell of the swamp was sweet.

With success so imminent, we decided not to tell anyone until he could actually walk. Each day, barring rain, we sneaked into Old Woman Swamp, and by cotton-picking time Doodle was ready to show what he could do. He still wasn't able to walk far, but we could wait no longer. Keeping a nice secret is very hard to do, like holding your breath. We chose to reveal all on October eighth, Doodle's sixth birthday, and for weeks ahead we mooned around the house, promising everybody a most spectacular surprise. Aunt Nicey said that, after so much talk, if we produced anything less tremendous than the Resurrection, she was going to be disappointed.

At breakfast on our chosen day, when Mama, Daddy, and Aunt Nicey were in the dining room, I brought Doodle to the door in the go-cart just as usual and had them turn their backs, making them cross their hearts and hope to die if they peeked. I helped Doodle up, and when he was standing alone I let them look. There wasn't a sound as Doodle walked slowly across the room and sat down at his place at the table. Then Mama began to cry and ran over to him, hugging him and kissing him. Daddy hugged him too, so I went to Aunt Nicey, who was thanks-praying in the doorway, and began to waltz her around. We danced together quite well until she came down on my big toe with her brogans, hurting me so badly I thought I was crippled for life.

Doodle told them it was I who had taught him to walk, so everyone wanted to hug me, and I began to cry.

"What are you crying for?" asked Daddy, but I couldn't answer. They did not know that I did it for myself; that pride, whose slave I was, spoke to me louder than all their voices, and that Doodle walked only because I was ashamed of having a crippled brother.

Within a few months Doodle had learned to walk well and his go-cart was put up in the barn loft (it's still there) beside his little mahogany coffin. Now, when we roamed off together, resting often, we never turned back until our destination had been reached, and to help pass the time, we took up lying. From the beginning Doodle was a terrible liar and he got me in the habit. Had anyone stopped to listen to us, we would have been sent off to Dix Hill.

My lies were scary, involved, and usually pointless, but Doodle's were twice as crazy. People in his stories all had wings and flew wherever they wanted to go. His favorite lie was about a boy named Peter who had a pet peacock with a ten-foot tail. Peter wore a golden robe that glittered so brightly that when he walked through the sunflowers they turned away from the sun to face him. When Peter was ready to go to sleep, the peacock spread his magnificent tail, enfolding the boy gently like a closing go-to-sleep flower, burying him in the gloriously iridescent, rustling vortex. Yes, I must admit it. Doodle could beat me lying.

Doodle and I spent lots of time thinking about our future.

We decided that when we were grown we'd live in Old Woman Swamp and pick dog-tongue for a living. Beside the stream, he planned, we'd build us a house of whispering leaves and the swamp birds would be our chickens. All day long (when we weren't gathering dog-tongue) we'd swing through the cypresses on the rope vines, and if it rained we'd huddle beneath an umbrella tree and play stickfrog. Mama and Daddy could come and live with us if they wanted to. He even came up with the idea that he could marry Mama and I could marry Daddy. Of course, I was old enough to know this wouldn't work out, but the picture he painted was so beautiful and serene that all I could do was whisper Yes, yes.

Once I had succeeded in teaching Doodle to walk, I began to believe in my own infallibility and I prepared a terrific development program for him, unknown to Mama and Daddy, of course. I would teach him to run, to swim, to climb trees, and to fight. He, too, now believed in my infallibility, so we set the deadline for these accomplishments less than a year away, when, it had been decided, Doodle could start to school.

That winter we didn't make much progress, for I was in school and Doodle suffered from one bad cold after another. But when spring came, rich and warm, we raised our sights again. Success lay at the end of summer like a pot of gold, and our campaign got off to a good start. On hot days, Doodle and I went down to Horsehead Landing and I gave him swimming lessons or showed him how to row a boat. Sometimes we descended into the cool greenness of Old Woman Swamp and climbed the rope vines or boxed scientifically beneath the pine where he had learned to walk. Promise hung about us like the leaves, and wherever we looked, ferns unfurled and birds broke into song.

That summer, the summer of 1918, was blighted. In May and June there was no rain and the crops withered, curled up, then died under the thirsty sun. One morning in July a hurricane came out of the east, tipping over the oaks in the yard and splitting the limbs of the elm trees. That afternoon it roared back out of the west, blew the fallen oaks around, snapping their roots and tearing them out of the earth like a hawk at the entrails of a chicken. Cotton bolls were wrenched from the stalks and lay like green walnuts in the valleys between the rows, while the cornfield leaned over uniformly so that the tassels touched the ground. Doodle and I followed Daddy out into the cotton field, where he stood, shoulders sagging, surveying the ruin. When his chin sank down onto his chest, we were frightened, and Doodle slipped his hand into mine. Suddenly Daddy straightened his shoulders, raised a giant knuckly fist, and with a voice that seemed to rumble out of the earth itself began cursing heaven, hell, the weather, and the Republican Party. Doodle and I, prodding each other and giggling, went back to the house, knowing that everything would be all right.

And during that summer, strange names were heard through the house: Château Thierry, Amiens, Soissons, and in her blessing at the supper table, Mama once said, "And bless the Pearsons, whose boy Joe was lost at Belleau Wood."[2]

So we came to that clove of seasons. School was only a few weeks away, and Doodle was far behind schedule. He could barely clear the ground when climbing up the rope vines and his swimming was certainly not passable. We decided to double our efforts, to make that last drive and reach our pot of gold. I made him swim until he turned blue and row until he couldn't lift an oar. Wherever we went, I purposely walked fast, and although he kept up, his face turned red and his eyes became glazed. Once, he could go no further, so he collapsed on the ground and began to cry.

"Aw, come on, Doodle," I urged. "You can do it. Do you want to be different from everybody else when you start school?"

"Does it make any difference?"

2. Château Thierry (shä-tō′ tyē-rē′), Amiens (à-myăN′), Soissons (swä-sôN′), and Belleau (bĕl-ō′) are World War I battle sites in France.

"It certainly does," I said. "Now, come on," and I helped him up.

As we slipped through dog days, Doodle began to look feverish, and Mama felt his forehead, asking him if he felt ill. At night he didn't sleep well, and sometimes he had nightmares, crying out until I touched him and said, "Wake up, Doodle. Wake up."

It was Saturday noon, just a few days before school was to start. I should have already admitted defeat, but my pride wouldn't let me. The excitement of our program had now been gone for weeks, but still we kept on with a tired doggedness. It was too late to turn back, for we had both wandered too far into a net of expectations and had left no crumbs behind.

Daddy, Mama, Doodle, and I were seated at the dining-room table having lunch. It was a hot day, with all the windows and doors open in case a breeze should come. In the kitchen Aunt Nicey was humming softly. After a long silence, Daddy spoke. "It's so calm, I wouldn't be surprised if we had a storm this afternoon."

"I haven't heard a rain frog," said Mama, who believed in signs, as she served the bread around the table.

"I did," declared Doodle. "Down in the swamp."

"He didn't," I said contrarily.

"You did, eh?" said Daddy, ignoring my denial.

"I certainly did," Doodle reiterated, scowling at me over the top of his iced-tea glass, and we were quiet again.

Suddenly, from out in the yard, came a strange croaking noise. Doodle stopped eating, with a piece of bread poised ready for his mouth, his eyes popped round like two blue buttons. "What's that?" he whispered.

I jumped up, knocking over my chair, and had reached the door when Mama called, "Pick up the chair, sit down again, and say excuse me."

By the time I had done this, Doodle had excused himself and had slipped out into the yard. He was looking up into the bleeding tree. "It's a great big red bird!" he called.

The bird croaked loudly again, and Mama and Daddy came out into the yard. We shaded our eyes with our hands against the hazy glare of the sun and peered up through the still leaves. On the topmost branch a bird the size of a chicken, with scarlet feathers and long legs, was perched precariously. Its wings hung down loosely, and as we watched, a feather dropped away and floated slowly down through the green leaves.

"It's not even frightened of us," Mama said.

"It looks tired," Daddy added. "Or maybe sick."

Doodle's hands were clasped at his throat, and I had never seen him stand still so long. "What is it?" he asked.

Daddy shook his head. "I don't know, maybe it's—"

At that moment the bird began to flutter, but the wings were uncoordinated, and amid much flapping and a spray of flying feathers, it tumbled down, bumping through the limbs of the bleeding tree and landing at our feet with a thud. Its long, graceful neck jerked twice into an S, then straightened out, and the bird was still. A white veil came over the eyes and the long white beak unhinged. Its legs were crossed and its clawlike feet were delicately curved at rest. Even death did not mar its grace, for it lay on the earth like a broken vase of red flowers, and we stood around it, awed by its exotic beauty.

"It's dead," Mama said.

"What is it?" Doodle repeated.

"Go bring me the bird book," said Daddy.

I ran into the house and brought back the bird book. As we watched, Daddy thumbed through its pages. "It's a scarlet ibis," he said, pointing to a picture. "It lives in the tropics—South America to Florida. A storm must have brought it here."

Sadly, we all looked back at the bird. A scarlet ibis! How many miles it had traveled to die like this, in *our* yard, beneath the bleeding tree.

"Let's finish lunch," Mama said, nudging us back toward the dining room.

"I'm not hungry," said Doodle, and he knelt down beside the ibis.

"We've got peach cobbler for dessert," Mama tempted from the doorway.

Doodle remained kneeling. "I'm going to bury him."

"Don't you dare touch him," Mama warned. "There's no telling what disease he might have had."

"All right," said Doodle. "I won't."

Daddy, Mama, and I went back to the dining-room table, but we watched Doodle through the open door. He took out a piece of string from his pocket and, without touching the ibis, looped one end around its neck. Slowly, while singing softly "Shall We Gather at the River," he carried the bird around to the front yard and dug a hole in the flower garden, next to the petunia bed. Now we were watching him through the front window, but he didn't know it. His awkwardness at digging the hole with a shovel whose handle was twice as long as he was made us laugh, and we covered our mouths with our hands so he wouldn't hear.

When Doodle came into the dining room, he found us seriously eating our cobbler. He was pale and lingered just inside the screen door. "Did you get the scarlet ibis buried?" asked Daddy.

Doodle didn't speak but nodded his head.

"Go wash your hands, and then you can have some peach cobbler," said Mama.

"I'm not hungry," he said.

"Dead birds is bad luck," said Aunt Nicey, poking her head from the kitchen door. "Specially *red* dead birds!"

As soon as I had finished eating, Doodle and I hurried off to Horsehead Landing. Time was short, and Doodle still had a long way to go if he was going to keep up with the other boys when he started school. The sun, gilded with the yellow cast of autumn, still burned fiercely, but the dark green woods through which we passed were shady and cool. When we reached the landing, Doodle said he was too tired to swim, so we got into a skiff and floated down the creek with the tide. Far off in the marsh a rail was scolding, and over on the beach locusts were singing in the myrtle trees. Doodle did not speak and kept his head turned away, letting one hand trail limply in the water.

After we had drifted a long way, I put the oars in place and made Doodle row back against the tide. Black clouds began to gather in the southwest, and he kept watching them, trying to pull the oars a little faster. When we reached Horsehead Landing, lightning was playing across half the sky and thunder roared out, hiding even the sound of the sea. The sun disappeared and darkness descended, almost like night. Flocks of marsh crows flew by, heading inland to their roosting trees, and two egrets, squawking, arose from the oyster-rock shallows and careened away.

Doodle was both tired and frightened, and when he stepped from the skiff he collapsed onto the mud, sending an armada of fiddler crabs rustling off into the marsh grass. I helped him up, and as he wiped the mud off his trousers, he smiled at me ashamedly. He had failed and we both knew it, so we started back home, racing the storm. We never spoke (What are the words that can solder cracked pride?), but I knew he was watching me, watching for a sign of mercy. The lightning was near now, and from fear he walked so close behind me he kept stepping on my heels. The faster I walked, the faster he walked, so I began to run. The rain was coming, roaring through the pines, and then, like a bursting Roman candle, a gum tree ahead of us was shattered by a bolt of lightning. When the deafening peal of thunder had died, and in the moment before the rain arrived, I heard Doodle, who had fallen behind, cry out, "Brother, Brother, don't leave me! Don't leave me!"

The knowledge that Doodle's and my plans had come to naught was bitter, and that streak of cruelty within me awakened. I ran as fast as I could, leaving him far behind with a wall of rain dividing us. The drops stung my face like nettles, and the wind flared the wet, glistening leaves of the bordering trees. Soon I could hear his voice no more.

I hadn't run too far before I became tired, and the flood of childish spite evanesced[3] as well. I stopped and waited for Doodle. The sound of rain was everywhere, but the wind had died and it fell straight down in parallel paths like ropes hanging from the sky. As I waited, I peered through the downpour, but no one came. Finally I went back and found him huddled beneath a red nightshade bush beside the road. He was sitting on the ground, his face buried in his arms, which were resting on his drawn-up knees. "Let's go, Doodle," I said.

He didn't answer, so I placed my hand on his forehead and lifted his head. Limply, he fell backwards onto the earth. He had been bleeding from the mouth, and his neck and the front of his shirt were stained a brilliant red.

"Doodle! Doodle!" I cried, shaking him, but there was no answer but the ropy rain. He lay very awkwardly, with his head thrown far back, making his vermilion neck appear unusually long and slim. His little legs, bent sharply at the knees, had never before seemed so fragile, so thin.

I began to weep, and the tear-blurred vision in red before me looked very familiar. "Doodle!" I screamed above the pounding storm and threw my body to the earth above his. For a long long time, it seemed forever, I lay there crying, sheltering my fallen scarlet ibis from the heresy of rain.

3. *evanesced:* vanished, faded away.

The Facts of the Story

Write short answers to the following questions. Use complete sentences.

1. Doodle's older brother tells this story. What conflicts or problems does the older brother face?

2. By the end of the story, have the older brother's conflicts been resolved? Explain.

3. Does the older brother teach Doodle to walk for Doodle's sake or for his own sake? Explain.

4. Why do you think the people in Doodle's stories all have wings?

5. The narrator tells us at the end of the story that Doodle is watching him for "a sign of mercy." What sort of sign does he want? Why doesn't he get it?

The Ideas in the Story

For class discussion, prepare answers to the following questions about the story's theme.

1. Careful thinking about this story will tell you that its theme has something to do with the effects of pride. The narrator says that "pride is a wonderful, terrible thing, a seed that bears two vines, life and death." How does this statement relate to the events of the story? Do you agree that pride can be both destructive and fruitful? Do you think the brother's pride is entirely responsible for Doodle's death? Explain.

2. The story also seems to reveal something about people who are different from others, people who are made for a different, more generous kind of world. How is Doodle

unsuited to survive in his brother's world? How is Doodle's spirit different from his frail and sickly body? Do you think he could have survived somewhere else? Explain.

The Art of the Storyteller

Foreshadowing

In his first paragraph, Hurst foreshadows the fact that this story is going to be about loss. He tells us that summer is "dead," that the magnolia petals are "rotting brown," that the ironweeds grow "rank" (they smell of decay), that the oriole nest is "untenanted" and rocks "like an empty cradle," that the "last graveyard flowers" are blooming and that their odor speaks "the names of our dead." All these details foreshadow tragedy.

Another use of foreshadowing occurs when the narrator threatens to leave Doodle in the barn if he doesn't touch his own coffin. "Don't go leave me, Brother," Doodle cries. And again, "Don't leave me. Don't leave me." How does this cry foreshadow the circumstances of Doodle's death? How did you feel when this plea was repeated at the end of the story?

Symbols

A *symbol* is a thing or a person or an event that has meaning in itself but that also represents something broader than itself—such as a value, an attitude, or a human condition. The American flag, for example, is a symbol of the United States of America. A red cross on an ambulance symbolizes help for the injured and the sick. A skull and crossbones on a bottle symbolize danger. A red heart symbolizes love.

The color red appears several times in this story. There is a bleeding tree, the scarlet ibis, a red nightshade bush, and Doodle's blood. Red is a color that carries symbolic meaning. It usually suggests courage and a martyr's death. Why is red a suitable symbolic color for this story?

The scarlet ibis is a major symbol in this story—it is a real bird in the story, but it also is a symbol of something else. It is clear that the writer wants us to see similarities between Doodle and the fallen bird. In what specific ways are Doodle and the scarlet ibis alike? Remembering that the ibis is strange, beautiful, and away from its natural home, tell how it could be seen as a symbol of Doodle and of his unusual spirit.

Composition

Supporting a Topic Sentence

Select one of the following topic sentences and develop it into a one-paragraph composition (100 to 150 words). Support the topic with one or more examples or by telling an anecdote.

1. What appears to be an act of kindness, or generosity, is sometimes actually an act of selfishness.

2. Pride may lead a person to good or great deeds, but it may also lead to mean and self-serving actions.

3. Handicapped people want our respect; they do not want our pity.

4. People do not have to be physically strong and athletic to be productive and happy in life.

James Hurst

James Hurst first studied engineering; then he switched to music. When his efforts to get into opera in New York failed, he turned to writing, supporting himself by working at night as a bank clerk. "The Scarlet Ibis," which appeared in the *Atlantic Monthly,* was the first story that Hurst ever published in a national magazine.

Red Dress

ALICE MUNRO

A dance can mark a turning point in someone's life. This story is about a girl whose mother makes her a red dress to wear to the Christmas dance at school. The girl is thirteen years old and in the ninth grade. Through her experiences at the dance, she learns something about her mother, about herself—and about happiness and unhappiness.

The story takes place in a small town in Canada. The girl herself narrates the story, which is sometimes funny, sometimes sad. Whatever you think of the girl, and of what happens at home and at the dance, you will probably find something of yourself in her.

My mother was making me a dress. All through the month of November I would come from school and find her in the kitchen, surrounded by cut-up red velvet and scraps of tissue-paper pattern. She worked at an old treadle machine pushed up against the window to get the light, and also to let her look out, past the stubble fields and bare vegetable garden, to see who went by on the road. There was seldom anybody to see.

The red velvet material was hard to work with, it pulled, and the style my mother had chosen was not easy either. She was not really a good sewer. She liked to make things; that is different. Whenever she could she tried to skip basting and pressing, and she took no pride in the fine points of tailoring, the finishing of buttonholes and the overcasting of seams, as, for instance, my aunt and my grandmother did. Unlike them she started off with an inspiration, a brave and dazzling idea; from that moment on, her pleasure ran downhill. In the first place she could never find a pattern to suit her. It was no wonder; there were no patterns made to match the ideas that blossomed in her head. She had made me, at various times when I was younger, a flowered organdy dress with a high Victorian neckline edged in scratchy lace, with a poke bonnet to match; a Scottish plaid outfit with a velvet jacket and tam; an embroidered peasant blouse worn with a full, red skirt and black-laced bodice. I had worn these clothes with docility, even pleasure, in the days when I was unaware of the world's opinion. Now, grown wiser, I wished for dresses like those my friend Lonnie had, bought at Beale's store.

I had to try it on. Sometimes Lonnie came home from school with me and she would sit on the couch watching. I was

230

embarrassed by the way my mother crept around me, her knees creaking, her breath coming heavily. She muttered to herself. Around the house she wore no corset or stockings, she wore wedge-heeled shoes and ankle socks; her legs were marked with lumps of blue-green veins. I thought her squatting position shameless, even obscene; I tried to keep talking to Lonnie so that her attention would be taken away from my mother as much as possible. Lonnie wore the composed, polite, appreciative expression that was her disguise in the presence of grown-ups. She laughed at them and was a ferocious mimic, and they never knew.

My mother pulled me about, and pricked me with pins. She made me turn around, she made me walk away, she made me stand still. "What do you think of it, Lonnie?" she said around the pins in her mouth.

"It's beautiful," said Lonnie, in her mild, sincere way. Lonnie's own mother was dead. She lived with her father, who never noticed her, and this, in my eyes, made her seem both vulnerable and privileged.

"It *will* be, if I can ever manage the fit," my mother said. "Ah, well," she said theatrically, getting to her feet with a woeful creaking and sighing, "I doubt if she appreciates it." She enraged me, talking like this to Lonnie, as if Lonnie were grown up and I were still a child. "Stand still," she said, hauling the pinned and basted dress over my head. My head was muffled in velvet, my body exposed, in an old cotton school slip. I felt like a great raw lump, clumsy and goose-pimpled. I wished I was like Lonnie, light-boned, pale and thin; she had been a Blue Baby.

"Well, nobody ever made me a dress when I was going to high school," my mother said, "I made my own, or I did without." I was afraid she was going to start again on the story of her walking seven miles to town and finding a job waiting on tables in a boarding house, so that she could go to high school. All the stories of my mother's life which had once interested me had begun to seem melodramatic, irrelevant, and tiresome.

"One time I had a dress given to me," she said. "It was a cream-colored cashmere wool with royal blue piping down the front and lovely mother-of-pearl buttons, I wonder whatever became of it?"

When we got free Lonnie and I went upstairs to my room. It was cold, but we stayed there. We talked about the boys in our class, going up and down the rows and saying, "Do you like him? Well, do you half like him? Do you *hate* him? Would you go out with him if he asked you?" Nobody had asked us. We were thirteen, and we had been going to high school for two months. We did questionnaires in magazines, to find out whether we had personality and whether we would be popular. We read articles on how to make up our faces to accentuate our good points and how to carry on a conversation on the first date. We had made a pact to tell each other everything. But one thing I did not tell was about this dance, the high school Christmas Dance for which my mother was making me a dress. It was that I did not want to go.

At high school I was never comfortable for a minute. I did not know about Lonnie. Before an exam, she got icy hands and palpitations, but I was close to despair at all times. When I was asked a question in class, any simple little question at all, my voice was apt to come out squeaky, or else hoarse and trembling. My hands became slippery with sweat when they were required to work the blackboard compass. I could not hit the ball in volleyball; being called upon to perform an action in front of others made all my reflexes come undone. I hated Business Practice because you had to rule pages for an account book, using a straight pen, and when the teacher looked over my shoulder all the delicate lines wobbled and ran together. I hated Science; we perched on stools under harsh lights behind tables of unfamiliar, fragile equipment, and were taught by the principal of the school, a man with a cold, self-relishing voice—he read the Scriptures every morning—and a great talent for inflicting humiliation. I hated English because the boys played bingo at the back of the room while the teacher, a stout, gentle girl, slightly cross-eyed, read Wordsworth at the front. She threatened them, she begged them, her face red and her voice as unreliable as mine. They offered burlesqued apologies and when she started to read again they took up rapt postures, made swooning faces, crossed their eyes, flung their hands over their hearts. Sometimes she would burst into tears, there was no help for it, she had to run out into the hall. Then the boys made loud mooing noises; our hungry laughter—oh, mine too—pursued her. There was a carnival atmosphere of brutality in the room at such times, scaring weak and suspect people like me.

But what was really going on in the school was not Business Practice and Science and English; there was something else that gave life its urgency and brightness. That old building, with its rock-walled clammy basements and black cloakrooms and pictures of dead royalties and lost explorers, was full of the tension and excitement of sexual competition, and in this, in spite of daydreams of vast successes, I had premonitions of total defeat. Something had to happen, to keep me from that dance.

With December came snow, and I had an idea. Formerly I had considered falling off my bicycle and spraining my ankle and I had tried to manage this, as I rode home along the hard-frozen, deeply rutted country roads. But it was too difficult. However, my throat and bronchial tubes were supposed to be weak; why not expose them? I started getting out of bed at night and opening my window a little. I knelt down and let the wind, sometimes stinging with snow, rush in around my bared throat. I took off my pajama top. I said to myself the words "blue with cold" and as I knelt there, my eyes shut, I pictured my chest and throat turning blue, the cold, grayed blue of veins under the skin. I stayed until I could not stand it any more, and then I took a handful of snow from the windowsill and smeared it all over my chest, before I buttoned my pajamas. It would melt against the flannelette and I would be sleeping in wet clothes, which was supposed to be the worst thing of all. In the morning, the moment I woke up, I cleared my throat, testing for soreness, coughed experimentally, hopefully, touched my forehead to see if I had fever. It was no good. Every morning, including the day of the dance, I rose defeated, and in perfect health.

The day of the dance I did my hair up in steel curlers. I had never done this before, because my hair was naturally curly, but today I wanted the protection of all possible female rituals. I lay on the couch in the kitchen, reading *The Last Days of Pompeii* and wishing I was there. My mother, never satisfied, was sewing a white lace collar on the dress; she had decided it was too grown-up-looking. I watched the hours. It was one of the shortest days of the year. Above the couch, on the wallpaper, were old games of X's and O's, old drawings and scribblings my brother and I had done when we were sick with bronchitis. I looked at them and longed to be back safe behind the boundaries of childhood.

When I took out the curlers my hair, both naturally and artificially stimulated, sprang out in an exuberant glossy bush. I wet it, I combed it, beat it with the brush and tugged it down along my cheeks. I applied face powder, which stood out chalkily on my hot face. My mother got out her Ashes of Roses cologne, which she never used, and let me splash it over my arms. Then she zipped up the dress and turned me around to the mirror. The dress was princess-style, very tight in the midriff.

"Well, I wish I could take a picture," my mother said. "I am really, genuinely proud of that fit. And you might say thank you for it."

"Thank you," I said.

The first thing Lonnie said when I opened the door to her was, "What did you do to your hair?"

"I did it up."

"You look like a Zulu. Oh, don't worry. Get me a comb and I'll do the front in a roll. It'll look all right. It'll even make you look older."

I sat in front of the mirror and Lonnie stood behind me, fixing my hair. My mother seemed unable to leave us. I wished she would. She watched the roll take shape and said, "You're a wonder, Lonnie. You should take up hairdressing."

"That's a thought," Lonnie said. She had on a pale blue crepe dress, with a peplum and bow; it was much more grown-up than mine even without the collar. Her hair had come out as sleek as the girl's on the bobby-pin card. I had always thought secretly that Lonnie could not be pretty because she had crooked teeth, but now I saw that crooked teeth or not, her stylish dress and smooth hair made me look a little like a golliwog, stuffed into red velvet, wide-eyed, wild-haired, with a suggestion of delirium.

My mother followed us to the door and called out into the dark, "Au reservoir!" This was a traditional farewell of Lonnie's and mine; it sounded foolish and desolate coming from her, and I was so angry with her for using it that I did not reply. It was only Lonnie who called back cheerfully, encouragingly, "Good night!"

The gymnasium smelled of pine and cedar. Red and green bells of fluted paper hung from the basketball hoops; the high, barred windows were hidden by green boughs. Everybody in the upper grades seemed to have come in couples. Some of the Grade Twelve and Thirteen girls had brought boy friends who had already graduated, who were young businessmen around the town. These young men smoked in the gymnasium, nobody could stop them, they were free. The girls stood beside them, resting their hands casually on male sleeves, their faces bored, aloof and beautiful. I longed to be like that. They behaved as if only they–the older ones–were really at the dance, as if the rest of us, whom they moved among and peered around, were, if not invisible, inanimate; when the first dance was announced–a Paul Jones–they moved out languidly, smiling at each other as if they had been asked to take part in some half-forgotten childish game. Holding hands and shivering, crowding up together, Lonnie and I and the other Grade Nine girls followed.

I didn't dare look at the outer circle as it passed me, for fear I should see some unmannerly hurrying-up. When the music stopped I stayed where I was, and half raising my eyes I saw a boy named Mason Williams coming reluctantly towards me. Barely touching my waist and my fingers, he began to dance with me. My legs were hollow, my arms trembled from the shoulder, I could not have spoken. This Mason Williams was one of the heroes of the school; he played basketball and hockey and walked the halls with an air of royal sullenness and barbaric contempt. To have to dance with a nonentity like me was as offensive to him as having to memorize Shakespeare. I felt this as keenly as he did, and imagined that he was exchanging looks of dismay with his friends. He steered me, stumbling, to the edge of the floor. He took his hand from my waist and dropped my arm.

"See you," he said. He walked away.

It took me a minute or two to realize what had happened and that he was not coming back. I went and stood by the wall alone. The Physical Education teacher, dancing past energetically in the arms of a Grade Ten boy, gave me an inquisitive look. She was the only teacher in the school who made use of the words "social adjustment," and I was afraid that if she had seen, or if she found out, she might make some horribly public attempt to make Mason finish out the dance with me. I myself was not angry or surprised at Mason; I accepted his position, and mine, in the world of school and I saw that what he had done was the realistic thing to do. He was a Natural Hero, not a Student Council type of hero bound for success beyond the school; one of those would have danced with me courteously and patronizingly and left me feeling no better off. Still, I hoped not many people had seen. I hated people seeing. I began to bite the skin on my thumb.

When the music stopped I joined the surge of girls to the end of the gymnasium. Pretend it didn't happen, I said to myself. Pretend this is the beginning, now.

The band began to play again. There was movement in the dense crowd at our end of the floor; it thinned rapidly. Boys came over, girls went out to dance. Lonnie went. The girl on the other side of me went. Nobody asked me. I remembered a magazine article Lonnie and I had read, which said *Be gay! Let the boys see your eyes sparkle, let them hear laughter in your voice! Simple, obvious, but how many girls forget!* It was true, I had forgotten. My eyebrows were drawn together with tension; I must look scared and ugly. I took a deep breath and tried to loosen my face. I smiled. But I felt absurd, smiling at no one. And I observed that girls on the dance floor, popular girls, were not smiling; many of them had sleepy, sulky faces and never smiled at all.

Girls were still going out to the floor. Some, despairing, went with each other. But most went with boys. Fat girls, girls with pimples, a poor girl who didn't own a good dress and had to wear a skirt and sweater to the dance; they were claimed, they danced away. Why take them and not me? Why everybody else and not me? I have a red velvet dress, I did my hair in curlers, I used a deodorant and put on cologne. *Pray*, I thought. I couldn't close my eyes but I said over and over again in my mind, *Please, me, please*, and I locked my fingers behind my back in a sign more potent than crossing, the same secret sign Lonnie and I used not to be sent to the blackboard in Math.

It did not work. What I had been afraid of was true. I was going to be left. There was something mysterious the matter with me, something that could not be put right like bad breath or overlooked like pimples, and everybody knew it, and I knew it; I had known it all along. But I had not known it for sure, I had hoped to be mistaken. Certainty rose inside me like sickness. I hurried past one or two girls who were also left and went into the girls' washroom. I hid myself in a cubicle.

There was where I stayed. Between dances girls came in and went out quickly. There were plenty of cubicles; nobody noticed that I was not a temporary occupant. During the dances, I listened to the music which I liked but had no part of any more. For I was not going to try any more. I only wanted to hide in here, get out without seeing anybody, get home.

One time after the music started somebody stayed behind. She was taking a long time running the water, washing her hands, combing her hair. She was going to think it funny that I stayed in so long. I had better go out and wash my hands, and maybe while I was washing them she would leave.

It was Mary Fortune. I knew her by name, because she was an officer of the Girls' Athletic Society and she was on the Honor Roll and she was always organizing things. She had something to do with organizing this dance; she had been around to all the classrooms asking for volunteers to do the decorations. She was in Grade Eleven or Twelve.

"Nice and cool in here," she said. "I came in to get cooled off. I get so hot."

She was still combing her hair when I finished my hands. "Do you like the band?" she asked.

"It's all right." I didn't really know what to say. I was surprised at her, an older girl, taking this time to talk to me.

"I don't. I can't stand it. I hate dancing when I don't like the band. Listen. They're so choppy. I'd just as soon not dance as dance to that."

I combed my hair. She leaned against a basin, watching me.

"I don't want to dance and don't particularly want to stay in here. Let's go and have a cigarette."

"Where?"

"Come on, I'll show you."

At the end of the washroom there was a door. It was unlocked and led into a dark closet full of mops and pails. She had me hold the door open, to get the washroom light until she found the knob of another door. This door opened into darkness.

"I can't turn on the light or somebody might see," she said. "It's the janitor's room." I reflected that athletes always seemed to know more than the rest of us about the school as a building; they knew where things were kept and they were always coming out of unauthorized doors with a bold, preoccupied air. "Watch out where you're going," she said. "Over at the far end there's some stairs. They go up to a closet on the second floor. The door's locked at the top, but there's like a partition between the stairs and the room. So if we sit on the steps, even if by chance someone did come in here, they wouldn't see us."

"Wouldn't they smell smoke?" I said.

"Oh, well. Live dangerously."

There was a high window over the stairs which gave us a little light. Mary Fortune had cigarettes and matches in her purse. I had not smoked before except the cigarettes Lonnie and I made ourselves, using papers and tobacco stolen from her father; they came apart in the middle. These were much better.

"The only reason I even came tonight," Mary Fortune said, "is because I am responsible for the decorations and I wanted to see, you know, how it looked once people got in there and everything. Otherwise, why bother? I'm not boy-crazy."

In the light from the high window I could see her narrow, scornful face, her dark skin pitted with acne, her teeth pushed together at the front, making her look adult and commanding.

"Most girls are. Haven't you noticed that? The greatest collection of boy-crazy girls you could imagine is right here in this school."

I was grateful for her attention, her company and her cigarette. I said I thought so too.

"Like this afternoon. This afternoon I was trying to get them to hang the bells and junk. They just get up on the ladders and fool around with boys. They don't care if it ever gets decorated. It's just an excuse. That's the only aim they have in life, fooling around with boys. As far as I'm concerned, they're idiots."

We talked about teachers, and things at school. She said she wanted to be a physical education teacher and she would have to go to college for that, but her parents did not have enough money. She said she planned to work her own way through, she wanted to be independent anyway, she would work in the cafeteria and in the summer she would do farm work, like picking tobacco. Listening to her, I felt the acute phase of my unhappiness passing. Here was someone who had suffered the same defeat as I had—I saw that—but she was full of energy and self-respect. She had thought of other things to do. She would pick tobacco.

We stayed there talking and smoking during the long pause in the music, when, outside, they were having doughnuts and coffee. When the music started again Mary said, "Look, do we have to hang around here any longer? Let's get our coats and go. We can go down to Lee's and have a hot chocolate and talk in comfort, why not?"

We felt our way across the janitor's room, carrying ashes and cigarette butts in our hands. In the closet, we stopped and listened to make sure there was nobody in the washroom. We came back into the light and threw the ashes into the toilet. We had to go out and cut across the dance floor to the cloakroom, which was beside the outside door.

A dance was just beginning. "Go around the edge of the floor," Mary said. "Nobody'll notice us."

I followed her. I didn't look at anybody. I didn't look for Lonnie. Lonnie was probably not going to be my friend any more, not as much as before anyway. She was what Mary would call boy-crazy.

I found that I was not so frightened, now that I had made up my mind to leave the dance behind. I was not waiting for anybody to choose me. I had my own plans. I did not have to smile or make signs for luck. It did not matter to me. I was on my way to have a hot chocolate, with my friend.

A boy said something to me. He was in my way. I thought he must be telling me that I had dropped something or that I couldn't go that way or that the cloakroom was locked. I didn't understand that he was asking me to dance until he said it over again. It was Raymond Bolting from our class, whom I had never talked to in my life. He thought I meant yes. He put his hand on my waist and almost without meaning to, I began to dance.

We moved to the middle of the floor. I was dancing. My legs had forgotten to tremble and my hands to sweat. I was dancing with a boy who had asked me. Nobody told him to, he didn't have to, he just asked me. Was it possible, could I believe it, was there nothing the matter with me after all?

I thought that I ought to tell him there was a mistake, that I was just leaving, I was going to have a hot chocolate with my girl friend. But I did not say anything. My face was making certain delicate adjustments, achieving with no effect at all the grave, absent-minded look of those who were chosen, those who danced. This was the face that Mary Fortune saw, when she looked out of the cloakroom door, her scarf already around her head. I made a weak waving motion with the hand that lay on the boy's shoulder, indicating that I apologized, that I didn't know what had happened and also that it was no use waiting for me. Then I turned my head away, and when I looked again she was gone.

Raymond Bolting took me home and Harold Simons took Lonnie home. We all walked together as far as Lonnie's corner. The boys were having an argument about a hockey game, which Lonnie and I could not follow. Then we separated into couples and Raymond continued with me the conversation he had been having with Harold. He did not seem to notice that he was now talking to me instead. Once or twice I said, "Well, I don't know, I didn't see that game," but after a while I decided just to say "H'm hmm," and that seemed to be all that was necessary.

One other thing he said was, "I didn't realize you lived such a long ways out." And he sniffled. The cold was making my nose run a little too, and I worked my fingers through the candy wrappers in my coat pocket until I found a shabby Kleenex. I didn't know whether I ought to offer it to him or not, but he sniffled so loudly that I finally said, "I just have this one Kleenex, it probably isn't even clean, it probably has ink on it. But if I was to tear it in half we'd each have something."

"Thanks," he said. "I sure could use it."

It was a good thing, I thought, that I had done that, for at my gate, when I said, "Well, good night," and after he said, "Oh, yeah. Good night," he leaned towards me and kissed me, briefly, with the air of one who knew his job when he saw it, on the corner of my mouth. Then he turned back to town, never knowing he had been my rescuer, that he had brought me from Mary Fortune's territory into the ordinary world.

I went around the house to the back door, thinking, I have been to a dance and a boy has walked me home and kissed me. It was all true. My life was possible. I went past the kitchen window and I saw my mother. She was sitting with her feet on the open oven door, drinking tea out of a cup without a saucer. She was just sitting and waiting for me to come home and tell her everything that had happened. And I would not do it, I never would. But when I saw the waiting kitchen, and my mother in her faded, fuzzy paisley kimono, with her sleepy but doggedly expectant face, I understood what a mysterious and oppressive obligation I had, to be happy, and how I had almost failed it, and would be likely to fail it, every time, and she would not know.

The Facts of the Story

Write short answers to the following questions. Most answers require only a word or a phrase. A few require a complete sentence. Look back at the story if you wish.

1. The girl in the story is critical of her mother. Name two things about her mother that she finds objectionable.

2. What fact about her attitude toward the dance does the girl keep from her closest friend?

3. What personal characteristic accounts for the girl's unhappiness in school?

4. The girl feels sure that she will be defeated in the competition among the girls for the attention of _____.

5. Why does she, at one point, consider her good health a disadvantage?

6. What two experiences at the dance increase her unhappiness?

7. How does she try to escape from her unhappy situation at the dance?

8. Mary Fortune criticizes the other girls because, she says, they are all _____.

9. What happens that makes the girl feel that her life is possible after all?

10. What decision does she make when she sees her mother waiting for her, eager to hear about her evening at the dance?

The Ideas in the Story

This story is not about a dress, but about a girl who wears the dress to a school dance. We learn that the girl is afraid of leaving the "safe" boundaries of her childhood, and that she sees the dance as a big test which she would prefer to avoid. Two things happen to her as a result of her experiences at the dance: one has to do with her feelings about her mother; the other has to do with her feelings about herself.

1. One of the ideas in the story is about parents and children – about parents' hopes for their children and about the children's reactions to these hopes. What does the girl realize about her mother's hopes for her, as she sees the older woman sitting alone in the kitchen? Why would a parent "oblige" a child to be happy? Why does the girl feel that this could be "oppressive"?

2. Another idea in the story has to do with our anxiety to "keep up a good front." At one time or another, most of us do not want to admit that we are insecure or unhappy, or that we feel rejected or unpopular. Do you think Mary Fortune means what she says so scornfully about the "boy-crazy girls"? Why do you think someone would behave as Mary does?

3. Think about the girl's discovery of Mary Fortune in the washroom, her "rescue" by Raymond Bolting, and her relief at being released from Mary's "territory." How did you feel about her desertion of Mary? Do you think the girl cares for Raymond, or is she just relieved to be like everyone else? Is there any evidence that Raymond is especially taken with her, or does he seem to be doing a job that is expected of him? Explain why you feel the way you do.

4. The girl says she fears something is wrong with her. Only when Raymond invites her to dance (after she has stopped caring) does the girl think it might be possible that there is nothing wrong with her at all. Why do you suppose a mere invitation to dance would have such an impact on the girl? Did you find her response to Raymond's invitation and to his rather businesslike kiss believable? Tell why or why not.

5. Do you think young boys have the same feelings of insecurity that this girl has? Explain.

The Art of the Storyteller

Characterization

In life you get to know people well by watching what they do, by hearing what they say, by noticing what they look like, and by hearing what others say about them. Writers bring characters to life in the same ways. (1) They show us characters in action. (2) They let us know what the characters say and think. (3) They tell us what the characters look like. (4) They tell us how other people react to the characters. (5) Often, writers will tell us directly something about their characters. James Hurst does this in "The Scarlet Ibis" (page 211), when he tells us directly that Doodle is "a nice crazy, like someone you meet in your dreams." In "To Build a Fire" (page 32), Jack London tells us directly that his main character is "without imagination." In "The Bridge" (page 134), Chukovski tells us directly that his main character has become "shy and unsure of himself."

Each of the following quotations from "Red Dress" characterizes the girl's mother. Tell which of the five methods of characterization are being used, and what traits of the mother are revealed.

We also learn about the girl in the story from what she says about others. What do these comments reveal about the girl herself?

1. She was not really a good sewer. She liked to make things; that is different. . . . she took no pride in the fine points of tailoring. . . . she started off with an inspiration, a brave and dazzling idea; from that moment on, her pleasure ran downhill. In the first place she could never find a pattern to suit her. It was no wonder; there were no patterns made to match the ideas that ᵇlossomed in her head.

2. Around the house she wore no corset or stockings, she wore wedge-heeled shoes and ankle socks; her legs were marked with lumps of blue-green veins. I thought her squatting position shameless, even obscene. . . .

3. "Ah, well," she said theatrically, getting to her feet with a woeful creaking and sighing, "I doubt if she appreciates it."

4. She enraged me, talking like this to Lonnie, as if Lonnie were grown up and I were still a child.

5. She was sitting with her feet on the open oven door, drinking tea out of a cup without a saucer. She was just sitting and waiting for me to come home and tell her everything that had happened.

Composition

Expressing an Opinion About a Story

Everyone who reads a story has an opinion about it. It is important that you learn to express your opinions clearly and to explain why you hold them. Write a paragraph in which you give your opinion of "Red Dress." Express this opinion in your opening sentence. Try to say more than "I liked the story," or "I didn't like the story." Say something more specific and interesting, such as "I felt as if I were reading about myself in this story," or "I don't believe this gives a realistic picture of a thirteen-year-old girl." Support your opening statement with at least three reasons that explain why you hold this opinion.
Write approximately 150 words.

Alice Munro

Alice Munro's (1931-   ) stories and novels are about the day-to-day lives of ordinary people who live in the small towns and farms of Ontario, Canada, where she grew up and attended college. "Red Dress" is part of a collection of stories called *Dance of the Happy Shades.* The book won the Governor General's Award for Fiction in Canada in 1968.

All Summer in a Day

RAY BRADBURY

Successful writers of fantasy and science fiction like Ray Bradbury must have powerful imaginations, since they describe places where no one on earth has ever been. They must imagine what those places are like, and they may imagine anything they wish. In this story the setting is the planet Venus.

Bradbury imagines Venus as a place where rain falls continuously, except for two hours every seven years, when the sun comes out. Even in this dreary climate, however, settlers from Earth live, work, and raise families. But Bradbury's purpose in telling this story is not to describe life on Venus as he imagines it. He is writing about people who are no different from us even though they live on an island in space. All of us, sadly, can understand the ideas about human beings, especially about children, that Bradbury expresses in this story.

"Ready?"

"Ready."

"Now?"

"Soon."

"Do the scientists really know? Will it happen today, will it?"

"Look, look; see for yourself!"

The children pressed to each other like so many roses, so many weeds, intermixed, peering out for a look at the hidden sun.

It rained.

It had been raining for seven years; thousands upon thousands of days compounded and filled from one end to the other with rain, with the drum and gush of water, with the sweet crystal fall of showers and the concussion of storms so heavy they were tidal waves come over the islands. A thousand forests had been crushed under the rain and grown up a thousand times to be crushed again. And this was the way life was forever on the planet Venus, and this was the schoolroom of the children of the rocket men and women who had come to a raining world to set up civilization and live out their lives.

"It's stopping, it's stopping!"

"Yes, yes!"

Margot stood apart from them, from these children who could never remember a time when there wasn't rain and rain and rain. They were all nine years old, and if there had been a day, seven years ago, when the sun came out for an hour and showed its face to the stunned world, they could not recall.

249

Sometimes, at night, she heard them stir, in remembrance, and she knew they were dreaming and remembering gold or a yellow crayon or a coin large enough to buy the world with. She knew they thought they remembered a warmness, like a blushing in the face, in the body, in the arms and legs and trembling hands. But then they always awoke to the tatting drum, the endless shaking down of clear bead necklaces upon the roof, the walk, the gardens, the forests, and their dreams were gone.

All day yesterday they had read in class about the sun. About how like a lemon it was, and how hot. And they had written small stories or essays or poems about it:

> *I think the sun is a flower,*
> *That blooms for just one hour.*

That was Margot's poem, read in a quiet voice in the still classroom while the rain was falling outside.

"Aw, you didn't write that!" protested one of the boys.

"I did," said Margot, "I *did.*"

"William!" said the teacher.

But that was yesterday. Now the rain was slackening, and the children were crushed in the great thick windows.

"Where's teacher?"

"She'll be back."

"She'd better hurry, we'll miss it!"

They turned on themselves, like a feverish wheel, all tumbling spokes.

Margot stood alone. She was a very frail girl who looked as if she had been lost in the rain for years and the rain had washed out the blue from her eyes and the red from her mouth and the yellow from her hair. She was an old photograph dusted from an album, whitened away, and if she spoke at all her voice would be a ghost. Now she stood, separate, staring at the rain and the loud wet world beyond the huge glass.

"What're *you* looking at?" said William.

Margot said nothing.

"Speak when you're spoken to." He gave her a shove. But

she did not move; rather she let herself be moved only by him and nothing else.

They edged away from her, they would not look at her. She felt them go away. And this was because she would play no games with them in the echoing tunnels of the underground city. If they tagged her and ran, she stood blinking after them and did not follow. When the class sang songs about happiness and life and games her lips barely moved. Only when they sang about the sun and the summer did her lips move as she watched the drenched windows.

And then, of course, the biggest crime of all was that she had come here only five years ago from Earth, and she remembered the sun and the way the sun was and the sky was when she was four in Ohio. And they, they had been on Venus all their lives, and they had been only two years old when last the sun came out and had long since forgotten the color and heat of it and the way it really was. But Margot remembered.

"It's like a penny," she said once, eyes closed.

"No it's not!" the children cried.

"It's like a fire," she said, "in the stove."

"You're lying, you don't remember!" cried the children.

But she remembered and stood quietly apart from all of them and watched the patterning windows. And once, a month ago, she had refused to shower in the school shower rooms, had clutched her hands to her ears and over her head, screaming the water musn't touch her head. So after that, dimly, dimly, she sensed it, she was different and they knew her difference and kept away.

There was talk that her father and mother were taking her back to Earth next year; it seemed vital to her that they do so, though it would mean the loss of thousands of dollars to her family. And so, the children hated her for all these reasons of big and little consequence. They hated her pale snow face, her waiting silence, her thinness, and her possible future.

"Get away!" The boy gave her another push. "What're you waiting for?"

Then, for the first time, she turned and looked at him. And what she was waiting for was in her eyes.

"Well, don't wait around here!" cried the boy savagely. "You won't see nothing!"

Her lips moved.

"Nothing!" he cried. "It was all a joke, wasn't it?" He turned to the other children. "Nothing's happening today. *Is* it?"

They all blinked at him and then, understanding, laughed and shook their heads. "Nothing, nothing!"

"Oh, but," Margot whispered, her eyes helpless. "But this is the day, the scientists predict, they say, they *know*, the sun . . ."

"All a joke!" said the boy, and seized her roughly. "Hey, everyone, let's put her in a closet before teacher comes!"

"No," said Margot, falling back.

They surged about her, caught her up and bore her, protesting, and then pleading, and then crying, back into a tunnel, a room, a closet, where they slammed and locked the door. They stood looking at the door and saw it tremble from her beating and throwing herself against it. They heard her muffled cries. Then, smiling, they turned and went out and back down the tunnel, just as the teacher arrived.

"Ready, children?" She glanced at her watch.

"Yes!" said everyone.

"Are we all here?"

"Yes!"

The rain slackened still more.

They crowded to the huge door.

The rain stopped.

It was as if, in the midst of a film, concerning an avalanche, a tornado, a hurricane, a volcanic eruption, something had, first, gone wrong with the sound apparatus, thus muffling and finally cutting off all noise, all of the blasts and repercussions and thunders, and then, second, ripped the film from the projector and inserted in its place a peaceful tropical slide which did not move or tremor. The world ground to a standstill. The silence was so immense and unbelievable that you felt your ears had been stuffed or you had lost your hearing altogether. The children put their hands to their ears. They stood apart. The door slid back and the smell of the silent, waiting world came in to them.

The sun came out.

It was the color of flaming bronze and it was very large. And the sky around it was a blazing blue tile color. And the jungle burned with sunlight as the children, released from their spell, rushed out, yelling, into the springtime.

"Now, don't go too far," called the teacher after them. "You've only two hours, you know. You wouldn't want to get caught out!"

But they were running and turning their faces up to the sky and feeling the sun on their cheeks like a warm iron; they were taking off their jackets and letting the sun burn their arms.

"Oh, it's better than the sunlamps, isn't it?"

"Much, much better!"

They stopped running and stood in the great jungle that covered Venus, that grew and never stopped growing, tumultuously, even as you watched it. It was a nest of octopi, clustering up great arms of fleshlike weed, wavering, flowering this brief spring. It was the color of rubber and ash, this jungle, from the many years without sun. It was the color of stones and white cheeses and ink, and it was the color of the moon.

The children lay out, laughing, on the jungle mattress, and heard it sigh and squeak under them, resilient and alive. They ran among the trees, they slipped and fell, they pushed each other, they played hide-and-seek and tag, but most of all they squinted at the sun until the tears ran down their faces, they put their hands up to that yellowness and that amazing blueness and they breathed of the fresh, fresh air and listened and listened to the silence which suspended them in a blessed sea of no sound and no motion. They looked at everything and savored everything. Then, wildly, like animals escaped from their caves, they ran and ran in shouting circles. They ran for an hour and did not stop running.

And then—

In the midst of their running one of the girls wailed.

Everyone stopped.

The girl, standing in the open, held out her hand.

"Oh, look, look," she said, trembling.

They came slowly to look at her opened palm.

In the center of it, cupped and huge, was a single raindrop.

She began to cry, looking at it.

They glanced quietly at the sky.

"Oh. Oh."

A few cold drops fell on their noses and their cheeks and their mouths. The sun faded behind a stir of mist. A wind blew cool around them. They turned and started to walk back toward the underground house, their hands at their sides, their smiles vanishing away.

A boom of thunder startled them and like leaves before a new hurricane, they tumbled upon each other and ran. Lightning struck ten miles away, five miles away, a mile, a half mile. The sky darkened into midnight in a flash.

They stood in the doorway of the underground for a moment until it was raining hard. Then they closed the door and heard the gigantic sound of the rain falling in tons and avalanches, everywhere and forever.

"Will it be seven more years?"

"Yes. Seven."

Then one of them gave a little cry.

"Margot!"

"What?"

"She's still in the closet where we locked her."

"Margot."

They stood as if someone had driven them, like so many

stakes, into the floor. They looked at each other and then looked away. They glanced out at the world that was raining now and raining and raining steadily. They could not meet each other's glances. Their faces were solemn and pale. They looked at their hand and feet, their faces down.

"Margot."

One of the girls said, "Well . . . ?"

No one moved.

"Go on," whispered the girl.

They walked slowly down the hall in the sound of cold rain. They turned through the doorway to the room in the sound of the storm and thunder, lightning on their faces, blue and terrible. They walked over to the closet door slowly and stood by it.

Behind the closet door was only silence.

They unlocked the door, even more slowly, and let Margot out.

The Facts of the Story

Write answers to the following questions. Answers should be complete sentences, not just single words or phrases.

1. This story opens with the question "Ready?" What are the characters getting ready for?

2. In what way is Margot's reaction to the constant rain different from the reactions of the other children?

3. What is the major conflict in this story, and how is it resolved?

4. What is the climax of the story?

5. The children's feelings have changed by the time they release Margot from the closet. What accounts for this change in their attitude?

The Ideas in the Story

For class discussion, prepare answers to the following questions.

1. The main idea in this story has something to do with why people are sometimes cruel to one another. The author says the children hated Margot for "all these reasons of big and little consequence. They hated her pale snow face, her waiting silence, her thinness, and her possible future." Tell which of these four reasons you think are of "big consequence" and which are of "little consequence."

2. How important is the *group* feeling? Do you think that the children would have treated Margot as they did if there had not been many against one? What has your own experience, or your reading, shown you about group behavior versus individual behavior? What is the meaning of "mob psychology"? What are its dangers?

The Art of the Storyteller

Similes and Metaphors

Often in our speaking, and especially in our writing, we compare one thing to another, very different thing. When the children in Bradbury's story hear that the sun is like a lemon, they immediately understand something about the sun's appearance, even though the sun and a lemon are not actually alike in any way other than in color and, perhaps, in shape. When Margot uses a comparison and says, "I think the sun is a flower, / That blooms for just one hour," she immediately helps us understand her idea of the beauty of the sun, and of its brief "bloom."

Comparisons can be made in two ways. When a comparison is made with words such as *like* or *as,* it is called a *simile.* (The sun is *like* a lemon. The sun is *as* yellow *as* a lemon.) When a comparison is expressed without words such as *like* or *as,* it is called a *metaphor.* (The sun *is* a flower.)

Read the following comparisons from "All Summer in a Day" and decide whether each is a simile or a metaphor. What points of comparison are being made in each statement?

1. She [Margot] was an old photograph dusted from an album, whitened away. . . .

2. But they were . . . feeling the sun on their cheeks like a warm iron. . . .

3. They stood as if someone had driven them, like so many stakes, into the floor.

Composition

Using Similes and Metaphors

Write a description of a scene or of an experience in which you include at least three similes or metaphors. As you think about what you want to describe, ask yourself, "What is it like? What does it remind me of?" Here are some suggestions for subjects:

A walk–in a city, in a park, on a country road, around a neighborhood

A beach or a pool or a shower on a hot August afternoon

The stadium at game time

A night ride

Eating ice cream

A carnival

A cellar or an attic or an old familiar house

A storm

Be sure to compare things that are not actually alike in most respects. "Her dress is like mine" is *not* a simile. "Her dress is like a tent" *is* a simile.

Write approximately 150 words.

Ray Bradbury

Ray Bradbury's (1920-   ) childhood was spent in the city of his birth, Waukegan, Illinois. After moving to Southern California, he went to high school in Los Angeles, where he still lives. Bradbury is probably America's foremost writer of fantasy and science fiction. In addition to his short stories, for which he is best known, he has written novels and plays, including screenplays. In 1956, he received the Boys' Clubs of America Junior Book Award. One of his most popular books is *The Martian Chronicles,* which was made into a television serial.

Bad Characters

JEAN STAFFORD

Emily Vanderpool, the principal character in this story, says about herself at the age of eleven, "I had a bad character, I know that, but my badness never gave me half the enjoyment Jack and Stella thought it did." Jack and Stella are her older brother and sister. But if you think Emily had a bad character, Lottie Jump, her friend for a short time, had a much worse one—Lottie seemed to get plenty of enjoyment from her "badness."

Events in our past that we took quite seriously and suffered painfully from at the time sometimes seem very funny when we look back on them. In looking back on the events described in this story, Jean Stafford finds them hilariously funny. Her character Emily says she did not enjoy her "badness," but Stafford certainly makes us enjoy reading about it, and also about the greater "badness" of Lottie.

Up until I learned my lesson in a very bitter way, I never had more than one friend at a time, and my friendships, though ardent, were short. When they ended and I was sent packing in unforgetting indignation, it was always my fault; I would swear vilely in front of a girl I knew to be pious and prim (by the time I was eight, the most grandiloquent gangster could have added nothing to my vocabulary—I had an awful tongue), or I would call a Tenderfoot Scout a sissy or make fun of athletics to the daughter of the high-school coach. These outbursts came without plan; I would simply one day, in the middle of a game of Russian bank or a hike or a conversation, be possessed with a passion to be by myself, and my lips instantly and without warning would accommodate me. My friend was never more surprised than I was when this irrevocable slander, this terrible, talented invective, came boiling out of my mouth.

Afterward, when I had got the solitude I had wanted, I was dismayed, for I did not like it. Then I would sadly finish the game of cards as if someone were still across the table from me; I would sit down on the mesa and through a glaze of tears would watch my friend departing with outraged strides; mournfully, I would talk to myself. Because I had already alienated everyone I knew, I then had nowhere to turn, so a famine set in and I would have no companion but Muff, the cat, who loathed all human beings except, significantly, me—truly. She bit and scratched the hands that fed her, she arched her back like a Halloween cat if someone kindly tried to pet her, she hissed, laid her ears flat to her skull, growled, fluffed up her tail into a great bush and flailed it like a bullwhack. But she purred for me, she patted me with her paws, keeping her claws in their velvet scabbards. She was not only an ill-natured cat, she was also badly dressed. She was a calico, and the distribution of her colors was a mess; she looked as if she had been left out in the rain and her paint had run. She had a Roman nose as the result of some early injury, her tail was skinny, she had a perfectly venomous look in her eye. My family said—my family discriminated against me—that I was much closer kin to Muff than I was to any of them. To tease me into a tantrum, my brother Jack and my sister Stella often called me Kitty instead of Emily. Little Tess did not dare, because she knew I'd chloroform her if she did. Jack, the meanest boy I have ever known in my life, called me Polecat and talked about my mania for fish, which, it so happened, I despised. The name would have been far more appropriate for *him*, since he trapped skunks up in the foothills—we lived in Adams, Colorado—and quite often, because he was careless and foolhardy, his clothes had to be buried, and even when that was done, he sometimes was sent home from school on the complaint of girls sitting next to him.

Along about Christmas time when I was eleven, I was making a snowman with Virgil Meade in his backyard, and all of a sudden, just as we had got around to the right arm, I had to be alone. So I called him a son of a sea cook, said it was common knowledge that his mother had bedbugs and that his father, a dentist and the deputy marshal, was a bootlegger on the side. For a moment, Virgil was too aghast to speak—a little earlier we had agreed to marry someday and become millionaires—and then, with a bellow of fury, he knocked me down and washed my face in snow. I saw stars, and black balls bounced before my eyes. When finally he let me up, we were both crying, and he hollered that if I didn't get off his property that instant, his father would arrest me and send me to Canon City. I trudged slowly home, half frozen, critically sick at heart. So it was old Muff again for me for quite some time. Old Muff, that is, until I met Lottie Jump, although "met" is a euphemism for the way I first encountered her.

I saw Lottie for the first time one afternoon in our own kitchen, stealing a chocolate cake. Stella and Jack had not come home from school yet—not having my difficult disposition, they were popular, and they were at their friends' houses, pulling taffy, I suppose, making popcorn balls, playing casino, having fun—and my mother had taken Tess with her to visit a friend in one of the TB sanitariums. I was alone in the house, and making a funny-looking Christmas card, although I had no one to send it to. When I heard someone in the kitchen, I thought it was Mother home early, and I went out to ask her why the green pine tree I had pasted on a square of red paper looked as if it were falling down. And there, instead of Mother and my baby sister, was this pale, conspicuous child in the act of lifting the glass cover from the devil's-food my mother had taken out of the oven an hour before and set on the plant shelf by the window. The child had her back to me, and when she heard my footfall, she wheeled with an amazing look of fear and hatred on her pinched and pasty face. Simultaneously, she put the cover over the cake again, and then she stood motionless as if she were under a spell.

I was scared, for I was not sure what was happening, and anyhow it gives you a turn to find a stranger in the kitchen in the middle of the afternoon, even if the stranger is only a skinny child in a moldy coat and sopping-wet basketball shoes. Between us there was a lengthy silence, but there was a great deal of noise in the room: the alarm clock ticked smugly; the teakettle simmered patiently on the back of the stove; Muff, cross at having been waked up, thumped her tail against the side of the flower box in the window where she had been sleeping—contrary to orders—among the geraniums. This went on, it seemed to me, for hours and hours while that tall, sickly girl and I confronted each other. When, after a long time, she did open her mouth, it was to tell a prodigious lie. "I came to see if you'd like to play with me," she said. I think she sighed and stole a sidelong and regretful glance at the cake.

Beggars cannot be choosers, and I had been missing Virgil so sorely, as well as all those other dear friends forever lost to me, that in spite of her flagrance (she had never clapped eyes on me before, she had had no way of knowing there was a creature of my age in the house—she had come in like a hobo to steal my mother's cake), I was flattered and consoled. I asked her name and, learning it, believed my ears no better than my eyes: Lottie Jump. What on earth! What on earth—you surely will agree with me—and yet when I told her mine, Emily Vanderpool, she laughed until she coughed and gasped. "Beg pardon," she said. "Names like them always hit my funny bone. There was this towhead boy in school named Delbert Saxonfield." I saw no connection and I was insulted (what's so funny about Vanderpool, I'd like to know), but Lottie Jump was, technically, my guest and I *was* lonesome, so I asked her, since she had spoken of playing with me, if she knew how to play Andy-I-Over. She said, "Naw." It turned out that she did not know how to play any games at all; she couldn't do anything and didn't want to do anything; her only recreation and her only gift was, and always had been, stealing. But this I did not know at the time.

As it happened, it was too cold and snowy to play outdoors that day anyhow, and after I had run through my list of indoor games and Lottie had shaken her head at all of them (when I spoke of Parcheesi, she went "Ugh!" and pretended to be sick), she suggested that we look through my mother's bureau drawers. This did not strike me as strange at all, for it was one of my favorite things to do, and I led the way to Mother's bedroom without a moment's hesitation. I loved the smell of the lavender she kept in gauze bags among her chamois gloves and linen handkerchiefs and filmy scarves; there was a pink fascinator[1] knitted of something as fine as spider's thread, and it made me go quite soft—I wasn't soft as a rule, I was hard as nails and I

---

1. *fascinator*: scarf.

gave my mother a rough time—to think of her wearing it around her head as she waltzed on the ice in the bygone days. We examined stockings, nightgowns, camisoles, strings of beads, and mosaic pins, keepsake buttons from dresses worn on memorial occasions, tortoise-shell combs, and a transformation[2] made from Aunt Joey's hair when she had racily had it bobbed. Lottie admired particularly a blue cloisonné perfume flask with ferns and peacocks on it. "Hey," she said, "this sure is cute. I like thing-daddies like this here." But very abruptly she got bored and said, "Let's talk instead. In the front room." I agreed, a little perplexed this time, because I had been about to show her a remarkable powder box that played "The Blue Danube." We went into the parlor, where Lottie looked at her image in the pier glass for quite a while and with great absorption, as if she had never seen herself before. Then she moved over to the window seat and knelt on it, looking out at the front walk. She kept her hands in the pockets of her thin dark red coat; once she took out one of her dirty paws to rub her nose for a minute and I saw a bulge in that pocket, like a bunch of jackstones. I know now that it wasn't jackstones, it was my mother's perfume flask; I thought at the time her hands were cold and that that was why she kept them put away, for I had noticed that she had no mittens.

Lottie did most of the talking, and while she talked, she never once looked at me but kept her eyes fixed on the approach to our house. She told me that her family had come to Adams a month before from Muskogee, Oklahoma, where her father, before he got tuberculosis, had been a brakeman on the Frisco. Now they lived down by Arapahoe Creek, on the west side of town, in one of the cottages of a wretched settlement made up of people so poor and so sick—for in nearly every ramshackle house someone was coughing himself to death—that each time I went past I blushed with guilt because my shoes were sound and my coat was warm and I was well. I

---

2. *transformation:* wig.

wished that Lottie had not told me where she lived, but she was
not aware of any pathos in her family's situation, and, indeed,
it was with a certain boastfulness that she told me her mother
was the short-order cook at the Comanche Café (she pronounced this word in one syllable), which I knew was the
dirtiest, darkest, smelliest place in town, patronized by coal
miners who never washed their faces and sometimes had such
dangerous fights that the sheriff had to come. Laughing, Lottie
told me that her brother didn't have any brains and had never
been to school. She herself was eleven years old, but she was
only in the third grade, because teachers had always had it in
for her—making her go to the blackboard and all like that when
she was tired. She hated school—she went to Ashton, on North
Hill, and that was why I had never seen her, for I went to
Carlyle Hill—and she especially hated the teacher, Miss Cudahy, who had a head shaped like a pine cone and who had
killed several people with her ruler. Lottie loved the movies
("Not them Western ones or the ones with apes in," she said.
"Ones about hugging and kissing. I love it when they die in
that big old soft bed with the curtains up top, and he comes in
and says, 'Don't leave me, Marguerite de la Mar' "), and she
loved to ride in cars. She loved Mr. Goodbars, and if there was
one thing she despised worse than another it was tapioca. ("Pa
calls it fish eyes. He calls floating island horse spit. He's a big
piece of cheese. I hate him.") She did not like cats (Muff was
now sitting on the mantelpiece, glaring like an owl); she kind of
liked snakes—except cottonmouths and rattlers—because she
found them kind of funny; she had once seen a goat eat a tin
can. She said that one of these days she would take me downtown—it was a slowpoke town, she said, a one-horse burg (I had
never heard such gaudy, cynical talk and was trying to memorize it all)—if I would get some money for the trolley fare; she
hated to walk, and I ought to be proud that she had walked all
the way from Arapahoe Creek today for the sole solitary purpose of seeing me.

Seeing our freshly baked dessert in the window was a more

likely story, but I did not care, for I was deeply impressed by this bold, sassy girl from Oklahoma and greatly admired the poise with which she aired her prejudices. Lottie Jump was certainly nothing to look at. She was tall and made of skin and bones; she was evilly ugly, and her clothes were a disgrace, not just ill-fitting and old and ragged but dirty, unmentionably so; clearly she did not wash much or brush her teeth, which were notched like a saw, and small and brown (it crossed my mind that perhaps she chewed tobacco); her long, lank hair looked as if it might have nits. But she had personality. She made me think of one of those self-contained dogs whose home is where his handout is and who travels alone but, if it suits him to, will become the leader of a pack. She was aloof, never looking at me, but amiable in the way she kept calling me "kid." I liked her enormously, and presently I told her so.

At this, she turned around and smiled at me. Her smile was the smile of a jack-o'-lantern—high, wide, and handsome. When it was over, no trace of it remained. "Well, that's keen, kid, and I like you, too," she said in her downright Muskogee accent. She gave me a long, appraising look. Her eyes were the color of mud. "Listen, kid, how much do you like me?"

"I like you loads, Lottie," I said. "Better than anybody else, and I'm not kidding."

"You want to be pals?"

"Do I!" I cried. So *there*, Virgil Meade, you big fat hoot-nanny, I thought.

"All right, kid, we'll be pals." And she held out her hand for me to shake. I had to go and get it, for she did not alter her position on the window seat. It was a dry, cold hand, and the grip was severe, with more a feeling of bones in it than friend-liness.

Lottie turned and scanned our path and scanned the side-walk beyond, and then she said, in a lower voice, "Do you know how to lift?"

"Lift?" I wondered if she meant to lift *her*. I was sure I could do it, since she was so skinny, but I couldn't imagine why she would want me to.

"Shoplift, I mean. Like in the five-and-dime."

I did not know the term, and Lottie scowled at my stupidity.

"*Steal*, for crying in the beer!" she said impatiently. This she said so loudly that Muff jumped down from the mantel and left the room in contempt.

I was thrilled to death and shocked to pieces. "Stealing is a sin," I said. "You get put in jail for it."

"Ish ka bibble! I should worry if it's a sin or not," said Lottie, with a shrug. "And they'll never put a smart old whatsis like *me* in jail. It's fun, stealing is—it's a picnic. I'll teach you if you want to learn, kid." Shamelessly she winked at me and grinned again. (That grin! She could have taken it off her face and put it on the table.) And she added, "If you don't, we can't be pals, because lifting is the only kind of playing I like. I hate those dumb games like Statues. Kick-the-Can—phooey!"

I was torn between agitation (I went to Sunday School and knew already about morality; Judge Bay, a crabby old man who loved to punish sinners, was a friend of my father's and once had given Jack a lecture on the criminal mind when he came to call and found Jack looking up an answer in his arithmetic book) and excitement over the daring invitation to misconduct myself in so perilous a way. My life, on reflection, looked deadly prim; all I'd ever done to vary the monotony of it was to swear. I knew that Lottie Jump meant what she said—that I could have her friendship only on her terms (plainly, she had gone it alone for a long time and could go it alone for the rest of her life)—and although I trembled like an aspen and my heart went pitapat, I said, "I want to be pals with you, Lottie."

"All right, Vanderpool," said Lottie, and got off the window seat. "I wouldn't go braggin' about it if I was you. I wouldn't go telling my ma and pa and the next-door neighbor that you and

Lottie Jump are going down to the five-and-dime next Saturday aft and lift us some nice rings and garters and things like that. I mean it, kid." And she drew the back of her forefinger across her throat and made a dire face.

"I won't. I promise I won't. My *gosh*, why would I?"

"That's the ticket," said Lottie, with a grin. "I'll meet you at the trolley shelter at two o'clock. You have the money. For both down and up. I ain't going to climb up that ornery hill after I've had my fun."

"Yes, Lottie," I said. Where was I going to get twenty cents? I was going to have to start stealing before she even taught me how. Lottie was facing the center of the room, but she had eyes in the back of her head, and she whirled around back to the window; my mother and Tess were turning in our front path.

"Back way," I whispered, and in a moment Lottie was gone; the swinging door that usually squeaked did not make a sound as she vanished through it. I listened and I never heard the back door open and close. Nor did I hear her, in a split second, lift the glass cover and remove that cake designed to feed six people.

I was restless and snappish between Wednesday afternoon and Saturday. When Mother found the cake was gone, she scolded me for not keeping my ears cocked. She assumed, naturally, that a tramp had taken it, for she knew I hadn't eaten it; I never ate anything if I could help it (except for raw potatoes, which I loved) and had been known as a problem feeder from the beginning of my life. At first it occurred to me to have a tantrum and bring her around to my point of view: my tantrums scared the living daylights out of her because my veins stood out and I turned blue and couldn't get my breath. But I rejected this for a more sensible plan. I said, "It just so happens I didn't hear anything. But if I had, I suppose you wish I had gone out in the kitchen and let the robber cut me up into a million little tiny pieces with his sword. You wouldn't even bury me. You'd just put me on the dump. *I* know who's wanted in this family and who isn't." Tears of sorrow, not of anger, came in powerful tides and I groped blindly to the bedroom I shared with Stella, where I lay on my bed and shook with big, silent *weltschmerzlich*[3] sobs. Mother followed me immediately, and so did Tess, and both of them comforted me and told me how much they loved me. I said they didn't; they said they did. Presently, I got a headache, as I always did when I cried, so I got to have an aspirin and a cold cloth on my head, and when Jack and Stella came home, they had to be quiet. I heard Jack say, "Emily Vanderpool is the biggest polecat in the USA. Whyn't she go in the kitchen and say, 'Hands up'? He woulda lit out." And Mother said, "Sh-h-h! You don't want your sister to be sick, do you?" Muff, not realizing that Lottie had replaced her, came in and curled up at my thigh, purring lustily; I found myself glad that she had left the room before Lottie Jump made her proposition to me, and in gratitude I stroked her unattractive head.

Other things happened. Mother discovered the loss of her perfume flask and talked about nothing else at meals for two whole days. Luckily, it did not occur to her that it had been stolen—she simply thought she had mislaid it—but her monomania got on my father's nerves and he lashed out at her and at the rest of us. And because I was the cause of it all and my conscience was after me with red-hot pokers, I finally *had* to have a tantrum. I slammed my fork down in the middle of supper on the second day and yelled, "If you don't stop fighting, I'm going to kill myself. Yammer, yammer, nag, nag!" And I put my fingers in my ears and squeezed my eyes tight shut and screamed so the whole country could hear, "Shut *up!*" And then I lost my breath and began to turn blue. Daddy hastily apologized to everyone, and Mother said she was sorry

---

3. *weltschmerzlich*: German for "sorrowful over the state of the world."

for carrying on so about a trinket that had nothing but sentimental value—she was just vexed with herself for being careless, that was all, and she wasn't going to say another word
about it.

I never heard so many references to stealing and cake, and
even to Oklahoma (ordinarily no one mentioned Oklahoma
once in a month of Sundays) and the ten-cent store as I did
throughout those next days. I myself once made a ghastly slip
and said something to Stella about "the five-and-dime." "The
five-and-*dime!*" she exclaimed. "Where'd you get *that* kind of
talk? Do you by any chance have reference to the *ten-cent
store?*"

The worst of all was Friday night—the very night before I was
to meet Lottie Jump—when Judge Bay came to play two-hand-
ed pinochle with Daddy. The Judge, a giant in intimidating
haberdashery[4]—for some reason, the white piping on his vest
bespoke, for me, handcuffs and prison bars—and with an aura
of disapproval for almost everything on earth except what per-
tained directly to himself, was telling Daddy, before they began
their game, about the infamous vandalism that had been going
on among the college students. "I have reason to believe that
there are girls in this gang as well as boys," he said. "They
ransack vacant houses and take everything. In one house on
Pleasant Street, up there by the Catholic Church, there wasn't
anything to take, so they took the kitchen sink. Wasn't a question of taking everything *but*—they took the kitchen sink."

"Whatever would they want with a kitchen sink?" asked my
mother.

"Mischief," replied the Judge. "If we ever catch them and if
they come within my jurisdiction, I can tell you I will give
them no quarter. A thief, in my opinion, is the lowest of the
low."

Mother told about the chocolate cake. By now, the fiction
was so factual in my mind that each time I thought of it I saw a

---

4. *haberdashery:* men's clothing.

funny-paper bum in baggy pants held up by rope, a hat with holes through which tufts of hair stuck up, shoes from which his toes protruded, a disreputable stubble on his face; he came up beneath the open window where the devil's-food was cooling and he stole it and hotfooted it for the woods, where his companion was frying a small fish in a beat-up skillet. It never crossed my mind any longer that Lottie Jump had hooked that delicious cake.

Judge Bay was properly impressed. "If you will steal a chocolate cake, if you will steal a kitchen sink, you will steal diamonds and money. The small child who pilfers a penny from his mother's pocketbook has started down a path that may lead him to holding up a bank."

It was a good thing I had no homework that night, for I could not possibly have concentrated. We were all sent to our rooms, because the pinochle players had to have absolute quiet. I spent the evening doing cross-stitch. I was making a bureau runner for a Christmas present; as in the case of the Christmas card, I had no one to give it to, but now I decided to give it to Lottie Jump's mother. Stella was reading *Black Beauty*, crying. It was an interminable evening. Stella went to bed first; I saw to that, because I didn't want her lying there awake listening to me talking in my sleep. Besides, I didn't want her to see me tearing open the cardboard box—the one in the shape of a church, which held my Christmas Sunday School offering. Over the door of the church was this shaming legend: "My mite[5] for the poor widow." When Stella had begun to grind her teeth in her first deep sleep, I took twenty cents away from the poor widow, whoever she was (the owner of the kitchen sink, no doubt), for the trolley fare, and secreted it and the remaining three pennies in the pocket of my middy. I wrapped the money well in a handkerchief and buttoned the pocket and hung my skirt over the middy. And then I tore the paper church into bits—the heavens opened and Judge Bay came

5. *mite:* small bit of money.

toward me with a double-barreled shotgun—and hid the bits under a pile of pajamas. I did not sleep one wink. Except that I must have, because of the stupendous nightmares that kept wrenching the flesh off my skeleton and caused me to come close to perishing of thirst; once I fell out of bed and hit my head on Stella's ice skates. I would have waked her up and given her a piece of my mind for leaving them in such a lousy place, but then I remembered: I wanted *no* commotion of any kind.

I couldn't eat breakfast and I couldn't eat lunch. Old Johnny-on-the-spot Jack kept saying, "*Poor* Polecat. Polecat wants her fish for dinner." Mother made an abortive attempt to take my temperature. And when all that hullabaloo subsided, I was nearly in the soup because Mother asked me to mind Tess while she went to the sanitarium to see Mrs. Rogers, who, all of a sudden, was too sick to have anyone but grown-ups near her. Stella couldn't stay with the baby, because she had to go to ballet, and Jack couldn't, because he had to go up to the mesa and empty his traps. ("No, they *can't* wait. You want my skins to rot in this hot-one-day-cold-the-next weather?") I was arguing and whining when the telephone rang. Mother went to answer it and came back with a look of great sadness; Mrs. Rogers, she had learned, had had another hemorrhage. So Mother would not be going to the sanitarium after all and I needn't stay with Tess.

By the time I left the house, I was as cross as a bear. I felt awful about the widow's mite and I felt awful for being mean about staying with Tess, for Mrs. Rogers was a kind old lady, in a cozy blue hug-me-tight[6] and an old-fangled boudoir cap, dying here all alone; she was a friend of Grandma's and had lived just down the street from her in Missouri, and all in the world Mrs. Rogers wanted to do was go back home and lie down in her own big bedroom in her own big, high-ceilinged house and have Grandma and other members of the Eastern

6. *hug-me-tight:* bed jacket.

Star come in from time to time to say hello. But they wouldn't let her go home; they were going to kill or cure her. I could not help feeling that my hardness of heart and evil of intention had had a good deal to do with her new crisis; right at the very same minute I had been saying, "Does that old Mrs. Methuselah *always* have to spoil my fun?" the poor wasted thing was probably coughing up her blood and saying to the nurse, "Tell Emily Vanderpool not to mind me, she can run and play."

I had a bad character, I know that, but my badness never gave me half the enjoyment Jack and Stella thought it did. A good deal of the time I wanted to eat lye. I was certainly having no fun now, thinking of Mrs. Rogers and of depriving that poor widow of bread and milk; what if this penniless woman without a husband had a dog to feed, too? Or a baby? And besides, I didn't want to go downtown to steal anything from the ten-cent store; I didn't want to see Lottie Jump again—not really, for I knew in my bones that that girl was trouble with a capital T. And still, in our short meeting she had mesmerized me; I would think about her style of talking and the expert way she had made off with the perfume flask and the cake (how had she carried the cake through the streets without being noticed?) and be bowled over, for the part of me that did not love God was a blackhearted villain. And apart from these considerations, I had some sort of idea that if I did not keep my appointment with Lottie Jump, she would somehow get revenge; she had seemed a girl of purpose. So, revolted and fascinated, brave and lily-livered, I plodded along through the snow in my flopping galoshes up toward the Chautauqua,[7] where the trolley stop was. On my way, I passed Virgil Meade's house; there was not just a snowman, there was a whole snow family in the backyard, and Virgil himself was throwing a stick for his dog. I was delighted to see that he was alone.

Lottie, who was sitting on a bench in the shelter eating a Mr.

---

7. *Chautauqua:* meeting house for *Chautauquas,* educational get-togethers.

Goodbar, looked the same as she had the other time, except that she was wearing an amazing hat. I think I had expected her to have a black handkerchief over the lower part of her face or to be wearing a Jesse James waistcoat. But I had never thought of a hat. It was felt; it was the color of cooked meat; it had some flowers appliquéd on the front of it; it had no brim, but rose straight up to a very considerable height, like a monument. It sat so low on her forehead and it was so tight that it looked, in a way, like part of her.

"How's every little thing, bub?" she said, licking her candy wrapper.

"Fine, Lottie," I said, freshly awed.

A silence fell. I drank some water from the drinking fountain, sat down, fastened my galoshes, and unfastened them again.

"My mother's teeth grow wrong way to," said Lottie, and showed me what she meant: the lower teeth were in front of the upper ones. "That so-called trolley car takes its own sweet time. This town is blah."

To save the honor of my hometown, the trolley came scraping and groaning up the hill just then, its bell clanging with an idiotic frenzy, and ground to a stop. Its broad, proud cowcatcher was filled with dirty snow, in the middle of which rested a tomato can, put there, probably, by somebody who was bored to death and couldn't think of anything else to do—I did a lot of pointless things like that on lonesome Saturday afternoons. It was the custom of this trolley car, a rather mysterious one, to pause at the shelter for five minutes while the conductor, who was either Mr. Jansen or Mr. Peck, depending on whether it was the A.M. run or the P.M., got out and stretched and smoked and spit. Sometimes the passengers got out, too, acting like sightseers whose destination was this sturdy stucco gazebo instead of, as it really was, the Piggly Wiggly or the Nelson Dry. You expected them to take snapshots of the drinking fountain or of the Chautauqua meeting house up on the hill.

And when they all got back in the car, you expected them to exchange intelligent observations on the aborigines and the ruins they had seen.

Today there were no passengers, and as soon as Mr. Peck got out and began staring at the mountains as if he had never seen them before while he made himself a cigarette, Lottie, in her tall hat (was it something like the Inspector's hat in the Katzenjammer Kids?), got into the car, motioning me to follow. I put our nickels in the empty box and joined her on the very last double seat. It was only then that she mapped out the plan for the afternoon, in a low but still insouciant[8] voice. The hat—she did not apologize for it, she simply referred to it as "my hat"—was to be the repository of whatever we stole. In the future, it would be advisable for me to have one like it. (How? Surely it was unique. The flowers, I saw on closer examination, were tulips, but they were blue, and a very unsettling shade of blue.) I was to engage a clerk on one side of the counter, asking her the price of, let's say, a tube of Daggett & Ramsdell vanishing cream, while Lottie would lift a round comb or a barrette or a hairnet or whatever on the other side. Then, at a signal, I would decide against the vanishing cream and would move on to the next counter that she indicated. The signal was interesting; it was to be the raising of her hat from the rear—"like I've got the itch and gotta scratch," she said. I was relieved that I was to have no part in the actual stealing, and I was touched that Lottie, who was going to do all the work, said we would "go halvers" on the take. She asked me if there was anything in particular I wanted—she herself had nothing special in mind and was going to shop around first—and I said I would like some rubber gloves. This request was entirely spontaneous; I had never before in my life thought of rubber gloves in one way or another, but a psychologist—or Judge Bay—might have said that this was most significant and

8. *insouciant* (in-sōō′sē-ənt): carefree.

that I was planning at that moment to go on from petty larceny to bigger game, armed with a weapon on which I wished to leave no fingerprints.

On the way downtown, quite a few people got on the trolley, and they all gave us such peculiar looks that I was chicken-hearted until I realized it must be Lottie's hat they were looking at. No wonder. I kept looking at it myself out of the corner of my eye; it was like a watermelon standing on end. No, it was like a tremendous test tube. On this trip—a slow one, for the trolley pottered through that part of town in a desultory,[9] neighborly way, even going into areas where no one lived—Lottie told me some of the things she had stolen in Muskogee and here in Adams. They included a white satin prayer book (think of it!), Mr. Goodbars by the thousands (she had probably never paid for a Mr. Goodbar in her life), a dinner ring valued at two dollars, a strawberry emery, several cans of corn, some shoelaces, a set of poker chips, countless pencils, four spark plugs ("Pa had this old car, see, and it was broke, so we took 'er to get fixed; I'll build me a radio with 'em sometime—you know? Listen in one them earmuffs to Tulsa?"), a Boy Scout knife, and a Girl Scout folding cup. She made a regular practice of going through the pockets of the coats in the cloakroom every day at recess, but she had never found anything there worth a red cent and was about to give that up. Once, she had taken a gold pencil from a teacher's desk and had got caught—she was sure that this was one of the reasons she was only in the third grade. Of this unjust experience, she said, "The old hoot owl! If I was drivin' in a car on a lonesome stretch and she was settin' beside me, I'd wait till we got to a pile of gravel and then I'd stop and say, 'Git out, Miss Priss.' She'd git out, all right."

Since Lottie was so frank, I was emboldened at last to ask her what she had done with the cake. She faced me with her grin;

9. *desultory* (dĕs'əl-tôr'-ē): aimless.

this grin, in combination with the hat, gave me a surprise from which I have never recovered. "I ate it up," she said. "I went in your garage and sat on your daddy's old tires and ate it. It was pretty good."

There were two ten-cent stores side by side in our town, Kresge's and Woolworth's, and as we walked down the main street toward them, Lottie played with a yo-yo. Since the street was thronged with Christmas shoppers and farmers in for Saturday, this was no ordinary accomplishment; all in all, Lottie Jump was someone to be reckoned with. I cannot say that I was proud to be seen with her; the fact is that I hoped I would not meet anyone I knew, and I thanked my lucky stars that Jack was up in the hills with his dead skunks, because if he had seen her with that lid and that yo-yo, I would never have heard the last of it. But in another way I *was* proud to be with her; in a smaller hemisphere, in one that included only her and me, I was swaggering—I felt like Somebody, marching along beside this lofty Somebody from Oklahoma who was going to hold up the dime store.

There is nothing like Woolworth's at Christmas time. It smells of peanut brittle and terrible chocolate candy, Djer-Kiss talcum powder and Ben Hur perfume—smells sourly of tinsel and waxily of artificial poinsettias. The crowds are made up largely of children and women, with here and there a deliberative old man; the women are buying ribbons and wrappings and Christmas cards, and the children are buying asbestos potholders for their mothers and, for their fathers, suede bookmarks with a burnt-in design that says "A good book is a good friend" or "Souvenir from the Garden of the Gods." It is very noisy. The salesgirls are forever ringing their bells and asking the floorwalker to bring them change for a five; babies in gocarts are screaming as parcels fall on their heads; the women, waving rolls of red tissue paper, try to attract the attention of the harried girl behind the counter. ("Miss! All I want is this one batch of the red. Can't I just give you the dime?" And the girl, beside herself, mottled[10] with vexation, cries back, "Has to be rung up, Moddom, that's the rule.") There is pandemonium at the toy counter, where things are being tested by the customers—wound up, set off, tooted, pounded, made to say "Maaaah-Maaaah!" There is very little gaiety in the scene and, in fact, those baffled old men look as if they were walking over their own dead bodies, but there is an atmosphere of carnival, nevertheless, and as soon as Lottie and I entered the doors of Woolworth's golden-and-vermilion bedlam, I grew giddy and hot—not pleasantly so. The feeling, indeed, was distinctly disagreeable, like the beginning of a stomach upset.

Lottie gave me a nudge and said softly, "Go look at the envelopes. I want some rubber bands."

This counter was relatively uncrowded (the seasonal stationery supplies—the Christmas cards and wrapping paper and stickers—were at a separate counter), and I went around to examine some very beautiful letter paper; it was pale pink and it had a border of roses all around it. The clerk here was a cheerful middle-aged woman wearing an apron, and she was giving all her attention to a seedy old man who could not make up his mind between mucilage and paste. "Take your time, Dad," she said. "Compared to the rest of the girls, I'm on my vacation." The old man, holding a tube in one hand and a bottle in the other, looked at her vaguely and said, "I want it for stamps. Sometimes I write a letter and stamp it and then don't mail it and steam the stamp off. Must have ninety cents' worth of stamps like that." The woman laughed. "I know what you mean," she said. "I get mad and write a letter and then I tear it up." The old man gave her a condescending look and said, "That so? But I don't suppose yours are of a political nature." He bent his gaze again to the choice of adhesives.

This first undertaking was duck soup for Lottie. I did not even have to exchange a word with the woman; I saw Miss

10. *mottled*: blotched (with a rash).

Fagin[11] lift up *that hat* and give me the high sign, and we moved away, she down one aisle and I down the other, now and again catching a glimpse of each other through the throngs. We met at the foot of the second counter, where notions were sold.

"Fun, huh?" said Lottie, and I nodded, although I felt wholly dreary. "I want some crochet hooks," she said. "Price the rickrack."

This time the clerk was adding up her receipts and did not even look at me or at a woman who was angrily and in vain trying to buy a paper of pins. Out went Lottie's scrawny hand, up went her domed chimney. In this way for some time she bagged sitting birds: a tea strainer (there was no one at all at that counter), a box of Mrs. Carpenter's All Purpose Nails, the rubber gloves I had said I wanted, and four packages of mixed seeds. Now you have some idea of the size of Lottie Jump's hat.

I was nervous, not from being her accomplice but from being in this crowd on an empty stomach, and I was getting tired—we had been in the store for at least an hour—and the whole enterprise seemed pointless. There wasn't a thing in her hat I wanted—not even the rubber gloves. But in exact proportion as my spirits descended, Lottie's rose; clearly she had only been target-practicing and now she was moving in for the kill.

We met beside the books of paper dolls, for reconnaissance. "I'm gonna get me a pair of pearl beads," said Lottie. "You go fuss with the hairpins, hear?"

Luck, combined with her skill, would have stayed with Lottie, and her hat would have been a cornucopia by the end of the afternoon if, at the very moment her hand went out for the string of beads, that idiosyncrasy of mine had not struck me full force. I had never known it to come with so few preliminaries;

11. *Miss Fagin:* the narrator is calling Lottie a feminine Fagin, the character in Dickens' *Oliver Twist* who trains boys to be thieves.

probably this was so because I was oppressed by all the masses of bodies poking and pushing me, and all the open mouths breathing in my face. Anyhow, right then, at the crucial time, I *had to be alone.*

I stood staring down at the bone hairpins for a moment, and when the girl behind the counter said, "What kind does Mother want, hon? What color is Mother's hair?" I looked past her and across at Lottie and I said, "Your brother isn't the only one in your family that doesn't have any brains." The clerk astonished, turned to look where I was looking and caught Lottie in the act of lifting up her hat to put the pearls inside. She had unwisely chosen a long strand and was having a little trouble; I had the nasty thought that it looked as if her brains were leaking out.

The clerk, not able to deal with this emergency herself, frantically punched her bell and cried, "Floorwalker! Mr. Bellamy! I've caught a thief!"

Momentarily there was a violent hush—then such a clamor as you have never heard. Bells rang, babies howled, crockery crashed to the floor as people stumbled in their rush to the arena.

Mr. Bellamy, nineteen years old but broad of shoulder and jaw, was instantly standing beside Lottie, holding her arm with one hand while with the other he removed her hat to reveal to the overjoyed audience that incredible array of merchandise. Her hair was wild, her face a mask of innocent bewilderment; Lottie Jump, the scurvy thing, pretended to be deaf and dumb. She pointed at the rubber gloves and then she pointed at me, and Mr. Bellamy, able at last to prove his mettle, said "Aha!" and, still holding Lottie, moved around the counter to me and grabbed *my* arm. He gave the hat to the clerk and asked her kindly to accompany him and his red-handed catch to the manager's office.

I don't know where Lottie is now—whether she is on the

stage or in jail. If her performance after our arrest meant anything, the first is quite as likely as the second. (I never saw her
again, and for all I know she lit out of town that night on a
freight train. Or perhaps her whole family decamped as suddenly as they had arrived; ours was a most transient population.
You can be sure I made no attempt to find her again, and for
months I avoided going anywhere near Arapahoe Creek or
North Hill.) She never said a word but kept making signs with
her fingers, ad-libbing the whole thing. They tested her hearing by shooting off a popgun right in her ear and she never
batted an eyelid.

They called up my father, and he came over from the Safe-
way on the double. I heard very little of what he said because I
was crying so hard, but one thing I did hear him say was,
"Well, young lady, I guess you've seen to it that I'll have to part
company with my good friend Judge Bay." I tried to defend
myself, but it was useless. The manager, Mr. Bellamy, the
clerk, and my father patted Lottie on the shoulder, and the
clerk said, "Poor, afflicted child." For being a poor, afflicted
child, they gave her a bag of hard candy, and she gave them the
most fraudulent smile of gratitude, and slobbered a little, and
shuffled out, holding her empty hat in front of her like a beg-
garman. I hate Lottie Jump to this day, but I have to hand it to
her—she was a genius.

The floorwalker would have liked to see me sentenced to the
reform school for life, I am sure, but the manager said that,
considering this was my first offense, he would let my father
attend to my punishment. The old-maid clerk, who looked
precisely like Emmy Schmalz, clucked her tongue and shook
her head at me. My father hustled me out of the office and out
of the store and into the car and home, muttering the entire
time; now and again I'd hear the words *morals* and *nowadays*.

What's the use of telling you the rest? You know what happened. Daddy, on second thoughts, decided not to hang his

head in front of Judge Bay but to make use of his friendship in this time of need, and he took me to see the scary old curmudgeon at his house. All I remember of that long declamation, during which the Judge sat behind his desk, never taking his eyes off me, was the warning: "I want you to give this a great deal of thought, miss. I want you to search and seek in the innermost corners of your conscience and root out every bit of badness." Oh, *him!* Why, listen, if I'd rooted out all the badness in me, there wouldn't have been anything left of me. My mother cried for days because she had nurtured an outlaw and was ashamed to show her face at the neighborhood store; my father was silent, and he often looked at me. Stella, who was a prig, said, "And to think you did it at *Christmas* time!" As for Jack—well, Jack a couple of times did not know how close he came to seeing glory when I had a butcher knife in my hand. It was Polecat this and Polecat that until I nearly went off my rocker. Tess, of course, didn't know what was going on and asked so many questions that finally I told her to go to Helen Hunt Jackson[12] in a savage tone of voice.

Good old Muff.

It is not true that you don't learn by experience. At any rate, I did that time. I began immediately to have two or three friends at a time—to be sure, because of the stigma on me, they were by no means the elite of Carlyle Hill Grade—and never again when that terrible need to be alone arose did I let fly. I would say, instead, "I've got a headache. I'll have to go home and take an aspirin," or "Gosh all hemlocks, I forgot—I've got to go to the dentist."

After the scandal died down, I got into the Camp Fire Girls. It was through pull, of course, since Stella had been a respected member for two years and my mother was a friend of the leader. But it turned out all right. Even Muff did not miss our periods of companionship, because about that time she grew up and started having literally millions of kittens.

---

12. Helen Hunt Jackson is the author of a popular love story called **Ramona**.

The Facts of the Story

Write answers to the following questions. Answers may be one word or a phrase or a sentence. You can probably answer all the questions without rereading the story, but look back if you wish.

1. Whenever Emily feels a strong need "to be alone," she achieves her goal by _____.

2. When Emily's friends have left her, her only companion is _____.

3. Emily says Lottie's "only recreation and her only gift" is, and always has been, _____.

4. Why is Emily so attracted to Lottie and willing to go along with her schemes?

5. Does Emily take to stealing easily, or does she feel guilty about it?

6. Lottie puts what she steals in Woolworth's into her_____.

7. How does Lottie get caught in the act at Woolworth's?

8. Lottie escapes punishment by pretending _____.

9. As a result of this experience with Lottie, Emily learns to control her _____.

10. How is Emily's "badness" different from Lottie's?

The Art of the Storyteller

Tone

The *tone* of a story or an article is the attitude the writer takes toward the subject. The tone of "Bad Characters," as we have seen, is humorous. The events of the story are not, in themselves, comic, but Stafford takes a humorous view of them.

A writer may have a number of different attitudes toward different subjects. In an article about crime in our city streets, a writer might take a bitter or an angry tone. A writer expressing disapproval of the vast sums paid to our professional athletes might take a sarcastic tone, referring to the poor, underpaid prizefighter who makes a million in one bout.

Tone is revealed by the writer's style, or manner of expression, and by the words used. The tone of "Bad Characters" is not only humorous, but also light and informal.

The tone of a piece of writing may be humorous, sarcastic, satirical (poking fun), critical, sentimental, romantic, frivolous, bitter, angry, solemn, and so on. As an intelligent reader, you must recognize the tone of a piece of writing, or you may misunderstand the whole point of a story or an article.

Look back at "All Summer in a Day" (page 248) and describe the tone used there.

A Humorous Style

Most readers agree that Jean Stafford has a sense of humor. She creates humor not through the events in the story, which are not in themselves very funny, but by her *style*—by her particular way of telling the story. Two aspects of Stafford's style that make us laugh are her comic descriptions and her *exaggerations,* or overstatements.

Comic Description

She was not only an ill-natured cat, she was also badly dressed. She was a calico, and the distribution of her colors was a mess; she looked as if she had been left out in the rain and her paint had run. She had a Roman nose as the result of some early injury, her tail was skinny, she had a perfectly venomous look in her eye. My family said—my family discriminated against me—that I was much closer kin to Muff than I was to any of them.

Comic Exaggeration

To tease me into a tantrum, my brother Jack and my sister Stella often called me Kitty instead of Emily. Little Tess did not dare, because she knew I'd chloroform her if she did.

Leaf through the story and find other descriptions and exaggerations that make this a comical story.

Composition

Writing a Story

Using an actual experience or a made-up one, write a story of your own which could be entitled "Bad Characters." Of course, you could be the Lottie Jump of your story, who gets someone else into trouble, or you could be the Emily type, who is given a taste of "badness" by another character. As every storyteller knows, you can "improve" on a true story by using your imagination to add some events that did not actually happen. Your story need not be funny, but if you write like Jean Stafford, it probably will be. To create humor, try the methods she uses.

Write between 200 and 300 words.

Jean Stafford

Born in California, Jean Stafford (1915-1979) grew up in Colorado, the setting of many of her stories, including "Bad Characters." Her mother ran a boarding house there; her father spent his time writing unsuccessful Westerns. She won a scholarship, graduated from Colorado University, and spent her adult life in the East, in Boston and New York. Many of Stafford's stories appeared in *The New Yorker* magazine. Her *Collected Stories* won the Pulitzer Price for fiction in 1970.

The Animals' Fair

JAMES GOULD COZZENS

If you enjoyed "Bad Characters," Jean Stafford's story of how Lottie Jump, the shoplifter, almost led her new and innocent friend into a life of crime, you will enjoy "The Animals' Fair." There are interesting similarities between the two stories. In fact, the title "Bad Characters" would apply as well to Cozzens' story as it does to Stafford's.

"The Animals' Fair" is also the title of an old song, which you may know:

> *I went to the animal fair,*
> *The birds and the beasts were there,*
> *The big baboon, by the light of the moon,*
> *Was combing his auburn hair.*
> *The monkey, he got drunk,*
> *And sat on the elephant's trunk.*
> *The elephant sneezed and fell on his knees*
> *And what became of the monk, the monk,*
> *And what became of the monk?*

As you will see, an important character in "The Animals' Fair" is a teacher named Miss Monk.

Miss Monk had handsome dark brown eyes. Although she was nothing like as old as that, her hair was almost entirely white. This gave her face a curious, clean, tanned appearance. She had a light graceful figure, and though she could not have been called pretty, she was a pleasant person to look at. Moreover, she and I were old friends, for I was one of the members of the eighth grade who, five years earlier, had been in the third grade when Miss Monk was teaching that. I knew, because she had told me so, that she had to rely a lot on old academy boys like myself, and I was always glad to help her out.

On the day, a couple of weeks after school opened this fall, Hicksey first appeared at the academy, Miss Monk glanced over the class at recess and signaled to me. I stopped at her desk and she said, "John, this is Emerson Hicks. I want you to show Emerson around and help him to feel at home."

As it was meant to, this gave me a feeling of importance and responsibility, which I greatly enjoyed. I said, "Yes, Miss Monk." Also, it gave me a good look at Emerson Hicks. I had been trying to get one ever since I raced in, about five seconds late, and noticed only when I was past him that somebody new had the desk in the second row heretofore empty. I had spent a good deal of time speculating on the back of the newcomer's head—which was small, and a dusty, silvery blond. His hair, I observed now, had a kind of crinkly ripple or wave in it. Emerson Hicks's nose and cheeks were covered with small pale freckles, which made his face much the same dusty tone as his head. His eyes were a very bright, arresting blue. I decided that he was all right, and, since he was rather small, that I could certainly lick him. Not that I had any intention of trying, nor that I liked fighting, but I was, as we said, eleven going on twelve, and the atavistic[1] savage, unsubdued, wisely took notes for war in time of peace. I said, "Oh, hello." I put out my hand a little uncertainly and, bumping his, gave it as hard a grip as I could.

What Emerson Hicks thought at first glance I shall never know. I suspect, for he was a shrewd little boy, that he sized me up at once as promising material. It isn't likely that he named or clearly classified such points, but he doubtless took in the fact that I was naturally bossy and vain; that I had not been around much; that under my officious manner I was timid and uncertain. Thus reassured, he squeezed my hand back, entirely at ease. We went out of the classroom, down the wide, echoing stairs, which were lined on one side with twenty-eight large engravings of the Presidents of the United States, with their signatures in facsimile under each. I could see Emerson Hicks looking at them; not with interest, exactly, but with an automatic attention, not missing anything. Neither of us had said a word until we reached the main hall. He suddenly asked then: "What was her name?"

When I realized what he was talking about, I answered, "Oh, Miss Monk."

Emerson Hicks's blue eyes rested on me with a shining pleasure. "The elephant sneezed," he whispered in a low sing-song voice, "and fell on his knees, and what became of the monk, the monk—" He giggled. Seeing me staring at him with perplexed suspicion, he added, "It's a song. I thought everybody knew that. I'll teach it to you."

"All right," I answered, though not with enthusiasm, for I didn't think the song made any sense, and the obvious jibe at Miss Monk failed to strike me as funny.

The academy was one of those advanced and enlightened schools with methods then fairly new. I suppose I was living

---

1. *atavistic:* primitive.

proof of one form of their success; for, though most of their theories greatly encouraged my strong inclination to waste my time and to do only that part of my work which I could do with little or no effort, I did not hate school, and it had never crossed my mind that a teacher was my natural enemy.

Not liking Emerson Hicks very well, I said, "Well, what do you want to see? That's the fourth grade in there. And the fifth grade over there. And down here is the reception room and Mr. Apgar's office. At the end, that opens onto the gallery in the gymnasium; and—"

"I know," Emerson Hicks said. There had been a brief flicker of surprise or curiosity in his glance. He smiled in a very friendly and engaging way and dropped the subject of Miss Monk. "I saw the gymnasium," he said. "Come on. Let's go outside."

We came out on the wide sandstone steps and he stood a moment, sniffing the sharp October air, considering the groups playing in the big yard. The academy was a massive building of red brick, here and there overgrown with ivy. It stood on a sloping plot of ground, a couple of acres of banked lawn hedged with high privet in front and up on the side. Behind, it backed against a higher street, with deep areaways bridged by railed concrete entries to doors on the second floor. Emerson Hicks looked at all this carefully. Then he said, "Let's go to that store at the corner."

"No, we can't," I answered. "We aren't allowed to leave the grounds at recess."

"It would be a cinch," he said. "You could go through there and out along the hedge without them seeing you. What do they do to you if you do?"

"Oh, I don't know," I responded. "You might get sent to Mr. Apgar."

"What's he do to you?"

"Plenty," I said, though the truth was I did not know. I regarded Mr. Apgar with awe. He was a large, rather tall and stately man. His broad mild face was crowned by a dense high pompadour of well-combed black hair. His manner of speaking was slow and impressive. Monday mornings the school started the week with an assembly, and Mr. Apgar would come into the auditorium wearing what I later learned was a Master of Arts gown. At the time it impressed me all the more, for I could not imagine what it was. In a sober voice he read the part from the eighth chapter of Proverbs about knowledge rather than choice gold. Then he coughed and made a few solemn announcements. The only other glimpses I got of him were accidental—momentarily, through an open door, I might see him sitting at the extensive polished desk in his office, looking over papers which his secretary, Miss Tyrrell, was handing to him. Sometimes, effacing myself as much as possible, I would pass him in the halls. I suppose I must have been shown to him when I first came to the academy, but I couldn't remember that we had ever exchanged a word.

Emerson Hicks said, "Listen—at one school where I went once, the principal would wallop you with a stick so you couldn't sit down for a week." What he had seen of the academy doubtless satisfied him that no such barbarities were likely to be practiced here. "Come on," he said. "We should worry!"

He had judged me very well. In the face of his airy tone and manner, I did not see how I could refuse without, in the humiliating presence of a person not so big as I was, reflecting injuriously on my courage and spirit. "All right," I said, "I'm certainly not worried if you're not."

We got back before the bell—safely, I decided, to my relief, as we went in the side entry. However, when I was in my seat, with the period started, I looked to Miss Monk and began to wonder. I could very soon see that all was not well. Soon after I entered, Miss Monk eyed me gravely a moment. After that she never looked in my direction until the last bell rang. She beckoned to me then. "Wait," she told me, "I want to speak to you."

I attempted an expression of innocent wonder, but it was poorly simulated, for I could feel in my pocket the lump made by the bag of jelly beans. Emerson Hicks had munificently bought two, one for him and one for me.

From where I sat, I had been able to see Emerson, with a highly accomplished technique, eating his. After Miss Monk's first disturbing glance, I had decided to leave mine untouched; not only because my appetite for them had departed, but because, when I feared that I had been caught doing something I ought not to do, it was an idea of mine that I could better matters by behaving in all other respects with ostentatious[2] virtue.

Miss Monk said, "Why did you take Emerson down to the store? It's not a bit like you, John. I've always said to myself: 'I know John is a boy I can trust.' Don't you see how it makes me feel when you deliberately—"

The outcome was that I lost my privilege of being the one to collect homework papers when they were called for, and got down to the lunchroom so late that the only dessert left was tapioca. Though my sense of self-importance was dashed by the loss of my informal office, and I was genuinely aggrieved about the tapioca, I did not feel that I had been unjustly treated. I merely repented the folly of falling in with Emerson Hicks's suggestion.

When I discovered that he had got through his own lunch without waiting, or showing any interest in my fate, I was, in addition, indignant and offended. "All right for him," I told myself somberly while I took a tray and collected my food. While I ate I was busy imagining various scenes and conversational exchanges in which I injured or tellingly humiliated him. I was too absorbed to notice when Elizabeth Jones, a large, strong girl from my class, paused in front of me on her way out. She got my attention by giving my head a shove. I started half up in anger, but she skipped heavily aside, jeering,

2. *ostentatious* (ŏs′tĕn-tā′shəs): showy.

"Well, smarty! You thought nobody saw you. Miss Monk saw you from the corner window all the time."

She gave me no time to make a response, and, indeed, I could not think of any to make. When I wandered glumly out into the hall afterward, almost the first person I saw was Emerson Hicks. I met him with a hostile look. He winked at me. "Come on," he whispered.

I said indignantly, "Like fun! I—"

From his pocket he produced an object the color of gun metal. I got only a glimpse of it, but I was able to recognize a water pistol of an expensive and desirable type.

"You'd better not shoot that around here," I said. "You'd better not take it into class. If Miss Monk spots it you'll have to hand it in. And you won't get it back either."

"Come on," he said, "we'll go down to the washroom and fill it."

I tagged along unwillingly. While he was immersing the pistol in a basin, letting it suck up water, he said, "How'd she catch you?" His tone was sympathetic but casual, as though I, too, were hardened to the fortunes of war, and it would take more than that to down me.

Enjoying this novel view of myself, I shrugged and said, "Oh, Elizabeth Jones snitched on me, I guess."

"Which one is she?" he said, lifting the water pistol from the basin and squinting down the barrel. "The big fat lummox?"

I nodded, interested in his pistol. "We'll get her for that," he said, with assurance. He held the pistol out to me. "Want to try it?" he asked generously.

As I had foretold, before school was out Miss Monk had the pistol. Aiming under his desk, Hicksey—he had already told me that he was to be called that; that only girls, sissies, and teachers called him Emerson—picked a moment when Elizabeth Jones was standing to recite to drive the thin jet of water against the back of her ankle where the top of her buttoned shoe met her brown lisle stocking. It made her yell, all right, and the shot was a remarkable one, but it was obvious who did it.

Hicksey gave up his weapon with composure, and Miss Monk kept him afterward to explain that at the academy we didn't do things like that. She probably thought Emerson just didn't understand, especially after I had set him such a bad example in the morning. I was, naturally, not present at the interview, but I'm sure that Hicksey put on a good show—not of the amateur, pretending-he-hadn't-done-anything sort, but a subtler, embarrassed business of its being all just a foolish impulse, for which he was really sorry. He shouldn't have done it, and he didn't try to excuse himself, but you could see he meant no actual harm, and he was touched and much impressed by what was being said to him, for he looked you straight in the eye, like the manly little fellow he was—somewhat shamefaced, yet in brave agreement. I'm sure Miss Monk accepted it all and was pleased with his attitude. For myself, I mistook the whole matter for simple bad judgment—just throwing away a good water pistol. To Hicksey it must have been a necessary reconnaissance in force, a demonstration to make Miss Monk develop her strength and position.

I duly waited to hear how this came out, but, waiting, I got into a game, and so missed Hicksey. The next day he was cordial enough, only I soon found that he was making friends with several other boys. This left him little time for me. He had realized that though I was bigger than he was, there were boys in the class bigger than I was, or, if no bigger, nonetheless more than a match for me. Of course, he meant to find out if one of them would make a more useful best friend.

When he decided not, as he did suddenly about two weeks later, it must have been because whatever else he was offered, he had found no one so amenable and easily impressed. I had been offended by his neglect and was cool toward him. That made no difference. Coming up from the gymnasium period one afternoon, he got himself into line next to me, gave me one of his winks. He put his hand to his mouth and spit out a wad of gum. When the file of girls came from their locker rooms and we were moving in the constricted stairs from the basketball floor, I saw him eyeing Elizabeth Jones. By crowding on the way up, he got almost abreast of her. At the dark turn he made an effort to clap the wad of gum into her hair.

I wished Elizabeth Jones all possible bad luck. I appreciated the friendly gesture on Hicksey's part. Yet I would have dissuaded him if he had let me see what he was planning to do before he did it. I knew Elizabeth Jones. Girl or no girl, she was hefty, and wouldn't take it lying down.

As it proved, Elizabeth was also quick. Exactly what happened was lost in the shadow, but some intuition must have warned her. She wheeled, ducking her head aside, and caught Hicksey by the wrist. She bumped him so suddenly and hard against the wall that she was able to force his hand up before he recovered, and so to get the gum into Hicksey's own hair. With her other hand she smacked him across the cheek.

It created only an instant's disturbance. Both lines were jostled a little, but they kept moving. Not many people had really seen it, though I heard Katherine Boyd, her small pretty face wrinkled with mirth, giggle, "Serves you right!"

Hicksey was scarlet, not only at his failure but at the appalling disgrace of learning, as he must have, that Elizabeth Jones was twice as strong as he was. He could not speak for a moment. Then he muttered to me, "Gee, I can't hit a girl back, can I?" implying hopefully that all that saved her was his chivalry and forbearance. A boy named Geoffrey Allen, behind me, said eagerly, "What'd she do?"

Hicksey muttered something more, dropped out, and ran down to the washroom. We were into class then, and with much presence of mind, I went straight to Miss Monk. I said that Emerson had to be excused a moment; so no formal notice was taken when he entered. I observed, as he sat down, that he had been obliged to cut hair off the side of his head to get the gum out. Elizabeth Jones, at Miss Monk's desk with some papers, also saw it. She gave Hicksey a derisive grin, turned, and started jauntily up the aisle, still grinning.

Hicksey had gazed back at her with miraculous blandness, as though he wondered what on earth she meant, so, perhaps, I ought to have realized that he had the situation well in hand. Instead, angry and indignant—for I had already forgotten Hicksey's neglect and my coolness—I saw a possible opportunity to fix Elizabeth. I didn't seriously hope for much, but, anyway, I shot my left leg out. As sometimes happens, unconsidered impulse served better than any careful plan. Still looking at Hicksey, Elizabeth Jones walked directly into the obstruction. Her other foot, which she had been lifting to complete the interrupted step, came forward fast in automatic reflex to save her balance. That bumped my leg, too, so she fell forward, flat in the aisle.

To any eighth grade, such a tripping is one of the supreme comic spectacles. No one who saw it could help laughing. I had to laugh myself, but I got out no more than a quick giggle. Scrambling up, Elizabeth turned in main fury, like an Amazon, on me. I slid from my seat with a hasty side motion, putting the desk between us, poised ready for any emergencies. Perhaps fortunately for me, none arose. Elizabeth Jones had to realize that she was hurt. Her knee and elbow had been banged hard enough to bring her up wincing. The fight went out of her and she burst abruptly into furious, painful tears.

This produced an appalled hush.

"Excuse me," I stammered, not without sincerity, for though I had intended to trip her, I hadn't planned on anything so thorough and spectacular.

As Miss Monk had told Hicksey, at the academy, tricks of this kind and roughhousing in general were not common in class. As far as she knew, they were not much in my line anyway. For an instant she may have imagined that it was really an accident; but when she heard my "Excuse me," of course, she knew it wasn't. She came down the aisle to see how badly Elizabeth was hurt. Then she motioned to Katherine Boyd, who stood up with earnest alacrity,[3] and the three of them went into the hall.

"Gee. I never meant—" I began in abashed[4] general defense. A sharp-eyed, dark-haired girl named Mabel Parsons, whom I deeply disliked, said contemptuously, "Oh, you! You think you're so clever!"

Abashed, I looked toward Emerson Hicks. He was sitting calmly, without expression, and for an instant I thought he had turned against me too. Then, casually, he let an eyelid drop in his unmistakable wink. Setting both elbows on the desk, he put his hands together and shook them warmly.

"Oh, tell it to Sweeney!" I said to Mabel Parsons, for I had experienced one of my mercurial lifts in spirit and now saw the episode as a good job, well done. I sat down at my desk and waited defiantly.

Miss Monk came back soon. She was alone, which meant that Elizabeth had gone down to the nurse with Katherine Boyd, but it also meant that she was not hurt seriously, or Miss Monk would have gone down with her. I had been ready to be dealt with at once, and perhaps Miss Monk saw that I was, and deliberately let me wait. She simply took up the lesson and went on with it. Elizabeth Jones duly returned with some adhesive tape around her knee under the stocking and her arm stained with arnica, but nothing was said. By three o'clock, when the last bell rang and school was over, I no longer felt very defiant. By half past three I felt about the way I deserved to.

Against one wall in Miss Tyrrell's office there was a long wooden settee. Hicksey and I sat on it. I had been surprised to see Hicksey kept after school too. Hicksey had been a good deal

3. *alacrity:* eager readiness.
4. *abashed:* ashamed.

more than surprised. He was injured and outraged. It was easy to guess that Elizabeth—or Katherine Boyd, more likely—had told about the chewing gum as a possible reason for my act, and Hicksey might reasonably have blamed them, or even me. Instead, though he came docilely, it was obvious that he held Miss Monk responsible. I could see his blue eyes fixed, narrow and reflective, on her back as she led us downstairs.

However angry he may have felt, Hicksey had seated himself on the bench with quiet dignity. I think he had no nerves. As for me, I took no comfort from his company. My stomach, a large distressing lump, quaked and thrilled, making it hard for me to breathe the thin and tasteless air. From Mr. Apgar's office beyond kept coming the sounds of prolonged conversation. A good deal louder, a voice in my own head repeated knowingly, "Now you're going to get it. Now you're going to get it." I stared, while my sensations grew more and more intolerable, at the bookcase against the opposite wall. It had glass doors and was filled with bound volumes of some educational journal. On top was a bust marked Cicero. In despair I studied the bust, until I noticed suddenly that someone had sometime given it a mustache, either in ink or crayon. The mustache had been rubbed off, but not entirely. With a kind of relief, I uttered an unplanned feeble giggle.

This brought me to Hicksey's attention. He had hitched himself along the bench until he was close to the door. He hissed now, "Shut up, will you? Can't you see I'm listening?" Apparently he misinterpreted my sickly laugh, for he added, "And look serious, you sap! Do you want to make him mad?"

Steps sounded and the door was drawn open. Hicksey had moved like magic on the bench, back toward me, composing his face into a meek, injured expression. Miss Monk came out and did not look at us. On her heels was Miss Tyrrell, who eyed us coldly and said only, "Go in now."

Hicksey stood up. His air was so solemn and guileless that he gave me a quite a shock when, reaching the door, he hit me inconspicuously in the ribs with his elbow. Under his breath, he said, "You keep your trap shut!"

Mr. Apgar had been standing by the large window behind his desk, looking out at the afternoon sunlight on the playground. He turned with impressive deliberation. I could see Hicksey looking right back at him, but my own eyes fell immediately, for his sober brown ones made me wish I could get under something. When he said in his measured voice, "John, you may close the door," I stood like an idiot, unable to move. There was an awful silence.

"The door," Mr. Apgar said, still more deeply and carefully, "behind you." I turned, bumped into it, and somehow got it shut.

"Thank you," he said, with a ponderous politeness which set me shaking worse than ever. "Now you may sit down. Both of you."

Things have happened since which frightened me badly, and with much better reason, but I don't think I was ever again frightened to the degree I reached then. Mr. Apgar had begun to speak in his Monday-morning voice. I literally did not hear a word he was saying. The light from the window behind him was in my face and made it hard to see him clearly. Outside, the declining sunlight shone reddish on some bare treetops, and I tried to look at them instead of him. It was his voice finally stopping which startled me into partial awareness. After a little while, I realized that he had asked me a question. Having no idea what it was, I moved my head in a motion meant to combine yes and no. Mr. Apgar said then, "What about you, Emerson? Have you anything you want to say?"

I looked at Hicksey with a vague remote curiosity. His face had pinkened to what looked like embarrassment. When he spoke, his voice was distressed and low. "Well, gee, Mr. Apgar, only one thing—" He stopped as though he had thought better of it. "No, sir," he said.

"Come," said Mr. Apgar, not unkindly, "if you have something to say in your defense, you owe it to yourself to say it. I want to hear it. That's the only way we can understand each other."

Hicksey seemed to be struggling with himself. Then, with an obvious brave resolve, he put his chin up as though he were facing a firing squad and intended his words to be a last statement. "Well, Mr. Apgar," he said, "it's just Miss Monk, I guess. Miss Monk always playing favorites, I mean. We don't think it's fair." He made a sound something like a gulp, but restrained himself stoically. "If she doesn't happen to like you—"

"Now, now," said Mr. Apgar gently, "when you try to put chewing gum in a girl's hair, you are not making yourself very likable. No one likes a boy who behaves that way."

On Hicksey's face spread an expression of alarm and anguish. Noting it, Mr. Apgar said, "Or haven't I understood you, Emerson? What did you mean?"

Hicksey composed himself. He started to mutter, but his voice cleared suddenly and he proved to be saying, "—wasn't trying to get out of anything. I just mean, why we did it. Sort of seeing Elizabeth Jones getting away with things all the time, I guess it made us sore. And then—well, like before we knew it—I didn't say it was any excuse or anything—"

"I see," said Mr. Apgar. He sat silent, his large sober face turned steadily on Hicksey, while Hicksey, red but resolute, met his eye. "I see," he repeated at last. "Of course, you're right. That is no valid excuse. But I am glad that you explained how you felt. All of us sometimes feel impulses of anger or jealousy. What we must do is learn to control them." He took up a paper knife from his desk and looked at it a moment. He put it down then, arose, and, ignoring us, stood gazing out the window a little while. When he turned around he said, "Now, I think we will all forget about this. I feel that you are both sorry. That is the principal thing. Tomorrow I want each of you to go to Elizabeth Jones and apologize to her for your ungentlemanly conduct. John, I want you to apologize to Miss Monk for disturbing the class." He paused. Then he said, "I think that will be all." He reached and pressed a button on his desk. Miss Tyrrell opened the door.

"Good night, boys," he said, inclining his head.

"Good night, sir," we said, or, rather, Hicksey did. I made a kind of croak. We turned and stiffly we walked past Miss Tyrrell to the outer door. The hall was deep in late-afternoon shadows. There was no one in sight, and no sound in the big building but the bump and shuffle made by Dennis, the janitor, or one of his assistants, while they swept some classroom.

"Jimminy crickets!" whistled Hicksey softly. He gave an exultant skip, and suddenly, with a skill and ease I had to admire, turned a cartwheel down the twilit hall. "You'd better not go doing stunts," I told him, "not in the building."

A fountain pen had dropped clattering out of his pocket in the process and now he returned to pick that up.

"Oh, you kid!" he said, giving me a push.

My various emotional ups and downs had left me shaky and irritable. "Quit it!" I cried. "What's so wonderful?"

"Didn't you get it?" he asked, pausing.

"Get what?"

"Brains he has nix!" said Hicksey.

"I suppose you know a lot," I answered, sullen.

"Well, she'd better go easy, see? I can fix her, all right. At one school I went to once, I got a teacher who picked on me fired, see?"

"Yes, you did!" I said. "Just because we happened to get away with it this time, don't think—"

"We?" said Hicksey. "You didn't get away with anything. You were so scared you—"

"Oh, was I?" I said. I was suddenly impelled to punch him.

No doubt it hurt, for his cheekbone stung my knuckles. "You big slob!" he cried. "Don't you hit me!" I started for him again, and he retreated. "All right," he said, his tone changing entirely, "I take it back. I'll show you whether you're scared or not. Come on."

I stood at the bottom of the stairs, looking up at him suspiciously, for already, by the invitation, he had shown me whether I was scared or not. I was. His jubilant conspiratorial friendliness, replacing so suddenly his outraged yell, made me feel approximately the way a flyer who has just crashed must feel when, crawling, by a miracle, uninjured from the wreckage, he looks at a new plane which, for his soul's good, he is advised to take up right away.

"Where are you going?" I asked feebly.

"Come on. We aren't going to let her get away with sending us to the principal. We'll fix her an ink bomb."

"A what?" I said.

"Say, don't you know anything?" said Hicksey. "You fix an ink bottle in her desk, so when she opens the drawer it shoots all over."

"She'll think right away we did it," I said gloomily, for, although I abhorred the whole idea, I knew, with a sort of sad fatality, that I was going to embark on it.

"Let her think!" said Hicksey. "When I fix something, believe me, she can think all she wants, but she can't prove anything. We'll show her she'd better leave us alone."

As I had foreseen, I went, lagging a little, upstairs after him. The still twilight of the swept and tidied classroom, the clean blackboards still damp from washing, gave me an ominous sense of being where I ought not to be. "No," I said faintly, "I'm not going to do it."

"You don't have to," Hicksey whispered, "if you'll just please give me your ink bottle. And look in my desk and get some thumbtacks and some big rubber bands, not the little ones." He watched me while I collected these things. "There's nothing to be scared of," he said impatiently. "There's no one on this floor." He opened the top drawer of Miss Monk's desk carefully. "Look," he said. "See what you do?"

"No," I said. I put the things down and moved away a little. "You go on and do it if you want to. I've done all I'm going to."

Hicksey looked pained. "Did I ask you to?" he said. "I'm not scared. I'll do it. I've done it hundreds of times. I never got caught yet. You can bet your life I won't get caught this time." I don't know whether his choice of pronoun was conscious or unconscious, but, in any event, I was far too agitated for it to make an impression on me.

I was still agitated the following morning. When the weather was good I rode my bicycle to school, and usually I liked to arrive early, so that there would be plenty of time to fool around before class; but that morning I put off getting there as long as I possibly could. I think I was hoping that Miss Monk would try that drawer of Hicksey's and get the whole thing over before I appeared. This, it seemed to me, might somehow show that I didn't have anything to do with it.

I wasted what time I could getting to school and when I got there, after I had locked my bicycle in the long rack in the basement hall, I gave it a thorough, needless tightening-up until the first bell rang. After that I washed my hands, which didn't leave any spare time. I raced upstairs. I had gained the turn of the second flight, still at full speed, when I saw, to my consternation, Mr. Apgar's monumental, somberly clad figure moving with precise dignity around the corner and into the eighth-grade classroom.

This brought me up, stumbling, and I scraped my shin on the next step. Clasping the injury in anguish, I was not too occupied to jump to alarming conclusions—somebody had seen us last night; Mr. Apgar had reconsidered his decision to do nothing about yesterday's matter; the so-called ink bomb had gone off and Miss Monk had sent for Mr. Apgar to question the class. I climbed the last few steps numbly, as though my feet and even my sore shin belonged to somebody else. I came quaking into the room.

To my vast relief, everything seemed to be in order. Miss Monk was standing by her desk with that immaculate, gracefully erect and alert air which so became her, speaking calmly to Mr. Apgar, who bulked over her, inclining his torso a little in elephantine courtliness. Trying not to see Hicksey, I walked by with elaborate casualness, went past my seat on up the aisle until I got to Elizabeth Jones's desk. Not without a feeling of virtue, I looked her detestable large round face almost in the eyes, and said, "Sorry I tripped you yesterday. I beg your pardon." As I was praying it would, the second bell rang then and I was able to conclude the ceremony with a conscientious dash back to my seat.

Miss Monk said, "Quiet, please. Mr. Apgar has a few words to say to you about conduct in the library," I got in a deep grateful breath and relaxed, for I had not been in the library for weeks. I looked down, but there was a pause, and so I looked up. I was in time to see Mr. Apgar apparently ask Miss Monk for something. She nodded, and, horrified, I saw her put a hand toward the desk drawer.

Though I had not dared or cared to look at Hicksey before, I did look at him now, stricken. For an instant Hicksey seemed perfectly placid, bright-faced, sitting straight in his seat, but, while I watched, the freckles started suddenly out on his cheeks. He had gone white. Looking where he looked, I saw the drawer must have stuck quite hard. Mr. Apgar, moving around to that side, said, "Allow me," in his majestic voice. He took the knob and gave it a powerful tug.

I suppose Hicksey's self-control had never been more magnificent. He, after all, knew what was going to happen. I almost yelled myself, though I had expected little more than an overturned ink bottle. Doubtless Mr. Apgar's powerful pull greatly improved the effect. The drawer yielded suddenly. Into the air, perhaps three feet above the level of the desk, the uncorked bottle sprang, spinning a wide gush of ink far and wide, over the desk, floor, and Mr. Apgar.

In the room arose a sound like one tremendous drawn breath, and there was total silence. Though in itself the drenching of an unwary person with ink was certainly funny enough, we were not amused. We simply stared in horror, as though we expected a thunderclap or the heavens to fall.

On Mr. Apgar dignity's obligations rested easily. He took a handkerchief from his breast pocket and wiped away the ink dripping from his chin. In a mild and measured voice, as though nothing had happened, he said to Miss Monk, "I must ask you to excuse me for a few minutes." Without any sign of haste, he walked to the door and disappeared.

Miss Monk had been standing frozen, not, I suppose, with quite our horrified sense of lese majesty,[5] but with shock enough. It must have been hard for her to believe that such a thing could actually happen in a class of hers. To remain, as she did, perfectly self-possessed, was a feat. The phrase I vaguely associated with her appearance and manner I had heard my elders use. It was: cool as a cucumber.

First of all, she looked at the desk and floor, and then at the empty ink bottle, which had rolled to one side. Raising her eyes, she looked at us, her gaze traveling from face to face. In the end it settled on a boy sitting in the first row just in front of Hicksey. "Carl," she said quietly, "go down and find Dennis, please. I want him to clean up." She walked around to the front of her desk. "I am going to ask if anyone knows anything about this," she said. "Before I find out for myself, whoever did it has a chance to tell me. I strongly advise him to." I saw the flicker of Hicksey's eyes shot guardedly in my direction, but no one moved and no one spoke.

5. *lese majesty* (lēz maj'ĭs-tē): offense against authority (literally, a crime against the king).

"Very well," Miss Monk said. "I know of two boys who were in the building late yesterday. I wonder if either of them knows anything about it?" She gave me a long steady look and then said suddenly, "Emerson, did you come up here after you left Mr. Apgar's office?"

Hicksey's color had got a good deal better. He gave a start of surprise and said, "No, Miss Monk."

"You're quite sure about that?"

Hicksey assumed an injured look. "Yes, Miss Monk."

"You and John left the building as soon as Mr. Apgar let you go?"

Hicksey opened his mouth and then closed it. "Sure, I guess so," he stammered.

"Either you did or you didn't," said Miss Monk. "You don't have to guess."

Hicksey remained silent.

"Emerson," said Miss Monk, "you must answer my question."

"Well, all I know is, we came out, and then we had a kind of argument. And then I went home."

"What did you argue about?"

"Oh, nothing. John had something he wanted me to do, and I didn't want to. He hit me and—" Hicksey raised a hand and touched his cheek. There was, sure enough, a slight red mark below the eye.

"What were you arguing about?" Miss Monk repeated.

Hicksey had looked down at his hands, frowning. "I won't tell you," he muttered.

A kind of icy paralysis had come over me. The sense of fury and outrage, swelling in me, made me want to shriek, "You're a liar!" but I wasn't able to utter a sound. Hicksey shot me a second sidelong glance, and I suppose my imbecile appearance of stupor and guilt more than satisfied him. "I'm not going to tell you," he said in a low, defiant voice. "You can't make me."

"I don't think it will be necessary," Miss Monk said. "Let me see your ink bottle, please."

At the words, I gave myself up for lost. Even I could see that when it came my turn to produce mine, I was simply caught, that Hicksey had me hopelessly entangled. The only thing not clear to me was Miss Monk's attitude, what she was waiting for, why she didn't ask everyone to produce his ink bottle then and there. This must have puzzled Hicksey too. His expression never changed, but there was a slight tightening and flaring of his nostrils, as though he scented danger. He waited a moment, no doubt thinking, and then he said sullenly, "Why don't you ask John for his bottle?"

"I want to see yours."

Hicksey still hesitated. I have seen that hesitation since. It is the one affected by a professional magician who has allowed his audience to imagine they have seen through his trick—in fact, to be sure that they have caught him—before he dumbfounds them by showing that the hat is perfectly empty. Hicksey raised his desk lid with a reluctant movement. He put his hands in. There was a moment's delay, and suddenly he raised the desk lid higher, turning over books and papers.

"Haven't you got it, Emerson?" said Miss Monk calmly.

"Gee, I don't know what happened to it," he began. He gave a wild look around, his composure dissolving. "Somebody took it!" he cried. "Somebody took it to make them think I did it!" He turned his congested[6] face toward me. "And I know who!" he shrilled. He must have been casting about in his mind, frantic, for some clue as to how I had made the change. I suppose he could not find one, since everything had been done at his direction, under his eyes. "John was up here!" he shouted. "Ask him, why don't you? Ask him!"

Miss Monk seemed willing to take his suggestion. She

---

6. *congested*: red (with anger); literally, overfilled with blood.

turned a profound appraising glance in my direction. I can imagine what I looked like, for the next thing to a smile went across her face. "John," she said, "did you put Emerson's bottle in this drawer?"

With a great effort I managed to move my tongue. I licked my lips and said, "I was up here. But I never touched his bottle."

"So you were both here," said Miss Monk. "I thought so. . . . Now, Emerson, think carefully. Did—"

Hicksey had got hold of himself. His voice took on that old, frank, manly ring, and he interrupted quickly, "All right. I admit it too. I tried not to tell you. I didn't want to go telling on anybody. But if he thinks he can take my ink bottle when I'm not looking—"

"This much is clear," said Miss Monk. "Somebody used somebody's ink bottle. The question is who?"

Hicksey gave an admirable shrug. He scratched his head. "Gee," he said. "Well, would I use my own bottle, if I did it? That's all I can say."

Miss Monk looked toward the door. It proved to be Dennis, carrying a mop and pail. He ambled in, gave a nod to Miss Monk, and looked at the floor. He made a clicking sound with his tongue. "Fine mess!" he said cheerfully.

"Yes," said Miss Monk. She looked at me and then at Hicksey. "But we're going to clear it up." Her messenger had entered behind Dennis, and she waited until he took his seat. "Carl," she said then, "I think Emerson may want to get his school things together after he has seen Mr. Apgar. Have you anything of his?"

I have forgotten Carl's last name, but I can remember his guileless vacant face and short whitish hair perfectly. He blinked in the bewildered way he had. "Why, no, Miss Monk." The words weren't out of his mouth when he blushed, struck his knuckles against his head. "Nobody home!" he said.

He reached into his desk, faced about, and set an ink bottle in front of Hicksey. "Say, thanks," he stuttered. "I borrowed it before you came in. I hope you don't mind."

"Emerson," Miss Monk said, "you may go down to Mr. Apgar's office now."

Hicksey sat motionless. His expression was distraught, and I was not sorry to think how he must be feeling. Still angry, still outraged by his attempt to betray me, I looked at him with scorn and hatred, unable to imagine what I had ever seen in him. A moment passed while he continued to stare at Carl's amiable, somewhat witless face, and then I suppose Hicksey showed me—in fact, he showed us all. He got to his feet. He made a kind of bow to Carl. "Oh," he said with some elegance, "don't mention it. You're quite welcome, I'm sure."

The Facts of the Story

Write the numbers 1 to 10 in a column on a piece of paper. Each of the following statements of fact has three possible conclusions. Write the letter of the answer that best completes each statement after the proper number.

1. John knows Miss Monk better than some of his classmates do because (a) she is a neighbor (b) she has been his teacher before (c) she constantly picks on John.

2. John (a) likes Miss Monk (b) likes Miss Monk, but enjoys causing trouble for her (c) dislikes Miss Monk.

3. John looks upon Mr. Apgar with a feeling of (a) awe (b) dislike (c) affection.

4. Miss Monk feels that John is (a) a natural troublemaker (b) a boy she could trust (c) a born leader.

5. Hicksey decides to make John his best friend because (a) he finds John impressionable and agreeable (b) he knows John is as eager as he is to make trouble (c) he wants to learn some new tricks from John.

6. When Hicksey and John are taken to the principal's office, Hicksey (a) hints that Miss Monk lets Elizabeth Jones get away with things (b) takes full responsibility for putting gum in Elizabeth's hair (c) yells at Mr. Apgar.

7. Mr. Apgar deals with the problem by (a) expelling the boys from school (b) firing Miss Monk (c) insisting that the boys apologize to Elizabeth Jones.

8. When Hicksey makes the ink bomb, he deliberately (a) uses his own ink bottle (b) uses John's ink bottle (c) uses Miss Monk's ink bottle.

9. Miss Monk knows that Hicksey made the ink bomb because (a) he falsely accuses John when he finds his ink

bottle is missing (b) she saw Hicksey plant the bomb (c) John tells on Hicksey.

10. At the end of the story, John's feeling about Hicksey is (a) admiration for Hicksey's cleverness (b) regret that Hicksey got caught (c) anger and hatred toward Hicksey.

The Ideas in the Story

For class discussion, prepare answers to the following questions.

1. One idea worth considering in this story is how a trusted and well-behaved student can be led astray by a different kind of boy. Even though John does not want to go along with Hicksey's schemes, he does go along with them. Read the part of the story (page 289) where Hicksey persuades John to break the rule about leaving the school grounds during recess. Explain why John goes to the store with Hicksey.

2. Reread the part (page 291) in which John, after his late lunch and after repenting "the folly of falling in with Emerson Hicks's suggestion," meets Emerson in the hall. John is determined not to be drawn into trouble again, but his determination fades. Explain how John is drawn back into Emerson's grip.

3. Reread the scene (page 301) in which Hicksey is explaining his ink-bomb plan. Find details that reveal that John himself knows he is helpless in Hicksey's hands. Why do you think John does not simply walk out of the building and go home, choosing to ignore whatever mischief Hicksey is planning?

4. Why do some people, like Emerson Hicks, naturally want to defy authority? The opposite attitude is taken by John, who says, ". . . I did not hate school, and it had never

crossed my mind that a teacher was my natural enemy."
How can you account for this difference in attitude?

5. What do you think the "animals' fair" in the title refers
to? What do you think of this as a title?

The Art of the Storyteller

Characterization

Cozzens is an expert at revealing character. Sometimes he
lets his narrator tell us directly what a character is like; for example, John tells us that he is "naturally bossy and vain," that he
has "not been around much," that under his "officious manner"
he is "timid and uncertain."

Sometimes Cozzens reveals character indirectly by showing
the person in action and then letting us draw our own conclusions about what the person is like. For example, in the following passage, Hicksey's actions tell us something about his
character and personality:

> Hicksey was scarlet, not only at his failure but at the
> appalling disgrace of learning, as he must have, that Eliz-
> abeth Jones was twice as strong as he was. He could not
> speak for a moment. Then he muttered to me, "Gee, I
> can't hit a girl back, can I?" implying hopefully that all
> that saved her was his chivalry and forbearance.

What other passages in the story lead us to conclude that
Hicksey is a liar?

Look at how Cozzens characterizes Miss Monk and Mr.
Apgar. He uses direct characterization on page 287 when he
tells us that Miss Monk has "handsome dark brown eyes," and
is "graceful" and "pleasant" to look at. Mr. Apgar, on page 290,
is described directly as being "stately," with a "mild face" and a
"slow and impressive" manner of speaking. What do Mr.
Apgar's actions when the boys are in his office reveal about his
character and personality? What do Miss Monk's and Mr.

Apgar's actions in the final scene with the ink bomb reveal about their characters?

How does Cozzens make you feel about the characters in this story—about John, Hicksey, Miss Monk, and Mr. Apgar?

Irony

When a character makes a prediction about future events, and the events turn out to be the opposite of what was expected, the prediction becomes ironic. For example, when John gloomily says that Miss Monk will "think right away we did it," Hicksey predicts, "she can think all she wants, but she can't prove anything." We feel the irony of Hicksey's remark later, when Miss Monk does indeed think "all she wants," and does prove that it was Hicksey, not John, who set the ink bomb.

Explain, in the light of the end of the story, the irony in Hicksey's remark: "I've done it hundreds of times. I never got caught yet. You can bet your life I won't get caught this time."

Another kind of irony occurs when the readers of a story know something that a character does *not* know. This kind of irony is found in the scene where Mr. Apgar is about to open the desk drawer. *We* know, and John and Hicksey know, that Mr. Apgar is about to be doused with ink, but no one else knows, including the unfortunate victim. This kind of ironic situation is common in plays, when the audience knows something that the characters onstage do not know. It is referred to as *dramatic irony.* The use of dramatic irony almost always creates suspense. What were your feelings in the last scene of the story, as you waited for the ink bomb to explode?

Composition

Comparing Two Stories

Write a paragraph comparing the stories "Bad Characters" (page 259) and "The Animals' Fair." Before you begin, make a brief outline, listing the similar details in both stories. You may discuss only one point of similarity between the stories, or you may talk about several connections between the stories. Some obvious ways in which the stories are similar are in their ideas, events, and characters. You can find others.

Back up your ideas with references to the stories. It would not be enough, for example, just to say that a character in one story is like a character in the other story. You must tell in what ways they are alike.

Write 100 to 150 words.

James Gould Cozzens

James Gould Cozzens (1903-1978) was born in Chicago and grew up on Staten Island, New York. He graduated from the Kent School in Connecticut and attended Harvard University. Cozzens' career was devoted to writing adult novels not likely to be of much interest to young readers. An exception to his usual subject matter is his book of short stories, *Children and Others,* which contains "The Animals' Fair." His novel *Guard of Honor* won the Pulitzer Prize in 1949.

A Slander

ANTON CHEKHOV
Translated by Nathalie Wollard

*One of the greatest of all the European short-story writers is
the Russian Anton Chekhov. The story that follows is one of
his comic tales of small-town life in Russia, during the years
when the Czar was still in power. Though the story was
written many years ago, this uproar over a kiss could easily
happen today. Before you read, be sure you know what
"slander" is.*

*Don't worry about the names in the story. If you pro-
nounce them the way they look, you'll come close enough to
the way the Russians say them.*

The penmanship teacher Sergei Kapitonich Ahineyev was marrying his daughter Natalia to the history and geography teacher. The wedding gaiety was at its height. People sang, played, and danced in the ballroom. Hired waiters, dressed in black tails and dirty white ties, scurried back and forth like madmen. Noise filled the air. The mathematics teacher, the French teacher, and the tax assessor, sitting side by side on the sofa, talked hurriedly, interrupting each other to tell the guests about cases of people buried alive, and expressing their opinions of spiritualism.[1] None of the three believed in spiritualism, but all admitted that there are many things in this world which a human mind will never understand. In the next room the literature teacher was explaining the cases in which a sentry has the right to shoot at passers-by. As you can see, the conversations were terrifying but highly pleasant. From the yard, people whose social standing did not give them the right to enter looked through the windows.

Exactly at midnight, Ahineyev, the host, walked into the kitchen to see whether everything was ready for supper. The kitchen was full of fumes from the goose and duck, mixed with many other smells. Appetizers and drinks were spread in artistic disorder on two tables. Marfa, the cook, a red-faced woman whose figure was like a balloon with a belt around it, bustled near the tables.

"Show me the sturgeon,[2] Marfa," said Ahineyev, rubbing his hands and licking his lips. "What an aroma! I could eat up the whole kitchen. Now then, show me the sturgeon!"

Marfa went to a bench and carefully lifted a greasy newspaper. Under the paper, on an enormous platter, rested a big jellied sturgeon, dazzling with olives and carrots. Ahineyev looked at the sturgeon and gasped. His faced beamed, his eyes

1. *spiritualism:* the belief that spirits of the dead can communicate with the living.
2. *sturgeon:* a large fresh-water fish.

rolled up. He bent over and made a sound like an ungreased wheel. After a while he snapped his fingers with pleasure and smacked his lips once more.

"Oh, the sound of a passionate kiss! . . . Who are you kissing in there, little Marfa?" asked a voice from the next room, and Vankin, an assistant teacher, stuck his cropped head through the door. "Who are you with? Ah, ah, ah . . . very nice! With Sergei Kapitonich! You're a fine grandfather, alone here with a woman!"

"Not at all, I am not kissing her," said Ahineyev with embarrassment. "Who told you that, you fool? I just . . . smacked my lips because of . . . my pleasure . . . at the sight of the fish."

"Tell me another one!" Vankin's head smiled broadly and disappeared behind the door. Ahineyev blushed.

"What now?" he thought. "The scoundrel will go now and gossip. He will put me to shame before the whole town, the beast . . ."

Ahineyev timidly entered the ballroom and looked around: where was Vankin? Vankin was standing at the piano and dashingly bent over to whisper something to the laughing sister-in-law of the inspector.

"It is about me," thought Ahineyev, "about me. He should be torn apart! And she believes . . . believes! She's laughing. I can't let this go on . . . no . . . I must arrange it so that no one will believe him . . . I will talk to everybody and show what a fool and gossip he is."

Ahineyev scratched himself and, still embarrassed, approached the French teacher.

"I was just in the kitchen, arranging the supper," he told the Frenchman. "I know you love fish and I have a sturgeon, old chap. Two yards long. Ha, ha, ha . . . oh, yes, I almost forgot . . . in the kitchen now, with the sturgeon . . . it was a real joke! I went to the kitchen and wanted to examine the food . . . I looked at the sturgeon and from the pleasure, the aroma of it, I smacked my lips! But at this moment suddenly this fool Vankin came in and said . . . ha, ha, ha . . . and said . . . 'Ah, are you kissing in here?' Kissing Marfa, the cook! He made it all up, the fool. The woman looks like a beast, such a face, such skin . . . and he . . . kissing! Funny man!"

"Who is funny?" asked the mathematics teacher, coming over.

"That one there, Vankin! I came into the kitchen . . ." and he told the story of Vankin. "He made me laugh, he's so funny! I think I'd rather kiss a stray dog than Marfa," added Ahineyev, turning around and seeing the tax assessor behind him.

"We are talking about Vankin," said he. "Such a funny man! He came in the kitchen, saw me near Marfa . . . well, he started to invent all kinds of stories. 'Why,' he says, 'are you kissing?' He was drunk and made it up. And I said, 'I would rather kiss a turkey than Marfa. I have a wife,' I told him, 'you are such a fool.' He made me laugh."

"Who made you laugh?" asked the priest who taught Scripture in the school, coming to Ahineyev.

"Vankin. I was, you know, standing in the kitchen and looking at the sturgeon . . ."

And so forth. In half an hour all the guests knew the story of the sturgeon and Vankin.

"Let him tell the stories now!" thought Ahineyev, rubbing his hands. "Let him! He'll start telling stories, and everyone will say right away: 'Stop talking nonsense, you fool! We know all about it.' "

And Ahineyev was so reassured that he drank four glasses too much from joy. After supper he saw the newlyweds to their room, went home, and slept like an innocent child, and the next day he had already forgotten the story of the sturgeon. But, alas! Man supposes, but God disposes. Wicked tongues will wag, and Ahineyev's cunning did not help him. Exactly a week later, after the third lesson on Wednesday, when Ahineyev was standing in the staff room discussing the evil ways of one of his students, the principal came to him and called him aside.

"Well, Sergei Kapitonich," said the principal, "excuse me

. . . it is not my business, but still I must explain . . . my duty. You see, there is talk that you have kissed this . . . cook. It is not my business, but . . . kiss her . . . anything you want but, please, not so publicly. Please! Don't forget, you are a teacher."

Ahineyev got chilly and faint. He felt as if he had been stung by a swarm of bees and scalded in boiling water. As he walked home, it seemed to him that the whole town was looking at him as if he were smeared with tar. New trouble awaited him at home.

"Why don't you eat anything?" his wife asked him during dinner. "What are you thinking about? Your love life? Lonesome without little Marfa? I know all about it, Mohammedan![3] Good people opened my eyes! O-o-oh, barbarian!"

And she slapped him on the cheek. He left the table in a daze, without his hat and coat, and wandered to Vankin. Vankin was home.

"You scoundrel!" Ahineyev addressed Vankin. "Why did you smear me with mud before the entire world? Why did you slander me?"

"What slander? What are you inventing?"

"Who gossiped that I kissed Marfa? Not you? Not you, robber?"

Vankin blinked and winked with all his worn face, raised his eyes to the icon,[4] and said, "Let God punish me! Let my eyes burst, let me die, if I ever said one word about you! Bad luck to me! Cholera is not enough!"

The sincerity of Vankin could not be doubted. Evidently he had not gossiped.

"But who? Who?" thought Ahineyev, turning over in his mind all his acquaintances and beating his breast. "Who else?"

"Who else?" we will also ask the reader . . .

3. *Mohammedan:* a reference to a follower of Islam, which allows a man four wives.
4. *icon:* a sacred picture.

The Facts of the Story

Write brief answers to the following questions. Use complete sentences. You should be able to answer the questions without referring back to the story.

1. What slander does Ahineyev fear will spread about town?

2. What incident begins the slander?

3. Who does Ahineyev fear will spread the slander?

4. How does Ahineyev try to head off the slander?

5. Who actually does spread the slander?

The Ideas in the Story

For class discussion, prepare answers to the following questions.

1. One of the ideas in this story has to do with gossip. Why do you think the wedding guests do not believe Ahineyev's story about the kiss? (Do you think they prefer a scandal?) Do you think this quickness to gossip is a common human trait? Why, or why not?

2. Another idea in this story has to do with snobbery. The story is set in Russia during the rule of the Czar, when people belonged to clearly defined social classes. Ahineyev, Vankin, and the other people at the party are schoolteachers, members of the middle class. Below them would be people like Marfa, members of the servant class. Above these classes, and looking "down" on them both, would be the aristocracy. What does Ahineyev say about Marfa? How do his comments about her reveal his snobbery? How does the principal indicate that the scandal is disturbing because it is a *teacher* who has kissed a *cook*?

The Art of the Storyteller

Irony

This story is based on an *ironic situation* – a situation that turns out to be completely different from what is expected. Poor Ahineyev expects to head off a scandal. What is the ironic result of his efforts? How do you know that Ahineyev learns nothing from his errors in judgment?

Ahineyev says that he will show everyone what a "fool and gossip" Vankin is. Ironically, who is shown to be the "fool"?

Composition

Writing an Explanation

Just as Ahineyev thinks he has put a lid on the scandal, it erupts in his face. At this point (page 317), Chekhov quotes an old proverb: "Man supposes, but God disposes." (A proverb is a wise saying that expresses some truth about human experience; this one sometimes goes "Man proposes, but God disposes.") In a brief paragraph, explain what the proverb means, and tell how it applies to the events in this story.

Write about 100 words.

Anton Chekhov

Chekhov (1860-1904) knew well the kinds of people he wrote about. His father was a failed shopkeeper; his grandfather was a freed serf. Chekhov himself studied to be a doctor, but he did not practice medicine for long. Instead he wrote, producing over a thousand short stories and several plays, which are still staged today. Though Chekhov often wrote about the sad side of human life, "A Scandal" shows his light, humorous touch.

The Lady or the Tiger?

or the

FRANK R. STOCKTON

"The Lady or the Tiger?," one of the most popular short stories ever written, became famous almost the instant it was published. The title includes a question mark, for reasons that will soon become clear to you. By now generations of readers have enjoyed this story and have tried to answer the question in its title. Stockton's tale has humor and suspense. It also makes people think. You yourself just may be arguing in favor of the lady, or of the tiger, for some time to come.

In the very olden time, there lived a semi-barbaric king, whose ideas, though somewhat polished and sharpened by the progressiveness of distant Latin neighbors, were still large, florid, and untrammeled,[1] as became the half of him which was barbaric. He was a man of exuberant fancy, and of an authority so irresistible that, at his will, he turned his varied fancies into facts. He was greatly given to self-communing; and, when he and himself agreed upon anything, the thing was done. When every member of his domestic and political systems moved smoothly in its appointed course, his nature was bland and genial; but whenever there was a little hitch, and some of his orbs got out of their orbits, he was blander and more genial still, for nothing pleased him so much as to make the crooked straight, and crush down uneven places.

Among the borrowed notions by which his barbarism had become semified was that of the public arena, in which, by exhibitions of manly and beastly valor, the minds of his subjects were refined and cultured.

But even here the exuberant and barbaric fancy asserted itself. The arena of the king was built, not to give the people an opportunity of hearing the rhapsodies of dying gladiators, nor to enable them to view the inevitable conclusion of a conflict between religious opinions and hungry jaws, but for purposes far better adapted to widen and develop the mental energies of the people. This vast amphitheater, with its encircling galleries, its mysterious vaults, and its unseen passages, was an agent of poetic justice, in which crime was punished, or virtue rewarded, by the decrees of an impartial and incorruptible chance.

1. *untrammeled*: unrestrained.

When a subject was accused of a crime of sufficient importance to interest the king, public notice was given that on an
appointed day the fate of the accused person would be decided
in the king's arena—a structure which well deserved its name;
for, although its form and plan were borrowed from afar, its
purpose emanated solely from the brain of this man, who,
every barleycorn a king, knew no tradition to which he owed
more allegiance than pleased his fancy, and who ingrafted on
every adopted form of human thought and action the rich
growth of his barbaric idealism.

When all the people had assembled in the galleries, and the
king, surrounded by his court, sat high up on his throne of
royal state on one side of the arena, he gave a signal, a door
beneath him opened, and the accused subject stepped out into
the amphitheater. Directly opposite him, on the other side of
the enclosed space, were two doors exactly alike and side by
side. It was the duty and the privilege of the person on trial to
walk directly to these doors and open one of them. He could
open either door he pleased: he was subject to no guidance or
influence but that of the aforementioned impartial and incorruptible chance. If he opened the one, there came out of it a
hungry tiger, the fiercest and most cruel that could be pro-
cured, which immediately sprang upon him, and tore him to
pieces, as a punishment for his guilt. The moment that the
case of the criminal was thus decided, doleful iron bells were
clanged, great wails went up from the hired mourners posted
on the outer rim of the arena, and the vast audience, with
bowed heads and downcast hearts, wended slowly their home-
ward way, mourning greatly that one so young and fair, or so
old and respected, should have merited so dire a fate.

But, if the accused person opened the other door, there
came forth from it a lady, the most suitable to his years and
station that his majesty could select among his fair subjects;
and to this lady he was immediately married, as a reward of his
innocence. It mattered not that he might already possess a wife

and family, or that his affections might be engaged upon an object of his own selection; the king allowed no such subordinate arrangements to interfere with his great scheme of retribution and reward. The exercises, as in the other instance, took place immediately, and in the arena. Another door opened beneath the king, and a priest, followed by a band of choristers, and dancing maidens blowing joyous airs on golden horns, advanced to where the pair stood, side by side; and the wedding was promptly and cheerily solemnized. Then the gay brass bells rang forth their merry peals, the people shouted glad hurrahs, and the innocent man, preceded by children strewing flowers on his path, led his bride to his home.

This was the king's semi-barbaric method of administering justice. Its perfect fairness is obvious. The criminal could not know out of which door would come the lady; he opened either he pleased, without having the slightest idea whether, in the next instant, he was to be devoured or married. On some occasions the tiger came out of one door, and on some out of the other. The decisions of this tribunal were not only fair, they were positively determinate: the accused person was instantly punished if he found himself guilty; and, if innocent, he was rewarded on the spot, whether he liked it or not. There was no escape from the judgments of the king's arena.

The institution was a very popular one. When the people gathered together on one of the great trial days, they never knew whether they were to witness a bloody slaughter or a hilarious wedding. This element of uncertainty lent an interest to the occasion which it could not otherwise have attained. Thus, the masses were entertained and pleased, and the thinking part of the community could bring no charge of unfairness against this plan; for did not the accused person have the whole matter in his own hands?

This semi-barbaric king had a daughter as blooming as his most florid fancies, and with a soul as fervent and imperious as his own. As is usual in such cases, she was the apple of his eye, and was loved by him above all humanity. Among his courtiers was a young man of that fineness of blood and lowness of station common to the conventional heroes of romance who love royal maidens. This royal maiden was well satisfied with her lover, for he was handsome and brave to a degree unsurpassed in all this kingdom; and she loved him with an ardor that had enough of barbarism in it to make it exceedingly warm and strong. This love affair moved on happily for many months, until one day the king happened to discover its existence. He did not hesitate nor waver in regard to his duty in the premises. The youth was immediately cast into prison, and a day was appointed for his trial in the king's arena. This, of course, was an especially important occasion; and his majesty, as well as all the people, was greatly interested in the workings and development of this trial. Never before had such a case occurred; never before had a subject dared to love the daughter of a king. In afteryears such things became commonplace enough; but then they were, in no slight degree, novel and startling.

The tiger cages of the kingdom were searched for the most savage and relentless beasts, from which the fiercest monster might be selected for the arena; and the ranks of maiden youth and beauty throughout the land were carefully surveyed by competent judges, in order that the young man might have a fitting bride in case fate did not determine for him a different destiny. Of course, everybody knew that the deed with which the accused was charged had been done. He had loved the princess, and neither he, she, nor anyone else thought of denying the fact; but the king would not think of allowing any fact of this kind to interfere with the workings of the tribunal, in which he took such great delight and satisfaction. No matter how the affair turned out, the youth would be disposed of; and the king would take an aesthetic pleasure in watching the course of events, which would determine whether or not the young man had done wrong in allowing himself to love the princess.

The appointed day arrived. From far and near the people

gathered, and thronged the great galleries of the arena; and crowds, unable to gain admittance, massed themselves against its outside walls. The king and his court were in their places, opposite the twin doors—those fateful portals, so terrible in their similarity.

All was ready. The signal was given. A door beneath the royal party opened, and the lover of the princess walked into the arena. Tall, beautiful, fair, his appearance was greeted with a low hum of admiration and anxiety. Half the audience had not known so grand a youth had lived among them. No wonder the princess loved him! What a terrible thing for him to be there!

As the youth advanced into the arena, he turned, as the custom was, to bow to the king; but he did not think at all of that royal personage; his eyes were fixed upon the princess, who sat to the right of her father. Had it not been for the semi-barbarism in her nature, it is probable that lady would not have been there; but her intense and fervid soul would not allow her to be absent on an occasion in which she was so terribly interested. From the moment that the decree had gone forth that her lover should decide his fate in the king's arena, she had thought of nothing, night or day, but this great event and the various subjects connected with it. Possessed of more power, influence, and force of character than anyone who had ever before been interested in such a case, she had done what no other person had done—she had possessed herself of the secret of the doors. She knew in which of the two rooms that lay behind those doors stood the cage of the tiger, with its open front, and in which waited the lady. Through these thick doors, heavily curtained with skins on the inside, it was impossible that any noise or suggestion should come from within to the person who should approach to raise the latch of one of them; but gold, and the power of a woman's will, had brought the secret to the princess.

And not only did she know in which room stood the lady

ready to emerge, all blushing and radiant, should her door be opened, but she knew who the lady was. It was one of the fairest and loveliest of the damsels of the court who had been selected as the reward of the accused youth, should he be proved innocent of the crime of aspiring to one so far above him; and the princess hated her. Often had she seen, or imagined that she had seen, this fair creature throwing glances of admiration upon the person of her lover, and sometimes she thought these glances were perceived and even returned. Now and then she had seen them talking together; it was but for a moment or two, but much can be said in a brief space; it may have been on most unimportant topics, but how could she know that? The girl was lovely, but she had dared to raise her eyes to the loved one of the princess; and, with all the intensity of the savage blood transmitted to her through long lines of wholly barbaric ancestors, she hated the woman who blushed and trembled behind that silent door.

When her lover turned and looked at her, and his eye met hers as she sat there paler and whiter than anyone in the vast ocean of anxious faces about her, he saw, by that power of quick perception which is given to those whose souls are one, that she knew behind which door crouched the tiger, and behind which stood the lady. He had expected her to know it. He understood her nature, and his soul was assured that she would never rest until she had made plain to herself this thing, hidden to all other lookers-on, even to the king. The only hope for the youth in which there was any element of certainty was based upon the success of the princess in discovering the mystery; and the moment he looked upon her, he saw she had succeeded, as in his soul he knew she would succeed.

Then it was that his quick and anxious glance asked the question: "Which?" It was as plain to her as if he shouted it from where he stood. There was not an instant to be lost. The question was asked in a flash; it must be answered in another.

Her right arm lay on the cushioned parapet[2] before her. She raised her hand, and made a slight, quick movement toward the right. No one but her lover saw her. Every eye but his was fixed on the man in the arena.

He turned, and with a firm and rapid step he walked across the empty space. Every heart stopped beating, every breath was held, every eye was fixed immovably upon that man. Without the slightest hesitation, he went to the door on the right, and opened it.

Now, the point of the story is this: Did the tiger come out of that door, or did the lady?

The more we reflect upon this question, the harder it is to answer. It involves a study of the human heart which leads us through devious mazes of passion, out of which it is difficult to find our way. Think of it, fair reader, not as if the decision of the question depended upon yourself, but upon that hot-blooded, semi-barbaric princess, her soul at a white heat beneath the combined fires of despair and jealousy. She had lost him, but who should have him?

How often, in her waking hours and in her dreams, had she started in wild horror, and covered her face with her hands, as she thought of her lover opening the door on the other side of which waited the cruel fangs of the tiger!

But how much oftener had she seen him at the other door! How in her grievous reveries had she gnashed her teeth, and torn her hair, when she saw his start of rapturous delight as he opened the door of the lady! How her soul had burned in agony when she had seen him rush to meet that woman, with her flushing cheek and sparkling eye of triumph; when she had seen him lead her forth, his whole frame kindled with the joy of recovered life; when she had heard the glad shouts from the multitude, and the wild ringing of the happy bells; when she

2. *parapet:* wall.

had seen the priest, with his joyous followers, advance to the couple, and make them man and wife before her very eyes; and when she had seen them walk away together upon their path of flowers, followed by the tremendous shouts of the hilarious multitude, in which her one despairing shriek was lost and drowned!

Would it not be better for him to die at once, and go to wait for her in the blessed regions of semi-barbaric futurity?

And yet, that awful tiger, those shrieks, that blood!

Her decision had been indicated in an instant, but it had been made after days and nights of anguished deliberation. She had known she would be asked, she had decided what she would answer, and, without the slightest hesitation, she had moved her hand to the right.

The question of her decision is one not to be lightly considered, and it is not for me to presume to set myself up as the one person able to answer it. And so I leave it with all of you: Which came out of the opened door—the lady, or the tiger?

The Facts of the Story

Number 1 to 10 on a piece of paper. Read the following statements. If a statement is true, write T after its number on your paper; if a statement is false, write F.

1. The king believes it is fair and just to let *chance* determine whether an accused person is guilty or innocent.

2. The accused person has to make a choice between taking a chance in the arena or having a trial by jury.

3. Any accused person who opens the door with the lady has the choice of marrying her or of not marrying her.

4. Everyone knows that the young man who has dared to love the king's daughter is guilty of the crime with which he is charged.

5. The tiger is muzzled, for if it roars at the right moment, the accused will know which door to open.

6. The sympathy of the audience is with the young man.

7. The princess has persuaded her father to tell her which door is the lady's and which is the tiger's.

8. The princess knows the girl who stands behind one of the doors, and she hates her.

9. The two conflicting emotions in the mind of the princess are her love for the young man and her jealousy of the lady.

10. The young man opens the door the princess points to.

The Ideas in the Story

For class discussion, prepare answers to the following questions.

1. "After days and nights of anguished deliberation," the princess makes her decision. What do you think her decision is? Be prepared, in the light of your understanding of human nature, to support your view. Be prepared also to refer to evidence in the story.

One thing you may wish to consider is the author's continued emphasis on the semi-barbarism of the king and the princess. He refers to the king's semi-barbaric method of administering justice. He says the princess loves the young man with an ardor that has "enough of barbarism in it to make it exceedingly warm and strong." He says it is probable that the princess would not have attended the arena trial had it not been for "the semi-barbarism in her nature." Do you think Stockton is trying to tell us something about the ending?

Another question you may want to discuss is this: which is the more powerful emotion: jealousy or love?

2. You may also wonder if we can ever really know another person well enough to be able to foretell accurately how he or she will act in a difficult situation. In other words, can the young man tell, on the basis of what he knows about the princess, whether she would prefer his death or his marriage to the lady? If you had been the accused young man, would you have opened the door the princess suggested? Explain.

The Art of the Storyteller

Satire

Stockton has a sense of humor and uses it effectively in *satirizing* (or poking fun at) romantic fairy tales set in "the very olden time." For example, he says his hero "was a young man of that fineness of blood and lowness of station common to the conventional heroes of romance who love royal maidens." Do other passages seem to poke fun at fairy tales?

Stockton's satire is not limited to fairy-tale fiction. What attitudes of real-life rulers is he mocking in this passage?

But, if the accused person opened the other door, there came forth from it a lady, the most suitable to his years and station that his majesty could select among his fair subjects; and to this lady he was immediately married, as a reward of his innocence. It mattered not that he might already possess a wife and family, or that his affections might be engaged upon an object of his own selection; the king allowed no such subordinate arrangements to interfere with his great scheme of retribution and reward.

Stockton's satire turns to sarcasm, as satire often does, when he says of the king: "Among the borrowed notions by which his barbarism had become semified was that of the public arena, in which, by exhibitions of manly and beastly valor, the minds of his subjects were refined and cultured." What is ironic about this statement—that is, can minds be "refined" and "cultured" by exhibitions of tigers eating people?

Composition

Supporting an Opinion

Write a composition in which you express your opinion as to who came through the door, the lady or the tiger. Use details from the story to explain the reasons why you hold that opinion. Devote a paragraph to each reason. You will have to show that you are an amateur psychologist, a student of human nature, and a careful reader.

Write between 150 and 200 words.

Frank R. Stockton

Frank R. Stockton (1834-1902) was born in Philadelphia. He worked as a newspaper reporter and magazine editor before devoting himself to writing short stories and novels. Although his collected works fill twenty-three volumes and although he achieved fame for his humorous fiction, Stockton is known today principally as the author of "The Lady or the Tiger?" People used to corner him at parties and ask him, confidentially, who *really* came out of that arena door.

The Secret Life of Walter Mitty

JAMES THURBER

Walter Mitty's secret life is lived in his daydreams. Since all of us have our daydreams and our secret lives, we are all "Walter Mittys" at one time or another.

But not Mrs. Mitty, an amazingly practical person. "You're tensed up again," says Mrs. Mitty, as she observes one of Walter's spells of absent-mindedness. "It's one of your days." Thurber's story describes a few hours in one of Walter Mitty's tensed-up days.

The story is very funny, but it also has a point. When we laugh at Walter Mitty as he escapes into his secret life, we are really laughing at ourselves and at our own escapes into daydreams. The ability to laugh at ourselves is a valuable one. It prevents us from taking ourselves too seriously.

"We're going through!" The Commander's voice was like thin ice breaking. He wore his full-dress uniform, with the heavily braided white cap pulled down rakishly over one cold gray eye. "We can't make it, sir. It's spoiling for a hurricane, if you ask me." "I'm not asking you, Lieutenant Berg," said the Commander. "Throw on the power lights! Rev her up to 8,500! We're going through!" The pounding of the cylinders increased: ta-pocketa-pocketa-pocketa-*pocketa-pocketa*. The Commander stared at the ice forming on the pilot window. He walked over and twisted a row of complicated dials. "Switch on No. 8 auxiliary!" he shouted. "Switch on No. 8 auxiliary!" repeated Lieutenant Berg. "Full strength in No. 3 turret!" shouted the Commander. "Full strength in No. 3 turret!" The crew, bending to their various tasks in the huge, hurtling eight-engined Navy hydroplane, looked at each other and grinned. "The Old Man'll get us through," they said to one another. "The Old Man ain't afraid of Hell!" . . .

"Not so fast! You're driving too fast!" said Mrs. Mitty. "What are you driving so fast for?"

"Hmm?" said Walter Mitty. He looked at his wife, in the seat beside him, with shocked astonishment. She seemed grossly unfamiliar, like a strange woman who had yelled at him in a crowd. "You were up to fifty-five," she said. "You know I don't like to go more than forty. You were up to fifty-five." Walter Mitty drove on toward Waterbury in silence, the roaring of the SN202 through the worst storm .in twenty years of Navy flying fading in the remote, intimate airways of his mind. "You're tensed up again," said Mrs. Mitty. "It's one of your days. I wish you'd let Dr. Renshaw look you over."

Walter Mitty stopped the car in front of the building where

his wife went to have her hair done. "Remember to get those overshoes while I'm having my hair done," she said. "I don't need overshoes," said Mitty. She put her mirror back into her bag. "We've been all through that," she said, getting out of the car. "You're not a young man any longer." He raced the engine a little. "Why don't you wear your gloves? Have you lost your gloves?" Walter Mitty reached in a pocket and brought out the gloves. He put them on, but after she had turned and gone into the building and he had driven on to a red light, he took them off again. "Pick it up, brother!" snapped a cop as the light changed, and Mitty hastily pulled on his gloves and lurched ahead. He drove around the streets aimlessly for a time, and then he drove past the hospital on his way to the parking lot.

. . . "It's the millionaire banker, Wellington McMillan," said the pretty nurse. "Yes?" said Walter Mitty, removing his gloves slowly. "Who has the case?" "Dr. Renshaw and Dr. Benbow, but there are two specialists here, Dr. Remington from New York and Mr. Pritchard-Mitford from London. He flew over." A door opened down a long, cool corridor and Dr. Renshaw came out. He looked distraught and haggard. "Hello, Mitty," he said. "We're having the devil's own time with McMillan, the millionaire banker and close personal friend of Roosevelt. Obstreosis of the ductal tract. Tertiary. Wish you'd take a look at him." "Glad to," said Mitty.

In the operating room there were whispered introductions: "Dr. Remington, Dr. Mitty. Mr. Pritchard-Mitford, Dr. Mitty." "I've read your book on streptothricosis," said Pritchard-Mitford, shaking hands. "A brilliant performance, sir." "Thank you," said Walter Mitty. "Didn't know you were in the States, Mitty," grumbled Remington. "Coals to Newcastle, bringing Mitford and me up here for a tertiary." "You are very kind," said Mitty. A huge, complicated machine, connected to the operating table, with many tubes and wires, began at this moment to go pocketa-pocketa-pocketa. "The new anesthetizer is giving way!" shouted an intern. "There is no one in the

East who knows how to fix it!" "Quiet, man!" said Mitty, in a low, cool voice. He sprang to the machine, which was now going pocketa-pocketa-queep-pocketa-queep. He began fingering delicately a row of glistening dials. "Give me a fountain pen!" he snapped. Someone handed him a fountain pen. He pulled a faulty piston out of the machine and inserted the pen in its place. "That will hold for ten minutes," he said. "Get on with the operation." A nurse hurried over and whispered to Renshaw, and Mitty saw the man turn pale. "Coreopsis has set in," said Renshaw nervously. "If you would take over, Mitty?" Mitty looked at him and at the craven figure of Benbow, who drank, and at the grave, uncertain faces of the two great specialists. "If you wish," he said. They slipped a white gown on him; he adjusted a mask and drew on thin gloves; nurses handed him shining . . .

"Back it up, Mac! Look out for that Buick!" Walter Mitty jammed on the brakes. "Wrong lane, Mac," said the parking-lot attendant, looking at Mitty closely. "Gee. Yeh," muttered Mitty. He began cautiously to back out of the lane marked "Exit Only." "Leave her sit there," said the attendant. "I'll put her away." Mitty got out of the car. "Hey, better leave the key." "Oh," said Mitty, handing the man the ignition key. The attendant vaulted into the car, backed it up with insolent skill, and put it where it belonged.

They're so damn cocky, thought Walter Mitty, walking along Main Street; they think they know everything. Once he had tried to take his chains off, outside New Milford, and he had got them wound around the axles. A man had had to come out in a wrecking car and unwind them, a young, grinning garageman. Since then Mrs. Mitty always made him drive to a garage to have the chains taken off. The next time, he thought, I'll wear my right arm in a sling; they won't grin at me then. I'll have my right arm in a sling and they'll see I couldn't possibly take the chains off myself. He kicked at the slush on the sidewalk. "Overshoes," he said to himself, and he began looking for a shoe store.

When he came out into the street again, with the overshoes in a box under his arm, Walter Mitty began to wonder what the other thing was his wife had told him to get. She had told him, twice, before they set out from their house for Waterbury. In a way he hated these weekly trips to town—he was always getting something wrong. Kleenex, he thought, Squibb's, razor blades? No. Toothpaste, toothbrush, bicarbonate, carborundum, initiative and referendum? He gave it up. But she would remember it. "Where's the what's-its-name?" she would ask. "Don't tell me you forgot the what's-its-name." A newsboy went by shouting something about the Waterbury trial.

. . . "Perhaps this will refresh your memory." The District Attorney suddenly thrust a heavy automatic at the quiet figure on the witness stand. "Have you ever seen this before?" Walter Mitty took the gun and examined it expertly. "This is my Webley-Vickers 50.80," he said calmly. An excited buzz ran around the courtroom. The Judge rapped for order. "You are a crack shot with any sort of firearms, I believe?" said the District Attorney, insinuatingly. "Objection!" shouted Mitty's attorney. "We have shown that the defendant could not have fired the shot. We have shown that he wore his right arm in a sling on the night of the fourteenth of July." Walter Mitty raised his hand briefly and the bickering attorneys were stilled. "With any known make of gun," he said evenly, "I could have killed Gregory Fitzhurst at three hundred feet *with my left hand.*" Pandemonium broke loose in the courtroom. A woman's scream rose above the bedlam and suddenly a lovely, dark-haired girl was in Walter Mitty's arms. The District Attorney struck at her savagely. Without rising from his chair, Mitty let the man have it on the point of the chin. "You miserable cur!" . . .

"Puppy biscuit," said Walter Mitty. He stopped walking and the buildings of Waterbury rose up out of the misty courtroom and surrounded him again. A woman who was passing laughed. "He said 'Puppy biscuit,' " she said to her companion. "That man said 'Puppy biscuit' to himself." Walter Mitty hurried on. He went into an A & P, not the first one he came to but a smaller one farther up the street. "I want some biscuit for small, young dogs," he said to the clerk. "Any special brand, sir?" The greatest pistol shot in the world thought a moment. "It says 'Puppies Bark for It' on the box," said Walter Mitty.

His wife would be through at the hairdresser's in fifteen minutes, Mitty saw in looking at his watch, unless they had trouble drying it; sometimes they had trouble drying it. She didn't like to get to the hotel first; she would want him to be there waiting for her as usual. He found a big leather chair in the lobby, facing a window, and he put the overshoes and the puppy biscuit on the floor beside it. He picked up an old copy of *Liberty* and sank down into the chair. "Can Germany Conquer the World Through the Air?" Walter Mitty looked at the pictures of bombing planes and of ruined streets.
. . . "The cannonading has got the wind up in young Raleigh, sir," said the sergeant. Captain Mitty looked up at him through tousled hair. "Get him to bed," he said wearily. "With the others. I'll fly alone." "But you can't, sir," said the sergeant anxiously. "It takes two men to handle that bomber and the Archies[1] are pounding hell out of the air. Von Richtman's circus is between here and Saulier." "Somebody's got to get that ammunition dump," said Mitty. "I'm going over. Spot of brandy?" He poured a drink for the sergeant and one for himself. War thundered and whined around the dugout and battered at the door. There was a rending of wood and splinters flew through the room. "A bit of a near thing," said Captain Mitty carelessly. "The box barrage is closing in," said the sergeant. "We only live once, Sergeant," said Mitty, with his faint, fleeting smile. "Or do we?" He poured another brandy and tossed it off. "I never see a man could hold his brandy like you, sir," said the sergeant. "Begging your pardon, sir." Captain Mitty stood up and strapped on his huge Webley-Vickers

1. *Archies:* antiaircraft guns of the enemy.

automatic. "It's forty kilometers through hell, sir," said the sergeant. Mitty finished one last brandy. "After all," he said softly, "what isn't?" The pounding of the cannon increased; there was the rat-tat-tatting of machine guns, and from somewhere came the menacing pocketa-pocketa-pocketa of the new flame-throwers. Walter Mitty walked to the door of the dugout humming "Auprès de Ma Blonde." He turned and waved to the sergeant. "Cheerio!" he said. . . .

Something struck his shoulder. "I've been looking all over this hotel for you," said Mrs. Mitty. "Why do you have to hide in this old chair? How did you expect me to find you?" "Things close in," said Walter Mitty vaguely. "What?" Mrs. Mitty said. "Did you get the what's-its-name? The puppy biscuit? What's in that box?" "Overshoes," said Mitty. "Couldn't you have put them on in the store?" "I was thinking," said Walter Mitty. "Does it ever occur to you that I am sometimes thinking?" She looked at him. "I'm going to take your temperature when I get you home," she said.

They went out through the revolving doors that made a faintly derisive whistling sound when you pushed them. It was two blocks to the parking lot. At the drugstore on the corner she said, "Wait here for me. I forgot something. I won't be a minute." She was more than a minute. Walter Mitty lighted a cigarette. It began to rain, rain with sleet in it. He stood up against the wall of the drugstore, smoking. . . . He put his shoulders back and his heels together. "To hell with the handkerchief," said Walter Mitty scornfully. He took one last drag on his cigarette and snapped it away. Then, with that faint, fleeting smile playing about his lips, he faced the firing squad; erect and motionless, proud and disdainful, Walter Mitty the Undefeated, inscrutable to the last.

The Facts of the Story

Write answers to the following questions. Look at the story if you wish. Answers may be phrases or sentences.

1. List the five heroic roles Walter Mitty imagines himself playing.

2. Mrs. Mitty treats Walter as though he were a little boy. Give two examples of this.

3. Walter does, in fact, sometimes behave like a little boy. Give two examples of this.

4. What does Mrs. Mitty believe is the real cause of Walter's spells?

5. How does the Walter Mitty of the daydreams differ from the real Walter Mitty?

The Ideas in the Story

You have learned (page 148) that the main idea about life expressed in a short story is called its *theme.* You quickly realize that the theme, or main idea, of "The Secret Life of Walter Mitty" must have something to do with daydreams and reality. What events in real life trigger Mitty's fantasies? What unheroic situations snap Mitty out of his daydreams? What does the story say about *why* we might daydream?

How is this story like "Peter Two" (page 164)? In what ways is it different?

In one sentence try to state the theme of Thurber's story. Do not begin your sentence with "The theme of the story is . . ." or "I think the theme is . . ." Instead, state the main idea directly: "Daydreaming is . . ." or "Daydreams can be . . ."

The Art of the Storyteller

Satire

Thurber pokes fun at Walter Mitty and his fantasies. Literature that pokes fun at human foolishness or vice is called *satire.* Thurber actually satirizes all of us when he satirizes Walter Mitty. When Thurber makes us realize how our own daydreams contrast with our own ordinary lives, he makes us laugh at ourselves.

What kind of behavior is Thurber satirizing in the characters of the meek Walter Mitty and of the formidable Mrs. Mitty?

Stock Characters

You may have noticed that the characters in Walter Mitty's daydreams seem to come right out of TV shows. Like most characters in soap operas, Mitty's imagined characters are immediately recognizable and predictable. We recognize the clipped speech of the doctors going about their serious tasks. We recognize the character of Dr. Mitty, the great surgeon, arriving just in time to "take over," facing the emergency calmly and saving a life ingeniously. The whole operating-room scene, in fact, has been done on TV a hundred times. The forceful commander of the Navy plane ("The Old Man'll get us through") and the very British captain in the Air Force are also recognizable types. Characters like these that we encounter over and over again in our reading and viewing are called *stock characters*—as though they are stored in large quantities in a stockroom and brought out whenever a writer needs them.

Some other common stock characters are the tough detective who always outsmarts the crooks; the ruthless gangster who smokes a cigar; the innocent child who melts the miser's heart; the temperamental movie star; the tough guy or gal with a heart of gold. You can add to the list.

Stock characters often appear in popular fiction and popular plays. Writers of quality literature, however, who try to make their characters more complex, usually avoid stock characters, unless, like Thurber, they want to satirize them.

Walter Mitty himself is a "stock character"—the little guy who is bossed by his wife and by just about everyone else. Are there any "Walter Mittys" in TV shows or movies you've seen recently? Are there any "Mrs. Mittys"?

Composition

Describing a Stock Character

We often think of people from real life as certain "types." If placed in a story, they would be stock characters. A few examples are the hand-grabbing politician, the star athlete, the brain, the gossip, the practical joker, the teacher's pet.

Write a sketch of a character "type." You can do this without having any real person in mind. You can simply create a character to show the traits of a certain recognizable type. Use descriptive details and include at least one anecdote to illustrate the person's main characteristic. You might follow your character through a day or an hour, telling what he or she does and says. Try to use some dialogue.

Write approximately 200 words.

James Thurber

James Thurber (1894-1961) was born in Columbus, Ohio, where he attended the public schools and Ohio State University. He began his writing career as a newspaper reporter in Columbus and then went to Paris. In New York he started his lifelong association with *The New Yorker* magazine, to which he regularly contributed humorous stories and cartoons. Thurber was the foremost American humorist of his time. Although his writings are funny, most of them, like "The Secret Life of Walter Mitty," have a serious comment to make about contemporary life and about the relationships between men and women. "The Secret Life of Walter Mitty" was made into a movie starring Danny Kaye.

Harrison
Bergeron

KURT VONNEGUT

In "Harrison Bergeron," Kurt Vonnegut imagines a society (the United States in 2081) from which all competition has been removed. By assigning handicaps to persons who have above-average mental or physical abilities, the agents of the United States Handicapper General have forced everybody to be equal in every way. Harrison Bergeron is the name of a boy who dares to rebel against this handicap system. For a few beautiful moments, Harrison shows everyone what excellence is—but he pays a heavy price for his freedom.

The year was 2081, and everybody was finally equal. They weren't only equal before God and the law. They were equal every which way. Nobody was smarter than anybody else. Nobody was better-looking than anybody else. Nobody was stronger or quicker than anybody else. All this equality was due to the 211th, 212th, and 213th Amendments to the Constitution, and to the unceasing vigilance of agents of the United States Handicapper General.

Some things about living still weren't quite right, though. April, for instance, still drove people crazy by not being springtime. And it was in that clammy month that the H-G men took George and Hazel Bergeron's fourteen-year-old son, Harrison, away.

It was tragic, all right, but George and Hazel couldn't think about it very hard. Hazel had a perfectly average intelligence, which meant she couldn't think about anything except in short bursts. And George, while his intelligence was way above normal, had a little mental handicap radio in his ear. He was required by law to wear it at all times. It was tuned to a government transmitter. Every twenty seconds or so, the transmitter would send out some sharp noise to keep people like George from taking unfair advantage of their brains.

George and Hazel were watching television. There were tears on Hazel's cheeks, but she'd forgotten for the moment what they were about.

On the television screen were ballerinas.

A buzzer sounded in George's head. His thoughts fled in panic, like bandits from a burglar alarm.

"That was a real pretty dance, that dance they just did," said Hazel.

"Huh?" said George.

"That dance—it was nice," said Hazel.

"Yup," said George. He tried to think a little about the ballerinas. They weren't really very good—no better than anybody else would have been, anyway. They were burdened with sashweights and bags of birdshot, and their faces were masked, so that no one, seeing a free and graceful gesture or a pretty face, would feel like something the cat drug in. George was toying with the vague notion that maybe dancers shouldn't be handicapped. But he didn't get very far with it before another noise in his ear radio scattered his thoughts.

George winced. So did two out of the eight ballerinas.

Hazel saw him wince. Having no mental handicap herself, she had to ask George what the latest sound had been.

"Sounded like somebody hitting a milk bottle with a ball-peen hammer," said George.

"I'd think it would be real interesting, hearing all the different sounds," said Hazel, a little envious. "All the things they think up."

"Um," said George.

"Only, if I was Handicapper General, you know what I would do?" said Hazel. Hazel, as a matter of fact, bore a strong resemblance to the Handicapper General, a woman named Diana Moon Glampers. "If I was Diana Moon Glampers," said Hazel, "I'd have chimes on Sunday—just chimes. Kind of in honor of religion."

"I could think, if it was just chimes," said George.

"Well—maybe make 'em real loud," said Hazel. "I think I'd make a good Handicapper General."

"Good as anybody else," said George.

"Who knows better'n I do what normal is?" said Hazel.

"Right," said George. He began to think glimmeringly about his abnormal son who was now in jail, about Harrison, but a twenty-one-gun salute in his head stopped that.

"Boy!" said Hazel, "that was a doozy, wasn't it?"

It was such a doozy that George was white and trembling, and tears stood on the rims of his red eyes. Two of the eight ballerinas had collapsed to the studio floor, were holding their temples.

"All of a sudden you look so tired," said Hazel. "Why don't you stretch out on the sofa, so's you can rest your handicap bag on the pillows, honeybunch." She was referring to the forty-seven pounds of birdshot in a canvas bag which was padlocked around George's neck. "Go on and rest the bag for a little while," she said. "I don't care if you're not equal to me for a while."

George weighed the bag with his hands. "I don't mind it," he said. "I don't notice it any more. It's just a part of me."

"You been so tired lately—kind of wore out," said Hazel. "If there was just some way we could make a little hole in the bottom of the bag, and just take out a few of them lead balls. Just a few."

"Two years in prison and two thousand dollars fine for every ball I took out," said George. "I don't call that a bargain."

"If you could just take a few out when you come home from work," said Hazel. "I mean—you don't compete with anybody around here. You just set around."

"If I tried to get away with it," said George, "then other people'd get away with it—and pretty soon we'd be right back to the dark ages again, with everybody competing against everybody else. You wouldn't like that, would you?"

"I'd hate it," said Hazel.

"There you are," said George. "The minute people start cheating on laws, what do you think happens to society?"

If Hazel hadn't been able to come up with an answer to this question, George couldn't have supplied one. A siren was going off in his head.

"Reckon it'd fall all apart," said Hazel.

"What would?" said George blankly.

"Society," said Hazel uncertainly. "Wasn't that what you just said?"

"Who knows?" said George.

The television program was suddenly interrupted for a news bulletin. It wasn't clear at first as to what the bulletin was about, since the announcer, like all announcers, had a serious speech impediment. For about half a minute, and in a state of high excitement, the announcer tried to say, "Ladies and gentlemen—"

He finally gave up, handed the bulletin to a ballerina to read.

"That's all right—" Hazel said of the announcer, "he tried. That's the big thing. He tried to do the best he could with what God gave him. He should get a nice raise for trying so hard."

"Ladies and gentlemen—" said the ballerina, reading the bulletin. She must have been extraordinarily beautiful, because the mask she wore was hideous. And it was easy to see that she was the strongest and most graceful of all the dancers, for her handicap bags were as big as those worn by two-hundred-pound men.

And she had to apologize at once for her voice, which was a very unfair voice for a woman to use. Her voice was a warm, luminous, timeless melody. "Excuse me—" she said, and she began again, making her voice absolutely uncompetitive.

"Harrison Bergeron, age fourteen," she said in a grackle squawk, "has just escaped from jail, where he was held on suspicion of plotting to overthrow the government. He is a genius and an athlete, is under-handicapped, and should be regarded as extremely dangerous."

A police photograph of Harrison Bergeron was flashed on the screen—upside down, then sideways, upside down again, then right side up. The picture showed the full length of Harrison against a background calibrated in feet and inches. He was exactly seven feet tall.

The rest of Harrison's appearance was Halloween and hardware. Nobody had ever borne heavier handicaps. He had outgrown hindrances faster than the H-G men could think them up. Instead of a little ear radio for a mental handicap, he wore a tremendous pair of earphones, and spectacles with thick wavy lenses. The spectacles were intended to make him not only half blind, but to give him whanging headaches besides.

Scrap metal was hung all over him. Ordinarily, there was a certain symmetry, a military neatness to the handicaps issued to strong people, but Harrison looked like a walking junkyard. In the race of life, Harrison carried three hundred pounds.

And to offset his good looks, the H-G men required that he wear at all times a red rubber ball for a nose, keep his eyebrows shaved off, and cover his even white teeth with black caps at snaggle-tooth random.

"If you see this boy," said the ballerina, "do not—I repeat, do not—try to reason with him."

There was the shriek of a door being torn from its hinges.

Screams and barking cries of consternation came from the television set. The photograph of Harrison Bergeron on the screen jumped again and again, as though dancing to the tune of an earthquake.

George Bergeron correctly identified the earthquake, and well he might have—for many was the time his own home had danced to the same crashing tune. "My God—" said George, "that must be Harrison!"

The realization was blasted from his mind instantly by the sound of an automobile collision in his head.

When George could open his eyes again, the photograph of Harrison was gone. A living, breathing Harrison filled the screen.

Clanking, clownish, and huge, Harrison stood in the center of the studio. The knob of the uprooted studio door was still in his hand. Ballerinas, technicians, musicians, and announcers cowered on their knees before him, expecting to die.

"I am the Emperor!" cried Harrison. "Do you hear? I am the Emperor! Everybody must do what I say at once!" He stamped his foot and the studio shook.

"Even as I stand here—" he bellowed, "crippled, hobbled, sickened—I am a greater ruler than any man who ever lived! Now watch me become what I *can* become!"

Harrison tore the straps of his handicap harness like wet tissue paper, tore straps guaranteed to support five thousand pounds.

Harrison's scrap-iron handicaps crashed to the floor.

Harrison thrust his thumbs under the bar of the padlock that secured his head harness. The bar snapped like celery. Harrison smashed his headphones and spectacles against the wall.

He flung away his rubber-ball nose, revealed a man that would have awed Thor, the god of thunder.

"I shall now select my Empress!" he said, looking down on the cowering people. "Let the first woman who dares rise to her feet claim her mate and her throne!"

A moment passed, and then a ballerina arose, swaying like a willow.

Harrison plucked the mental handicap from her ear, snapped off her physical handicaps with marvelous delicacy. Last of all, he removed her mask.

She was blindingly beautiful.

"Now—" said Harrison, taking her hand, "shall we show the people the meaning of the word *dance?* Music!" he commanded.

The musicians scrambled back into their chairs, and Harrison stripped them of their handicaps, too. "Play your best," he told them, "and I'll make you barons and dukes and earls."

The music began. It was normal at first—cheap, silly, false. But Harrison snatched two musicians from their chairs, waved them like batons as he sang the music as he wanted it played. He slammed them back into their chairs.

The music began again and was much improved.

Harrison and his Empress merely listened to the music for a while—listened gravely, as though synchronizing their heart-beats with it.

They shifted their weights to their toes.

Harrison placed his big hands on the girl's tiny waist, letting her sense the weightlessness that would soon be hers.

And then, in an explosion of joy and grace, into the air they sprang!

Not only were the laws of the land abandoned, but the law of gravity and the laws of motion as well.

They reeled, whirled, swiveled, flounced, capered, gam-boled, and spun.

They leaped like deer on the moon.

The studio ceiling was thirty feet high, but each leap brought the dancers nearer to it.

It became their obvious intention to kiss the ceiling.

They kissed it.

And then, neutralizing gravity with love and pure will, they remained suspended in air inches below the ceiling, and they kissed each other for a long, long time.

It was then that Diana Moon Glampers, the Handicapper General, came into the studio with a double-barreled ten-gauge shotgun. She fired twice, and the Emperor and the Empress were dead before they hit the floor.

Diana Moon Glampers loaded the gun again. She aimed it at the musicians and told them they had ten seconds to get their handicaps back on.

It was then that the Bergerons' television tube burned out.

Hazel turned to comment about the blackout to George. But George had gone out into the kitchen for a can of beer.

George came back in with the beer, paused while a handicap signal shook him up. And then he sat down again. "You been crying?" he said to Hazel.

"Yup," she said.

"What about?" he said.

"I forget," she said. "Something real sad on television."

"What was it?" he said.

"It's all kind of mixed-up in my mind," said Hazel.

"Forget sad things," said George.

"I always do," said Hazel.

"That's my girl," said George. He winced. There was the sound of a riveting gun in his head.

"Gee—I could tell that one was a doozy," said Hazel.

"You can say that again," said George.

"Gee—" said Hazel, "I could tell that one was a doozy."

The Facts of the Story

Write brief answers to the following questions. Answers should be complete sentences. Look at the story if you wish.

1. What kind of handicap has been imposed on people with better-than-average mental capacity?

2. What kind of handicap has been imposed on people with better-than-average physical ability?

3. Is George right when he says that Hazel would be as good a Handicapper General as anybody else? Explain.

4. Why has Harrison Bergeron been put in jail?

5. What penalty do Harrison and his ballerina partner pay for refusing to wear their handicaps?

The Ideas in the Story

Prepare to discuss the following questions in class.

1. "Harrison Bergeron" is a *satire,* a kind of writing that ridicules people's actions and beliefs. What belief does Vonnegut ridicule, or satirize, in this story? What kind of society is he mocking?

2. Even if it were possible by some practical method to remove all competition from society, would such a removal be a good thing? Why? Consider the effect the lack of competition would have on business, on sports, on education.

3. What do you think would be the most damaging result of removing all individual talents and skills from society? What is the difference between believing people are equals under the law and believing that everyone should be "equal every which way" (that is, the same)?

4. What do you think of Hazel's comments about the radio announcer who fails in his attempt to read the news? " 'That's all right—' Hazel said of the announcer, 'he tried. That's the big thing. He tried to do the best he could with what God gave him. He should get a nice raise for trying so hard.' " Do you think people should be rewarded for effort as well as for accomplishment? Explain why or why not.

5. Do you think that Harrison, by his heroic defiance of the system, may have accomplished something good? Explain.

Composition

Writing an Explanation

Write a composition that explains how our society would be affected if everybody were "equal" in Vonnegut's sense of the word. Use ideas mentioned in the class discussion of this story. In your essay, discuss the possible advantages and disadvantages of eliminating competition.
Write approximately 150 words.

Kurt Vonnegut

Kurt Vonnegut (1922-   ), was born in Indianapolis, Indiana. He attended Cornell University and the University of Chicago. Since 1950, he has pursued a literary career as a writer of short stories, novels, and plays. He has also been a teacher at the Hopefield School, in Sandwich, Massachusetts. Vonnegut's writing is often satirical and humorous, sometimes bordering on fantasy, but always serious in purpose. He says he is concerned about the dehumanization of the individual in a society dominated by science and technology. His novel *Slaughterhouse-Five* has won Vonnegut a strong following among college students.

₼e *Fatalist*

ISAAC BASHEVIS SINGER
Translated by Joseph Singer

*A fatalist, of course, is a person who believes in fatalism.
This story explains just what "fatalism" is. It tells how one
fatalist risks his life to show how strong his belief is.*

*You will find the story easier to understand if you pay
attention to quotation marks. The narrator introduces the
story of the Fatalist, but then he has the secretary of the
Young Zion organization tell the story. Since what the secretary says is quoted, his story is enclosed in quotation marks.
The conversation of characters within this story is enclosed in
single quotation marks. After the secretary finishes telling the
Fatalist's story, the narrator concludes with a brief conversation between himself and the secretary.*

*This is a kind of love story, but its ending may not be what
you expect.*

Nicknames given in small towns are the homely, familiar ones: Haim Bellybutton, Yekel Cake, Sarah Gossip, Gittel Duck, and similar names. But in the Polish town where I came as a teacher in my young days I heard of someone called Benjamin Fatalist. I promptly became curious. How did they come to the word *fatalist* in a small town? And what did that person do to earn it? The secretary of the Young Zion organization where I taught Hebrew told me about it.

The man in question wasn't a native here. He stemmed from somewhere in Courland. He had come to town in 1916 and posted notices that he was a teacher of German. It was during the Austrian occupation, and everyone wanted to learn German. German is spoken in Courland and he, Benjamin Schwartz—that was his real name—got many students of both sexes. Just as the secretary was talking, he pointed to the window and exclaimed: "There he goes now!"

I looked through the window and saw a short man, dark, in a derby and with a curled mustache that was already long out of style. He was carrying a briefcase. After the Austrians left, the secretary continued, no one wanted to study German any more and the Poles gave Benjamin Schwartz a job in the archives. If someone needed a birth certificate, they came to him. He had a fancy handwriting. He had learned Polish, and he also became a kind of hedge-lawyer.[1]

The secretary said: "He came here as if dropping from heaven. At that time, he was a bachelor of some twenty-odd. The young people had a club and when an educated person came to our town this was cause for a regular celebration. He was invited to our club and a box evening was arranged in his honor.

1. *hedge-lawyer*: unofficial lawyer.

Questions were placed in a box, and he was supposed to draw them out and answer them. A girl asked whether he believed in Special Providence, and, instead of replying in a few words, he spoke for a whole hour. He said that . . . all things were determined, every trifle. If one ate an onion for supper, it was because one *had* to eat an onion. It had been so preordained a billion years ago. If you walked in the street and tripped over a pebble, it was fated that you should fall. He described himself as a fatalist. It had been destined that he come to our town, though it appeared accidental.

"He spoke too long; nevertheless, a discussion followed. 'Is there no such thing as chance?' someone asked, and he replied: 'No such thing as chance.' 'If that is so,' another asked, 'what's the point of working, of studying? Why learn a trade or bring up children? Well, and why contribute to Zionism and agitate for a Jewish homeland?'

" 'The way it is written in the books of fate, that's how it has to be,' Benjamin Schwartz replied. 'If it was destined that someone open a store and go bankrupt, he has to do this.' All the efforts man made were fate, too, because free choice is nothing but an illusion. The debate lasted well into the night and from that time on, he was called the Fatalist. A new word was added to the town's vocabulary. Everyone here knows what a fatalist is, even the beadle[2] of the synagogue and the poorhouse attendant.

"We assumed that after that evening the crowd would get tired of these discussions and turn back to the real problems of our time. Benjamin himself said that this wasn't a thing that could be decided by logic. Either one believed in it or not. But somehow, all our youth became preoccupied with the question. We would call a meeting about certificates to Palestine or about education, but instead of sticking to these subjects, they would discuss fatalism. At that time our library acquired a copy

---

2. *beadle*: minor official.

of Lermontov's A *Hero of Our Time*, translated into Yiddish, which describes a fatalist, Petchorin. Everyone read this novel, and there were those among us who wanted to test their luck. We already knew about Russian roulette and some of us might have tried it if a revolver were available. But none of us had one.

"Now listen to this. There was a girl among us, Heyele Minz, a pretty girl, smart, active in our movement, a daughter of a wealthy man. Her father had the biggest dry-goods store in town, and all the young fellows were crazy about her. but Heyele was choosy. She found something wrong in everybody. She had a sharp tongue, what the Germans call *schlagfertig*. If you said something to her she came right back at you with a sharp and cutting retort. When she wanted to, she could ridicule a person in a clever, half-joking way. The Fatalist fell in love with her soon after he arrived. He wasn't at all bashful. One evening he came up to her and said: 'Heyele, it's fated that you marry me, and since that is so, why delay the inevitable?'

"He said this aloud so that everyone would hear, and it created an uproar. Heyele answered: 'It's fated that I should tell you that you're an idiot and that you've got lots of nerve besides, and therefore I'm saying it. You'll have to forgive me, it was all preordained in the celestial books a billion years ago.'

"Not long afterward, Heyele became engaged to a young man from Hrubieszów, the chairman of the Paole Zion there. The wedding was postponed for a year because the fiancé had an older sister who was engaged and who had to be married first. The boys chided the Fatalist, and he said: 'If Heyele is to be mine, she will be mine,' and Heyele replied: 'I am to be Ozer Rubinstein's, not yours. That's what fate wanted.'

"One winter evening the discussion flared up again about fate, and Heyele spoke up: 'Mr. Schwartz, or Mr. Fatalist, if you really believe in what you say, and you are even ready to play Russian roulette if you had a revolver, I have a game for you that's even more dangerous.'

"I want to mention here that at that time, the railroad didn't reach to our town yet. It passed two miles away, and it never stopped there at all. It was the train from Warsaw to Lvov. Heyele proposed to the Fatalist that he lie down on the rails a few moments before the train passed over them. She argued: 'If it's fated that you live, you will live and have nothing to fear. However, if you don't believe in fatalism, then . . .'

"We all burst out laughing. Everyone was sure that the Fatalist would come up with some pretext to get out of it. Lying down on the tracks meant certain death. But the Fatalist said: 'This, like Russian roulette, is a game, and a game requires another participant who must risk something, too.' He went on: 'I'll lie down on the tracks as you propose, but you must make a sacred vow that if I should live, you'll break your engagement with Ozer Rubinstein and marry me.'

"A deadly silence fell over the hall. Heyele grew pale, and she said: 'Good, I accept your conditions.' 'Give me your sacred vow on it,' the Fatalist said, and Heyele gave him her hand and said: 'I have no mother, she died of the cholera. But I swear on her soul that if you will keep your word, I will keep mine. If not, then let my honor be stained forever.' She turned to us and went on: 'You are all witnesses. If I should break my word, you can all spit in my face.'

"I'll make it short. Everything was settled that evening. The train would pass our town around two in the afternoon. At one thirty, our whole group would meet by the tracks and the Fatalist would demonstrate whether he was a real fatalist or just a braggart. We all promised to keep the matter secret because if the older people had found out about it, there would have been a terrible fuss.

"I didn't sleep a wink that night, and, as far as I know, none of the others did either. Most of us were convinced that at the last minute the Fatalist would have second thoughts and back out. Some also suggested that when the train came into sight or the rails started to hum, we should drag the Fatalist away by force. Well, but all this posed a gruesome danger. Even now as I speak of it a shudder runs through me.

"The next day we all got up early. I was so scared that I couldn't swallow any food at breakfast. The whole thing might not have happened if we hadn't read Lermontov's book. Not all of us went; there were only six boys and four girls, including Heyele Minz. It was freezing cold outside. The Fatalist, I remember, wore a light jacket and a cap. We met on the Zamosc Road, on the outskirts of town. I asked him: 'Schwartz, how did you sleep last night?' and he answered: 'Like any other night.' You actually couldn't tell what he was feeling, but Heyele was as white as if she had just gotten over the typhoid. I went up to her and said: 'Heyele, do you know that you're sending a person to his death?' And she said: 'I'm not sending him. He has plenty of time to change his mind.'

"I'll never forget that day as long as I live. None of us will ever forget it. We walked along and the snow kept falling on us the whole time. We came to the tracks. I thought that on account of the snow the train might possibly not be running, but apparently someone had cleared the rails. We had arrived a good hour too early, and, believe me, this was the longest hour I ever spent. Around fifteen minutes before the train was due to come by, Heyele said: 'Schwartz, I've thought it all over and I don't want you to lose your life because of me. Do me a favor and let's forget the whole thing.' The Fatalist looked at her and asked: 'So you've changed your mind? You want that fellow from Hrubieszów at any price, huh?' She said: 'No, it's not the fellow from Hrubieszów, it's your life. I hear that you have a mother and I don't want her to lose a son on account of me.' Heyele could barely utter these words. She spoke and she trembled. The Fatalist said: 'If you will keep your promise, I'm ready to keep mine, but under one condition: stand a little farther away. If you try to force me back at the last minute, the game is over.' Then he cried out: 'Let everyone move twenty paces back!' He seemed to hypnotize us with his words, and we began to back up. He cried again: 'If someone tries to pull me away, I'll grab him by his coat and he will share my fate.' We realized how dangerous this could be. It happens more than once that when you try to save someone from drowning, you both get pushed down and drown.

"As we moved back, the rails began to vibrate and hum and we heard the whistle of the locomotive. We began to yell as one: 'Schwartz, don't do it! Schwartz, have pity!' But even as we yelled he stretched out across the tracks. There was then just one line of track. One girl fainted. We were sure that in a second we would see a person cut in half. I can't tell you what I went through in those few seconds. My blood literally began to seethe from excitement. At that moment, a loud screech was heard and a thud and the train came to a halt no more than a yard away from the Fatalist. I saw in a mist how the engineer and fireman jumped down from the locomotive. They yelled at him and dragged him away. Many passengers disembarked. Some of us ran away out of fear of being arrested. It was a real commotion. I myself stayed where I was and watched everything. Heyele ran up to me, put her arms around me and started to cry. It was more than a cry, it was like the howling of a beast—give me a cigarette. I can't talk about it. It chokes me. Excuse me. . . ."

I gave the secretary a cigarette and watched how it shook between his fingers. He drew in the smoke and said: "That is actually the whole story."

"She married him?" I asked.

"They have four children."

"I guess the engineer managed to halt the train in time," I remarked.

"Yes, but the wheels were only one yard away from him."

"Did this convince you about fatalism?" I asked.

"No. I wouldn't make such a bet even if you offered me all the fortunes in the world."

"Is he still a fatalist?"

"He still is."

"Would he do it again?" I asked.

The secretary smiled. "Not for Heyele."

The Facts of the Story

Write short answers to the following questions. Your answers may be phrases or sentences. Refer to the story, if you wish.

1. What game does Heyele propose to test the Fatalist's belief?

2. On what condition does the Fatalist accept Heyele's test?

3. What do some of the young people by the railroad track plan to do, if necessary, to prevent the death of the Fatalist? Why do they have to abandon their plan?

4. According to the story, is the Fatalist telling the truth when he says, "Heyele, it's fated that you marry me"? Explain.

5. Years later, how does the Fatalist feel about his fate?

The Ideas in the Story

"The Fatalist" is concerned with only one idea. It is the idea held by Benjamin Schwartz: that "all things were determined, every trifle." Schwartz believes that things do not happen to us by chance or by accident or by coincidence, or even because we will them. Rather, he believes that everything that happens to us has been prearranged and *has* to happen. The Fatalist says, "The way it is written in the books of fate, that's how it has to be." According to this belief, even the person we marry, our success or failure in life, the time and place of our dying–all are predetermined. Does Singer's story suggest that there is truth in the belief of a fatalist, or does it suggest that fatalism is ridiculous? Refer to the story to support your opinion.

What do you think a fatalist's answer would be to the question "Why should I work hard to get what I want when everything that is going to happen has already been determined?" Would the answer suggest that the determination to work hard is itself preordained?

Composition

Backing Up an Opinion

Write a paragraph in which you state and support your opinion of fatalism. If you are a fatalist, explain why. If you are not, give your reasons. You may, if you wish, use ideas and events from this story to back up your opinion.
Write approximately 100 words.

Isaac Bashevis Singer

Isaac Bashevis Singer (1904-   ) was born in Poland. He grew up in Warsaw, where, as an adult, he worked as a journalist and as a writer of novels and stories. He emigrated to the United States in 1935 and became a United States citizen in 1943. He says that when he arrived in America, he knew only three words in English–"Take a chair." His language was Yiddish, which is a language written in Hebrew letters and used by Jews in Eastern Europe, and wherever Jewish emigrés from Eastern Europe have settled. Although Singer mastered the English language long ago, he still writes in Yiddish. In 1978, he was awarded the Nobel Prize for literature. As for information about the authors of the books we read, Singer says, "A real reader, especially a young reader, never cares too much about the author. He wants to read the book and he enjoys it."

A Sunrise on the Veld

DORIS LESSING

The veld is a part of Rhodesia and South Africa—a vast area of great plains covered with tall grass, scattered bush areas, and trees. Although there are farms on the veld, some of it is unspoiled wilderness filled with wildlife of many kinds.

The story tells of a fifteen-year-old boy, healthy, strong, confident, excited by a sense of well-being and by the sheer joy of living as he goes out onto the veld before dawn. On the morning of the story, however, his high spirits are dampened by a horrible and thought-provoking experience. Nature seems to be teaching him a lesson, one he does not fully understand, a lesson about life—and death.

This is a serious story that touches on the great questions that have always puzzled philosophers. It may not strike you as pleasant, but it should hold your interest, and it may make you think about the great questions yourself.

The story is beautifully written. Do not read rapidly. Take time to appreciate Lessing's descriptions of the veld, and of the boy's exultation in his own happiness before he witnesses the event that deeply disturbs him.

Every night that winter he said aloud into the dark of the pillow: Half past four! Half past four! till he felt his brain had gripped the words and held them fast. Then he fell asleep at once, as if a shutter had fallen, and lay with his face turned to the clock so that he could see it first thing when he woke.

It was half past four to the minute, every morning. Triumphantly pressing down the alarm knob of the clock, which the dark half of his mind had outwitted, remaining vigilant all night and counting the hours as he lay relaxed in sleep, he huddled down for a last warm moment under the clothes, playing with the idea of lying abed for this once only. But he played with it for the fun of knowing that it was a weakness he could defeat without effort; just as he set the alarm each night for the delight of the moment when he woke and stretched his limbs, feeling the muscles tighten, and thought: Even my brain—even that! I can control every part of myself.

Luxury of warm rested body, with the arms and legs and fingers waiting like soldiers for a word of command! Joy of knowing that the precious hours were given to sleep voluntarily!—for he had once stayed awake three nights running, to prove that he could, and then worked all day, refusing even to admit that he was tired; and now sleep seemed to him a servant to be commanded and refused.

The boy stretched his frame full-length, touching the wall at his head with his hands, and the bed foot with his toes; then he sprung out, like a fish leaping from water. And it was cold, cold.

He always dressed rapidly, so as to try and conserve his night-warmth till the sun rose two hours later; but by the time he had on his clothes his hands were numbed and he could scarcely hold his shoes. These he could not put on for fear of waking his parents, who never came to know how early he rose.

As soon as he stepped over the lintel, the flesh of his soles contracted on the chilled earth, and his legs began to ache with cold. It was night: the stars were glittering, the trees standing black and still. He looked for signs of day, for the graying of the edge of a stone, or a lightening in the sky where the sun would rise, but there was nothing yet. Alert as an animal he crept past the dangerous window, standing poised with his hand on the sill for one proudly fastidious moment, looking in at the stuffy blackness of the room where his parents lay.

Feeling for the grass-edge of the path with his toes, he reached inside another window further along the wall, where his gun had been set in readiness the night before. The steel was icy, and numbed fingers slipped along it, so that he had to hold it in the crook of his arm for safety. Then he tiptoed to the room where the dogs slept, and was fearful that they might have been tempted to go before him; but they were waiting, their haunches crouched in reluctance at the cold, but ears and swinging tails greeting the gun ecstatically. His warning undertone kept them secret and silent till the house was a hundred yards back; then they bolted off into the bush, yelping excitedly. The boy imagined his parents turning in their beds and muttering: Those dogs again! before they were dragged back in sleep; and he smiled scornfully. He always looked back over his shoulder at the house before he passed a wall of trees that shut it from sight. It looked so low and small, crouching there under a tall and brilliant sky. Then he turned his back on it, and on the frowsting sleepers,[1] and forgot them.

He would have to hurry. Before the light grew strong he must be four miles away; and already a tint of green stood in the hollow of a leaf, and the air smelled of morning and the stars were dimming.

1. *frowsting sleepers:* people sleeping in a stuffy, musty room.

He slung the shoes over his shoulder, veld *skoen* that were crinkled and hard with the dews of a hundred mornings. They would be necessary when the ground became too hot to bear. Now he felt the chilled dust push up between his toes, and he let the muscles of his feet spread and settle into the shapes of the earth; and he thought: I could walk a hundred miles on feet like these! I could walk all day, and never tire!

He was walking swiftly through the dark tunnel of foliage that in daytime was a road. The dogs were invisibly ranging the lower travelways of the bush, and he heard them panting. Sometimes he felt a cold muzzle on his leg before they were off again, scouting for a trail to follow. They were not trained, but free-running companions of the hunt, who often tired of the long stalk before the final shots, and went off on their own pleasure. Soon he could see them, small and wild-looking in a wild strange light, now that the bush stood trembling on the verge of color, waiting for the sun to paint earth and grass afresh.

The grass stood to his shoulders; and the trees were showering a faint silvery rain. He was soaked; his whole body was clenched in a steady shiver.

Once he bent to the road that was newly scored with animal trails, and regretfully straightened, reminding himself that the pleasure of tracking must wait till another day.

He began to run along the edge of a field, noting jerkily how it was filmed over with fresh spider web, so that the long reaches of great black clods seemed netted in glistening gray. He was using the steady lope he had learned by watching the natives, the run that is a dropping of the weight of the body from one foot to the next in a slow balancing movement that never tires, nor shortens the breath; and he felt the blood pulsing down his legs and along his arms, and the exultation and pride of body mounted in him till he was shutting his teeth hard against a violent desire to shout his triumph.

Soon he had left the cultivated part of the farm. Behind him

the bush was low and black. In front was a long vlei, acres of
long pale grass that sent back a hollowing gleam of light to a
satiny sky. Near him thick swathes of grass were bent with the
weight of water, and diamond drops sparkled on each frond.

The first bird woke at his feet and at once a flock of them
sprang into the air, calling shrilly that day had come; and suddenly, behind him, the bush woke into song, and he could
hear the guinea fowl calling far ahead of him. That meant they
would now be sailing down from their trees into thick grass,
and it was for them he had come: he was too late. But he did
not mind. He forgot he had come to shoot. He set his legs
wide, and balanced from foot to foot, and swung his gun up
and down in both hands horizontally, in a kind of improvised
exercise, and let his head sink back till it was pillowed in his
neck muscles, and watched how above him small rosy clouds
floated in a lake of gold.

Suddenly it all rose in him; it was unbearable. He leapt up
into the air, shouting and yelling wild, unrecognizable noises.
Then he began to run, not carefully, as he had before, but
madly, like a wild thing. He was clean crazy, yelling mad with
the joy of living and a superfluity of youth. He rushed down
the vlei under a tumult of crimson and gold, while all the birds
of the world sang about him. He ran in great leaping strides,
and shouted as he ran, feeling his body rise into the crisp rushing air and fall back surely onto sure feet; and thought briefly,
not believing that such a thing could happen to him, that he
could break his ankle any moment, in this thick tangled grass.
He cleared bushes like a duiker,[2] leapt over rocks, and finally
came to a dead stop at a place where the ground fell abruptly
away below him to the river. It had been a two-mile-long dash
through waist-high growth, and he was breathing hoarsely and
could no longer sing. But he poised on a rock and looked down
at stretches of water that gleamed through stooping trees, and

---

2. *duiker* (dī´kər): kind of antelope.

thought suddenly: I am fifteen! Fifteen! The words came new
to him, so that he kept repeating them wonderingly, with
swelling excitement; and he felt the years of his life with his
hands, as if he were counting marbles, each one hard and
separate and compact, each one a wonderful shining thing.
That was what he was: fifteen years of this rich soil, and this
slow-moving water, and air that smelt like a challenge whether
it was warm and sultry at noon, or as brisk as cold water, like it
was now.

There was nothing he couldn't do, nothing! A vision came
to him, as he stood there, like when a child hears the word
eternity and tries to understand it, and time takes possession of
the mind. He felt his life ahead of him as a great and wonderful
thing, something that was his; and he said aloud, with the
blood rising to his head: All the great men of the world have
been as I am now, and there is nothing I can't become, nothing I can't do; there is no country in the world I cannot make
part of myself, if I choose. I contain the world. I can make of it
what I want. If I choose, I can change everything that is going
to happen: it depends on me, and what I decide now.

The urgency and the truth and the courage of what his voice
was saying exulted him so that he began to sing again, at the
top of his voice, and the sound went echoing down the river
gorge. He stopped for the echo, and sang again; stopped and
shouted. That was what he was!—he sang, if he chose; and the
world had to answer him.

And for minutes he stood there, shouting and singing and
waiting for the lovely eddying sound of the echo; so that his
own new strong thoughts came back and washed round his
head, as if someone were answering him and encouraging him;
till the gorge was full of soft voices clashing back and forth from
rock to rock over the river. And then it seemed as if there was a
new voice. He listened, puzzled, for it was not his own. Soon
he was leaning forward, all his nerves alert, quite still: somewhere close to him there was a noise that was no joyful

bird, nor tinkle of falling water, nor ponderous movement of cattle.

There it was again. In the deep morning hush that held his future and his past, was a sound of pain, and repeated over and over: it was a kind of shortened scream, as if someone, something, had no breath to scream. He came to himself, looked about him, and called for the dogs. They did not appear: they had gone off on their own business, and he was alone. Now he was clean sober, all the madness gone. His heart beating fast, because of that frightened screaming, he stepped carefully off the rock and went towards a belt of trees. He was moving cautiously, for not so long ago he had seen a leopard in just this spot.

At the edge of the trees he stopped and peered, holding his gun ready; he advanced, looking steadily about him, his eyes narrowed. Then, all at once, in the middle of a step, he faltered, and his face was puzzled. He shook his head impatiently, as if he doubted his own sight.

There, between two trees, against a background of gaunt black rocks, was a figure from a dream, a strange beast that was horned and drunken-legged, but like something he had never even imagined. It seemed to be ragged. It looked like a small buck that had black ragged tufts of fur standing up irregularly all over it, with patches of raw flesh beneath . . . but the patches of rawness were disappearing under moving black and came again elsewhere; and all the time the creature screamed, in small gasping screams, and leaped drunkenly from side to side, as if it were blind.

Then the boy understood: it *was* a buck. He ran closer, and again stood still, stopped by a new fear. Around him the grass was whispering and alive. He looked wildly about, and then down. The ground was black with ants, great energetic ants that took no notice of him, but hurried and scurried towards the fighting shape, like glistening black water flowing through the grass.

And, as he drew in his breath and pity and terror seized him, the beast fell and the screaming stopped. Now he could hear nothing but one bird singing, and the sound of the rustling, whispering ants.

He peered over at the writhing blackness that jerked convulsively with the jerking nerves. It grew quieter. There were small twitches from the mass that still looked vaguely like the shape of a small animal.

It came into his mind that he should shoot it and end its pain; and he raised the gun. Then he lowered it again. The buck could no longer feel; its fighting was a mechanical protest of the nerves. But it was not that which made him put down the gun. It was a swelling feeling of rage and misery and protest that expressed itself in the thought: If I had not come it would have died like this; so why should I interfere? All over the bush things like this happen; they happen all the time; this is how life goes on, by living things dying in anguish. He gripped the gun between his knees and felt in his own limbs the myriad swarming pain of the twitching animal that could no longer feel, and set his teeth, and said over and over again under his breath: I can't stop it. I can't stop it. There is nothing I can do.

He was glad that the buck was unconscious and had gone past suffering, so that he did not have to make a decision to kill it even when he was feeling with his whole body: This is what happens, this is how things work.

It was right—that was what he was feeling. *It was right and nothing could alter it*.

The knowledge of fatality, of what has to be, had gripped him and for the first time in his life; and he was left unable to make any movement of brain or body, except to say: "Yes, yes. That is what living is." It had entered his flesh and his bones and grown into the furthest corners of his brain and would never leave him. And at that moment he could not have performed the smallest action of mercy, knowing as he did, having lived on it all his life, the vast, unalterable, cruel veld, where at any moment one might stumble over a skull or crush the skeleton of some small creature.

Suffering, sick, and angry, but also grimly satisfied with his new stoicism, he stood there leaning on his rifle, and watched the seething black mound grow smaller. At his feet, now, were ants trickling back with pink fragments in their mouths, and there was a fresh acid smell in his nostrils. He sternly controlled the uselessly convulsing muscles of his empty stomach, and reminded himself: The ants must eat too! At the same time he found that the tears were streaming down his face, and his clothes were soaked with the sweat of that other creature's pain.

The shape had grown small. Now it looked like nothing recognizable. He did not know how long it was before he saw the blackness thin, and bits of white showed through, shining in the sun—yes, there was the sun, just up, glowing over the rocks. Why, the whole thing could not have taken longer than a few minutes.

He began to swear, as if the shortness of the time was in itself unbearable, using the words he had heard his father say. He strode forward, crushing ants with each step, and brushing them off his clothes, till he stood above the skeleton, which lay sprawled under a small bush. It was clean-picked. It might have been lying there years, save that on the white bone were pink fragments of gristle. About the bones ants were ebbing away, their pincers full of meat.

The boy looked at them, big black ugly insects. A few were standing and gazing up at him with small glittering eyes.

"Go away!" he said to the ants, very coldly. "I am not for you—not just yet, at any rate. Go away." And he fancied that the ants turned and went away.

He bent over the bones and touched the sockets in the skull; that was where the eyes were, he thought incredulously, remembering the liquid dark eyes of a buck. And then he bent the slim foreleg bone, swinging it horizontally in his palm.

That morning, perhaps an hour ago, this small creature had been stepping proud and free through the bush, feeling the chill on its hide even as he himself had done, exhilarated by it. Proudly stepping the earth, tossing its horns, frisking a pretty white tail, it had sniffed the cold morning air. Walking like kings and conquerors it had moved through this free-held bush, where each blade of grass grew for it alone, and where the river ran pure sparkling water for its slaking.

And then—what had happened? Such a swift, sure-footed thing could surely not be trapped by a swarm of ants?

The boy bent curiously to the skeleton. Then he saw that the back leg that lay uppermost and strained out in the tension of death, was snapped midway in the thigh, so that broken bones jutted over each other uselessly. So that was it! Limping into the ant-masses it could not escape, once it had sensed the danger. Yes, but how had the leg been broken? Had it fallen, perhaps? Impossible, a buck was too light and graceful. Had some jealous rival horned it?

What could possibly have happened? Perhaps some Africans had thrown stones at it, as they do, trying to kill it for meat, and had broken its leg. Yes, that must be it.

Even as he imagined the crowd of running, shouting natives, and the flying stones, and the leaping buck, another picture came into his mind. He saw himself, on any one of these bright ringing mornings, drunk with excitement, taking a snapshot at some half-seen buck. He saw himself with the gun lowered, wondering whether he had missed or not, and thinking at last that it was late, and he wanted his breakfast, and it was not worthwhile to track miles after an animal that would very likely get away from him in any case.

For a moment he would not face it. He was a small boy again, kicking sulkily at the skeleton, hanging his head, refusing to accept the responsibility.

Then he straightened up, and looked down at the bones with

an odd expression of dismay, all the anger gone out of him. His mind went quite empty; all around him he could see trickles of ants disappearing into the grass. The whispering noise was faint and dry, like the rustling of a cast snakeskin.

At last he picked up his gun and walked homewards. He was telling himself half defiantly that he wanted his breakfast. He was telling himself that it was getting very hot, much too hot to be out roaming the bush.

Really, he was tired. He walked heavily, not looking where he put his feet. When he came within sight of his home he stopped, knitting his brows. There was something he had to think out. The death of that small animal was a thing that concerned him, and he was by no means finished with it. It lay at the back of his mind uncomfortably.

Soon, the very next morning, he would get clear of everybody and go to the bush and think about it.

The Facts of the Story

Write answers to the following questions. Some can be answered in a word; others will require a phrase or a complete sentence. Look at the story, if you wish.

1. Find a statement at the opening of the story that tells how the boy feels about control over his own body.

2. Why does the boy go out onto the veld?

3. Think of three words to describe the boy's feelings as he runs over the veld.

4. What does the boy see that changes his feelings?

5. Why doesn't the boy shoot the dying buck?

6. How was the buck like the boy at one time?

7. Why was the buck unable to escape from the ants?

8. What makes the boy feel that he may have been responsible for the buck's death?

9. What excuses does he make for returning home?

10. What does he plan to do the following morning?

The Ideas in the Story

Reread these key passages from the story. For class discussion, prepare answers to the questions that follow.

I

There was nothing he couldn't do, nothing! . . . He felt his life ahead of him as a great and wonderful thing, something that was his; and he said aloud, with the blood rising to his head: All the great men of the world have been as I am now, and there is nothing I can't become, nothing I can't do. . . .

He gripped the gun between his knees and felt in his own limbs the myriad swarming pain of the twitching animal that could no longer feel, and set his teeth, and said over and over again under his breath: I can't stop it. I can't stop it. There is nothing I can do.

1. What change has taken place in the boy? Why do you think his feelings about his power have changed?

2. Select the adjectives that best complete this statement: The lesson the boy learns from his experience makes him feel (a) afraid (b) sorry (c) angry (d) self-confident (e) helpless (f) dejected. Explain your choices by referring to the story.

3. Why is it significant that on this particular day, of all days, the boy witnesses the death of the buck?

II

It came into his mind that he should shoot it and end its pain; and he raised the gun. Then he lowered it again. The buck could no longer feel; its fighting was a mechanical protest of the nerves. But it was not that which made him put down the gun. It was a swelling feeling of rage and misery and protest that expressed itself in the thought: If I had not come it would have died like this; so why should I interfere? All over the bush things like this happen; they happen all the time; this is how life goes on, by living things dying in anguish. . . . This is what happens, this is how things work.

It was right—that was what he was feeling. *It was right and nothing could alter it.*

1. Explain why you do or do not agree with the boy's statement: ". . . this is how life goes on, by living things dying in anguish."

2. If you agree that there must be death in order that there be life, do you also agree that death must be "in anguish"? Explain.

3. Are the boy's statements about life and death applicable to human life, or do they apply only to life in the wild? Explain.

III

The knowledge of fatality, of what has to be, had gripped him and for the first time in his life; and he was left unable to make any movement of brain or body, except to say: "Yes, yes. That is what living is." It had entered his flesh and his bones and grown into the furthest corners of his brain and would never leave him. And at that moment he could not have performed the smallest action of mercy, knowing as he did, having lived on it all his life, the vast, unalterable, cruel veld, where at any moment one might stumble over a skull or crush the skeleton of some small creature.

Suffering, sick, and angry, but also grimly satisfied with his new stoicism, he stood there leaning on his rifle, and watched the seething black mound grow smaller.

1. A key word in the first sentence is *fatality,* which is related to the word *fatalism.* If you read Singer's story "The Fatalist" (page 355), you know what is meant by fatalism. What indication is there in this passage that the boy, after his first "knowledge" of fatality, feels it is futile to attempt to change "what has to be"? How does the boy's awareness of *fatality* ("what has to be") differ from *fatalism?*

2. The boy had once said, "I contain the world. I can make of it what I want. If I choose, I can change everything that is going to happen: it depends on me, and what I decide now." Do you think the "knowledge of fatality" has changed the boy forever, or do you think he will once again feel he can control what happens? Why or why not?

3. A key word in the second paragraph is *stoicism.* Use the dictionary to find out what this means. How are the "knowledge of fatality" and "his new stoicism" related?

4. Many of our greatest thinkers and philosophers have difficulty understanding what life is, why our destiny often seems beyond our control, how our fate is determined, why there must be suffering and death. These are some of the things that the boy will probably want to think about after his experience on the veld. What conclusions do you think he will reach? What advice would you give him?

The Art of the Storyteller

A Descriptive Style

Everything we experience, we experience through our senses—sight, hearing (or sound), feeling (or touch), smell, and taste. Lessing, of course, knows this very well, and she uses language that appeals to our senses. She does this because she wants us to experience vividly what the boy in her story experiences.

Read the following descriptions from the story. Tell which of the five senses (sight, hearing, feeling, smell, and taste) each description appeals to.

1. As soon as he stepped over the lintel, the flesh of his soles contracted on the chilled earth, and his legs began to ache with cold.

2. He began to run along the edge of a field, noting jerkily how it was filmed over with fresh spider web, so that the long reaches of great black clods seemed netted in glistening gray.

3. At his feet, now, were ants trickling back with pink fragments in their mouths, and there was a fresh acid smell in his nostrils.

4. The whispering noise was faint and dry, like the rustling of a cast snakeskin.

Composition

Appealing to the Senses

Write an account in which you make an event or an experience real and vivid by using descriptive phrases that appeal to one or two of the senses (sight, sound, touch, smell, taste). Perhaps, for good measure, you can also slip in a few similes or metaphors. (See the composition assignment following "All Summer in a Day," page 257.) The following list may suggest a subject:

A picnic
A feast—Thanksgiving dinner, Christmas dinner, Passover dinner, etc.
A crowd—a parade, a religious festival, a party, a disco, an airport, the gymnasium during a game, a crowded school corridor

Write approximately 150-200 words. Underline the phrases that appeal to the senses and, if you have used any, the similes and metaphors.

Doris Lessing

Doris Lessing (1919-   ), a British novelist and short-story writer, lived for twenty-five years (1924-1949) in Southern Rhodesia, the setting of "A Sunrise on the Veld" and other stories in her collection called *African Stories*. After moving to England in 1949, she continued to write novels, stories, and plays, gradually breaking away from the African settings of her earlier works. She is regarded today as one of England's most important writers of fiction. She says she began writing when she was fourteen or fifteen, "but everything I wrote for years was rubbish. The only advice I would ever give to a young writer is 'just go on writing.' "

The Boscombe Valley Mystery

ARTHUR CONAN DOYLE

A collection of stories would not be complete without a detective story. The best-known detective in literature is Sherlock Holmes. He is portrayed so realistically that many readers find it hard to believe he was not real. Holmes is, however, a fictional character, created by the great British writer of detective stories, Arthur Conan Doyle. Almost all modern writers of detective fiction have learned some of their art from the Sherlock Holmes stories.

Holmes's adventures are usually told by his friend Dr. Watson. Watson is a physician who seems able, with remarkable ease, to take time off from his medical practice to accompany Holmes on various crime-solving missions. The Sherlock Holmes stories usually take place in England, during the 1880's and 1890's.

We were seated at breakfast one morning, my wife and I, when the maid brought in a telegram. It was from Sherlock Holmes and ran in this way:

> Have you a couple of days to spare? Have just been wired for from the west of England in connection with Boscombe Valley tragedy. Shall be glad if you will come with me. Air and scenery perfect. Leave Paddington Station by the 11:15.

"What do you say, dear?" said my wife, looking across at me. "Will you go?"

"I really don't know what to say. I have a fairly long list at present."

"Oh, Anstruther would do your work for you. You have been looking a little pale lately. I think that the change would do you good, and you are always so interested in Mr. Sherlock Holmes's cases."

"I should be ungrateful if I were not, seeing what I gained through one of them,"[1] I answered. "But if I am to go, I must pack at once, for I have only half an hour."

My experience of camp life in Afghanistan had at least had the effect of making me a prompt and ready traveler. My wants were few and simple, so that in less than the time stated I was in a cab with my valise, rattling away to Paddington Station. Sherlock Holmes was pacing up and down the platform, his tall, gaunt figure made even gaunter and taller by his long gray traveling cloak and close-fitting cloth cap.

"It is really very good of you to come, Watson," said he. "It makes a considerable difference to me, having someone with

1. Watson met his wife through the case called "The Sign of the Four."

me on whom I can thoroughly rely. Local aid is always either worthless or else biased. If you will keep the two corner seats I shall get the tickets."

We had the carriage to ourselves save for an immense litter of papers which Holmes had brought with him. Among these he rummaged and read, with intervals of note-taking and of meditation, until we were past Reading. Then he suddenly rolled them all into a gigantic ball and tossed them up onto the rack.

"Have you heard anything of the case?" he asked.

"Not a word. I have not seen a paper for some days."

"The London press has not had very full accounts. I have just been looking through all the recent papers in order to master the particulars. It seems, from what I gather, to be one of those simple cases which are so extremely difficult."

"That sounds a little paradoxical."

"But it is profoundly true. Singularity is almost invariably a clue. The more featureless and commonplace a crime is, the more difficult it is to bring it home. In this case, however, they have established a very serious case against the son of the murdered man."

"It is a murder, then?"

"Well, it is conjectured to be so. I shall take nothing for granted until I have the opportunity of looking personally into it. I will explain the state of things to you, as far as I have been able to understand it, in a very few words.

"Boscombe Valley is a country district not very far from Ross, in Herefordshire. The largest landed proprietor in that part is a Mr. John Turner, who made his money in Australia and returned some years ago to the old country. One of the farms which he held, that of Hatherley, was let to Mr. Charles McCarthy, who was also an ex-Australian. The men had known each other in the colonies, so that it was not unnatural that when they came to settle down they should do so as near each other as possible. Turner was apparently the richer man, so McCarthy became his tenant but still remained, it seems, upon terms of perfect equality, as they were frequently together. McCarthy had one son, a lad of eighteen, and Turner had an only daughter of the same age, but neither of them had wives living. They appear to have avoided the society of the neighboring English families and to have led retired lives, though both the McCarthys were fond of sport and were frequently seen at the race meetings of the neighborhood. McCarthy kept two servants—a man and a girl. Turner had a considerable household, some half-dozen at the least. That is as much as I have been able to gather about the families. Now for the facts.

"On June 3rd, that is, on Monday last, McCarthy left his house at Hatherley about three in the afternoon and walked down to the Boscombe Pool, which is a small lake formed by the spreading out of the stream which runs down the Boscombe Valley. He had been out with his serving man in the morning at Ross, and he had told the man that he must hurry, as he had an appointment of importance to keep at three. From that appointment he never came back alive.

"From Hatherley Farmhouse to the Boscombe Pool is a quarter of a mile, and two people saw him as he passed over this ground. One was an old woman whose name is not mentioned, and the other was William Crowder, a gamekeeper in the employ of Mr. Turner. Both these witnesses depose[2] that Mr. McCarthy was walking alone. The gamekeeper adds that within a few minutes of his seeing Mr. McCarthy pass he had seen his son, Mr. James McCarthy, going the same way with a gun under his arm. To the best of his belief, the father was actually in sight at the time, and the son was following him. He thought no more of the matter until he heard in the evening of the tragedy that had occurred.

"The two McCarthys were seen after the time when William

2. *depose:* testify.

Crowder, the gamekeeper, lost sight of them. The Boscombe Pool is thickly wooded round, with just a fringe of grass and of reeds round the edge. A girl of fourteen, Patience Moran, who is the daughter of the lodge keeper of the Boscombe Valley estate, was in one of the woods picking flowers. She states that while she was there she saw, at the border of the wood and close by the lake, Mr. McCarthy and his son, and that they appeared to be having a violent quarrel. She heard Mr. McCarthy the elder using very strong language to his son, and she saw the latter raise up his hand as if to strike his father. She was so frightened by their violence that she ran away and told her mother when she reached home that she had left the two McCarthys quarreling near Boscombe Pool, and that she was afraid that they were going to fight. She had hardly said the words when young Mr. McCarthy came running up to the lodge to say that he had found his father dead in the wood, and to ask for the help of the lodge keeper. He was much excited, without either his gun or his hat, and his right hand and sleeve were observed to be stained with fresh blood. On following him they found the dead body stretched out upon the grass beside the pool. The head had been beaten in by repeated blows of some heavy and blunt weapon. The injuries were such as might very well have been inflicted by the butt end of his son's gun, which was found lying on the grass within a few paces of the body. Under these circumstances the young man was instantly arrested, and a verdict of 'willful murder' having been returned at the inquest on Tuesday, he was, on Wednesday, brought before the magistrates at Ross, who have referred the case to the next Assizes.[3] Those are the main facts of the case as they came out before the coroner and the police court."

"I could hardly imagine a more damning case," I remarked. "If ever circumstantial evidence pointed to a criminal, it does so here."

---

3. *Assizes:* court sessions.

"Circumstantial evidence is a very tricky thing," answered Holmes thoughtfully. "It may seem to point very straight to one thing, but if you shift your own point of view a little, you may find it pointing in an equally uncompromising manner to something entirely different. It must be confessed, however, that the case looks exceedingly grave against the young man, and it is very possible that he is indeed the culprit. There are several people in the neighborhood, however, and among them Miss Turner, the daughter of the neighboring landowner, who believe in his innocence, and who have retained Lestrade, whom you may recollect in connection with 'A Study in Scarlet,'[4] to work out the case in his interest. Lestrade, being rather puzzled, has referred the case to me, and hence it is that two middle-aged gentlemen are flying westward at fifty miles an hour instead of quietly digesting their breakfasts at home."

"I am afraid," said I, "that the facts are so obvious that you will find little credit to be gained out of this case."

"There is nothing more deceptive than an obvious fact," he answered, laughing. "Besides, we may chance to hit upon some other obvious facts which may have been by no means obvious to Mr. Lestrade. You know me too well to think that I am boasting when I say that I shall either confirm or destroy his theory by means which he is quite incapable of employing, or even of understanding. To take the first example to hand, I very clearly perceive that in your bedroom the window is upon the right-hand side, and yet I question whether Mr. Lestrade would have noted even so self-evident a thing as that."

"How on earth—"

"My dear fellow, I know you well. I know the military neatness which characterizes you. You shave every morning, and in this season you shave by the sunlight; but since your shaving is less and less complete as we get farther back on the left side, until it becomes positively slovenly as we get round the angle of

---

4. A reference to another case. Lestrade is the official inspector from Scotland Yard, who figures in several of Holmes's adventures.

the jaw, it is surely very clear that that side is less illuminated than the other. I could not imagine a man of your habits looking at himself in an equal light and being satisfied with such a result. I only quote this as a trivial example of observation and inference. Therein lies my *métier*,[5] and it is just possible that it may be of some service in the investigation which lies before us. There are one or two minor points which were brought out in the inquest, and which are worth considering."

"What are they?"

"It appears that his arrest did not take place at once, but after the return to Hatherley Farm. On the inspector of constabulary informing him that he was a prisoner, he remarked that he was not surprised to hear it, and that it was no more than his deserts.[6] This observation of his had the natural effect of removing any traces of doubt which might have remained in the minds of the coroner's jury."

"It was a confession," I ejaculated.

"No, for it was followed by a protestation of innocence."

"Coming on the top of such a damning series of events, it was at least a most suspicious remark."

"On the contrary," said Holmes, "it is the brightest rift which I can at present see in the clouds. However innocent he might be, he could not be such an absolute imbecile as not to see that the circumstances were very black against him. Had he appeared surprised at his own arrest, or feigned indignation at it, I should have looked upon it as highly suspicious, because such surprise or anger would not be natural under the circumstances, and yet might appear to be the best policy to a scheming man. His frank acceptance of the situation marks him as either an innocent man, or else as a man of considerable self-restraint and firmness. As to his remark about his deserts, it was also not unnatural if you consider that he stood beside the dead body of his father, and that there is no doubt that he had that very day so far forgotten his filial duty as to

5. *métier* (mā-tyā'): the work he is uniquely qualified to do.
6. *deserts:* what he deserved.

bandy words with him, and even, according to the little girl whose evidence is so important, to raise his hand as if to strike him. The self-reproach and contrition which are displayed in his remark appear to me to be the signs of a healthy mind rather than of a guilty one."

I shook my head. "Many men have been hanged on far slighter evidence," I remarked.

"So they have. And many men have been wrongfully hanged."

"What is the young man's own account of the matter?"

"It is, I am afraid, not very encouraging to his supporters, though there are one or two points in it which are suggestive. You will find it here, and may read it for yourself."

He picked out from his bundle a copy of the local Herefordshire paper, and, having turned down the sheet, he pointed out the paragraph in which the unfortunate young man had given his own statement of what had occurred. I settled myself down in the corner of the carriage and read it very carefully. It ran in this way:

> Mr. James McCarthy, the only son of the deceased, was then called and gave evidence as follows: "I had been away from home for three days at Bristol, and had only just returned upon the morning of last Monday, the 3rd. My father was absent from home at the time of my arrival, and I was informed by the maid that he had driven over to Ross with John Cobb, the groom. Shortly after my return, I heard the wheels of his trap[7] in the yard, and, looking out of my window, I saw him get out and walk rapidly out of the yard, though I was not aware in which direction he was going. I then took my gun and strolled out in the direction of Boscombe Pool, with the intention of visiting the rabbit warren which is upon the other side. On my way I saw William Crowder, the gamekeeper, as he had

7. *trap:* horse-drawn carriage.

stated in his evidence; but he is mistaken in thinking that I was following my father. I had no idea that he was in front of me. When about a hundred yards from the pool, I heard a cry of 'Cooee!' which was a usual signal between my father and myself. I then hurried forward, and found him standing by the pool. He appeared to be much surprised at seeing me and asked me rather roughly what I was doing there. A conversation ensued which led to high words and almost to blows, for my father was a man of a very violent temper. Seeing that his passion was becoming ungovernable, I left him and returned toward Hatherley Farm. I had not gone more than 150 yards, however, when I heard a hideous outcry behind me, which caused me to run back. I found my father expiring upon the ground, with his head terribly injured. I dropped my gun and held him in my arms, but he almost instantly expired. I knelt beside him for some minutes, and then made my way to Mr. Turner's lodge keeper, his house being the nearest, to ask for assistance. I saw no one near my father when I returned, and I have no idea how he came by his injuries. He was not a popular man, being somewhat cold and forbidding in his manners; but he had, as far as I know, no active enemies. I know nothing further of the matter."

The Coroner: Did your father make any statement to you before he died?

Witness: He mumbled a few words, but I could only catch some allusion to a rat.

The Coroner: What did you understand by that?

Witness: It conveyed no meaning to me. I thought that he was delirious.

The Coroner: What was the point upon which you and your father had this final quarrel?

Witness: I should prefer not to answer.

The Coroner: I am afraid that I must press it.

Witness: It is really impossible for me to tell you. I can assure you that it has nothing to do with the sad tragedy which followed.

The Coroner: That is for the court to decide. I need not point out to you that your refusal to answer will prejudice your case considerably in any future proceedings which may arise.

Witness: I must still refuse.

The Coroner: I understand that the cry of "Cooee" was a common signal between you and your father?

Witness: It was.

The Coroner: How was it, then, that he uttered it before he saw you, and before he even knew that you had returned from Bristol?

Witness (with considerable confusion): I do not know.

A Juryman: Did you see nothing which aroused your suspicions when you returned on hearing the cry and found your father fatally injured?

Witness: Nothing definite.

The Coroner: What do you mean?

Witness: I was so disturbed and excited as I rushed out into the open, that I could think of nothing except my father. Yet I have a vague impression that as I ran forward something lay upon the ground to the left of me. It seemed to me to be something gray in color, a coat of some sort, or a plaid[8] perhaps. When I rose from my father I looked round for it, but it was gone.

"Do you mean that it disappeared before you went for help?"

"Yes, it was gone."

"You cannot say what it was?"

"No, I had a feeling something was there."

---

8. *a plaid*: a plaid piece of cloth.

"How far from the body?"

"A dozen yards or so."

"And how far from the edge of the wood?"

"About the same."

"Then if it was removed it was while you were within a dozen yards of it?"

"Yes, but with my back toward it."

This concluded the examination of the witness.

"I see," said I as I glanced down the column, "that the coroner in his concluding remarks was rather severe upon young McCarthy. He calls attention, and with reason, to the discrepancy about his father having signaled to him before seeing him, also to his refusal to give details of his conversation with his father, and his singular account of his father's dying words. They are all, as he remarks, very much against the son."

Holmes laughed softly to himself and stretched himself out upon the cushioned seat. "Both you and the coroner have been at some pains," said he, "to single out the very strongest points in the young man's favor. Don't you see that you alternately give him credit for having too much imagination and too little? Too little, if he could not invent a cause of quarrel which would give him the sympathy of the jury; too much, if he evolved from his own inner consciousness anything so *outré*[9] as a dying reference to a rat, and the incident of the vanishing cloth. No, sir, I shall approach this case from the point of view that what this young man says is true, and we shall see whither that hypothesis will lead us. And now here is my pocket Petrarch,[10] and not another word shall I say of this case until we are on the scene of action. We lunch at Swindon, and I see that we shall be there in twenty minutes."

9. *outré* ($\overline{oo}$-trā'): bizarre, exaggerated.
10. A reference to a pocket-sized edition of Petrarch's sonnets.

It was nearly four o'clock when we at last, after passing through the beautiful Stroud Valley, and over the broad gleaming Severn, found ourselves at the pretty little country town of Ross. A lean, ferret-like man, furtive and sly-looking, was waiting for us upon the platform. In spite of the light brown dustcoat and leather leggings which he wore in deference to his rustic surroundings, I had no difficulty in recognizing Lestrade, of Scotland Yard. With him we drove to the Hereford Arms, where a room had already been engaged for us.

"I have ordered a carriage," said Lestrade, as we sat over a cup of tea. "I knew your energetic nature, and that you would not be happy until you had been on the scene of the crime."

"It was very nice and complimentary of you," Holmes answered. "It is entirely a question of barometric pressure."

Lestrade looked startled. "I do not quite follow," he said.

"How is the glass? Twenty-nine, I see. No wind, and not a cloud in the sky. I have a caseful of cigarettes here which need smoking, and the sofa is very much superior to the usual country hotel abomination. I do not think that it is probable that I shall use the carriage tonight."

Lestrade laughed indulgently. "You have, no doubt, already formed your conclusions from the newspapers," he said. "The case is as plain as a pikestaff, and the more one goes into it the plainer it becomes. Still, of course, one can't refuse a lady, and such a very positive one, too. She had heard of you, and would have your opinion, though I repeatedly told her that there was nothing which you could do which I had not already done. Why, bless my soul! here is her carriage at the door."

He had hardly spoken before there rushed into the room one of the most lovely young women that I have ever seen in my life. Her violet eyes shining, her lips parted, a pink flush upon her cheeks, all thought of her natural reserve lost in her overpowering excitement and concern.

"Oh, Mr. Sherlock Holmes!" she cried, glancing from one

to the other of us, and finally, with a woman's quick intuition, fastening upon my companion, "I am so glad that you have come. I have driven down to tell you so. I know that James didn't do it. I know it, and I want you to start upon your work knowing it, too. Never let yourself doubt upon that point. We have known each other since we were little children, and I know his faults as no one else does; but he is too tenderhearted to hurt a fly. Such a charge is absurd to anyone who really knows him."

"I hope we may clear him, Miss Turner," said Sherlock Holmes. "You may rely upon my doing all that I can."

"But you have read the evidence. You have formed some conclusion? Do you not see some loophole, some flaw? Do you not yourself think that he is innocent?"

"I think that it is very probable."

"There, now!" she cried, throwing back her head and looking defiantly at Lestrade. "You hear! He gives me hopes."

Lestrade shrugged his shoulders. "I am afraid that my colleague has been a little quick in forming his conclusions," he said.

"But he is right. Oh! I know that he is right. James never did it. And about his quarrel with his father, I am sure that the reason why he would not speak about it to the coroner was because I was concerned in it."

"In what way?" asked Holmes.

"It is no time for me to hide anything. James and his father had many disagreements about me. Mr. McCarthy was very anxious that there should be a marriage between us. James and I have always loved each other as brother and sister; but, of course, he is young and has seen very little of life yet, and—and—well, he naturally did not wish to do anything like that yet. So there were quarrels, and this, I am sure, was one of them."

"And your father?" asked Holmes. "Was he in favor of such a union?"

"No, he was averse to it also. No one but Mr. McCarthy was

in favor of it." A quick blush passed over her fresh young face as Holmes shot one of his keen, questioning glances at her.

"Thank you for this information," said he. "May I see your father if I call tomorrow?"

"I am afraid the doctor won't allow it."

"The doctor?"

"Yes, have you not heard? Poor Father has never been strong for years back, but this has broken him down completely. He has taken to his bed, and Dr. Willows says that he is a wreck and that his nervous system is shattered. Mr. McCarthy was the only man alive who had known Dad in the old days in Victoria."[11]

"Ha! In Victoria! That is important."

"Yes, at the mines."

"Quite so; at the gold mines, where, as I understand, Mr. Turner made his money."

"Yes, certainly."

"Thank you, Miss Turner. You have been of material assistance to me."

"You will tell me if you have any news tomorrow. No doubt you will go to the prison to see James. Oh, if you do, Mr. Holmes, do tell him that I know him to be innocent."

"I will, Miss Turner."

"I must go home now, for Dad is very ill, and he misses me so if I leave him. Goodbye, and God help you in your undertaking." She hurried from the room as impulsively as she had entered, and we heard the wheels of her carriage rattle off down the street.

"I am ashamed of you, Holmes," said Lestrade, with dignity, after a few minutes' silence. "Why should you raise up hopes which you are bound to disappoint? I am not over-tender of heart, but I call it cruel."

---

11. *Victoria:* a state in Australia.

"I think that I see my way to clearing James McCarthy," said Holmes. "Have you an order to see him in prison?"

"Yes, but only for you and me."

"Then I shall reconsider my resolution about going out. We have still time to take a train to Hereford and see him tonight?"

"Ample."

"Then let us do so. Watson, I fear that you will find it very slow, but I shall only be away a couple of hours."

I walked down to the station with them and then wandered through the streets of the little town, finally returning to the hotel, where I lay upon the sofa and tried to interest myself in a yellow-backed novel. The puny plot of the story was so thin, however, when compared to the deep mystery through which we were groping, and I found my attention wander so continually from the fiction to the fact, that I at last flung it across the room and gave myself up entirely to a consideration of the events of the day. Supposing that this unhappy young man's story were absolutely true, then what hellish thing, what absolutely unforeseen and extraordinary calamity could have occurred between the time when he parted from his father and the moment when, drawn back by his screams, he rushed into the glade? It was something terrible and deadly. What could it be? Might not the nature of the injuries reveal something to my medical instincts? I rang the bell and called for the weekly county paper, which contained a verbatim account of the inquest. In the surgeon's deposition it was stated that the posterior third of the left parietal bone and the left half of the occipital bone had been shattered by a heavy blow from a blunt weapon.[12] I marked the spot upon my own head. Clearly such a blow must have been struck from behind. That was to some extent in favor of the accused, as when seen quarreling, he was

---

12. Parietal bones form the skull's top and side; the occipital forms the skull's back.

face to face with his father. Still, it did not go for very much, for the older man might have turned his back before the blow fell. Still, it might be worthwhile to call Holmes's attention to it. Then there was the peculiar dying reference to a rat. What could that mean? It could not be delirium. A man dying from a sudden blow does not commonly become delirious. No, it was more likely to be an attempt to explain how he met his fate. But what could it indicate? I cudgeled my brains to find some possible explanation. And then the incident of the gray cloth seen by young McCarthy. If that were true, the murderer must have dropped some part of his dress, presumably his overcoat, in his flight, and must have had the hardihood to return and to carry it away at the instant when the son was kneeling with his back turned not a dozen paces off. What a tissue of mysteries and improbabilities the whole thing was! I did not wonder at Lestrade's opinion, and yet I had so much faith in Sherlock Holmes's insight that I could not lose hope as long as every fresh fact seemed to strengthen his conviction of young McCarthy's innocence.

It was late before Sherlock Holmes returned. He came back alone, for Lestrade was staying in lodgings in the town.

"The glass still keeps very high," he remarked as he sat down. "It is of importance that it should not rain before we are able to go over the ground. On the other hand, a man should be at his very best and keenest for such nice work as that, and I did not wish to do it when fatigued by a long journey. I have seen young McCarthy."

"And what did you learn from him?"

"Nothing."

"Could he throw no light?"

"None at all. I was inclined to think at one time that he knew who had done it and was screening him or her, but I am convinced now that he is as puzzled as everyone else. He is not a very quick-witted youth, though comely to look at and, I should think, sound at heart."

"I cannot admire his taste," I remarked, "if it is indeed a fact that he was averse to a marriage with so charming a young lady as this Miss Turner."

"Ah, thereby hangs a rather painful tale. This fellow is madly, insanely, in love with her, but some two years ago, when he was only a lad, and before he really knew her, for she had been away five years at a boarding school, what does the idiot do but get into the clutches of a barmaid in Bristol and marry her at a registry office? No one knows a word of the matter, but you can imagine how maddening it must be to him to be upbraided for not doing what he would give his very eyes to do, but what he knows to be absolutely impossible. It was sheer frenzy of this sort which made him throw his hands up into the air when his father, at their last interview, was goading him on to propose to Miss Turner. On the other hand, he had no means of supporting himself, and his father, who was by all accounts a very hard man, would have thrown him over utterly had he known the truth. It was with his barmaid wife that he had spent the last three days in Bristol, and his father did not know where he was. Mark that point. It is of importance. Good has come out of evil, however, for the barmaid, finding from the papers that he is in serious trouble and likely to be hanged, has thrown him over utterly and has written to him to say that she has a husband already in the Bermuda Dockyard, so that there is really no tie between them. I think that that bit of news has consoled young McCarthy for all that he has suffered."

"But if he is innocent, who has done it?"

"Ah! who? I would call your attention very particularly to two points. One is that the murdered man had an appointment with someone at the pool, and that the someone could not have been his son, for his son was away, and he did not know when he would return. The second is that the murdered man was heard to cry 'Cooee!' before he knew that his son had returned. Those are the crucial points upon which the case depends. And now let us talk about George Meredith,[13] if you

13. George Meredith was a novelist and poet, a contemporary of Doyle's.

please, and we shall leave all minor matters until tomorrow."

There was no rain, as Holmes had foretold, and the morning broke bright and cloudless. At nine o'clock Lestrade called for us with the carriage, and we set off for Hatherley Farm and the Boscombe Pool.

"There is serious news this morning," Lestrade observed. "It is said that Mr. Turner, of the Hall, is so ill that his life is despaired of."

"An elderly man, I presume?" said Holmes.

"About sixty; but his constitution has been shattered by his life abroad, and he has been in failing health for some time. This business has had a very bad effect upon him. He was an old friend of McCarthy's, and, I may add, a great benefactor to him, for I have learned that he gave him Hatherley Farm rent-free."

"Indeed! That is interesting," said Holmes.

"Oh, yes! In a hundred other ways he has helped him. Everybody about here speaks of his kindness to him."

"Really! Does it not strike you as a little singular that this McCarthy, who appears to have had little of his own, and to have been under such obligations to Turner, should still talk of marrying his son to Turner's daughter, who is, presumably, heiress to the estate, and that in such a very cocksure manner, as if it were merely a case of a proposal and all else would follow? It is the more strange, since we know that Turner himself was averse to the idea. The daughter told us as much. Do you not deduce something from that?"

"We have got to the deductions and the inferences," said Lestrade, winking at me. "I find it hard enough to tackle facts, Holmes, without flying away after theories and fancies."

"You are right," said Holmes demurely; "you do find it very hard to tackle the facts."

"Anyhow, I have grasped one fact which you seem to find it

difficult to get hold of," replied Lestrade, with some warmth.

"And that is—"

"That McCarthy senior met his death from McCarthy junior and that all theories to the contrary are the merest moonshine."

"Well, moonshine is a brighter thing than fog," said Holmes, laughing. "But I am very much mistaken if this is not Hatherley Farm upon the left."

"Yes, that is it." It was a widespread, comfortable-looking building, two-storied, slate-roofed, with great yellow blotches of lichen upon the gray walls. The drawn blinds and the smokeless chimneys, however, gave it a stricken look, as though the weight of this horror still lay heavy upon it. We called at the door, when the maid, at Holmes's request, showed us the boots which her master wore at the time of his death, and also a pair of the son's, though not the pair which he had then had. Having measured these very carefully from seven or eight different points, Holmes desired to be led to the courtyard, from which we all followed the winding track which led to Boscombe Pool.

Sherlock Holmes was transformed when he was hot upon such a scent as this. Men who had only known the quiet thinker and logician of Baker Street would have failed to recognize him. His face flushed and darkened. His brows were drawn into two hard black lines, while his eyes shone out from beneath them with a steely glitter. His face was bent downward, his shoulders bowed, his lips compressed, and the veins stood out like whipcord in his long, sinewy neck. His nostrils seemed to dilate with a purely animal lust for the chase, and his mind was so absolutely concentrated upon the matter before him that a question or remark fell unheeded upon his ears, or, at the most, only provoked a quick, impatient snarl in reply. Swiftly and silently he made his way along the track which ran through the meadows, and so by way of the woods to the Boscombe Pool. It was damp, marshy ground, as is all that district, and there were marks of many feet, both upon the path and amid the short grass which bounded it on either side. Sometimes Holmes would hurry on, sometimes stop dead, and once he made quite a little detour into the meadow. Lestrade and I walked behind him, the detective indifferent and contemptuous, while I watched my friend with the interest which sprang from the conviction that every one of his actions was directed toward a definite end.

The Boscombe Pool, which is a little reed-girt sheet of water some fifty yards across, is situated at the boundary between the Hatherley Farm and the private park of the wealthy Mr. Turner. Above the woods which lined it upon the farther side we could see the red, jutting pinnacles which marked the site of the rich landowner's dwelling. On the Hatherley side of the pool the woods grew very thick, and there was a narrow belt of sodden grass twenty paces across between the edge of the trees and the reeds which lined the lake. Lestrade showed us the exact spot at which the body had been found, and, indeed, so moist was the ground that I could plainly see the traces which had been left by the fall of the stricken man. To Holmes, as I could see by his eager face and peering eyes, very many other things were to be read upon the trampled grass. He ran round, like a dog who is picking up a scent, and then turned upon my companion.

"What did you go into the pool for?" he asked.

"I fished about with a rake. I thought there might be some weapon or other trace. But how on earth—"

"Oh, tut, tut! I have no time! That left foot of yours with its inward twist is all over the place. A mole could trace it, and there it vanishes among the reeds. Oh, how simple it would all have been had I been here before they came like a herd of buffalo and wallowed all over it. Here is where the party with the lodge keeper came, and they have covered all tracks for six or eight feet round the body. But here are three separate tracks of the same feet." He drew out a lens and lay down upon his waterproof[14] to have a better view, talking all the time rather to himself than to us. "These are young McCarthy's feet. Twice he was walking, and once he ran swiftly, so that the soles are deeply marked and the heels hardly visible. That bears out his story. He ran when he saw his father on the ground. Then here are the father's feet as he paced up and down. What is this, then? It is the butt end of the gun as the son stood listening. And this? Ha, ha! What have we here? Tiptoes! tiptoes! Square, too, quite unusual boots! They come, they go, they come again—of course, that was for the cloak. Now, where did they come from?" He ran up and down, sometimes losing, sometimes finding the track, until we were well within the edge of the wood and under the shadow of a great beech, the largest tree in the neighborhood. Holmes traced his way to the farther side of this and lay down once more upon his face, with a little cry of satisfaction. For a long time he remained there, turning over the leaves and dried sticks, gathering up what seemed to me to be dust into an envelope, and examining with his lens not only the ground but even the bark of the tree as far as he could reach. A jagged stone was lying among the moss, and this also he carefully examined and retained. Then he followed a pathway through the wood until he came to the highroad, where all traces were lost.

"It has been a case of considerable interest," he remarked, returning to his natural manner. "I fancy that this gray house on the right must be the lodge. I think that I will go in and have a word with Moran, and perhaps write a little note. Having done that, we may drive back to our luncheon. You may walk to the cab, and I shall be with you presently."

14. *waterproof:* raincoat.

"It was about ten minutes before we regained our cab and drove back into Ross, Holmes still carrying with him the stone which he had picked up in the wood.

"This may interest you, Lestrade," he remarked, holding it out. "The murder was done with it."

"I see no marks."

"There are none."

"How do you know, then?"

"The grass was growing under it. It had only lain there a few days. There was no sign of a place whence it had been taken. It corresponds with the injuries. There is no sign of any other weapon."

"And the murderer?"

"Is a tall man, left-handed, limps with the right leg, wears thick-soled shooting boots and a gray cloak, smokes Indian cigars, uses a cigar holder, and carries a blunt penknife in his pocket. There are several other indications, but these may be enough to aid us in our search."

Lestrade laughed. "I am afraid that I am still a skeptic," he said. "Theories are all very well, but we have to deal with a hardheaded British jury."

"Nous verrons,"[15] answered Holmes calmly. "You work your own method, and I shall work mine. I shall be busy this afternoon, and shall probably return to London by the evening train."

"And leave your case unfinished?"

"No, finished."

"But the mystery?"

"It is solved."

"Who was the criminal, then?"

"The gentleman I describe."

"But who is he?"

"Surely it would not be difficult to find out. This is not such a populous neighborhood."

---

15. *Nous verrons* (noo və-rōN'): French for "We will see."

Lestrade shrugged his shoulders. "I am a practical man," he said, "and I really cannot undertake to go about the country looking for a left-handed gentleman with a game leg. I should become the laughingstock of Scotland Yard."

"All right," said Holmes quietly. "I have given you the chance. Here are your lodgings. Goodbye. I shall drop you a line before I leave."

Having left Lestrade at his rooms, we drove to our hotel, where we found lunch upon the table. Holmes was silent and buried in thought, with a pained expression upon his face, as one who finds himself in a perplexing position.

"Look here, Watson," he said, when the cloth was cleared; "just sit down in this chair and let me preach to you for a little. I don't know quite what to do, and I should value your advice. Light a cigar and let me expound."

"Pray do so."

"Well, now, in considering this case there are two points about young McCarthy's narrative which struck us both instantly, although they impressed me in his favor and you against him. One was the fact that his father should, according to his account, cry 'Cooee!' before seeing him. The other was his singular dying reference to a rat. He mumbled several words, you understand, but that was all that caught the son's ear. Now from this double point our research must commence, and we will begin it by presuming that what the lad says is absolutely true."

"What of this 'Cooee!' then?"

"Well, obviously it could not have been meant for the son. The son, as far as he knew, was in Bristol. It was mere chance that he was within earshot. The 'Cooee!' was meant to attract the attention of whoever it was that he had the appointment with. But 'Cooee' is a distinctly Australian cry, and one which is used between Australians. There is a strong presumption that the person whom McCarthy expected to meet him at Boscombe Pool was someone who had been in Australia."

"What of the rat, then?"

Sherlock Holmes took a folded paper from his pocket and flattened it out on the table. "This is a map of the Colony of Victoria," he said. "I wired to Bristol for it last night." He put his hand over part of the map. "What do you read?"

"ARAT," I read.

"And now?" He raised his hand.

"BALLARAT."

"Quite so. That was the word the man uttered, and of which his son only caught the last two syllables. He was trying to utter the name of his murderer. So and so, of Ballarat."

"It is wonderful!" I exclaimed.

"It is obvious. And now, you see, I had narrowed the field down considerably. The possession of a gray garment was a third point which, granting the son's statement to be correct, was a certainty. We have come now out of mere vagueness to the definite conception of an Australian from Ballarat with a gray cloak."

"Certainly."

"And one who was at home in the district, for the pool can only be approached by the farm or by the estate, where strangers could hardly wander."

"Quite so."

"Then comes our expedition of today. By an examination of the ground I gained the trifling details which I gave to that imbecile Lestrade, as to the personality of the criminal."

"But how do you gain them?"

"You know my method. It is founded upon the observation of trifles."

"His height I know that you might roughly judge from the length of his stride. His boots, too, might be told from their traces."

"Yes, they were peculiar boots."

"But his lameness?"

"The impression of his right foot was always less distinct

than his left. He put less weight upon it. Why? Because he limped—he was lame."

"But his left-handedness."

"You were yourself struck by the nature of the injury as recorded by the surgeon at the inquest. The blow was struck from immediately behind, and yet was upon the left side. Now, how can that be unless it were by a left-handed man? He had stood behind that tree during the interview between the father and son. He had even smoked there. I found the ash of a cigar, which my special knowledge of tobacco ashes enables me to pronounce as an Indian cigar. I have, as you know, devoted some attention to this, and written a little monograph[16] on the ashes of 140 different varieties of pipe, cigar, and cigarette tobacco. Having found the ash, I then looked round and discovered the stump among the moss where he had tossed it. It was an Indian cigar, of the variety which was rolled in Rotterdam."

"And the cigar holder?"

"I could see that the end had not been in his mouth. Therefore, he used a holder. The tip had been cut off, not bitten off, but the cut was not a clean one, so I deduced a blunt penknife."

"Holmes," I said, "you have drawn a net round this man from which he cannot escape, and you have saved an innocent human life as truly as if you had cut the cord which was hanging him. I see the direction in which all this points. The culprit is—"

"Mr. John Turner," cried the hotel waiter, opening the door of our sitting room, and ushering in a visitor.

The man who entered was a strange and impressive figure. His slow, limping step and bowed shoulders gave the appearance of decrepitude, and yet his hard, deep-lined, craggy fea-

---

16. *monograph:* scholarly article or paper written about some aspect of a subject.

tures and his enormous limbs showed that he was possessed of unusual strength of body and of character. His tangled beard, grizzled hair, and outstanding, drooping eyebrows combined to give an air of dignity and power to his appearance, but his face was of an ashen white, while his lips and the corners of his nostrils were tinged with a shade of blue. It was clear to me at a glance that he was in the grip of some deadly and chronic disease.

"Pray sit down on the sofa," said Holmes gently. "You had my note?"

"Yes, the lodge keeper brought it up. You say that you wished to see me here to avoid scandal."

"I thought people would talk if I went to the Hall."

"And why did you wish to see me?" He looked across at my companion with despair in his weary eyes, as though his question was already answered.

"Yes," said Holmes, answering the look rather than the words. "It is so. I know all about McCarthy."

The old man sank his face in his hands. "God help me!" he cried. "But I would not have let the young man come to harm. I give you my word that I would have spoken out if it went against him at the Assizes."

"I am glad to hear you say so," said Holmes gravely.

"I would have spoken now had it not been for my dear girl. It would break her heart—it will break her heart when she hears that I am arrested."

"It may not come to that," said Holmes.

"What?"

"I am no official agent. I understand that it was your daughter who required my presence here, and I am acting in her interests. Young McCarthy must be got off, however."

"I am a dying man," said old Turner. "I have had diabetes for years. My doctor says it is a question whether I shall live a month. Yet I would rather die under my own roof than in a jail."

Holmes rose and sat down at the table with his pen in his hand and a bundle of paper before him. "Just tell us the truth," he said. "I shall jot down the facts. You will sign it, and Watson here can witness it. Then I could produce your confession at the last extremity to save young McCarthy. I promise you that I shall not use it unless it is absolutely needed."

"It's as well," said the old man; "it's a question whether I shall live to the Assizes, so it matters little to me, but I should wish to spare Alice the shock. And now I will make the thing clear to you; it has been a long time in the acting, but will not take me long to tell.

"You didn't know this dead man, McCarthy. He was a devil incarnate. I tell you that. God keep you out of the clutches of such a man as he. His grip has been upon me these twenty years, and he has blasted my life. I'll tell you first how I came to be in his power.

"It was in the early '60's, at the diggings. I was a young chap then, hot-blooded and reckless, ready to turn my hand at anything; I got among bad companions, took to drink, had no luck with my claim, took to the bush, and in a word became what you would call over here a highway robber. There were six of us, and we had a wild, free life of it, sticking up a station from time to time, or stopping the wagons on the road to the diggings. Black Jack of Ballarat was the name I went under, and our party is still remembered in the colony as the Ballarat Gang.

"One day a gold convoy came down from Ballarat to Melbourne, and we lay in wait for it and attacked it. There were six troopers and six of us, so it was a close thing, but we emptied four of their saddles at the first volley. Three of our boys were killed, however, before we got the swag. [17] I put my pistol to the head of the wagon driver, who was this very man McCarthy. I wish to the Lord that I had shot him then, but I spared him,

---

17. *swag:* in Australia, a bundle or sack.

though I saw his wicked little eyes fixed on my face, as though to remember every feature. We got away with the gold, became wealthy men, and made our way over to England without being suspected. There I parted from my old pals and determined to settle down to a quiet and respectable life. I bought this estate, which chanced to be in the market, and I set myself to do a little good with my money, to make up for the way in which I had earned it. I married, too, and though my wife died young, she left me my dear little Alice. Even when she was just a baby her wee hand seemed to lead me down the right path, as nothing else had ever done. In a word, I turned over a new leaf and did my best to make up for the past. All was going well when McCarthy laid his grip upon me.

"I had gone up to town about an investment, and I met him in Regent Street with hardly a coat to his back or a boot to his foot.

" 'Here we are, Jack,' says he, touching me on the arm; 'we'll be as good as family to you. There's two of us, me and my son, and you can have the keeping of us. If you don't—it's a fine, law-abiding country is England, and there's always a policeman within hail.'

"Well, down they came to the west country, there was no shaking them off, and there they have lived rent-free on my best land ever since. There was no rest for me, no peace, no forgetfulness; turn where I would, there was his cunning, grinning face at my elbow. It grew worse as Alice grew up, for he soon saw I was more afraid of her knowing my past than of the police. Whatever he wanted he must have, and whatever it was I gave him without question, land, money, houses, until at last he asked a thing which I could not give. He asked for Alice.

"His son, you see, had grown up, and so had my girl, and as I was known to be in weak health, it seemed a fine stroke to him that his lad should step into the whole property. But there I was firm. I would not have his cursed stock mixed with mine; not that I had any dislike to the lad, but his blood was in him, and that was enough. I stood firm. McCarthy threatened. I braved him to do his worst. We were to meet at the pool midway between our houses to talk it over.

"When I went down there I found him talking with his son, so I smoked a cigar and waited behind a tree until he should be alone. But as I listened to his talk all that was black and bitter in me seemed to come uppermost. He was urging his son to marry my daughter with as little regard for what she might think as if she were a slut from off the streets. It drove me mad to think that I and all that I held most dear should be in the power of such a man as this. Could I not snap the bond? I was already a dying and a desperate man. Though clear of mind and fairly strong of limb, I knew that my own fate was sealed. But my memory and my girl! Both could be saved if I could but silence that foul tongue. I did it, Mr. Holmes. I would do it again. Deeply as I have sinned, I have led a life of martyrdom to atone for it. But that my girl should be entangled in the same meshes which held me was more than I could suffer. I struck him down with no more compunction than if he had been some foul and venomous beast. His cry brought back his son; but I had gained the cover of the wood, though I was forced to go back to fetch the cloak which I had dropped in my flight. That is the true story, gentlemen, of all that occurred."

"Well, it is not for me to judge you," said Holmes as the old man signed the statement which had been drawn out. "I pray that we may never be exposed to such a temptation."

"I pray not, sir. And what do you intend to do?"

"In view of your health, nothing. You are yourself aware that you will soon have to answer for your deed at a higher court than the Assizes. I will keep your confession, and if McCarthy is condemned I shall be forced to use it. If not, it shall never be seen by mortal eye; and your secret, whether you be alive or dead, shall be safe with us."

"Farewell, then," said the old man solemnly. "Your own deathbeds, when they come, will be the easier for the thought of the peace which you have given to mine." Tottering and shaking in all his giant frame, he stumbled slowly from the room.

"God help us!" said Holmes, after a long silence. "Why does fate play such tricks with poor, helpless worms? I never hear of such a case as this that I do not think of Baxter's words, and say, 'There, but for the grace of God, goes Sherlock Holmes.' "

James McCarthy was acquitted at the Assizes on the strength of a number of objections which had been drawn out by Holmes and submitted to the defending counsel. Old Turner lived for seven months after our interview, but he is now dead; and there is every prospect that the son and daughter may come to live happily together in ignorance of the black cloud which rests upon their past.

The Facts of the Story

Write brief answers to the following questions. Most of the answers will require a phrase or a complete sentence. Look at the story if you wish.

1. In what country did John Turner and Charles McCarthy meet and become well acquainted?

2. How did Turner acquire his fortune?

3. What threat did McCarthy use to blackmail Turner?

4. Give one reason why James McCarthy, Charles McCarthy's son, is thought guilty of the murder.

5. What was the cause of the quarrel between Charles McCarthy and his son?

6. James McCarthy believes he cannot marry Miss Turner because _____.

7. Lestrade believes the murderer is _____.

8. What clues lead Sherlock Holmes to the identity of the murderer?

9. Sherlock Holmes finally establishes that the murderer is _____.

10. Why is Holmes able to keep the murderer's identity a secret?

The Ideas in the Story

A detective story is not usually a source of significant ideas. But the Sherlock Holmes stories do carry one idea that shouldn't go by unmentioned. Read the following quotations from the story. Each, in a different way, expresses the same idea. Explain how the story bears out the truth of these remarks by Holmes:

I shall take nothing for granted until I have the opportunity of looking personally into it.

Circumstantial evidence is a very tricky thing. . . . It may seem to point very straight to one thing, but if you shift your own point of view a little, you may find it pointing in an equally uncompromising manner to something entirely different.

There is nothing more deceptive than an obvious fact.

What we find in a typical Sherlock Holmes story is the careful tracking down of the truth. No matter how obvious the truth may seem to some persons, Holmes does not believe anything until he himself has investigated the matter thoroughly. While others leap to the wrong conclusions, Holmes, in his clever and thorough way, looks at the trifles and finds the truth.

Another idea central to most detective fiction is the notion that there is evil in the world trying to conquer or outsmart the good. Detective fiction always offers an explanation for the evil—it usually comes from a bad character, who, to our satisfaction, is discovered and brought to justice. In this story, the *victim* is the evil character. Tell how McCarthy is presented so that we think of him as evil, or as a "bad guy." Do you think McCarthy deserved what happened to him? Why? Do you approve of the way Holmes treated the murderer? Explain.

The Art of the Storyteller

Stock Characters

Three "stock characters" almost always found in the Sherlock Holmes stories were actually invented by the American short-story writer Edgar Allan Poe. In Poe's stories, we find forerunners of the brilliant but unofficial detective; the baffled friend to whom the detective must explain everything; and the bumbling police inspector whose intelligence is no match for the unofficial detective's reasoning power. Poe invented these characters and Arthur Conan Doyle established them forever as trademarks of the typical detective story.

The Baffled Friend

Dr. Watson not only tells the story, he also plays an important part in it. He is not stupid. He is a successful physician, well-educated and experienced. Still, he is, like the reader, often baffled by Holmes's actions. His function in the story is to ask the questions that we, as readers, would also like to ask Holmes. Which of Watson's puzzled questions would you have asked Holmes yourself? Have you seen this character of the "baffled friend" used in detective movies or television shows?

The Unofficial Detective vs. the Police Inspector

In modern detective fiction, not only is there a solid, Watson-like character asking questions and demanding explanations, but there is also a rather stupid, Lestrade-like character. What function does this Scotland Yard inspector fulfill in the story? How do Lestrade's opinions and errors of judgment affect our opinion of Holmes? As in the movies or on television, the private detective painstakingly searching for clues often seems smarter and more thorough than the police inspector, who often leaps to the obvious, but wrong, conclusions.

Think of detective stories you have read or watched in the movies or on television. Describe two characters who take the parts played by Holmes and Lestrade—that of the unofficial detective, an outsider brought into the case; and that of the official police detective who has been working on the case and drawn the wrong conclusions.

Composition

Expressing an Opinion

Sherlock Holmes's decision not to reveal the identity of the murderer raises moral questions. Should he have taken Turner to the police and let the courts determine Turner's fate? If asked who the murderer was, Holmes would probably say he did not know, thus telling a lie. If he were not asked, would his silence amount to the same thing as lying? Has anyone the right to withhold important information about a crime? Are breaking the law and lying ever excusable?

Write a composition in which you either criticize or defend Holmes's decision. Give reasons for your opinion. Plan your composition carefully so that your arguments will be clear and convincing.

Write approximately 150 words.

Arthur Conan Doyle

Arthur Conan Doyle (1859-1930) was born in Edinburgh, Scotland. He received his medical degree from the University of Edinburgh and practiced medicine for six years. During those years, while waiting for patients who did not come in sufficient numbers to afford him a living, Doyle invented the characters of Sherlock Holmes and his loyal friend, Dr. Watson. In 1891, Doyle gave up medicine for a career in writing. He modeled his detective-hero after a surgeon from the University, and named him after a famous cricket player and the Chief Justice of the U. S. Supreme Court. The character of the faithful Watson was modeled after Doyle himself. After he had written many successful stories about his detective, Doyle decided it was time to kill him off. When the "last" Sherlock Holmes story appeared, Doyle's life was even threatened by an outraged public. And so Sherlock Holmes was brought back to life. Hundreds of movies have been based on the Sherlock Holmes stories.

By the Waters of Babylon

STEPHEN VINCENT BENÉT

This is a story of a young man's strange adventures in a future world, one that has nearly been destroyed by war. (You might be surprised to know that Benét wrote this story before the invention of the atomic bomb.) Take a few minutes to imagine what a devastated world would be like:

> *What would life be like for the human survivors, after all forms of civilization as we know them had been destroyed—all schools, cities, churches, libraries, theaters, museums, businesses?*

> *How could the survivors find out about the world that had been destroyed?*

> *What myths and superstitions about the old days might develop among the survivors?*

"Babylon," in the title, was one of the greatest cities of the ancient world. It was destroyed—"leveled to the ground"—by the Assyrians under King Sennacherib in 689 B.C. Like New York, which is on a great river (the Hudson), Babylon was also situated on water (the Euphrates). The title itself is a quotation from Psalm 137: "By the waters of Babylon, there we sat down and wept . . ."

The north and the west and the south are good hunting ground, but it is forbidden to go east. It is forbidden to go to any of the Dead Places except to search for metal and then he who touches the metal must be a priest or the son of a priest. Afterward, both the man and the metal must be purified. These are the rules and the laws; they are well made. It is forbidden to cross the great river and look upon the place that was the Place of the Gods—this is most strictly forbidden. We do not even say its name though we know its name. It is there that spirits live, and demons—it is there that there are the ashes of the Great Burning. These things are forbidden—they have been forbidden since the beginning of time.

My father is a priest; I am the son of a priest. I have been in the Dead Places near us, with my father—at first, I was afraid. When my father went into the house to search for the metal, I stood by the door and my heart felt small and weak. It was a dead man's house, a spirit house. It did not have the smell of man, though there were old bones in a corner. But it is not fitting that a priest's son should show fear. I looked at the bones in the shadow and kept my voice still.

Then my father came out with the metal—a good, strong piece. He looked at me with both eyes but I had not run away. He gave me the metal to hold—I took it and did not die. So he knew that I was truly his son and would be a priest in my time. That was when I was very young—nevertheless, my brothers would not have done it, though they are good hunters. After that, they gave me the good piece of meat and the warm corner by the fire. My father watched over me—he was glad that I should be a priest. But when I boasted or wept without a reason, he punished me more strictly than my brothers. That was right.

After a time, I myself was allowed to go into the dead-houses and search for metal. So I learned the ways of those houses—and if I saw bones, I was no longer afraid. The bones are light and old—sometimes they will fall into dust if you touch them. But that is a great sin.

I was taught the chants and the spells—I was taught how to stop the running of blood from a wound and many secrets. A priest must know many secrets—that was what my father said. If the hunters think we do all things by chants and spells, they may believe so—it does not hurt them. I was taught how to read in the old books and how to make the old writings—that was hard and took a long time. My knowledge made me happy—it was like a fire in my heart. Most of all, I liked to hear of the Old Days and the stories of the gods. I asked myself many questions that I could not answer, but it was good to ask them. At night, I would lie awake and listen to the wind—it seemed to me that it was the voice of the gods as they flew through the air.

We are not ignorant like the Forest People—our women spin wool on the wheel, our priests wear a white robe. We do not eat grubs from the tree, we have not forgotten the old writings, although they are hard to understand. Nevertheless, my knowledge and my lack of knowledge burned in me—I wished to know more. When I was a man at last, I came to my father and said, "It is time for me to go on my journey. Give me your leave."

He looked at me for a long time, stroking his beard; then he said at last, "Yes. It is time." That night, in the house of the priesthood, I asked for and received purification. My body hurt but my spirit was a cool stone. It was my father himself who questioned me about my dreams.

He bade me look into the smoke of the fire and see—I saw and told what I saw. It was what I have always seen—a river, and, beyond it, a great Dead Place and in it the gods walking. I have always thought about that. His eyes were stern when I told him—he was no longer my father but a priest. He said, "This is a strong dream."

"It is mine," I said, while the smoke waved and my head felt light. They were singing the Star song in the outer chamber and it was like the buzzing of bees in my head.

He asked me how the gods were dressed and I told him how they were dressed. We know how they were dressed from the book, but I saw them as if they were before me. When I had finished, he threw the sticks three times and studied them as they fell.

"This is a very strong dream," he said. "It may eat you up."

"I am not afraid," I said and looked at him with both eyes. My voice sounded thin in my ears but that was because of the smoke.

He touched me on the breast and the forehead. He gave me the bow and the three arrows.

"Take them," he said. "It is forbidden to travel east. It is forbidden to cross the river. It is forbidden to go to the Place of the Gods. All these things are forbidden."

"All these things are forbidden," I said, but it was my voice that spoke and not my spirit. He looked at me again.

"My son," he said. "Once I had young dreams. If your dreams do not eat you up, you may be a great priest. If they eat you, you are still my son. Now go on your journey."

I went fasting, as is the law. My body hurt but not my heart. When the dawn came, I was out of sight of the village. I prayed and purified myself, waiting for a sign. The sign was an eagle. It flew east.

Sometimes signs are sent by bad spirits. I waited again on the flat rock, fasting, taking no food. I was very still—I could feel the sky above me and the earth beneath. I waited till the sun was beginning to sink. Then three deer passed in the valley, going east—they did not wind me or see me. There was a white fawn with them—a very great sign.

I followed them, at a distance, waiting for what would happen. My heart was troubled about going east, yet I knew that I must go. My head hummed with my fasting—I did not even see the panther spring upon the white fawn. But, before I knew it, the bow was in my hand. I shouted and the panther lifted his head from the fawn. It is not easy to kill a panther with one arrow but the arrow went through his eye and into his brain. He died as he tried to spring—he rolled over, tearing at the ground. Then I knew I was meant to go east—I knew that was my journey. When the night came, I made my fire and roasted meat.

It is eight suns' journey to the east and a man passes by many Dead Places. The Forest People are afraid of them but I am not. Once I made my fire on the edge of a Dead Place at night and, next morning, in the dead-house, I found a good knife, little rusted. That was small to what came afterward but it made my heart feel big. Always when I looked for game, it was in front of my arrow, and twice I passed hunting parties of the Forest People without their knowing. So I knew my magic was strong and my journey clean, in spite of the law.

Toward the setting of the eighth sun, I came to the banks of the great river. It was half a day's journey after I had left the god-road—we do not use the god-roads now, for they are falling apart into great blocks of stone, and the forest is safer going. A long way off, I had seen the water through the trees but the trees were thick. At last, I came out upon an open place at the top of a cliff. There was the great river below, like a giant in the sun. It is very long, very wide. It could eat all the streams we know and still be thirsty. Its name is Ou-dis-sun, the Sacred, the Long. No man of my tribe had seen it, not even my father, the priest. It was magic and I prayed.

Then I raised my eyes and looked south. It was there, the Place of the Gods.

How can I tell what it was like—you do not know. It was there, in the red light, and they were too big to be houses. It was there with the red light upon it, mighty and ruined. I knew that in another moment the gods would see me. I covered my eyes with my hands and crept back into the forest.

Surely, that was enough to do, and live. Surely it was enough to spend the night upon the cliff. The Forest People themselves do not come near. Yet, all through the night, I knew that I should have to cross the river and walk in the places of the gods, although the gods ate me up. My magic did not help me at all and yet there was a fire in my bowels, a fire in my mind. When the sun rose, I thought, "My journey has been clean. Now I will go home from my journey." But, even as I thought so, I knew I could not. If I went to the Place of the Gods, I would surely die, but, if I did not go, I could never be at peace with my spirit again. It is better to lose one's life than one's spirit, if one is a priest and the son of a priest.

Nevertheless, as I made the raft, the tears ran out of my eyes. The Forest People could have killed me without fight, if they had come upon me then, but they did not come. When the raft was made, I said the sayings for the dead and painted myself for death. My heart was cold as a frog and my knees like water, but the burning in my mind would not let me have peace. As I pushed the raft from the shore, I began my death song—I had the right. It was a fine song.

"I am John, son of John," I sang. "My people are the Hill
    People. They are the men.
I go into the Dead Places but I am not slain.
I take the metal from the Dead Places but I am not blasted.
I travel upon the god-roads and am not afraid. E-yah! I have
    killed the panther, I have killed the fawn!
E-yah! I have come to the great river. No man has come there
    before.
It is forbidden to go east, but I have gone, forbidden to go on
    the great river, but I am there.
Open your hearts, you spirits, and hear my song.

Now I go to the Place of the Gods, I shall not return.
My body is painted for death and my limbs weak, but my heart
is big as I go to the Place of the Gods!"

All the same, when I came to the Place of the Gods, I was
afraid, afraid. The current of the great river is very strong—it
gripped my raft with its hands. That was magic, for the river
itself is wide and calm. I could feel evil spirits about me, in the
bright morning; I could feel their breath on my neck as I was
swept down the stream. Never have I been so much alone—I
tried to think of my knowledge, but it was a squirrel's heap of
winter nuts. There was no strength in my knowledge any more
and I felt small and naked as a new-hatched bird—alone upon
the great river, the servant of the gods.

Yet, after a while, my eyes were opened and I saw. I saw
both banks of the river—I saw that once there had been god-
roads across it, though now they were broken and fallen like
broken vines. Very great they were, and wonderful and broken—broken in the time of the Great Burning, when the fire
fell out of the sky. And always the current took me nearer to the
Place of the Gods, and the huge ruins rose before my eyes.

I do not know the customs of rivers—we are the People of the
Hills. I tried to guide my raft with the pole but it spun around. I
thought the river meant to take me past the Place of the Gods
and out into the Bitter Water of the legends. I grew angry
then—my heart felt strong. I said aloud, "I am a priest and the
son of a priest!" The gods heard me—they showed me how to
paddle with the pole on one side of the raft. The current
changed itself—I drew near to the Place of the Gods.

When I was very near, my raft struck and turned over. I can
swim in our lakes—I swam to the shore. There was a great spike
of rusted metal sticking out into the river—I hauled myself up
upon it and sat there, panting. I had saved my bow and two
arrows and the knife I found in the Dead Place but that was all.
My raft went whirling downstream toward the Bitter Water. I

looked after it, and thought if it had trod me under, at least I would be safely dead. Nevertheless, when I had dried my bow-string and restrung it, I walked forward to the Place of the Gods.

It felt like ground underfoot; it did not burn me. It is not true what some of the tales say, that the ground there burns forever, for I have been there. Here and there were the marks and stains of the Great Burning, on the ruins, that is true. But they were old marks and old stains. It is not true either, what some of our priests say, that it is an island covered with fogs and enchant-ments. It is not. It is a great Dead Place—greater than any Dead Place we know. Everywhere in it there are god-roads, though most are cracked and broken. Everywhere there are the ruins of the high towers of the gods.

How shall I tell what I saw? I went carefully, my strung bow in my hand, my skin ready for danger. There should have been the wailings of spirits and the shrieks of demons, but there were not. It was very silent and sunny where I had landed—the wind and the rain and the birds that drop seeds had done their work—the grass grew in the cracks of the broken stone. It is a fair island—no wonder the gods built there. If I had come there, a god, I also would have built.

How shall I tell what I saw? The towers are not all bro-ken—here and there one still stands, like a great tree in a forest, and the birds nest high. But the towers themselves look blind, for the gods are gone. I saw a fish-hawk, catching fish in the river. I saw a little dance of white butterflies over a great heap of broken stones and columns. I went there and looked about me—there was a carved stone with cut letters, broken in half. I can read letters but I could not understand these. They said UBTREAS. There was also the shattered image of a man or a god. It had been made of white stone and he wore his hair tied back like a woman's. His name was ASHING, as I read on the cracked half of a stone. I thought it wise to pray to ASHING, though I do not know that god.

How shall I tell what I saw? There was no smell of man left, on stone or metal. Nor were there many trees in that wilderness of stone. There are many pigeons, nesting and dropping in the towers—the gods must have loved them, or, perhaps, they used them for sacrifices. There are wild cats that roam the god-roads, green-eyed, unafraid of man. At night they wail like demons but they are not demons. The wild dogs are more dangerous, for they hunt in a pack, but them I did not meet till later. Everywhere there are the carved stones, carved with magical numbers or words.

I went north—I did not try to hide myself. When a god or a demon saw me, then I would die, but meanwhile I was no longer afraid. My hunger for knowledge burned in me—there was so much that I could not understand. After a while, I knew that my belly was hungry. I could have hunted for my meat, but I did not hunt. It is known that the gods did not hunt as we do—they got their food from enchanted boxes and jars. Sometimes these are still found in the Dead Places—once, when I was a child and foolish, I opened such a jar and tasted it and found the food sweet. But my father found out and punished me for it strictly, for, often, that food is death. Now, though, I had long gone past what was forbidden, and I entered the likeliest towers, looking for the food of the gods.

I found it at last in the ruins of a great temple in the mid-city. A mighty temple it must have been, for the roof was painted like the sky at night with its stars—that much I could see, though the colors were faint and dim. It went down into great caves and tunnels—perhaps they kept their slaves there. But when I started to climb down, I heard the squeaking of rats, so I did not go—rats are unclean, and there must have been many tribes of them, from the squeaking. But near there, I found food, in the heart of a ruin, behind a door that still opened. I ate only the fruits from the jars—they had a very sweet taste. There was drink, too, in bottles of glass—the drink of the gods was strong and made my head swim. After I had eaten and drunk, I slept on the top of a stone, my bow at my side.

When I woke, the sun was low. Looking down from where I lay, I saw a dog sitting on his haunches. His tongue was hanging out of his mouth; he looked as if he were laughing. He was a big dog, with a gray-brown coat, as big as a wolf. I sprang up and shouted at him but he did not move—he just sat there as if he were laughing. I did not like that. When I reached for a stone to throw, he moved swiftly out of the way of the stone. He was not afraid of me; he looked at me as if I were meat. No doubt I could have killed him with an arrow, but I did not know if there were others. Moreover, night was falling.

I looked about me—not far away was a great, broken god-road, leading north. The towers were high enough, but not so high, and while many of the dead-houses were wrecked, there were some that stood. I went toward this god-road, keeping to the heights of the ruins, while the dog followed. When I had reached the god-road, I saw that there were others behind him. If I had slept later, they would have come upon me asleep and torn out my throat. As it was, they were sure enough of me; they did not hurry. When I went into the dead-house, they kept watch at the entrance—doubtless they thought they would have a fine hunt. But a dog cannot open a door and I knew, from the books, that the gods did not like to live on the ground but on high.

I had just found a door I could open when the dogs decided to rush. Ha! They were surprised when I shut the door in their faces—it was a good door, of strong metal. I could hear their foolish baying beyond it but I did not stop to answer them. I was in darkness—I found stairs and climbed. There were many stairs, turning around till my head was dizzy. At the top was another door—I found the knob and opened it. I was in a long small chamber—on one side of it was a bronze door that could not be opened, for it had no handle. Perhaps there was a magic word to open it but I did not have the word. I turned to the door in the opposite side of the wall. The lock of it was broken and I opened it and went in.

Within, there was a place of great riches. The god who lived there must have been a powerful god. The first room was a small anteroom—I waited there for some time, telling the spirits of the place that I came in peace and not as a robber. When it seemed to me that they had had time to hear me, I went on. Ah, what riches! Few, even, of the windows had been broken—it was all as it had been. The great windows that looked over the city had not been broken at all though they were dusty and streaked with many years. There were coverings on the floors, the colors not greatly faded, and the chairs were soft and deep. There were pictures upon the walls, very strange, very wonderful—I remember one of a bunch of flowers in a jar—if you came close to it, you could see nothing but bits of color, but if you stood away from it, the flowers might have been picked yesterday. It made my heart feel strange to look at this picture—and to look at the figure of a bird, in some hard clay, on a table and see it so like our birds. Everywhere there were books and writings, many in tongues that I could not read. The god who lived there must have been a wise god and full of knowledge. I felt I had right there, as I sought knowledge also.

Nevertheless, it was strange. There was a washing place but no water—perhaps the gods washed in air. There was a cooking place but no wood, and though there was a machine to cook food, there was no place to put fire in it. Nor were there candles or lamps—there were things that looked like lamps but they had neither oil nor wick. All these things were magic, but I touched them and lived—the magic had gone out of them. Let me tell one thing to show. In the washing place, a thing said "Hot" but it was not hot to the touch—another thing said "Cold" but it was not cold. This must have been a strong magic but the magic was gone. I do not understand—they had ways—I wish that I knew.

It was close and dry and dusty in their house of the gods. I have said the magic was gone but that is not true—it had gone from the magic things but it had not gone from the place. I felt the spirits about me, weighing upon me. Nor had I ever slept in a Dead Place before—and yet, tonight, I must sleep there. When I though of it, my tongue felt dry in my throat, in spite of my wish for knowledge. Almost I would have gone down again and faced the dogs, but I did not.

I had not gone through all the rooms when the darkness fell. When it fell, I went back to the big room looking over the city and made fire. There was a place to make fire and a box with wood in it, though I do not think they cooked there. I wrapped myself in a floor covering and slept in front of the fire—I was very tired.

Now I tell what is very strong magic. I woke in the midst of the night. When I woke, the fire had gone out and I was cold. It seemed to me that all around me there were whisperings and voices. I closed my eyes to shut them out. Some will say that I slept again, but I do not think that I slept. I could feel the spirits drawing my spirit out of my body as a fish is drawn on a line.

Why should I lie about it? I am a priest and the son of a priest. If there are spirits, as they say, in the small Dead Places near us, what spirits must there not be in that great Place of the Gods? And would not they wish to speak? After such long years? I know that I felt myself drawn as a fish is drawn on a line. I had stepped out of my body—I could see my body asleep in front of the cold fire, but it was not I. I was drawn to look out upon the city of the gods.

It should have been dark, for it was night, but it was not dark. Everywhere there were lights—lines of light—circles and blurs of light—ten thousand torches would not have been the same. The sky itself was alight—you could barely see the stars for the glow in the sky. I thought to myself, "This is strong magic," and trembled. There was a roaring in my ears like the rushing of rivers. Then my eyes grew used to the light and my ears to the sound. I knew that I was seeing the city as it had been when the gods were alive.

That was a sight indeed—yes, that was a sight: I could not have seen it in the body—my body would have died. Everywhere went the gods, on foot and in chariots—there were gods beyond number and counting and their chariots blocked the streets. They had turned night to day for their pleasure—they did not sleep with the sun. The noise of their coming and going was the noise of many waters. It was magic what they could do—it was magic what they did.

I looked out of another window—the great vines of their bridges were mended and the god-roads went east and west. Restless, restless, were the gods and always in motion! They burrowed tunnels under rivers—they flew in the air. With unbelievable tools they did giant works—no part of the earth was safe from them, for, if they wished for a thing, they summoned it from the other side of the world. And always, as they labored and rested, as they feasted and made love, there was a drum in their ears—the pulse of the giant city, beating and beating like a man's heart.

Were they happy? What is happiness to the gods? They were great, they were mighty, they were wonderful and terrible. As I looked upon them and their magic, I felt like a child—but a little more, it seemed to me, and they would pull down the moon from the sky. I saw them with wisdom beyond wisdom and knowledge beyond knowledge. And yet not all they did was well done—even I could see that—and yet their wisdom could not but grow until all was peace.

Then I saw their fate come upon them and that was terrible past speech. It came upon them as they walked the streets of their city. I have been in the fights with the Forest People—I have seen men die. But this was not like that. When gods war with gods, they use weapons we do not know. It was fire falling out of the sky and a mist that poisoned. It was the time of the

Great Burning and the Destruction. They ran about like ants in the streets of their city—poor gods, poor gods! Then the towers began to fall. A few escaped—yes, a few. The legends tell it. But, even after the city had become a Dead Place, for many years the poison was still in the ground. I saw it happen, I saw the last of them die. It was darkness over the broken city and I wept.

All this, I saw. I saw it as I have told it, though not in the body. When I woke in the morning, I was hungry, but I did not think first of my hunger for my heart was perplexed and confused. I knew the reason for the Dead Places but I did not see why it had happened. It seemed to me it should not have happened, with all the magic they had. I went through the house looking for an answer. There was so much in the house I could not understand—and yet I am a priest and the son of a priest. It was like being on one side of the great river, at night, with no light to show the way.

Then I saw the dead god. He was sitting in his chair, by the window, in a room I had not entered before and, for the first moment, I thought that he was alive. Then I saw the skin on the back of his hand—it was like dry leather. The room was shut, hot and dry—no doubt that had kept him as he was. At first I was afraid to approach him—then the fear left me. He was sitting looking out over the city—he was dressed in the clothes of the gods. His age was neither young nor old—I could not tell his age. But there was wisdom in his face and great sadness. You could see that he would have not run away. He had sat at his window, watching his city die—then he himself had died. But it is better to lose one's life than one's spirit—and you could see from the face that his spirit had not been lost. I knew that, if I touched him, he would fall into dust—and yet, there was something unconquered in the face.

That is all of my story, for then I knew he was a man—I knew then that they had been men, neither gods nor demons. It is a great knowledge, hard to tell and believe. They were men–they went a dark road, but they were men. I had no fear after that–I had no fear going home, though twice I fought off the dogs and once I was hunted for two days by the Forest People. When I saw my father again, I prayed and was purified. He touched my lips and my breast, he said, "You went away a boy. You come back a man and a priest." I said, "Father, they were men! I have been in the Place of the Gods and seen it! Now slay me, if it is the law–but still I know they were men."

He looked at me out of both eyes. He said, "The law is not always the same shape–you have done what you have done. I could not have done it my time, but you come after me. Tell!"

I told and he listened. After that, I wished to tell all the people but he showed me otherwise. He said, "Truth is a hard deer to hunt. If you eat too much truth at once, you may die of the truth. It was not idly that our fathers forbade the Dead Places." He was right–it is better the truth should come little by little. I have learned that, being a priest. Perhaps, in the old days, they ate knowledge too fast.

Nevertheless, we make a beginning. It is not for the metal alone we go to the Dead Places now–there are the books and the writings. They are hard to learn. And the magic tools are broken–but we can look at them and wonder. At least, we make a beginning. And, when I am chief priest we shall go beyond the great river. We shall go to the Place of the Gods–the place newyork–not one man but a company. We shall look for the images of the gods and find the god ASHING and the others–the gods Licoln and Biltmore and Moses. But they were men who built the city, not gods or demons. They were men. I remember the dead man's face. They were men who were here before us. We must build again.

The Facts of the Story

Write answers to the following questions. Some answers may be one word or a phrase. Others will require a complete sentence. Look at the story if you wish.

1. List three things that are forbidden by the rules and laws of John's people.

2. What thing of value do the priests get from the Dead Places?

3. John refers to the destruction of the Place of the Gods as the time of the Great _____.

4. John makes the journey to the east, to the Place of the Gods, (a) because his tribe needs new sources of food (b) because the Forest People are moving east (c) because he has a great hunger for knowledge.

5. Describe two "signs" that direct John to go east.

6. When and why does John paint his body for death?

7. Name two kinds of creatures that survive in the ruins of the great Dead Places.

8. List at least three things that John sees in the house of the gods that puzzle him.

9. The "Place of the Gods" is actually the ruins of _____.

10. What discovery, which he calls a "great knowledge," does John report to his father about the former inhabitants of the Place of the Gods?

The Ideas in the Story

"By the Waters of Babylon" contains a great many ideas to think about and discuss. What are your views on the following?

1. After his visit to the Place of the Gods, John wonders why the Great Burning had happened. He says, "I knew the reason for the Dead Places but I did not see why it had happened. It seemed to me it should not have happened, with all the magic they had." If you had the opportunity, how would you explain to John "why it had happened"?

2. John's world of survivors appears to be divided between the Hill People and the Forest People. What is the attitude of the Hill People, to whom John belongs, toward the Forest People? John says, "I have been in the fights with the Forest People–I have seen men die." What point do you think Benét may be trying to make by including warring tribes in the *new* world? Do you think this is a realistic view of human nature?

3. John's father says, "If you eat too much truth at once, you may die of the truth." And John thinks, "Perhaps, in the old days, they ate knowledge too fast." Apply John's statement to our world. In what sense may we be in danger because of our rapidly increasing scientific knowledge?

4. John's hunger for knowledge leads him to risk his life. Give examples of actual men and women whose hunger for knowledge led them to take the same risk.

5. What do you think John means when he says twice during the story, "It is better to lose one's life than one's spirit." An opposite view would be, "One's spirit is of no value after one is dead." Discuss these two conflicting views. Do you agree or disagree with John's statement?

6. How important do you think "the books and the writings" will be in the survivors' effort to build again?

7. How does this story show that fears and taboos and superstitions can change and even fade away in the strong light of truth? Do you think John's newly discovered knowledge at the end of this story will make life better and happier for his people? Do you think John has learned anything that might prevent another "Great Burning"? Explain.

The Art of the Storyteller

Theme

You have learned that, in addition to its plot and its characters, a short story contains ideas. The main idea or insight into life is the *theme* of the story. The theme of "By the Waters of Babylon" tells us something about the survival powers of the human race. Benét believes that human beings have the power and the spirit to survive and recover from the worst that can happen to them—destruction by their own creations. The story makes us feel that the human race will never be completely wiped out. People will, if necessary, always begin again the long task of throwing off superstition and ignorance in their quest for knowledge and truth. What four-word statement at the end of this story expresses this theme? What is your opinion of Benét's ideas?

Suspense

Since this story is told by John, who therefore must have survived his journey east, Benét could not keep us in suspense by making us wonder whether John lives or dies. Benét creates suspense by making us curious to discover *what* John will find in the Place of the Gods, and *how* he will react to his discoveries there. We read on in suspense, not because we fear for John, but because we share John's curiosity.

One of the pleasures of reading this story is in solving several puzzles about John's whereabouts. When did you know for certain the actual name of this dead city? What is the sacred river named "Ou-dis-sun" (page 419)? (If you sound out this word, you'll hear the river's actual name.) What is the "Bitter Water" of the legends (page 421)? The letters ASHING are fragments of the name of a great American hero. Can you figure this out? This statue of "ASHING" stands in front of the old Treasury Building; can you figure out what UBTREAS is? The "great temple" in mid-city is Grand Central Station, which has a domed ceiling decorated with the constellations. What are the "tunnels" (page 423)? What is the "bronze door" that cannot be opened in the god's house (page 424)? Who are the "gods Licoln and Biltmore and Moses" (page 429)?

Composition

Supporting an Opinion

If you discussed the seven questions on page 431, you should have many ideas of your own on those topics. Select one or two of the questions and write detailed answers to them. Support your answers with evidence from your own experience, from your reading, and from your knowledge of human nature and of history. You will need to cite facts and examples.

Write approximately 200 words.

Stephen Vincent Benét

Stephen Vincent Benét (1898-1943) was born in Bethlehem, Pennsylvania, into an Army family. His great-grandfather, grandfather, and father were Army officers. He grew up in California and Georgia and graduated from Yale University. Benét's generation of the family shifted from the military to the literary life. His brother, William Rose Benét, and his sister, Laura Benét, were writers, and he himself never followed any profession but writing. His best-known work is *John Brown's Body,* a long narrative poem with a Civil War background, which won the Pulitzer Prize in 1929. His most popular short story is "The Devil and Daniel Webster." Benét was deeply interested in America, its past and its future. "By the Waters of Babylon" is one of several works in which he shows an interest in the future of the human race. He pursued this theme in a series of "nightmare" poems, in one of which he imagines what would happen if termites quietly destroyed New York City—after developing a taste for steel.

A Glossary of Helpful Terms for Readers of Short Stories

An asterisk (*) next to a word means that there is an entry defining that word in this glossary. Page references refer to a discussion of the term elsewhere in the book.

ALLUSION   A reference in a story to something outside the story. A *historical allusion* is a reference to an event or a person in history. A *literary allusion* is a reference to an event or a character or a place in literature. Three stories in this book have titles that are allusions: "Antaeus" refers to a character in Greek mythology; "The Animals' Fair" refers to the title of a song; and "By the Waters of Babylon" refers to a psalm in the Bible. When writers use allusions, they hope their readers will understand what they are referring to. Allusions frequently have to be explained, however, for people who have not read widely enough to recognize them.

ANTAGONIST   The character or force that opposes the protagonist,* who is the central character in a story. The plot* is an account of the conflict* that takes place between the antagonist and the protagonist. In a few stories, the antagonist is not a person, but an animal or a force, such as a storm or a weakness of character, that the protagonist is trying to overcome. (See page 29.)

CHARACTERIZATION   The process by which a writer presents the personal traits of the people in a story. Through characterization, writers make clear what the characters in their stories are like. Writers commonly use five methods of characterization: (1) they show their characters in action; (2) they tell what the characters say; (2) they give a physical description of the characters; (4) they tell how others react to the characters; (5) they state directly what the characters are like. (See pages 131, 176, 246, 311.)

CLICHÉ   A commonplace expression that has grown stale because it has been used too much. Examples of clichés: busy as a bee, accidents will happen, clear as crystal, easier said than done, few and far between, ripe old age, white as a sheet. Good writers avoid clichés and try to find new, fresh ways of expressing themselves.

CLIMAX   The point in a story when we find out whether or not the protagonist* has won the conflict.* The climax is usually the moment of greatest suspense and interest in a story. (See pages 30, 101.)

CONFLICT   The struggle between opposing forces that is the basis of all of our stories. Usually the conflict is between two persons, but it may be between a person and a natural force, such as a flood, or between a person and society, or between a person and a weakness in that person's character. A conflict is *external* when it takes place between a character and some outside force (such as another person, an animal, or a storm). A conflict is *internal* when it takes place within a character's own mind or feelings. In "The Most Dangerous Game," a character faces an external conflict because he must struggle against another man who wants to kill him. In "To Build a Fire," a character faces an external conflict because he must struggle for survival against the severe cold. In "The Scarlet Ibis," a character faces an internal conflict because he must struggle in his own mind and feelings to accept his brother's handicap. In "Red Dress," a character faces an internal conflict because she must struggle to conquer her own feelings of insecurity and fear. There often may be more than one kind of conflict in a story. "Enemy Territory" is a story with both kinds of conflict. (See page 28.)

DESCRIPTION   The kind of writing that appeals to the reader's senses: sight, hearing, touch, smell, and taste. Description is important in all stories because it is through description of people, places, and actions that the writer helps the readers to feel as if they are experiencing the story firsthand. (See page 379.)

DIALOGUE   Conversation between two or more persons. Dialogue can make a story easy to read. It opens up the page and it often holds the reader's interest better than long passages of description or narration do. Dialogue is also an effective method of characterization,* since people reveal themselves through the way they talk and the things they say. Dialogue must be the natural speech of the person speaking: college professors usually do not talk like their teen-age children. (See page 209.)

DICTION   The words used by a writer or speaker. A writer's diction may be formal (big words) or informal (slang, dialect, common words). It may be humorous, solemn, light, or heavy. It may be wordy, long-winded, or concise. Diction is an important element in a writer's style.*

EXAGGERATION   Overstatement, usually to achieve a humorous effect. Toni Cade Bambara uses exaggeration when she writes: "Then here comes Mr. Pearson with his clipboard and his cards and pencils and whistles and safety pins and fifty million other things he's always dropping all over the place with his clumsy self." Jean Stafford uses exaggeration when she writes: ". . . she especially hated the teacher, Miss Cudahy, who had a head shaped like a pine cone and who had killed several people with her ruler." (See page 284.)

FANTASY   Very imaginative writing that is not set in the actual world as we know it. Fantasy presents strange places that do not exist or characters that no one has ever seen on earth (such as elves or talking rabbits). Fairy stories and science fiction are examples of fantasy. Daphne du Maurier's story "The Birds" is a fantasy, as is Ray Bradbury's story "All Summer in a Day." (See page 102.)

FLASHBACK   An interruption in the telling of a story, when the writer "flashes back" to tell us about events that happened earlier. Most stories follow a simple time order, but occasionally a writer will interrupt this order by inserting a scene or describing an event that preceded the beginning of the story. Flashbacks appear near the beginning of Chukovski's "The Bridge" and Bradbury's "All Summer in a Day." (See page 149.)

FORESHADOWING   A hint given by the writer about something that will happen later in the story. Foreshadowing increases the reader's feeling of suspense.* In "To Build a Fire," Jack London tells us the man realized that "to get his feet wet in such a temperature meant trouble and danger. At the very least it meant delay, for he would be forced to stop and build a fire, and under its protection to bare his feet while he dried his socks and mocassins." This statement foreshadows exactly what does happen in the story. (See pages 54, 227.)

IRONY   A contrast between what is said and what is really meant, or between what happens and what we feel *should* happen.
    1. *Verbal irony* is the use of words that say the opposite of what is really meant. For example, suppose someone clumsily upsets a vase of flowers on the teacher's desk, splashing water over important papers and books. Annoyed, the teacher exclaims, "Gracefully done, Joe!" The teacher really means that Joe is careless and clumsy. This sarcastic remark is a kind of irony.

2. *Irony of situation* occurs when an event in a story turns out the opposite of what would normally be expected. For example, suppose the villain in a story plans a murder. Instead of shooting his intended victim, however, he accidentally shoots himself. This is an ironic situation.

3. *Dramatic irony* occurs when the reader or, in a play, the audience knows something the characters do not know. For example, suppose two characters in a play are talking about a third character who, they think, has left the room. The audience knows that the third character is actually hiding in a closet where he can hear everything the others are saying about him. Scenes like this are common in drama. Hence, this kind of irony is called *dramatic irony.* (See pages 114, 177, 312, 320.)

METAPHOR   A figure of speech which compares two things that are really not alike in most respects, but which seem alike in one meaningful way. In a metaphor, the comparison is made without the use of such words as *like* or as. Three examples of metaphor are:

> The lake was a great inland finger of the Gulf of Mexico, twenty miles long, ten wide. (Thomas Sancton, "The Silver Horn")

> The billows [of the glacier] were no longer static but undulating, and from their crests darted long white lances of light that struck blindingly into my eyes. (James Ramsey Ullman, "Kilimanjaro!")

> . . . the Store was my favorite place to be. . . . Opening the front doors was pulling the ribbon off the unexpected gift. (Maya Angelou, *I Know Why the Caged Bird Sings*)

> (See page 257.)

NARRATOR   The character in a story who is telling the story, using the first-person or "I" point of view.* In Poe's story "The Cask of Amontillado," the character Montresor is the narrator. In most of the Sherlock Holmes stories, Dr. Watson is the narrator. Most stories are *not* told by a character in the story who uses "I," but by a storyteller who uses the third-person point of view. In such stories, we usually think of the author as the person telling the story.

PLOT   What happens in a story. Plot consists of a series of related events that are brought to some kind of conclusion. Most plots contain the following elements: a problem to be solved; a conflict;* suspense;* and a climax.* (See pages 28, 53, 100, 113, 208.)

POINT OF VIEW   The vantage point from which a story is told. When a story is told by a character in the story, it is told from the *first-person point of view.* The character telling such a story uses the pronoun *I,* which in grammar is called the *first-person pronoun.* The first-person point of view is therefore sometimes called the *"I" point of view.* A narrator* using the first person can tell us only what he or she can hear and see as a character in the story.

When a story is told by the writer as an outsider, not by a character in the story, it is told from the *third-person point of view.* Such a storyteller is not limited, but knows everything. Hence, the third-person point of view is sometimes called the *omniscient point of view.* (*Omnis* is Latin for "all" and *sciens* means "knowing.") (See pages 192, 208.)

PROTAGONIST   The central character in a story, the one upon whom the action centers. The protagonist faces a problem and must undergo some conflict* to solve it. The protagonist is opposed by an antagonist,* which may be a person, or some force of nature, or even a flaw in the protagonist's personality. (See page 29.)

SATIRE   A kind of writing that ridicules human beings and social institutions for their weaknesses and peculiarities, or that ridicules human vices and failures. Satire, although frequently humorous, is usually written with a serious purpose. Most satirists want to improve human life by making our faults seem so ridiculous that we will want to correct them. (See pages 331, 342.)

SETTING   The place and the time in which a story happens. In some stories the setting is very important; it may actually determine what happens, as it does in Edgar Allan Poe's "The Cask of Amontillado," which is set in the catacombs of Italy during carnival time. Setting also determines what happens to a character in Doris Lessing's "A Sunrise on the Veld," which is set in the wild veld country of southern Africa, where nature is seen in all its cruelty and indifference. Setting can also be used to create atmosphere or mood; in Jack London's "To Build a Fire," the frozen Yukon setting creates an atmosphere of bleakness and hostility.

SIMILE   A figure of speech that directly compares two things that are really not alike in most respects, but that are alike in some way that makes the comparison effective. In a simile, the comparison is always made by using specific comparing words such as *like* or *as.* Here are three similes:

. . . Marley's face, with a dismal light about it, like a bad lobster in a dark cellar. (Charles Dickens, *A Christmas Carol*)

His hair was long and tangled and greasy and hung down, and you could see his eyes shining through like he was behind vines. (Mark Twain, *The Adventures of Huckleberry Finn*)

Carefully she put her hand on his stomach and moved closer; it felt as though a little clock was ticking inside him . . . (Carson McCullers, *The Member of the Wedding*)

(See page 257.)

STEREOTYPE (OR STOCK CHARACTER)   A character type that has been portrayed so often in literature that it is recognized at once by the reader. Stereotypes lack individuality because they are standard types that always behave in the same expected way. Examples are the doting parent; the bratty, brainy child; the tough private detective with a heart of gold; the villain with a waxed mustache; the beautiful heroine with a head of golden curls. Stereotypes are also called *stock characters* because they seem to have been stored in a stockroom and brought out whenever a writer needs them. Writers of quality literature avoid stereotypes unless they want to make fun of them. Great characters in literature are great because they are interesting, realistic individuals, not stereotypes. (See pages 342, 412.)

STYLE   A writer's characteristic way of writing. Style is a composite of many things. Among them are choice of words; arrangement of words in sentences; length of sentences; use of figurative language, description,* dialogue,* and humor. For three distinct writing styles, see Toni Cade Bambara's "Raymond's Run," Frank R. Stockton's "The Lady or the Tiger?," and Stephen Vincent Benét's "By the Waters of Babylon." (See page 284.)

SUSPENSE   The element of plot* that makes us want to read on to find out what happens. We usually experience suspense when we are worried about whether or not a character will succeed in overcoming the obstacles in his or her path and win in the conflict* with other characters or forces. The writer holds our attention by making it seem possible, even likely, that our hero or heroine may fail when we desperately want him or her to succeed. Very suspenseful stories are referred to as *cliffhangers,* because few things cause more anxiety than a person hanging from a cliff only minutes from death. How long will the person's strength last? Will rescuers arrive in time? (See pages 29, 432.)

SYMBOL   An object, a person, a place, or an event which has meaning in itself but which also stands for something broader than itself, such as an idea or an emotion. A red heart (valentine) is a symbol of love; a dove is a symbol of peace; a book is a symbol of learning; a famous battlefield may be preserved for future generations as a symbol of patriotism, heroism, and self-sacrifice. (See page 227.)

THEME   The main idea in a story. The theme of a story usually is an idea about life or about people. Writers sometimes state the story's theme outright, but more often they simply tell the story and let the reader discover the theme. It is important to understand the difference between theme and plot.* Theme is an idea revealed by the events of the story; plot is simply what happens in a story. (See pages 148, 432.)

TONE   The attitude the writer takes toward the subject he or she is writing about. Just as we reveal our attitude by our tone of voice when we are speaking, so writers show their attitude (tone) by the style in which they write. A writer's tone may be humorous, sarcastic, satirical, critical, sentimental, romantic, frivolous, bitter, angry, solemn, cheerful, and so on. (See page 283.)

Index of Skills

Literary Terms and Techniques

Antagonist, 29
Characters and
    Characterization, 29,
    131, 176, 192, 246, 311,
    342, 412
Climax, 30, 101
Conflict, 28
Description, 284, 379
Exaggeration, 284
Fantasy, 102
Flashback, 149
Foreshadowing, 54, 101, 227
Humor, 284
Irony, 114, 177, 312, 320
Plot, 28, 53, 100, 113, 208
Point of View, 192, 208
Protoganist, 29
Satire, 331, 342, 353
Setting, 103, 104, 130
Similes and Metaphors, 257
Single Effect, 114
Style, 284, 379
Suspense, 29, 432
Symbols, 227
Theme, 148, 341, 432
Tone, 283

Composition Skills

DESCRIPTION

Creating a Single Effect, 115
Writing a Character Sketch,
    132
Using Similes and Metaphors,
    257
Describing a Stock Character,
    343
Appealing to the Senses, 380

DIALOGUE

Writing Dialogue, 209

EXPOSITION

Developing a Paragraph, 55
Supporting a Topic Sentence
    with Examples, 150
Supporting an Opinion with
    Facts, 178
Developing a Topic Sentence,
    193
Supporting a Topic Sentence,
    228
Expressing an Opinion about
    a Story, 247
Comparing Two Stories, 312
Writing an Explanation, 320
Supporting an Opinion, 332
Writing an Explanation, 354
Backing Up an Opinion, 364
Expressing an Opinion, 413
Supporting an Opinion, 433

NARRATION

Narrating an Imagined
    Action, 30
Writing a "What If" Story,
    102
Putting "The Birds" in a
    Different Setting, 103
Telling a Story That
    Illustrates a Lesson, 162
Writing a Story, 285

441

Index of Authors and Titles